WITHDRAWN

9

14/8/19

This Man Confessed

This Man Confessed

JODI ELLEN MALPAS

First published in Great Britain in 2012
by Jodi Ellen Malpas
This edition first published in 2013
by Orion Books
an imprint of The Orion Publishing Group Ltd
Orion House, 5 Upper Saint Martin's Lane
London WC2H 9EA
An Hachette UK Company

1 3 5 7 9 10 8 6 4 2

A CIP catalogue record for this book is
available from the British Library.

ISBN (Mass Market Paperback) 978 1 4091 5152 4
ISBN (Ebook) 978 1 4091 5153 1

Typeset by Input Data Services Ltd, Bridgwater, Somerset

Printed in Great Britain by Clays Ltd, St Ives plc

The Orion Publishing Group's policy is to use papers that
are natural, renewable and recyclable products and made
from wood grown in sustainable forests. The logging and
manufacturing processes are expected to conform to the
environmental regulations of the country of origin.

www.orionbooks.co.uk

For my boys

Acknowledgements

Beyond Central Jesse Cloud Nine is another Cloud Nine. It's where I'll always find my family. I would never have survived this madness without them.

To my table legs, Fanny, Fruth, and Flo. I love every moment I spend with you, and most of all . . . owning my s*&t with you. London is calling.

J & G at TotallyBooked. Your support and encouragement have been invaluable to me. Some amazing things have come from my This Man journey and you two coming into my life is one of those things. Thank you for everything.

I started off as a self-published author and landed in a world that I had no idea about. My success has undoubtedly been assisted by book bloggers who work tirelessly and for no gain, other than the pure enjoyment of reading and sharing their latest find. I had no pre-promotion, no marketing, no contacts. I just pressed that publish button and was lucky enough for my story to fall into the hands of bloggers, whether by default or by talk in the community. My story could have been lost among the millions of other self-published books for an eternity unnoticed. Incredibly, it didn't get lost. It was found, and I have the online reading community to thank for that. My gratitude is huge and my admiration immense.

And last, but never least, my lovely ladies. Each comment, message, 'like', tweet, and blog comment has been read, absorbed, and appreciated – all of them. You'll never know what your support and enthusiasm mean to me. Obsessive Jesse

Disorder is an epidemic, and I'm not even sorry-ish. You've shared and enjoyed each and every moment with me, shouted about my story, and spread the word to family, friends, and even the shop assistant. Your passion is as fierce as mine, and I love it.

This is it – the conclusion, the final part of Jesse and Ava's story. For me, Central Jesse Cloud Nine doesn't get any better than this. I hope you feel the same.

Enjoy.

Jodi

xxx

This Man Confessed

Chapter 1

My nerves are shot to bits. I don't know why, I know I'm doing the right thing, but damn I'm a stupid mass of nerves. I'm alone, my first few reflective moments of the day and probably the last. I need this moment, just me to myself, absorbing the massive leap that I'm taking. I know these moments will likely be precious from this day forward.

It's my wedding day.

It's the day I promise myself to this man for the rest of my life – not that I need a piece of paper or a metal band on my finger to do that. But he does. That's why only two weeks after he fell to his knee on the terrace of Lusso, I'm marrying this man. And why I'm now sitting in my robe on a chaise longue in one of the private suites of The Manor – the suite where Jesse cornered me all those weeks ago – trying to gather myself.

I'm getting married at The Manor.

The biggest day of my life is taking place at the plush sex haven of my Lord. My nerves aren't only a result of me being the bride. My parents, brother and family members are all roaming around the grounds of Jesse's supposed country retreat, poking around, taking it all in. The Manor has been closed to members for two days so preparations could be made, and that alone has cost Jesse a small fortune in reimbursed membership fees. I might be just as unpopular with the male members as I am with the female members now. They must all hate me – the women for snatching their Lord from under their noses, and now the men for putting a halt on their preferred sexual adventures.

Jesse has ensured all wooden, cross-like wall hangings and suspended gold-grid frames have been removed from the private suites, and he's had the doors to the communal room locked. I don't feel any better about it, though.

I look up to the ceiling and roll my shoulders in an attempt to dispel some of the growing tension. It's not working. Pulling myself up, I walk over to the mirror and gaze at my reflection. Despite my unease, I look fresh, I'm glowing, and my make-up is light and natural. My dark hair has been glossed to within an inch of its life, the long, heavy waves flouncing freely and loosely pinned on one side with an intricately jewelled hair comb. Jesse loves my hair down. He also loves me in lace.

I turn towards the door where my dress is hanging and drink in the vast expanse of lace – lots of lace, with explosions of tiny pearls sewn here and there. Zoe of Harrods came up trumps with this dress. The ivory lace sweeps over my bum, hugs my thighs, and puddles on the floor a metre in every direction. I smile. He'll stop breathing. This simple gown, with delicate shoulder straps, plunging back and nipped-in waist will have my Lord on his knees.

I scoop my phone up from the nightstand. It's midday. In just an hour, I'll be meeting Jesse in the summer room and taking my vows. My stomach does a swift three-sixty degree turn . . . again.

Slipping off my robe, I put my knickers on before taking my ivory lace strapless corset and stepping in, pulling it up over my stomach and arranging my cleavage in the cups. Only just, but it does conceal the perfectly round bruise on my breast. My mark.

There's a quiet knock at the door. My quiet, reflective time is up. 'Yes?' I call, slipping back into my robe.

'Ava, darling, are you decent?' It's Mum.

I open the door. 'I'm decent, and I need your help.'

She pushes her way in, shutting the door behind her. She looks stunning, adorned in a lovely oyster-coloured satin shift dress, her short, sweeping hairstyle arranged with a feather and pearl hairpiece. 'Sorry, darling. I was showing Aunty Angela the spa facilities. I think she'll be asking Jesse about joining up. She was most impressed. Do you need membership for the spa and gym, or is it just for guests?'

I cringe. 'Just for guests, Mum.'

'Oh, well, I'm sure he'll make an exception for family. Your grandparents would've thought they were in Buckingham Palace, God rest their souls.' She faffs with my hair, and I bat her fussing hands away. 'Have you wiggled your way into your underwear yet?' She runs her chocolate eyes up and down my robe-covered body. 'It's nearly time.'

I slip my robe off again and drape it on the bed. 'Yes, I need you to fasten it.' I turn my back to her and pull my hair over my shoulder. Two weeks of Jesse's hands working cream into my back has cleared all evidence of my thrashing. The physical marks are gone, but the mental images will be etched on my brain for ever.

She commences securing all of the hooks and eyes. 'You're so lucky to have such a wonderful place to get married.'

I'm glad she can't see my face because she would see a painfully uncomfortable expression. 'I know.' I've seen the summer room and it *does* look beautiful – Tessa, our wedding planner, made sure of it. Jesse presented me with Tessa the day after I agreed to marry him, a small indication that my challenging man had already sourced her to take on the role of organising our wedding – the wedding we were supposed to discuss together like adults. And, quite conveniently, The Manor also holds a wedding licence. All *I've* done for my wedding is visit Zoe to find my dress. I've had no planning stress, just location stress.

'There.' Mum turns me around and sweeps my hair back over

my shoulder. She's looking at me thoughtfully. 'Darling, can your mother offer you some advice?'

'No,' I answer quickly on a small smile.

She returns my smile and sits me on the end of the bed. 'When you become a wife, you become the core of your husband.' She smiles fondly. 'Let him think he's in charge, let him think you can't live without him, but never let him take your independence or identity, darling.' She laughs a little. 'They like to think they're wearing the trousers, and you have to let them believe it.'

I shake my head a little. 'Mum, this isn't necessary.'

'Yes, it is,' she insists. 'Men are complicated creatures.'

I scoff. She has no idea how complicated *my* creature is.

She pulls my blushing face to hers. 'Ava, I can see that Jesse loves you, and I admire his frankness when it comes to how he feels about you, but remember who you are. Never let him change you, darling.'

'He won't change me, Mum.' My parents stayed with us for two days after Jesse proposed, so they've had the full-on experience of Jesse's way with me, minus the countdowns and various degrees of fuckings. They have witnessed the smothering, the constant touching and affection, and their quiet observations haven't gone unnoticed. Not by me, anyway. Jesse is oblivious. No, not oblivious; he just doesn't care. Whenever and wherever.

Mum smiles. 'He wants to look after you, and he's made it quite clear you're precious to him. It makes me and your father so happy to know that you've found a man who adores you, a man who'll walk through fire for you.'

'I adore him, too,' I say quietly. The sincerity of my mum's words is tugging at my vocal cords, making my voice a little quivery. 'Please don't make me cry. My make-up will be ruined.'

She clasps my cheeks in her palms and plants a kiss on my lips. 'Yes, let's stop with the emotional stuff. Just don't ever do anything that you don't want to. I can also see he could be quite persuasive.' I actually laugh, and Mum laughs with me. Persuasive? 'It's such a shame his family couldn't be here,' she muses.

I wince a little. 'I've told you, they live abroad. They're not very close.' I've only vaguely outlined the reason for Jesse's lack of family.

'Money,' she sighs. 'It causes more family rifts than anything else.'

'It does,' I agree. So do sex houses and playboy uncles.

We're interrupted by another knock at the door and Mum leaves me on the bed to answer it. 'Oh, that'll be Kate.'

'I have drinks! Wow, Elizabeth, you look incredible!' Kate's excited voice creeps into the room before she barrels past my mother and hits me with delighted blue eyes. 'Aren't you dressed yet?' She sets a tray on the wooden chest. She looks fabulous in an ivory satin dress, her long curls a mass of red flames surrounding her pale face – my only bridesmaid, but with the enthusiasm of ten.

'Just about to.' I stand myself up and adjust my boobs in my cups.

'Here, have one of these.' She thrusts a glass of pink liquid at me.

'Oh, yes, you must!' Mum chants, closing the door and hastily making her way over to scoop one up for herself. She takes a long sip and gasps. 'Oh, that little Italian knows how to keep a lady happy.'

I shake my head at the glass that's floating in front of me. 'No, I'm fine.' I don't want alcohol breath under Jesse's nose.

'It'll sort your nerves,' Kate insists, taking my hand and placing the glass in it. 'Drink.'

She nods at the glass with raised eyebrows and I relent, taking a generous swig of Mario's Most Marvellous. It tastes as marvellous as ever, but no amount of alcohol is going to settle me.

'Where's Jesse?' I ask, setting my glass down. I've not seen him since last night. Knowing my mum's traditional views, I insisted we sleep separately on the night before our wedding. He refused to leave my room until one minute to midnight, and then he did so in a mighty huff when my mum was banging on the door. I could see he was dying to trample all over her but, surprisingly, he conceded without too much fuss, just a ferocious scowl at my mum as she guided him from the room.

'I think he's getting ready.' Kate downs a Most Marvellous.

'Katie Matthews, take it easy!' Mum scolds, taking the glass from her. 'You've got all day to go.'

'Sorry.' Kate flicks me a cheeky grin. I know why she's hitting the drink so early, and it's called Dan and Sam combined.

'What about Dad and Dan?'

'At the bar, Ava. *All* of the men are at the bar.' Kate emphasises *all*.

I wince. Today is going to be tough for Kate. Dan delayed his return to Australia so he could be here for my wedding, but he hasn't said much, neither on the night of the proposal or since. He doesn't need to. It's obvious he's struggling with both the direction of my life and being near Kate, especially with an oblivious Sam on the scene. Kate's struggling, too, although trying to appear unaffected.

'Come on then.' Kate claps her hands. 'Are you getting dressed or walking down the aisle in that? I'm sure he won't mind.'

I smile at my fiery friend. 'I'm getting dressed.' I unpack my heels from the tissue paper and slip them on, raising me by four inches. 'Right.' I take a deep breath and make my way over to the door, where my dress is waiting for me.

'Perhaps you should use the toilet before we get you into it,' Mum suggests, joining me by the dress. 'Oh, Ava. I've never seen anything like it.'

I hum my agreement, my eyes drifting up and down the full length. 'I know. And yes, I need a wee.' I leave my mum admiring my dress and head for the bathroom, catching Kate having another quick glug while my mum's back is turned. I shut the door quietly before using the toilet and relishing another private moment. Then I hear a loud knock on the suite door, followed by the unmistakable, panicked voice of my mother. Wondering what's going on, I make quick work of sorting myself out and washing my hands before exiting the bathroom.

'Jesse.' Mum is clearly exasperated. 'You and I are going to fall out if you don't do as you're told.'

I look over at Kate, who's drinking more Most Marvellous while Mum is distracted. She grins at me on a shrug. 'What's going on?' I ask.

'Jesse wants to see you, but Elizabeth is having none of it.'

I roll my eyes, turning my attention to the door, where Mum is blocking the small gap between the door and the frame.

'We won't fall out, Mum, if you let me in,' Jesse says. I know he's grinning at my mother, but his playfulness isn't fooling me. I can detect the threat in his tone. He's coming in this room, and not even Mum will stop him.

'Jesse Ward, you do not get to call me "Mum" when I'm only nine years older than you!' she spits. 'Now go, you'll be seeing her in half an hour.'

'Ava!' he yells.

I throw my eyes back to Kate, and she nods her head, instantly catching my drift. We both run towards the door where my dress is hanging, Kate unhooking it from the top and me gathering the bottom in my arms before we take it into the bathroom and rehang it on the back of the door.

Kate laughs. 'Will your mum learn or will she continue to try and tame him?'

'I don't know.' I smooth the front of my dress down and follow Kate back out, shutting the door behind me. Mum is still guarding the main door, her foot wedged at the bottom. That won't stop him.

'Jesse, no!' She's pushing against him now. 'It's bad luck. Have you no respect for tradition, you stubborn man?'

'Let me in, Elizabeth.' He's clenching his teeth, I know he is.

I glance at Kate and shake my head. He's trampling my mother, just like he promised if she ever got in his way, and she is most certainly in his way.

Kate takes another drink from the tray and walks casually over to the door. 'Elizabeth, just let him in, you'll never stop him. The man's a rhinoceros.'

'No!' Mum is really digging her heels in. 'He is not . . . oh! . . . Jesse Ward!'

I smile to myself as I watch my determined mother shoved back slightly before being lifted from her feet and placed neatly to the side. She rearranges her dress and straightens her hairpiece, all the while spitting nails at my challenging man. Then I cast my eyes back to the open doorway.

I swallow. His green pools are full of desire and studying me closely, his face expressionless, his jaw stubbled. My greedy stare trails slowly down his half nakedness as he stands before me in just his loose shorts, his solid chest damp and his hair dark with sweat. He's been running again.

'Well!' Mum huffs. 'Ava, tell him to leave!' She's not happy.

I meet his gaze. 'It's fine, Mum. Just give us five minutes.'

His eyes sparkle in approval as he stands patiently waiting for my mum to relent and leave us. Mum won't appreciate it, but even this small gesture is uncharacteristically respectful. He's trampling all right, but he could trample harder.

In my peripheral vision I see Kate approach my mum and take her arm. 'Come on, Elizabeth. Just a few minutes won't hurt.'

'It's tradition!' she argues, but still lets Kate lead her out. I smile. There is nothing traditional about my relationship with Jesse. 'What's that bruise on his chest?' I hear my mother ask as she's pushed from the room.

The door closes, and we maintain our deep eye connection, neither one of us saying anything for the longest time. I just drink him in, every finely tuned muscle, every perfect inch of pure beauty.

He finally speaks. 'I don't want to take my eyes away from your face.'

'No?'

He shakes his head mildly. 'There'll be lace if I do, won't there?'

I nod.

'White lace?'

'Ivory.'

His chest expands slightly. This could be dangerous for my hair, make-up and underwear if those eyes stray. It could also be dangerous for our strict time schedule. I'm expecting Tessa up here at any moment to check that I'm ready before she hits me with how many steps it is to the summer room and how long it should take me to get there.

He blinks a few times, and I know he'll never resist a peek; he'd just better control himself, and I'd better control myself, too. It's hard. Sweat beads are trailing down his temple, across his neck and onto his solid chest, before shimmering as they travel the waves of his stomach and disperse in the waistband of his shorts. I shift as his eyes break from mine and lazily drag down my body, his chest heaving more severely as his gaze makes its journey. I'm bombarded with tingles.

I make my move before he does, walking slowly across the room and stopping close to his sweat-coated body. Then I flick my gaze up to his lush lips. His breathing escalates.

'You've just trampled my mother.' I try to hide the lust in my voice, but fail miserably.

'She was in my way,' he says quietly, breathing down on me.

'This is bad luck. You're not supposed to see me before our wedding.'

'Stop me.' His head dips so his lips brush over mine gently, but he doesn't touch my body. 'I've missed you.'

'It's been twelve hours.'

'Too long.' He runs his tongue slowly across my bottom lip, enticing a quiet moan from me. I'm instantly fighting the natural instinct to grab his big shoulders. 'You've had a drink.'

'Just a sip.' He's like a bloodhound. 'We shouldn't be doing this.'

'You can't look like this and say things like that, Ava.' His lips push to mine, his tongue seeking entry, encouraging my lips to part and accept him into my mouth. The hot warmth of him dispels my nerves; everything is forgotten as he claims me, but still keeps his hands to himself. Our sweeping tongues are the only contact between us, but it's as consuming as ever. My senses are saturated, my mind scrambled, and my body begging for him. But he just maintains the slow, fluid movements of his tongue, withdrawing occasionally to tease my lips, before plunging back into my mouth. I hum at his exquisite pace, the inevitable bang dropping between my thighs as he worships me delicately.

'Jesse, we're going to be late for our wedding.' I need to halt this before one of us takes it to the next level. It might be me.

'Don't tell me to stop kissing you, Ava.' He bites my bottom lip and drags it slowly through his teeth. 'Never tell me to stop kissing you.' He lowers himself to his knees and takes my hands, pulling me down. I kick my shoes off and join him. He watches his thumbs circling over the tops of my hands for a while before lifting his glorious greens to find my eyes. 'Are you ready to do this?'

I frown. 'Are you asking me if I still want to marry you?'

His lips tip a little. 'No, you don't get a choice. I'm just asking if you're ready.'

I struggle to stop my own small smile at his candidness. 'And what if I say no?'

'You won't.'

'Then why ask?'

His lips turn into a shy smile, and he shrugs. 'You're nervous. I don't want you to be nervous.'

'I'm nervous because of *where* I'm getting married.'

His smile falls away. 'Ava, everything has been taken care of. I said not to worry so you shouldn't. End of.'

'I can't believe you convinced me to do this.' I drop my head, feeling a little guilty for doubting he'd keep his word. I know exactly why we're marrying at The Manor. No waiting list. No other bookings to work around. It's where he could get me down the aisle without delay.

'Hey.' He tips my chin back up, making me look at his achingly handsome face. 'Stop it now. Ava, baby, I want you to cherish today, not get your knickers in a twist over something that's never going to happen. They'll never know, I promise.'

I shake myself out of my uneasiness and smile, feeling better for hearing his reassuring words. I believe him. 'Okay.'

I watch as he stands and strolls over to a big chest, pulling something from the drawer and returning a few moments later with a bath sheet. My brow furrows as he drops back to his knees and wipes his face, then ruffles his damp hair before laying it across his chest.

He opens his arms. 'Come here.'

I waste no time crawling onto his lap and letting him surround me in his arms, my cheek resting on his chest through the towel.

'Better?' he asks, pulling me in closer.

'Much better,' I whisper. 'I love you, my Lord.'

I feel him jerk a little under me, a silent hint of his quiet laugh. 'I thought I was your god.'

'You're that, too.'

'And you are my temptress. Or you could be my Lady of The Manor.'

I jump off his chest and find him grinning at me. 'I am not being your Lady of the Sex Manor!'

He laughs and yanks me back down, making a meal of stroking my glossy hair and inhaling deeply on a satisfied pull of breath. 'Whatever you want, lady.'

'Just lady will do.' I'm aware of my hands sliding all over his damp back, but I really don't care. 'I'm so in love with you.'

'I know you are, Ava.'

'I need to get ready. I'm getting married, you know.'

'You are? Who's the lucky bastard?'

I smile and pull myself away from his body again. I need to see him. 'He's a challenging, neurotic control freak.' I reach up and cup his rough cheek. 'He's so handsome,' I whisper, searching his eyes, which are watching me so closely. 'This man stops me breathing when he touches me and fucks me until I'm delirious.' I wait for his scorn, but his lips just press into a straight line, so I lean up and kiss his chin, working my way to his lips. 'I can't wait to marry him.'

'What would this man say if he caught you kissing another man?' he asks around my mouth.

I grin. 'Oh, he'd probably castrate him, offer burial or cremation, that type of thing.'

His eyes widen. 'He sounds possessive. I don't think I want to take him on.'

'You really don't. He'll trample all over you.' I shrug, and he laughs. It's that eye-sparkling laugh, the one that has light creases fanning his beautiful greens. 'Happy?' I ask.

'No, I'm shitting myself.' He falls back, taking me with him. 'But I'm feeling brave. Kiss me.'

I dive right in, smothering his face with my lips and humming in sweet contentment, but I don't get long to indulge myself.

The door swings open. 'Jesse Ward! Get your sweat-covered

body off my daughter!' Mum's shocked cry pierces the privacy of our moment.

I start laughing, my mum's scorn not stopping me from getting my fix of Jesse. And he lets me.

'Ava! You'll smell. Get up!' Her angry heels start thumping towards us. 'Tessa, help me out here, will you?'

I suddenly feel a mass of hands grasping at different parts of my body, trying to pull me from Jesse. 'Mum! Stop it!' I laugh, gripping Jesse harder.

'Get up then! You're getting married in half an hour, your hair is a mess and you've broken an ancient tradition, rolling around on the floor with your husband-to-be.' She huffs and puffs a bit more. 'Tessa, tell her!'

'Yes, come on, Ava.' Tessa's harsh husk stabs at my skin. She's nice enough, but the woman is frighteningly fierce with organisation.

'Okay, okay,' I grumble, dragging myself from Jesse's body.

'Oh, look at you,' Mum moans, trying to smooth my wild mane. I struggle to keep a straight face as I watch Jesse make no attempt to leave, but rather brace his arms under his head so he can watch as my mum pulls and pokes at me. She turns angry chocolate eyes onto my challenging man. 'Out!'

'All right.' He rises from the floor in one fluid effort, his delicious muscles bunching and rippling as he does. Tessa's staring doesn't escape my notice, but she soon snaps out of her dumbstruck state when she catches me watching her with raised eyebrows.

'I'll take care of the groom!' she declares, averting her eyes. 'Jesse, come on.'

'Wait.' He looks at my chest. 'Where's your diamond?'

'Shit!' My hand instantly flies up to my breastbone, my eyes darting around on the floor. 'Shit, shit, shit! Mum!'

'Ava!' Jesse yells. 'Please! Watch your mouth!'

'Don't panic!' Mum drops to her knees and starts looking

under the bed, while I scan every inch of the plush carpet.

'Here it is!' Tessa sweeps it up from the floor, and Jesse abruptly snatches it from her hand before making his way over to me.

'Turn around,' he huffs, and I comply immediately, my heart hammering in my chest. That damn fucking diamond will be the death of me. 'There.' His lips fall onto my shoulder, his hips pushing into my bum.

'That'll teach you for frolicking on the floor,' Mum huffs. 'Now, out!' She starts tugging at Jesse's arm, but he doesn't brush her off.

I turn and wave at him, then curtsy, prompting another huff from my mother and a cheeky grin from Jesse, before he lets Tessa usher him out of the suite.

'Right. In that dress, Ava O'Shea. Where is it?'

I point to the bathroom and sit myself on the end of the bed. 'Bathroom. And you won't be able to call me that soon,' I say haughtily.

She stomps across the room. 'You will always be Ava O'Shea to me,' she grumbles. 'Up. Your father will be here in a minute to escort you downstairs.'

I stand and rearrange my underwear. 'Is he okay?'

'Your dad? Nervous, but it's nothing a few whiskies won't cure. He hates being in the limelight.'

He does. He'll be keen to hand me over to Jesse so he can escape the attention and blend back into the crowd.

My dress is removed from the hanger and held in front of me. I rest my hand on Mum's shoulder and step into it, letting her pull it up my front so I can slip my arms through the delicate straps before she turns me around and fastens the dozens of tiny pearl buttons running down my lower spine. She's quiet, and she's stopped moving. I know what I'm going to see if I turn around, and I'm not sure I can cope with it. Then I hear a small sniff.

'Mum, please don't.'

Her hands kick back into action. 'What?'

I turn around, and my suspicions are confirmed. Her eyes are clouded and she lets out a small sob. 'Mum,' I warn softly.

'Oh, Ava.' She runs to the bathroom and I hear the frantic yanking of toilet paper from the roll. She appears in the doorway, dabbing under her eyes with some tissue. 'I'm sorry. I was doing so well.'

'You were,' I confirm. 'Hey, help me out here.' Distraction, that's what she needs.

'Yes, yes. What should I do?'

'Shoes.' I point to my shoes where I kicked them off, and she scoops them up, placing them at my feet.

'Thank you.' I lift my pooling dress and slip my feet back into my Louboutins. 'How's my face?'

She laughs. 'You mean after you've just rubbed it over every inch of Jesse's?'

'Yes,' I answer, walking across to the bathroom to inspect it myself.

'You could probably do with an extra brush of powder.'

She's right; I could. I look a little flushed. I sweep my make-up brush across my cheeks before refreshing my nude lips and applying a little extra mascara. My hair isn't as silky smooth after my little roll around on the floor, but the comb is still securely in place. I feel better. He does that to me. He draws all of the anxiety right out of me with his presence, and now I can't wait to get my lace-clad arse downstairs to meet him.

I pull up the hem of my dress and walk out of the bathroom, flicking my hair over my shoulder and blowing out a calming breath. 'I'm ready,' I declare, coming to an abrupt halt when I see that my mum is no longer alone.

'Oh, Joseph, look at her!' Mum cries, turning into my dad's shoulder and blubbering all over his charcoal suit. Kate reaches up and strokes Mum's back on a small eye roll, and Dad tenderly wraps his arm around her waist. This is rare. He's not a touchy-feely man at all.

I smile at him, and he returns my beam. 'Don't you start,' I warn.

'I'm saying nothing.' He laughs. 'Except how beautiful you look. Really beautiful, Ava.'

'Really?' I ask, shocked by his open display of affection, even if it is just words.

'Yes, really.' He nods sharply. 'Now, are you ready?' He shifts my mum away from his body and brushes his suit down, pretending he hasn't just said some loving words to his daughter.

'Yes, I'm more than ready. Take me to Jesse,' I demand, and that has the desired effect, everyone laughing at my order. Much better. I can't cope with all of this intensity. Jesse provides me with enough of that.

Tessa barges in. 'Come on, then. What's the hold-up?' she asks, scanning the bodies that are all staring at me. 'Elizabeth, Kate, downstairs, please.' She escorts them from the room. 'Ava, I'll meet you at the summer room in three minutes.'

She exits sharply, leaving me and my dad alone. 'You know, Dad, you have to link arms with me now,' I tease.

His face screws up. 'For how long?'

'Well, for however long it takes you to walk me downstairs.' I pick up my calla lily – just one calla lily.

'Let's get our arses in gear, then.' He cocks his arm to the side, and I link it with mine. 'Ready?'

I nod and let my dad lead me down to the summer room, where my Lord of the Sex Manor is waiting for me.

Chapter 2

Kate and Tessa are waiting for us outside the doors to the summer room, my wedding planner looking pleased, Kate looking tipsy. Kate bends down to spread my dress neatly. 'I can't believe you're not wearing a veil.'

'He wants to see my face,' I say quietly, clenching my eyes shut, the enormity of what I'm about to do suddenly overwhelming me. I can feel my chest expanding, and I'm beginning to shake. I've known this man for only two months. How did this happen?

The doors to the summer room open and music immediately drifts into my ears. Only now when I'm hearing Etta James's 'At Last' does it occur to me that I didn't even pick the music for my wedding. I've done absolutely nothing. I have no idea what's happening or when and I'm feeling a bit overwhelmed. My eyes are flying all over the floor and I'm suddenly feeling tearful.

Dad nudges me with his elbow, and I glance up at him, finding a soft, reassuring gaze. He cocks his head to the side on a small smile, and I follow his indication to look, clenching my lips together and slowly turning my eyes. Damn, I've done so well. I know everyone is looking at me, but it's the green-eyed man at the end of the aisle who holds my attention. His hands are joined and draped loosely in front of his grey three-piece suit, his body turned fully towards me. His lips part and he shakes his head a little, never taking his eyes from mine. Dad nudges me again, and I let out the breath I've been holding, forcing my feet to lift and carry me onward, but I only make it two steps before he starts towards me. I hear Mum's shocked gasp, no doubt reeling at Jesse's lack of respect for tradition, and I stop, halting my dad's progression, to wait for him. His face is completely straight, and when he makes it to me, he blisters my skin with his scorching gaze, his eyes running over every part of my face before settling on my lips. Slowly lifting his arm, his hand cups my cheek and his thumb runs over my flesh. I nuzzle into it; I can't help it. All anxiety is drawn from me by his touch, my heart steadying and my body starting to relax again.

He bends down and puts his lips to my ear. 'Give me your hand,' he whispers.

I hold out my hand to him, and he pulls away from me, taking my offering gently and placing his lips on the back. Then he snaps a pair of handcuffs over my wrist.

I gasp, my eyes shooting to his face, finding a small smile tickling the edges of his beautiful lips. But he doesn't look at me. He keeps his eyes down and makes quick work of securing the cuffs. What the hell is he doing? I glance up at my dad, but he just shakes his head, and then I look across to my mother, seeing her head in her hands, obviously despairing. I'm released from my dad's hold before he makes his way to the front to join Mum, her shocked whisper attacking him as he arrives by her side. My eyes drift over the congregation, noting that all of the people who know Jesse are smiling, the ones who don't display-ing wide eyes and gaping mouths. Kate and Sam are chuckling, John's flashing his gold tooth, and then there's my brother. He's not impressed.

I find my senses then find Jesse's eyes. 'What are you doing?' I whisper.

He leans in and kisses me gently on the lips, then moves across my cheek to my ear. 'You look so fuckable.'

I gasp again, my face flashing red. 'Jesse, people are waiting.'

'Then they'll wait.' He trails his way back to my lips. 'I *really, really, really* like this dress.'

Of course he does; it's pure lace. I flick my eyes to my mother, seeing her looking at the registrar all apologetic, and a small smile breaks the corners of my lips. I reach up to thread my fingers through his dark, dirty-blond hair and tug. 'Mr Ward, you're keeping *me* waiting.'

I feel him grin against my ear. 'Are you ready to love, honour and *obey* me?'

'Yes. Marry me now.'

He pulls back and hits me with his smile, reserved only for me. 'Let's get married, my beautiful girl.' He joins our hand-cuffed hands and starts leading me down the aisle.

'Here.' He hands me a half-full flute of champagne. 'Take it easy, Mrs Ward.'

I take the glass with my free hand before he can withdraw his offer. He's been even more unreasonable about me drinking lately. 'Are you going to remove the cuffs now?'

'No,' he answers swiftly. 'You're not leaving my side all day long.' He signals for a bottle of water from Mario, and I'm suddenly reminded that I'll never enjoy a drink with Jesse, not even on our wedding day.

I glance around the bar, seeing everyone chatting, nibbling on canapés and drinking champagne. It's relaxed and calm, just how I feel myself. After Jesse insulted all things traditional, we made our vows and he took it upon himself to drown me in his mouth – prior to getting the go-ahead from the registrar. Then he picked me up and strode out of the summer room, leaving my poor mother chasing behind, demanding he wait for the music. Not a chance. I was placed neatly on my stool at the bar and smothered with his lips while the congregation made their way in behind us.

Dan catches my attention across the room. He's being so

quiet, his attention constantly pointed in Kate's direction, which means it's also pointed in Sam's.

'What are you thinking about?'

I pull my attention back to Jesse and smile. 'Nothing.'

He rests his palm on the back of my neck and massages me. 'Are you happy?'

'Yes,' I answer quickly. I'm delirious. He knows I am.

'Good, then my work here is done. Kiss me, wife.' He leans down, offering me his lips.

Reaching up, I pull him down to me, giving him exactly what he wants.

'Enough!' Mum's shrill voice stabs at my eardrums. 'Get those handcuffs off my daughter!' She starts fiddling with my wrist. 'Jesse Ward, you would try the patience of a saint! Where's the key?'

He pulls back and narrows his eyes on Mum. 'Somewhere you'll never want to venture, Elizabeth.'

She gasps and throws irritated eyes at me. 'Your husband is a menace.'

'I love him,' I declare, and she fights a fond smile from her cherry-red lips. She's desperate to maintain her grievance, but I know she loves him, too. I know she loves how much he loves me, and while he infuriates her, he also charms her, as he does all women. Just because Elizabeth happens to be my mother doesn't make her immune to his potency.

'I know you do, darling.' She turns her attention to the bar, calling Mario for some of his Most Marvellous.

'Right!' Tessa dives over and takes my glass from my hand. 'The photographer is ready. I thought we'd get the family shots done first, then have you two alone for a few. You'll need to remove those cuffs.'

I watch as my glass is placed on the bar before she makes a grab for Jesse's water, but he swipes it away, leaving Tessa grabbing at thin air. 'We're not in the photos, I told you.'

'We're not?' I blurt, completely shocked. He's trampling that tradition, too?

'You must be in the photos,' Tessa insists. 'What memories will you have?' She looks horrified.

'I don't need pictures for memories.'

I look at him in horror. 'We're not in the family shots?' Oh God, another reason for my mum to despair.

'No,' he answers decisively.

'You can't begrudge her mother a photo with her daughter!' Tessa pleads.

He doesn't answer; he just shrugs nonchalantly, completely unfazed.

I roll my eyes. 'You do it on purpose,' I grumble. 'We're having photos.'

'No, we're not.'

I glare at my delicious husband with narrowed, determined eyes. He is not trampling this. 'We are having photographs. This is my wedding, too, Ward.'

His mouth drops open, his bottle pausing halfway to his lips. 'But I want some quiet time. Just me and you.'

'We're having photos,' I say, full of authority. I feel a sulk coming on, but I'm not letting him win this one.

He scowls slightly, but he doesn't argue with me. Instead, he signals for Tessa to gather our guests and take them into the rear grounds of The Manor. I watch as she flies into commander role, shouting for everyone to follow on.

'Come on, then,' he grumbles, lifting me from the stool and placing me neatly on my feet. I mentally cheer to myself. He's learning, or perhaps it's me who's learning – learning how to deal with him. I'm not sure, but we're making immense progress. He knows when to relent, as do I.

He leads me out into the sunshine, where Tessa is directing people into various positions, but my mother is quickly repositioning bodies as we approach. I look across and see Kate being ravished by Sam, my eyes instantly darting towards Dan and finding what I knew I would. A filthy look. Is she doing this on purpose?

I look up at Jesse. 'Please, just do what you're told.' The more he plays up, the longer this will take and the more stressed my mum will get.

'If you promise me quiet time after.'

'I promise you quiet time,' I say on a laugh.

'Good. I hate sharing you,' he grumbles, and I smile. I know he does.

Jesse spends the next hour cooperating completely. He moves when asked, smiles when requested, and even releases me from the cuffs without complaint when I have some shots on my own. On the final click, I'm swiftly scooped up and carried back to The Manor.

It's not long before we're alone in one of The Manor's suites – the suite where he cornered me and tried to seduce me, the suite where I got myself ready for our wedding. The door closes softly behind us, and I'm led to the grand, satin-adorned bed. He lifts me and crawls up the bed, settling me beneath him.

Now I've got a set of lustful greens gazing down at me. 'Quiet time,' he whispers, dropping a soft kiss on my lips before his face burrows straight into my neck.

'You want to snuggle?' I ask, a little surprised.

'I do.' He nuzzles further. 'I want to snuggle with my wife. Are you going to deny me?'

'No.'

'Good. Our marriage is getting off to the best start, then.'

So I let him snuggle. I absorb his weight, his smell and his heart beating against my chest. I like quiet time, but as I gaze up at the high ceiling, my mind naturally wanders to the thoughts that have been lingering for weeks – the thoughts that I have tried my hardest to bat away. Impossible. The perfection of this moment, of our love for each other, is clouded by the reality of the challenges ahead.

There has been no contact from Mikael, so I assume he is still in Denmark. I've been spared that challenge for now. There's been no sight of Coral, either, and Sarah has been kicked out on her arse after admitting to everything I absolutely knew she did. I've not heard from Matt, so he's definitely got the message, but I'm still far too curious about his knowledge of Jesse's drinking issue. And then there's my period, which is due on Monday. I've never wished so hard for something.

Jesse would love to have me nailed to his side, he's made that clear, and perhaps he thinks a baby would achieve that. He would see it as the perfect excuse for me to give up work, something else he would like to happen. But I love my job. I love spending my days designing and interacting with clients. I'll battle with him on this ... if I'm not pregnant. I've no idea what I'll do if I am. I've been making him wear condoms for two weeks, and he's demonstrated his disgust, but if I'm not pregnant, then I want it to stay that way.

'Will you do something for me?' I ask quietly.

'Anything.' His hot breath on my neck has my face turning into him, encouraging him to look at me. His head lifts from its hiding place, his hair now a dishevelled mess, his greens finding my eyes. 'What do you want, baby?'

'Can you *please* resist talking to Patrick about Mikael?' I brace myself for his scoff. I've managed to keep him from my boss, but with Patrick and Irene arriving later for the evening reception, I'm not sure Jesse can hold himself back.

'I agreed not to visit Patrick if you spoke with him. And I don't believe you have.' He raises expectant eyebrows at me.

No, I haven't, because I have no idea how to approach this. He was shocked enough to hear I was marrying one of my clients. I could hardly hit him with the news that I'm about to jump ship on Rococo Union's most important client, the client who guarantees Patrick's comfortable retirement.

'Give me until Monday,' I plead. 'I'll talk to him on Monday.'

'Monday,' he affirms, his eyes slightly narrowed. 'I mean it, Ava. You've got till Monday, and then I'm stepping in.'

'Okay.'

He grunts a little, and then buries himself back in my neck. 'When do I get to take you away?'

'I did warn you there would be no honeymoon for a while. You accepted that, remember?'

He lifts his head and points a scowl at me. 'So when am I going to get my wife to myself? When am I going to be able to love her?'

'You always love me. When I'm not working, I'm with you. And you text and call me often enough, so I'm technically connected to you all day, anyway.' I need to approach this issue, too. He's relentless.

'I want you to give up working.' He's pouting, and I'm shaking my head, just like I have every time he's suggested this. He's not demanding yet, but that's coming, most likely when Mikael rears his ugly head. 'Be a lady of leisure,' he presses.

'How would I be a lady of leisure if I'm permanently nailed to you?'

His hips push into my groin, enticing a sharp intake of breath from me. 'Okay. Be a lady of pleasure, then.' He's grinning at me, the crafty arse, and I suspect a sense fuck is on the horizon. I'd love him to take me hard. It would make a nice change after the last few weeks of gentle Jesse.

'Ward, you're not taking me now. Anyway, we should get downstairs before Mum comes searching for us.'

He rolls his eyes and sighs. 'Your mother's a pain in the fucking arse.'

'Don't wind her up, then.' I laugh.

He shifts off me and pulls me to the edge of the bed. 'She

needs to accept who has the power,' he says candidly, starting to re-cuff me.

My amusement increases. 'You're touching me. Of course you have the power.' I attempt to pull my hand free from his grip, but the clanging of metal soon tells me he's already managed to secure me. I look up at him. He's grinning that roguish grin.

'I'm sorry.' He shakes our wrists, instigating further clanking. 'Who has the power?'

I scowl at him. 'You can have the power for today.' I brush my hair over my shoulder and rearrange my diamond.

'You're being very reasonable,' he says quietly, swooping down and tackling my mouth. I grip his shoulder and soak up his attentive tongue and the warmth of his big palm secured at the base of my back. 'Hmmm. You taste delicious, Mrs Ward. Ready?'

I shake myself back to life. 'Yes.' I'm all breathy and hot.

He goes quiet and his eyes drift down my body, his hand slowly lifting and resting lightly on my stomach. I flinch, and he freezes. I don't know why that happened. He doesn't look up; he just waits a few silent moments before spreading his fingers, and then circling big, soft rings on my tummy. I wish he would stop doing this. Neither of us has spoken about it but it can't be avoided for much longer. He must sense my lack of enthusiasm. This is my biggest burden of all. I don't want a baby.

I pull back and his hand drops. 'Come on, then.' I can't look at him. I start towards the door, but I'm soon halted when Jesse doesn't follow, the metal of the cuffs cutting into my flesh. I wince a little.

'Are we going to talk about this, Ava?' he asks shortly.

'Talk about what?' I can't do this, not now – not on my wedding day. We've had weeks of skirting around this, and for once it's me who's evading all talk. I'm in complete denial, but it's hitting me harder each day. I could be pregnant.

'You know what.'

I keep my eyes down, not knowing what else to say. Time seems to slow, enhancing the awkward silence between us, and as I hear him draw breath to speak when I'm clearly not going to, the door crashes open and Mum charges in. I've never been so pleased to see her.

'Can I ask,' she starts, all stern, 'why you didn't just run off somewhere to get married? I'm thoroughly fed up of running around trying to control you.'

'We're coming.' I pull at the cuffs, but he doesn't budge.

'We'll be a few minutes, Elizabeth,' Jesse counters shortly.

'No, we're coming,' I argue, silently begging him to leave this exactly where it is. I give him pleading eyes, and he shakes his head on a sigh. 'Please,' I say quietly.

His hand delves into his hair in frustration and his jaw tightens severely. He's not happy but he relents and lets me pull him from the room. I can't believe he has chosen today of all days to push for a *talk* on this. It's my wedding day.

Chapter 3

The summer room looks incredible. Hints of green foliage peek out from among the masses of calla lilies adorning every spare space. The chairs are draped in white organza with big green bows fastened to the back, and tall glass vases, full of crystal clear water and tall calla lilies, dominate the tables.

Simple, understated elegance.

I've picked my way through a three-course meal with no wine and indulged anyone who's approached in conversation. I've done anything to avoid looking at Jesse. John has given a short, sweet speech as Jesse's best man, but there was no talk of their history as friends, or mention of Uncle Carmichael and the early days. John doesn't do humour, although he seems to find Jesse's way with me quite amusing.

And my dad. I'm close to tears as I watch him battle his way through his notes, reminiscing on my youth and advising everyone of my feisty streak.

He raises his glass and turns towards us. 'Jesse, good luck,' he says seriously, prompting a chorus of laughter from our guests and a huge smile from Jesse, who raises his glass too, then stands himself, keeping his arm down so he doesn't yank at my wrist. My dad is applauded as he sits and downs a whisky, my mum rubbing his shoulder on a smile.

Jesse places his water on the table and turns to me, dropping to his knees and taking my hands in his. My back straightens, and my eyes make a quick scan of the room, noting all attention is pointed right at us. Why can't he just play by the rules?

His thumbs are working fast circles on the backs of my hands, and then he plays with my rings, turning them on my finger before straightening them up. He lifts his glorious greens and I'm blasted by twinkling pools of pure happiness. 'Ava,' he says quietly, but I've no doubt the whole room can hear him. 'My beautiful girl.' He smiles mildly. 'All mine.' Leaning up, he kisses me sweetly. 'I don't need to stand up and declare to everyone here how much I love you. I'm not interested in satisfying anyone of that. Except you.'

A lump is forming in my throat, and he's only just started.

He sighs. 'You've taken me completely, baby. You've swallowed me up and drowned me in your beauty and spirit. You know I can't function without you. You've made my life as beautiful as you are. You've made me want to live a worthy existence – a life with you. All I need is you – to look at you; to listen to you; to feel you.' He drops my hands and smoothes his palms over my thighs. 'To love you.'

I'm ruined. My mum's ruined. Everyone in the room is ruined. My teeth are clamped on my bottom lip to prevent a sob escaping, I'm choking on the lump in my throat and my eyes are welling with tears as I look down at Jesse's handsome face.

'I need you to let me do all of those things, Ava. I need you to let me look after you for ever.'

I hear my mum's sobs, and I can't help mine. Not now. He used to cripple me with just his touch. Now he cripples me with his words, too. I'm destined for a life of devastating pleasure, melting tenderness, and heart-stopping emotion. He's going to incapacitate me at every turn.

'I know,' I whisper.

He nods and exhales a long lungful of air before standing and pulling me up to his body. My face falls straight into his neck, and I breathe him into me, his fresh, minty scent prompting me to close my eyes on a contented sigh.

The room is no longer silent. When I pull out of Jesse's hold, I see people standing everywhere, a steady, respectful clapping of hands resonating through the room. I should feel embarrassed, but I don't. He's just spoken to me like we were alone, proving that he really doesn't care where he is and who's there – wherever and whenever, as it always has been and as it always will be.

I watch as my mum approaches and throws her arms around Jesse. 'Jesse Ward, I love you,' she says in his ear as he holds her with one arm, 'but please remove those handcuffs from my daughter.'

'Not going to happen, Elizabeth.'

She releases him and slaps his shoulder, and then Kate dives on him. 'Oh my God. I wanna kiss your feet.'

I roll my eyes, getting my arm yanked all over the place while people congratulate my neurotic ex-playboy on his little speech. It's our wedding day, and I don't want to be here. All of these people, including Kate and my mother, are getting in my way. I want him all to myself.

After I've been kissed on the cheek a million times, and Jesse has shaken hands with everyone, he starts leading me from the summer room.

'Ava?'

I turn, finding my brother close behind. I almost wish he wasn't here. He's struggling, and it's incredibly painful to see. Looking down at my wrist, I start wondering how I can convince Jesse to release me. He wouldn't for my mum, and I haven't much faith that he will for my brother. They're wary of each other. It can't be ignored.

I turn my eyes up to Jesse and find him watching me. He knows what I'm thinking, and I know he's not happy about it, but he still reaches into his pocket and pulls out a small key.

Without a word, he releases me from the cuffs and leaves

them dangling from his wrist. 'Go,' he says quietly, flicking threatening eyes at Dan.

Dan gives as good as he gets, flashing an equally warning glare. I don't need this, not with two of the most important men in my life.

I lean up to kiss Jesse's cheek and feel his hand glide around my hips, smoothing over my bum before he rips his eyes away from Dan and turns his face into my lips. 'Don't be long,' he says, releasing me and striding off.

'Come on.' I hold my hand out to Dan, and he takes it, letting me lead him out to the gardens.

We're silent for a short while as we wander down the gravel path, past the tennis courts, finding ourselves in the woodlands. The low evening sun is fighting through the canopy of trees and scattering dashes of sparkling light across the ground before us, and I focus my attention on tracking the puddles of light as they dance across the forest floor at my feet. There has never been discomfort between us, but the tension now feels *really* uncomfortable.

Dropping Dan's hand and lifting my dress, I step over a large twig and catch my heel, causing me to stagger. 'Oh!'

'Careful.' Dan grabs my elbow to steady me. 'I don't think those shoes were made for hiking.'

I relax immediately. 'No,' I laugh, straightening myself out. 'Ava . . .'

I give him a tired look. 'Just say it, Dan. Whatever you've been dying to say since you've met Jesse, just say it.'

'Okay. I don't like him.'

I recoil a little. 'Okay.' I laugh uncomfortably. 'I didn't think you'd be so blunt.'

He shrugs. 'What do you want me to say?'

'You don't even know him. The only attempt you've made to speak with him, to get to know him, was when you tried to warn him.' Mum might have intercepted Dan's older brother speech, but he still made a start, and Jesse's ticking jaw was a clear indication of what he thought of Dan's intended caution.

'Explain about this drink issue, then.'

My eyes widen. 'What are you talking about?' I don't like the reproachful look on his face, not at all.

'I'm talking about the drink issue Matt brought up – the drink issue that hasn't been mentioned since. The fact he hasn't touched alcohol all day hasn't gone unnoticed, Ava. Not on my part, anyway.'

I knew it was too much of a good thing. I don't need Dan unearthing an issue that really isn't an issue. Jesse hasn't had a drink since I found him at Lusso. He doesn't need it if he has me, and he most definitely has me.

'And where's his family?' he asks.

'I've told you. He doesn't speak to them.'

'Right.' He laughs. 'That's convenient. And to think I disliked Matt.'

'So now you're suddenly a Matt advocate, are you?' I snipe nastily. I point my finger in his face. I feel really fucking mad. 'There is no issue. He has no family, so back off. Let's talk about what's really eating you up. Let's talk about Kate.'

It's his eyes that are wide now. Yes, I've just homed in on the real *issue* here.

'Nothing's eating me up!' he yells. 'I couldn't give a fuck about Kate!'

'Of course!' I laugh. 'That's why you've barely pulled your eyes away from her all day.'

'Who the hell is that Sam?' His tone only confirms I've hit a nerve.

I might not be thrilled with Kate's life direction at the moment, but I would prefer her carrying on with Sam rather than heading for guaranteed disaster with Dan. It ended in tears before and it will again. 'He's good for her,' I spit. 'You need to leave this exactly where it is.' I gather up my dress, ready to make a retreat, but he grabs my arm.

'What if I don't want to?'

'Get your fucking hands off her.' The familiar, rampant growl pulls my head around fast. Jesse is standing nearby, his chest heaving, a murderous look on his face.

'It's fine. We're done,' I say, yanking my arm free. I need to get Jesse away before he tramples all over my brother. And it won't just be a verbal trample.

Dan steps forward. 'She's my sister.'

Jesse closes the gap between them, his eyes black. 'She's. My. Wife.'

My brother laughs a little, not a good thing, judging by Jesse's darkening glare and the balling of his fists by his side.

I place my hand on his arm and he flinches, too focused on Dan to realise it's me. As soon as he does, though, he breaks the glowering deadlock and turns his eyes to mine. They soften immediately.

'Let's go,' I say quietly, sliding my hand down his arm to grasp his.

He nods and turns with me, not giving Dan another look. I'm grateful. Dan's not in a good place, and I know how tenacious he can be when he's on the defence.

'Give me your hand,' Jesse orders, reaching down as we head for The Manor. I let him take it and re-cuff me. 'Don't ask me to remove them again.'

'I won't,' I grumble. I wish he'd never released me in the first place. Then I might not be seething with Dan's obvious *issue* with Kate and his inquisitiveness with regard to Jesse's *issue*. 'Throw away the key.'

His eyebrows raise. 'Wishing you'd stayed nailed to me?'

'Yes,' I admit. 'Don't free me again.'

'Okay,' he agrees. 'Would you like a drink?'

We continue toward the house, re-cuffed and reunited. 'I'd

love a drink.' I've hardly touched a drop all day, and I'm a little surprised that he's offered.

'Come on.' He pulls me in and kisses my forehead. 'I won't stand for it, Ava. Even if he is your brother.'

'I know,' I agree quietly. I'm surprised by his self-control. It doesn't matter to Jesse who he eliminates, and Dan has not helped his cause. He's just tried to restrain me, the worst thing he could do. I don't want my husband and brother to battle, but I know Jesse would never back down when it comes to me, and Dan would never lose face.

This is an issue.

The evening guests have arrived, and as we make our way through the bar, we're accosted, kissed, and wished well with every step we take. I'm finally placed on my stool and handed a glass of water. Water? I look at the clear glass and back to Jesse, who is doing a damn fine job of ignoring my obvious disbelief.

Tessa comes steaming over, looking as wound up as poor Mum. 'Where have you been?' she asks incredulously, flicking her eyes from me to Jesse. 'You were supposed to cut the cake!'

Jesse opens a bottle of water and takes a long swig, not in the least bit perturbed by Tessa's concern. 'It's fine.'

Tessa shakes her head in disbelief and stomps off towards the entrance hall. 'Don't you want to cut the cake?' I ask, my wrist being lifted as Jesse secures the lid on his water bottle. 'Kate went out of her way to make it at such short notice.'

He reaches forward and straightens my diamond. 'Then let's not ruin it.'

'You're impossible,' I sigh, glancing across the bar, spotting Sam and Drew entertaining my dad, who's looking a little rosy cheeked. My mum is revelling in the attention, undoubtedly offering tours of the grounds, and Kate is looking drunk. Tom flaps a limp wrist at me, Victoria gives a girly wave, and poor Sal just looks like she's trying to fit in. She's still sparkling, but her new fellow isn't here. I smile and turn my attention back to Jesse, just as Tessa storms back into the bar.

'Okay. I've spoken to Elizabeth,' Tessa huffs. 'We're cutting the cake and having the first dance shortly, so don't disappear again.' She storms off. She's definitely regretting taking this job.

'You okay, baby?' His warm palm slides across my cheek.

'Yes, fine,' I answer, but I'm not. I've fallen out with my brother, and that has absolutely never happened.

'You don't look fine. I said I wanted you to enjoy today.'

I inwardly laugh. Then he should let me have a drink and he shouldn't have broached the subject that has my brain the most twisted at the moment. 'I'm fine.' I sigh, taking a long sip of my water. Fucking water.

Patrick and Irene approach, my cuddly bear of a boss brandishing a huge ivory gift bag, his wife adorned in a mass of animal-print material. I think it might be a dress. I quickly direct my eyes to Jesse. 'Here's Patrick. You said Monday, remember?' I need to get that in quickly.

Jesse looks over his shoulder. 'Yes, Ava. Just until Monday, though.'

'Flower!' Patrick thrusts the gift bag at me, kisses my cheek, and then holds his hand out to Jesse. 'Mr Ward,' he greets, a frown popping up onto his wrinkled forehead when he clocks the cuffs.

'Please, it's Jesse. Thank you for coming.' Jesse takes Patrick's hand.

My boss drags his eyes away from our wrists. 'This is Irene.' He signals to his wife as she wobbles over with the biggest grin on her face. I smile to myself. She's affected.

'Nice to meet you,' she giggles.

'And you.' Jesse hits her with his smile, and she disintegrates on the spot. 'Please, the bar staff will see to you.'

'Thank you!' she gushes. 'This hotel is just wonderful!'

'Hello, Irene,' I say on a smile. She drags her greedy eyes away from my husband and brings them onto me. She's a frightening woman, but not at the moment. She's too busy straightening her back and pulling in her stomach. 'How are you?'

'Delightful!' she sings in my face.

Patrick grasps his wife's elbow and guides her away. 'We'll get a drink.' He rolls his eyes, and I smile fondly at my boss. I know he finds his wife exasperating.

'Interesting woman,' Jesse muses, looking a little alarmed at her leopard-print body wobbling away from us.

I laugh. 'She makes Patrick's life miserable.'

'I can imagine.'

'Here's John,' I say, glancing past Jesse at the big guy strolling over, wraparounds in place and his usual menacing expression plastered all over his face. His stare is pointed at the cuffs before he gives me the nod. I nod back.

'A word, Jesse,' he rumbles. He's too serious. I don't like it, and Jesse's quick flick of his eyes to me doesn't make me feel any better.

Jesse reaches into his pocket and pulls out the key to the handcuffs, and I watch as he brings it to my wrist. 'What are you doing?' I ask, yanking my arm away.

'John wants a quick word.'

'Oh no,' I laugh. 'You don't get to release me when it suits you. No way, Ward.' I look at John, who's still expressionless.

'Ava, I'll be back shortly.' He pulls my wrist back to him.

'No! Where are you going?' I look at John. 'Where is he going?'

'S'all good, girl.'

'No. It's not all fucking good!' I yell, a bit too loudly, earning myself a frightening scowl from Jesse. I don't care. He doesn't get to do this. He doesn't get to brush me off when it suits him. It's my wedding day.

'Watch your mouth!' he grates, leaning into me. 'I'll be a few minutes. You'll stay fucking put, Ava.'

I recoil at his animosity, completely stunned as he makes quick work of the handcuffs before striding out with John. I'm perched on a barstool, the bride in a stunning gown, adorned with diamonds, all of our guests laughing, chatting and drinking, and I want to go home. I feel tearful, slighted, and very, very hurt. I lower myself from the stool, deciding to escape to the toilets. I might have a little cry, too. I need to get away from these people before the tears start flowing freely.

'Where are you going, darling?' Mum asks as she makes her way over.

I spread a fake smile on my face. She's had too much Most Marvellous. Her hair isn't perfect and she doesn't seem to care, a clear indication that she's feeling a bit squiffy. 'Toilet. I won't be long.'

'Do you want some help? I'm not sure where Kate's gone.' She looks around the bar.

'No, I've got it.' I leave my mum and head for the toilets, looking forward to some privacy.

Pushing my way through the door, I place myself in front of the mirror to look at my sorry face. I'm not a blushing bride any more. There is no twinkle in my eye or happy smile on my lips. I sigh heavily and pinch my cheeks in an attempt to get some colour back into them.

'Ohhh myyy Goddd!'

My head flies up and my body swings around to face the source of the long moan. I still myself, holding my breath as I hear shuffling and shifting from one of the cubicles. Someone is having sex in the toilet? No! I quickly gather my dress up to leave. This could be embarrassing. I take my first urgent step, but then freeze when the door swings open and Kate stumbles out.

I gasp, my dress dropping from my hands. 'What are you doing?' I blurt, shocked. I know Sam was slightly miffed that all things kink have been removed and stored temporarily, but they could've waited.

She stiffens from head to toe, her red hair a wild mane of curls, half covering her shocked face. 'Oh shit!' she says quietly, rearranging her dress.

'Couldn't you have waited?' I ask, horrified but relieved that I haven't just caught one of our guests in the act.

'Ava . . .' she begins, and then a man strolls out behind. And it's not Sam.

My mouth falls open. 'Dan?' I don't believe this. 'What the hell are you doing?'

He shrugs, refusing to look at me, keeping all of his attention on refastening his trousers. My eyes are batting between them, waiting for an explanation, but I get nothing from either of them. They're just standing there, both looking anywhere except at me.

I throw furious eyes at Dan. 'I told you to leave it!' I shout, before turning my fury on Kate. 'And you're pissed! What's the matter with you two? Haven't you learned?'

'None of your business,' Dan says flatly, and then strides out of the Ladies, leaving me and my delinquent friend alone.

'Kate?' I push, but she's still refusing to meet my eyes. 'What about Sam?' I ask. The poor bloke is out there, completely oblivious. 'I can't believe this.' The heel of my hand meets my forehead, my brain aching with information overload.

She hiccups and giggles before reaching for the sink to steady her swaying body. 'Fun,' she says haughtily. 'And it's got nothing to do with you.'

'Oh, okay,' I exclaim, lifting my dress. 'I'll leave you to have your *fun*, in that case.' I turn and leave the toilets, heading straight to Jesse's office. Today couldn't get any worse.

The summer room has been cleared of tables but is now full of people, the band enticing everyone to the dance floor with classic Motown. I skirt through our guests, smiling, trying my hardest to look like the elated bride and cutting any lengthy conversation very short. I've fallen out with my brother, and now Kate, too. I want to escape with Jesse and be alone when we're at our happiest – when the world and its problems are not interfering with our little bubble of contentment, where we only have our own *issues* to contend with.

I steam down the corridor and straight into his office, my heart falling straight into my Louboutins as soon as I lay my eyes on the occupants.

There are just two people.

Jesse . . . and Coral.

Chapter 4

My day just got a whole lot worse.

They're seated at opposite ends of a couch, and both heads fly towards me while I just stand there feeling a little lost. All of my anger, all of my frustrations of the day have just transformed into unbearable pain. I can feel my eyes welling up with tears and my heart is thundering in my chest. I feel completely crushed.

Not knowing what else to do, but knowing for certain I don't want this woman to see me break down, I slowly step back, closing the door quietly behind me. I walk numbly down the corridor in a haze of misery and escape the happy chatter and dancing bodies of our guests, heading down the gravel pathway towards the woodlands.

Sitting my defeated arse on an old log, I start picking at the dried bark, crumbling it into grains between my fingers, while the cool evening air spikes at my exposed skin. They were just talking, but he knows how I feel about her – how I feel about any other woman who Jesse's had – yet he still sacrificed time with me on our special day to see her. I want to scream at him, bash my fists on his chest, and yell in his face. But I don't have the energy. All of the fight has been sucked out of me. My spirit has been stripped down by drama, mine and others', and it's left me feeling exposed and vulnerable. And doubtful, too. On my wedding day of all days, I'm doubtful I can maintain the strength I need to spend my life with Jesse – spend my life fighting off women and problems . . . *issues*. The tears I've been holding back jump straight from my eyes and onto my lace. I'm powerless. I can't make these women go away, I can't strip Jesse's past from him, and I can't control other people and what they do. The one thing I can do, though, is take my pills so I don't get pregnant. I drop my head in my hands and sob quietly to myself. I've not even got the energy to cry properly.

Through my low, pathetic weeping, I hear him approach behind me. I can smell his fresh water and minty scent. Even through my total numbness, I can still feel his presence. Every part of my being senses him, but I don't want to look at him.

I brush my tears away. 'I know you're there,' I say quietly, keeping my gaze downward.

'I know you do.' His evenly spaced steps crunch over the ground, getting louder as he nears, and in my peripheral vision I see him lower himself next to me. But he doesn't touch me. His hands are clasped in front of him, his thumbs circling each other slowly. I can hear the tail end of his heavy breathing subsiding from where he's been running around the grounds like a madman trying to find me. And now he's just sitting next to me, all silent when he should be explaining himself, explaining why he abandoned me on our wedding day so he could see a woman who's in love with him – another woman who's in love with him.

I laugh to myself. 'Isn't it funny how we're so in touch with each other, yet you sit here now and don't know what to say?' I see him shift next to me, and then his hand drifts across the space between us and rests on my thigh, his heated touch doing things I really don't want it to do. I look down at his spread fingers, his flat platinum and diamond band sparkling as he flexes his hand and squeezes my thigh. 'So he touches me,' I say quietly.

'He loves you,' he whispers. 'He wishes he could eliminate the past that's hurting you.'

I turn my face to his and see green puddles of regret. 'Then why did you see her? Why did you desert me on our wedding day to see her?'

'I couldn't leave her at the gates with guests arriving, Ava.'

'So tell her to go away.'

'And cause a scene?'

'What did she want?' I ask. She was here for a reason. 'Did she know we were getting married today?'

His frown line crawls across his brow and sets firmly in place, his lip disappearing between his teeth. 'Yes, she knew.'

So he's spoken to her? 'And she still came? Was she hoping to stop it? Was she going to barge into the summer room and declare that we shouldn't be joined in holy matrimony?' This is laughable.

'I don't know, Ava.' He looks away.

'When did you speak to her?'

He sighs. 'She's been calling and turning up at The Manor. I've told her repeatedly I'm not helping her. I'm not sure what else I can do.'

'What's your definition of an affair?' I ask.

His eyes swiftly return to mine, all confused by my question. 'What do you mean?'

'I mean, she's in love with you, and you've said it was only sex. It was obviously more to her.' I assess him, trying to gauge his reaction.

'Baby, I've told you before, just sex. They always wanted more but I never gave them any reason to expect it. Never.'

I wince at the referral to *they*. He means many – many women who want him, many women who've had him, many women who have fallen in love with him. I want to tell him what Coral said about him making her need him, but then he'll know that I intercepted her call. And after having him, who wouldn't want him again, maybe even think they need him? I know that *I* did, but now my need is a lot deeper than his physical touch. Now I need him to breathe. 'I don't want you to see her again.'

He returns his eyes to mine. 'I've no need to.'

I take a deep breath and return to scanning the ground. 'I've had enough of my wedding. I'd like to leave.'

'Ava, look at me.'

'Jesse, don't start making demands when I'm feeling like this.'

'Perhaps you didn't hear me right. I said, look at me.' He's not asking gently now, but my despondency prevents me from defying him.

'What?' I ask, following through on his unreasonable order.

He falls to his knees in front of me and takes my hands. 'I've fucked up. I'm so sorry, but I was trying to keep her away from you. I panicked. I didn't want her kicking up a stink on your special day.'

'It's your special day, too,' I remind him quietly. 'You should've just told me.'

'I know.' He leans up and wraps me in his arms. 'Let me make it up to you. What do you want me do, baby?'

I relax into him. 'Just take me to bed.'

'Deal.' He stands me up and reinforces his apology with a deep, meaningful kiss. 'We'll make friends properly.' He scoops me up and heads back to The Manor.

We enter the summer room and are immediately attacked by my mother's infuriated glare. 'There you are!' She scuttles towards us, still tipsy, but obviously annoyed. 'You've not cut the cake and you need to have your first dance. Tell me, are we having a wedding?'

I want to do none of those things. Evening guests are here, and we should socialise, but I just can't be bothered.

'I'm taking Ava upstairs. She's tired.' He doesn't stop for my mum, and he doesn't put me down. I'm being carried through the summer room, through all of our guests, and he isn't stopping for anyone.

'But it's only ten o'clock!' She's horrified, as I expected. 'What about your guests?'

'There's a bar, a band, and plenty to eat, Elizabeth. I'm sure they'll survive.' His tolerance of my mum is lessening by the hour.

'Ava, please. Talk some sense into him.' She's pleading, and I suddenly feel terrible. This is a special day for her, too, and my Lord has trampled all over it.

I clamp my palms around Jesse's cheeks as he continues with his long strides, and Mum continues to flank us. 'A little longer,' I say quietly, and he halts in his tracks.

'You're tired.' He's frowning a little. Yes, I am tired, but not physically. I'm mentally exhausted. 'Let me take you to bed, baby.'

'Dance with me.' I run my nose up his cheek and take a full-on hit of fresh-water loveliness. 'Let's dance.' I feel him turning, while pushing his cheek into my nuzzle.

'Thank God!' Mum cries, following keenly behind.

I'm placed on my feet in the middle of the dance floor before he makes his way over to the band and speaks into the lead singer's ear. He nods and smiles, then everyone clears the floor, and it's just me, feeling conspicuous and exposed. And then the singer removes himself from the stage, along with all of the other band members, and Snow Patrol breaks the silence with 'Chasing Cars'. He turns to face me and just stands there, watching me for the longest time. I'm tearing up, and I know that if I look at Mum she'll be blubbering, so I don't. I keep my eyes on my husband and watch as he slowly crosses the floor and takes me in his hold, pulling me close to his chest. My cheek rests on his shoulder, and he starts swaying us, holding me firmly in his big, strong arms. My hands slide around his back and my eyes close, my body naturally following his slow, soft movements.

'I'm sorry, baby,' he says quietly into my hair. 'I'm sorry I left you earlier.'

I sigh and squeeze him a little, a silent indication of my forgiveness.

He exhales and pushes his lips to the back of my head. 'The harder I try not to hurt you, the more I do. I'm hopeless.'

'Be quiet.'

'Okay, but I'm still sorry.' He holds me firmer still. 'I can't wait to crawl into bed with you.'

'Me neither,' I agree. Once again, everyone is in our way. 'Tomorrow, we stay in bed all day.'

'We need to go home first.'

I sag in disappointment at his reminder. We're staying here tonight. All of the rooms have been prepared for guests, mainly for my family. 'We go home first thing in the morning, then.' I know it's rude, leaving our guests, but I don't want to face Kate, and I definitely don't want to face Dan.

'We do,' he agrees, 'after we've soaked in the bath and had breakfast with your parents.'

I let him gently rock me, my eyes closing again and my mind relaxing a little, letting Jesse draw all of my stress away. 'I wish you had taken me away. Somewhere quiet, just us.'

'I wish I had, too. But your mother would've had something to say about it.'

I smile to myself. Opening my eyes, I see her pull my reluctant dad to the floor, and then Kate and Sam follow with Victoria and Tom. I let my eyes close again and melt into Jesse and his movements.

'Mrs Ward, are you falling asleep on me?' he asks quietly.

'Hmmm.' I'm far too content, held tight in his arms, all of the other couples around us invisible as I remain in the dark, just feeling him, smelling him.

'I love you.' He pushes his nose into my hair and inhales deeply. 'I love you so fucking much.'

'I know,' I whisper, turning my head into him and capturing his lips. He hums happily, pulling me up from the floor so I'm locked tightly against his chest, our tongues gliding softly between our mouths. 'Mr Ward, you're drawing attention.'

'Fuck them. Wherever, whenever, baby. You know that.' He pulls away. 'Let me see those eyes.'

I show him immediately. 'Why do you always demand to see them?'

He only smiles mildly, but his greens still twinkle madly. 'Because when I look into them, I know for sure that you're real.'

I match his faint smile. 'I'm real.'

'I often wonder. I didn't tell you how beautiful you look.' He pecks my lips and keeps swaying us gently. 'I thought it, but my beautiful girl renders me stupid every time I lay my eyes on her.' He searches my eyes and sighs. 'You keep my heart beating, baby. And it will only ever beat for you. Understand?'

I really do understand. I nod mildly and move my hands to the back of his head, relishing the feel of his hair between my fingers. 'I need you to take me to bed.'

The corners of his lips tip a little. 'Will my delightful mother-in-law allow that?'

I shrug. 'I don't care. I just want you to myself. Take me to bed.'

'Deal.' He drops me to my feet and swoops down to kiss me chastely. 'You don't have to ask me twice, Mrs Ward.'

'I just did.'

He frowns. 'That's your fucking mother's fault.' I'm turned in his arms and led from the floor, sidestepping all of the couples in tight clinches.

'Oh, look at Clive and Cathy!' I say, spying our concierge and Jesse's housekeeper stuck together as Clive shuffles her from side-to-side. They look so sweet. I hear Jesse laugh a little as I spy Kate being held up by Sam. And then I spot my brother in the distance, his attention and scowl pointed directly at my best friend. Jesse gives me a little tug, and I look up to see he's noticed who I'm focused on.

'It doesn't look like history to me.' He raises his eyebrows, and then lowers his body to pick me up, just as Snow Patrol fades out and is replaced with something else – something much louder and upbeat. I can feel my face breaking out in a smile as I watch Jesse freeze mid-bend. And then the male's voice kicks in.

'Hello, Justin,' I say quietly, watching him straighten up. He steps back thoughtfully and grabs the lapels of his suit jacket, giving them a little tug before brushing them off and hitting me with wide, excited eyes.

'Oh, Mrs Ward.' He shakes his head mildly. 'I'm about tear that floor up.' He grabs my hand and pulls me urgently back to the dance floor, weaving us through the crowds of drunken dancers until we're right in the middle of them. I'm grinning like a complete idiot as I watch him shrug his jacket off and dust his hands down before I'm seized and reminded of my god's moves. He does, indeed, tear the floor up.

Chapter 5

A whole hour later, after Jesse has won my mum over and graced everyone with his dance floor presence, I'm finally on my way upstairs in Jesse's arms. My heels have been kicked off and Jesse is holding them as he takes the staircase with my heavy head resting against his shoulder. My eyes won't stay open. I hear my heels tumble to the floor and a few moments later, I'm placed on my feet.

My forehead falls straight to his chest. 'We need to consummate our vows,' I mumble, rolling my head and drawing his scent into me. It's the most soothing smell in the world.

He laughs lightly. 'Baby, you're too tired. We'll consummate in the morning.' He clasps the back of my neck and pulls me out of his chest so he can look at me. I try my hardest to open my eyes fully, but it's just too much like hard work.

'I know.' I try to push my forehead back, but he holds me firmly in place, scanning my face – every square inch of it. 'What?' I ask quietly.

'Tell me you love me,' he demands.

'I love you.' I don't falter in the slightest.

'Tell me—'

'I need you,' I interrupt him. I know the drill.

He smiles thoughtfully. 'You'll never know how happy that makes me.'

'I do know,' I correct him. I know very well because I feel exactly the same.

He dips and kisses me lightly. 'I want you naked and spread

all over me. Let me get this dress off.' He turns me around and starts unbuttoning the dozens of tiny pearls running down my spine. 'What's happening with your brother and Kate?' he asks.

The question immediately snaps my sleepy eyes open. 'I don't know.' Nothing, I hope, but I won't hold my breath. I won't be telling Jesse about what I discovered in the toilets.

'Either you've learned to control your bad habit, or you're telling me the truth.' He pushes my dress from my shoulders and takes it down to my feet so I can step out of it.

'I'm telling the truth,' I say, turning to face him. He straightens himself up and walks over to the door to hang my dress. 'I think seeing each other has sparked memories, that's all.'

'Memories?' he asks, making his way back to me.

I'm turned around again so he can access my bodice. 'They were bad for each other.' I say. 'They clashed terribly. It was best for them both when Dan left.'

'But now he's back.'

'Yes, but he'll be gone soon. What about Kate and Sam?'

'I've told you, that's none of our business.'

'But she's a member of The Manor.' I sound accusing, which is fine because I am. 'Why did you allow that?'

'It's not my job to ask potential members why they want to join, Ava. I check for criminal records, medical issues and financials. If they can pay, they're clean, and have no serious offences, then they're in.'

I scowl at thin air in front of me. 'Members could screw anything between visits to The Manor and catch something, or be arrested for violence. How would you know?'

'Because they're required to undertake monthly tests, and I obtain regular reports. There is no penetrative sex without condoms, and their honesty and disclosure form part of their agreement.' He reaches the final fastener and removes my corset. 'These people are respected members of society, Ava.'

'Who love having kinky sex with strangers and weird contraptions?' I grumble.

'None of my business.'

That's just it. It *is* his business, and it was also his pleasure. I wince at the direction of my thoughts and try to concentrate on the feel of him gathering my hair and pulling it to the side. The unmistakable heat of his lips on my nape makes me shiver, and he laughs.

'She's going to get hurt,' I say quietly.

His arm snakes around my bare tummy, pulling me back against him. I'm more than awake now. 'What makes you think that?'

My shoulders tense. 'I know she likes him.'

His hips push forward into my lower back and slowly grind, lazily, purposefully. 'And I know Sam likes her.'

I moan as he dips and pushes upward, moving his mouth to my ear. I'm not even going to bother trying to sound unaffected. 'Then why can't they date like any normal couple?'

'None of our business,' he whispers.

That's it. That voice, those damn fucking hips and the sharpness of his chest through his suit has me lock stock. I spin around and start walking forwards, pushing him back towards the bed. 'This marriage is getting consummated.' I shove him on the bed and climb up to straddle his hips. He's looking up at me, thoroughly amused. 'Mr Ward, I'm taking the power. Any objections?'

He grins. 'Knock yourself out, baby.'

I smile and reach forward, grabbing his tie and yanking it so he's forced to sit up or be strangled. His eyes widen in alarm as I get nose to nose with him. 'Who has the power?' I ask quietly.

'It looks like you do, for now.' He's fighting a grin. 'Don't get used to it.'

I match his grin and push my lips to his, a collective moan mingling between us as I force my body into his, pressing him back down to the bed, while our mouths work each other in perfect harmony. I've been getting far too much gentle Jesse lately, but I'm going to remedy that now. I break away and work my way into his neck, savouring the feeling of his big hands sweeping across my naked back.

'Damn you, woman,' he moans.

'You don't want me?' I tease, nibbling at his ear, circling wet, firm strokes in the hollow below his lobe. His scent is intoxicating.

'Don't ask stupid fucking questions.' He pushes against me, and I know he's going to spin me over, seize control, and then probably instigate sleepy sex, so I force myself back down onto him.

'Oh no, Ward.' I watch his chest heaving, his stunning face strained. He is clearly fighting instinct to take over here, but I'm not giving in. I know he could tackle me onto my back in a split second, and with little energy or strength, but he won't. On top of being far too gentle with me, he's trying hard to prove a point – that he can relinquish the power, that he can be reasonable. He's trying so bloody hard . . . and failing.

I reach forward and take his hand, and he watches carefully as I lift it, the cuffs chinking as they unravel. My eyes flick to his to gauge his reaction, and I find a look of understanding surfacing. Then his arm tenses. I tug gently, but he won't budge. This is the ultimate test. I know how he feels when he's unable to access me, but it's an unreasonable fear, and we have got to get past it. I tug again with slightly raised eyebrows. He's reluctant, but he lets me guide it to the headboard.

'You won't leave this time,' he pants. 'Promise you won't leave me this time.'

'If you promise you won't get mad.' I snap the cuff over

the wooden bar and look down at him. 'Don't get mad with me.'

He shakes his head faintly and takes a deep breath. I know how hard this is for him. 'Kiss me,' he orders harshly.

'But I'm in charge,' I remind him.

'Jesus, baby, don't make this harder than it already is.' He reaches out with his free hand and grasps the top of my arm, pulling me down so I'm flush to his chest again. My lips land on his and his marvellous mouth saturates me.

I start working his tie loose, yanking it from his neck as he claims me with his tongue. Then I begin on the buttons of his shirt until I've got the lusciousness of his hard chest under my palms.

Slowing our kiss down, I pull away and he growls, his eyes clenching shut, but I ignore his obvious displeasure and start trailing my lips down his neck, onto his chest, across his solid stomach until I reach the zip of his trousers. My nose runs the length of his cock over the material, and his hips jerk up, a suppressed bark flying from his mouth. My plan is working. I'm going to work him up into a frenzy so when I release him, he'll be rampant and hopefully fuck me unconscious. We've got way too much hard fucking to catch up on.

His hand lands on the back of my head, and he yanks at my hair a little, making me smile in smug satisfaction as I slip the button of his trousers and slowly pull his zip down, sliding my hand into his boxers and firmly grabbing his rock-hard length.

His hips fly up, the metal of the cuffs clanking loudly. 'Fuck, Ava! Fucking hell!' His head shoots up and he hits me with desperate, hungry eyes. 'Mouth, now!'

I crawl back up his body and grab his cheeks in my palms. 'You want me to take you in my mouth?' I press my lips to his . . . hard.

'Do it.'

'Who has the power, Jesse?' I bite his lip, and he moans.

'You do, baby. Mouth.'

I smile against him and drift straight back down, pulling his cock free and licking a teasing, wet lash straight up his shaft.

'Oh fuck,' he groans. 'Oh Jesus, Ava.'

'Good?' I ask, taking him halfway, before drawing back again.

'I knew I married you for a reason.'

I bite into his flesh lightly, warningly. 'All the way?'

'Yes.'

I wrap my lips around him and glide down until he hits the back of my throat. He groans loudly, his groin pushing up. I try to relax my mouth, try to accept the invasion, but my gag reflex fails me and I'm suddenly retching.

What the hell?

I drop him fast and leap up from the bed, my stomach convulsing, a sweat breaking out across my brow. I'm going to throw up. I fly into the bathroom and collapse in front of the toilet, then proceed to evacuate the contents of my stomach, trying to hold my hair out of my face while aiming right.

'Ava!' he bellows. The sound of cuffs start clanging loudly. 'Ava!'

'I'm . . .' I throw up again, choking as I try to talk, try to assure him that I'm fine. Shit, I need to release him.

'Jesus, Ava!' The persistent clattering of metal on wood rings out through the suite, accompanied by Jesse's panicked yells. 'Fucking hell, *Ava*!'

I can't talk. My throat is blocked, my eyes are watering and my stomach is aching from turning so much. What the hell is wrong with me? I'd hardly started. I've taken him endlessly like that and it's never had this effect. Shit, I feel queasy. I grab some toilet tissue and dab at my forehead. I really need to get a grip and get my arse back in there to release him before he has heart failure.

'Ava!' There's an almighty crash, and then he steams into the bathroom, shirt open, trousers undone, and a look of pure dread on his face.

I try to wave an arm at him, anything to reassure him that I'm okay, but I'm quickly grasping the side of the toilet again, bracing my arms as I continue to gag and choke.

'Jesus, baby.' He sounds so worried, the neurotic fool. I'm only being sick. I feel him close in behind me and gather my tresses, holding them and rubbing my back.

'I'm fine.' I wipe my face and rub my palms over my cheeks when I know I can't possibly throw up any more.

'Clearly,' he mutters drily. 'Let me look at you.'

I shuffle around on a sigh. 'Still want to fuck me?' I ask in attempt to soothe his obvious worry.

He rolls his eyes, 'Ava, please.'

'I'm sorry.'

'Lady, you'll kill me off, I swear.' He pushes my hair from my face. 'You okay?'

'No, I feel sick.' I collapse forward, my cheek colliding with his bare chest where his shirt is open.

'Why do you think that is?' he asks quietly.

I stiffen. I'm really not ready to deal with it yet. I haven't got the energy right now, so I keep my mouth shut, but I need to take my head out of the sand and face reality – the reality that I'm most certainly pregnant. 'Take me to bed, please.'

I hear him exhale deeply. It's an obvious demonstration of frustration. I won't be allowed to live in denial for much longer, but his need to care for me at the moment is getting me off the hook. He stands and pulls me up. 'You are the most frustrating woman on the fucking planet. You want to brush your teeth?'

'Please.'

He smiles down at me and brushes his knuckles across my cheek. 'Everything will be fine.'

Will it? Fine for him. He gets what he wants. 'Okay,' I agree feebly, catching a glimpse of a hanging handcuff from his wrist ... and a huge red blister. 'Jesse! What have you done?' I grab his hand and turn it over, discovering that the inner side on his wrist displays a mass of angry red welts. I suck in a shocked breath. Shit, that looks sore.

He pulls his wrist from my grip and removes the cuffs, throwing them to the floor. 'You keep my heart beating, baby, but you can also make it fucking stop.' He shakes his head and lifts me onto the counter. 'You said you couldn't live without me, didn't you?'

'Yes.'

He narrows accusing eyes on me. 'Then stop trying to kill me off.'

I feel a grin surfacing. 'You're such a drama queen.'

'There is nothing dramatic about being worried when my wife throws up after I've just thrust my cock in her mouth.'

I burst into laughter. My head falls back, my eyes close and I laugh. Really hard. I have tears and all. I can't stop, and he lets me have my moment, waiting patiently with my toothbrush hovering in front of my mouth. 'I'm sorry!' I chuckle. 'I'm really sorry.' I wipe my eyes and home straight in on a pair of curious greens, a raised brow and a chewed lip.

'I'm glad you find it amusing. Open your mouth.'

I let my jaw drop open and he sets about brushing my teeth for me before running a cool washcloth over my brow and then scooping me up and transporting me to the bed. My eyes widen when I see the mangled headboard with strips of wood all splintered and hanging off. He's trampled the bed.

'In you get.' He places me on the edge, and I waste no time crawling up and snuggling down, letting out a long, contented sigh as I turn over and watch him undress, my greedy gaze drinking in his perfection.

'I can't believe I'm spending my first night as your wife in one of your torture chambers.' The unpleasant thought has me shifting slightly and wondering who has been in this bed and what has gone down. I want to get out.

He knows what I'm thinking. 'No one has slept in this bed, Ava.'

I frown. 'They've not?'

He smiles as he shrugs his shirt off. 'No one has been in this room since I cornered you.' He's watching me closely. 'And the bed's new.'

'Really?' I blurt, a little shocked.

He laughs. 'Really.'

'Why?'

'Because I'm not having you in a bed that others have . . .' his frown line surfaces again, 'frequented.'

'And no one has been in this room since me?'

He kicks his trousers off and draws his boxers down his legs. 'Only me. Get your underwear off. I want you naked.'

I reach down and push my knickers from my legs. 'Did you sit in here quietly and think about me?' I ask on a grin.

He strides over to a unit of drawers and pulls the top one open. 'More than you know,' he answers quietly, turning and holding up a bra.

'That's my bra!' I blurt. I have a sudden flurry of flashbacks. I left my bra when I ran, and he stored it there all this time?

He chucks it on the top of the drawers and shrugs sheepishly, then paces over to the bed and slips in beside me. I immediately crawl onto his chest and settle myself all over him, my face nuzzling straight into his neck.

'Comfy?'

'Hmmm,' I hum, my hands wandering all over the place, needing to feel him and relish in the flesh-on-flesh contact. He sat in here quietly and thought of me. He kept my bra. No one has been in here, except me. And he's replaced the bed.

'How do you feel?' he asks, letting me smother him.

'I'm fine,' I sigh.

He matches my sigh. 'She's fine.' I'm held tighter, his heart-beat thumping against my breastbone. 'Go to sleep, my beautiful girl.'

And I do. My eyes slowly close and I'm gone.

Chapter 6

I open my eyes and stretch. It's an over-the-top, completely contented extension of my body all over the bed. Then I smile to myself, listening to him in the bathroom – the sound of the tap jetting out streams of hot water, him collecting all of the cosmetics he'll need, and then the unmistakable sound of him swishing the water to instigate some bubbles. My self-professed bath man is keeping to his word. We're going to have a long soak in the bath and undoubtedly some tub-talk while we're there. Do I want tub-talk today?

Shuffling myself to the edge of the gigantic bed, I take my naked form over to the suite's bathroom and lean up against the doorframe. He's sitting on a chair by the window, elbows resting on his knees, looking out across The Manor's grounds. He's naked too, every finely tuned muscle protruding from his back and his dark-blond hair damp from the condensation filling the vast space. I could stand all day and watch him, but even from here and with his back to me, I can see the cogs of his mind racing at a hundred miles per hour. He's probably thinking about my denial, and he's undoubtedly thinking about how he can keep me at home. It's Monday tomorrow.

My unreasonable, challenging, neurotic control freak.

My ex-playboy.

And now my husband.

I need to touch him.

I approach quietly, my eyes getting more delighted the closer I get, my skin starting to prickle with the usual sparks that simmer between our bodies. 'I know when you're near, beautiful girl.' He doesn't look around. 'You'll never get away with that.'

Moving in front of him, I climb onto his lap, planting my cheek on his chest.

His arms engulf me and his face plummets into my hair. 'How are you feeling?'

I smile into his chest. 'Fine.'

'Fine,' he replies, pulling me in closer. 'Don't go to work tomorrow.'

I sag in his lap slightly. I had agreed to marry him quick if he accepted that there would be no honeymoon, and if he agreed to chill out on the overprotectiveness and unreasonableness. My instincts told me he'd fail on all counts.

I pull myself up and face him. 'I need to work.'

He shakes his head. 'You don't *need* to work at all. We *need* to be together.'

'We are together.'

'You know what I mean,' he grumbles.

I'm going to get nowhere with this, so I remove myself from his lap and head for the bath.

'What are you doing?'

I don't need to turn around to confirm the scowl that I know will be on his face. 'Having a bath.' I climb in and settle back, but almost instantly move forward to give him space.

He climbs in and settles behind me, pulling me back to rest on his chest and homing straight in on my ear, giving a little growl and a nibble. 'I've told you before, don't fight me off.'

'Then stop making unreasonable demands.'

He bites down harder on my lobe. 'And I've also told you that before. There is nothing unreasonable about wanting to keep you safe.'

'You mean keep me to yourself.' I close my eyes and let my head relax against him, my palms sliding onto his strong, wet thighs.

'No.' His fingers lace through mine. 'To keep you safe.'

'You use that as an excuse for your unreasonable behaviour.'

'No. You make me crazy.'

'You make yourself crazy. I'm going to work tomorrow and you are going to let me, and you're not going to make a fuss of it. You promised.'

I feel his mouth at my ear again, and I use every modicum of strength to restrain my moan. 'But you promised to obey me. I think marriage vows override any promises that were made before.' He pushes himself up against my bum. 'Does someone need some sense fucked into them?'

I jerk, sending water swishing around us. I'd love some sense fucked into me, but I still won't relent. 'You also promised to stop fucking sense into me because it was agreed that all of the sense only makes sense to you.' I'm beginning to wish we'd never made that agreement. Sense fucking equals hard fucking.

'Love, honour and obey,' he whispers, and my face naturally turns towards that low, husky voice, my lips finding his. 'That makes sense, doesn't it?'

'No,' I breathe. 'Hardly anything you demand makes sense.'

'We make sense.' He swamps me with his mouth. 'Tell me we make sense.'

'We make sense.'

'Good girl. Sit up so I can bathe you.' He drops my lips, leaving me feeling deserted, and pushes me forward. 'We'll have breakfast with your family, then I'm taking you home. Deal?'

'Deal.' I can't wait to go home but I absolutely *can* wait to go downstairs and face Kate and Dan. I'm not even going to try and work out what the hell Kate's thinking. Will she even remember? She was pretty pissed. And Sam. I inwardly groan. How am I going to face Sam knowing this?

'What are you thinking about?' Jesse asks, pulling me back to the here and now.

'Kate,' I answer immediately. 'I'm thinking about Kate and Sam.'

'I've told you—'

'Don't tell me it's none of my business, Jesse. She's my best friend. I feel like I'm watching a car crash in slow motion. I need to stop it.'

'No, you need to mind your own business, Ava,' he scorns me harshly. 'You're done.' He places the sponge on the edge of the bath and rises behind me, stepping out and grabbing a towel. 'Wash your hair.' He rubs himself down and wraps the towel around his waist. 'Maybe you could show as much concern for a little detail in our relationship that needs addressing.' He drills holes into me with an expectant look, and I immediately forget all issues relating to Sam and Kate, but I don't embrace his new-found talent for talking – a talent only used on subjects of his choice. Instead, I slide down into the bath and immerse myself in the bubbly water. I'm not looking at him, but I know he's just rolled his eyes. He can roll his eyes all he likes. I'm dealing with this in my own way. And that way is to wedge my head as far underground as I can get it.

We walk into restaurant of The Manor hand in hand and are immediately greeted by loud clapping and cheering. The first things I notice, apart from the noise, is Kate's obvious hang-over, and across the room, Dan's glacial glare, pointed right at Jesse.

My husband either notices neither or ignores them both, because he scoops me up and strides through the tables, places me neatly on a chair opposite Mum and Dad, then takes one up next to me.

'Darling!' Mum's excited shriek hammers at my ears. 'What a wonderful day it was, despite a certain difficult man.' She glares across the table at Jesse.

'Good morning, Elizabeth.' Jesse beams at my mum and she

rolls her eyes, but I can tell she's restraining a fond smile. 'How are you, Joseph?'

My dad nods while carving through a sausage. 'Very well. Did you two enjoy your day?'

'We did, thank you. Are you being looked after?' Jesse casts his eyes around the restaurant, checking that the staff are seeing to the remaining guests.

'Too well.' Dad laughs. 'We'll be hitting the road after breakfast, so I'll take this opportunity to thank you for your hospitality.'

I smile at my dad and his graciousness, his manners never failing him. 'Is Dan going back with you?' I ask, trying to sound casual.

'Oh no, has he not told you?' Mum asks.

Jesse butters some toast and takes my hand, placing the bread in my grasp and nodding at it, his silent instruction to eat. 'Told me what?' I ask before wrapping my lips around the edge.

'He's staying in London for a while.' Mum starts cutting the fat off Dad's bacon, and I cough.

'He's what?'

'Staying in London, darling.'

I swing my eyes across the room to Dan, finding his full attention is on Kate. 'Why?' I ask. 'I thought he has the surf school to expand.' This is bad news. I drop my toast on my plate and Jesse immediately picks it up and puts it back in my grasp.

'He says there's no rush, and I'm not complaining.' Mum accepts a coffee from Pete, and then he places one in front of me, too.

'No chocolate and no sugar, Ava,' he confirms.

I look up at him and smile fondly. 'Thank you, Pete.' I place my toast back on my plate and Jesse immediately picks it up again.

'Eat.' He thrusts it in my hand.

'I don't want the fucking toast!' I spit harshly, halting all chopping and sipping at our table.

'Ava. Mouth!' Jesse recoils, and I can feel my parents' shocked stares from across the table. I'm shocked myself, but I don't need him trying to force-feed me, and I most definitely don't need Dan hanging around and complicating an already complicated situation.

I ignore Jesse's incredulous stare and my parents' dumbstruck faces, and get up from the table.

'Where are you going?' Jesse stands with me. 'Ava, sit down.' His tone is a warning, even in front of my parents, but I should know by now that he couldn't give a flying fuck where he is and who is present. He'll be mad at me or ravish me wherever and whenever he likes. My parents aren't going to stop him.

'Sit down and eat your breakfast, Jesse.' I go to pass him but his hand flies out and grasps my wrist.

'Excuse me?' He laughs.

I look him straight in the eye. 'I said, sit down and eat your breakfast.'

'Yes, I thought you did.' He pulls me back down onto my chair and places my toast in my hand, then leans into me, pressing his mouth to my ear. 'Ava, this isn't the time or the place for you to start throwing your weight around. And have a little respect in front of your parents.' His hand moves to my knee and strokes up the inside of my bare thigh. 'I like this dress,' he whispers.

I smile sweetly at my parents across the table, who have resumed eating their breakfast. He has a nerve. Have some respect for my parents? My teeth clench when he brushes the seam of my knickers and blows in my ear. He was losing the battle, so he saturates me with his touch to regain the power. Damn him. I squeeze my thighs together and pick up my coffee with shaking hands while he continues to wreak havoc on me with his hot breath in my ear. Mum and Dad have spent time with us, and they have fast become used to Jesse's craving for constant contact.

He pulls away and hits me with a smug, satisfied stare. Yes, he's won now, but only because he's absolutely right. This really isn't the time or the place, especially with my mum and dad here.

'Jesse is right, Ava,' Dad pipes up, completely shocking me. 'You should watch your language.'

'Yes,' my mum agrees quickly. 'It's not very ladylike.'

I don't have to look at my husband to know his smugness has just expanded into slap-worthy territory. 'Thank you, Joseph.' His knee knocks mine under the table, and I knock him right back.

'So, when are you two honeymooning?' Mum smiles across the table at us.

'When my wife says so,' Jesse replies drily, eyeing my toast. 'When will that be, lady?'

I nibble a corner of toast and shrug. 'When I have time. I've got a lot to sort out at work. My husband knows that.' I turn accusing eyes on him, and he grins at me. 'What are you grinning at?'

'You.'

'What about me?'

'Everything about you. Your beauty, your spirit, your need to drive me insanely crazy.' He reaches over and straightens my diamond. 'And the fact you're mine.'

I see my mother in my peripheral vision swaying with giddiness at my challenging man and his open need to drown me in his adoration. 'Oh, Joseph,' she croons. 'Do you remember being that much in love?'

'No, I don't.' Dad laughs. 'Come on, I want to get on the road.' He brushes his mouth with his napkin and stands.

Mum doesn't reply. She's too busy smiling fondly across the table at us. Dad leaves the restaurant, and I turn my attention to

Kate. She looks terrible, her skin looking even paler than usual and her vibrant red hair appearing dull. She's picking at some cornflakes while Sam chats buoyantly to her, seemingly oblivious to her despondent state. It's obvious that she's struggling with more than just a bad head and a queasy tummy. Sam can't be *that* ignorant. My eyes leave Sam and Kate and travel back across the room to Dan. He's still staring at her.

'You've noticed it, too?' Jesse asks quietly when he's obviously caught the direction of my gaze.

'Yes, but I've been warned to mind my own business,' I answer without taking my eyes from Dan.

'You have, but I didn't say you couldn't tell your brother to back off.'

My eyes shoot to Jesse's profile, but he ignores my shock and stands when my mum rises from the table. 'I'll be back soon to say my goodbyes.' She brushes her skirt down and leaves the room, giving Kate a shoulder rub en route. Kate smiles a little, then looks over at me, but quickly diverts her eyes elsewhere. I sigh to myself and wonder what on earth I'm going to say to my usually fiery friend. She looks in complete turmoil, but I can't help but be mad with her.

I quickly remember what Jesse said before my mum left the table. 'You want me to warn my brother off?' I ask.

He looks at me carefully as he sits back down. 'I think he needs to be told. I don't want to upset you by doing it myself, so perhaps you should have a word with him.'

I've already tried to have a word, and I know it fell on deaf ears, but I won't be telling Jesse that because it will undoubtedly prompt him to intervene. 'I'll speak to him.' I put my unfinished toast back on the plate. 'And before you start, I'm not hungry.'

'You need to eat, baby.' He makes a play for my breakfast again, and I slap my hand over his.

'I'm not hungry.' I load my voice with lashings of confidence. 'Can we go home now?'

He shifts his hand and grips mine firmly, looking at me thoughtfully. 'We can go home now. Come on.'

After seeing my parents off, ignoring my brother and telling Kate I'll call her later, I'm deposited in the DBS and taken back to Lusso. My home – the place where Jesse and I will live together as husband and wife.

I open the door and step out, letting out a shocked yelp when I'm swept off my feet. 'I have legs,' I laugh, linking my hands over his neck.

'And I have arms, and they were made to hold you.' He plants a chaste kiss on my lips and kicks the car door shut before striding into the foyer of Lusso. 'I'm putting you in our bed, and I'm not letting you out until morning.'

'Deal,' I agree, but he better be set for some hard action. I'm not feeling like softly, softly.

My attention moves to the concierge desk when Jesse stops abruptly and his eyes widen.

My eyes widen slightly too. Standing behind the desk with a phone to his ear is a man – and it's not Clive. It most certainly is *not* Clive. I purse my lips and grin to myself. Oh, this is going to provoke some serious possessive, trampling-like behaviour. I remain silent as I assess the situation. It doesn't take much assessing, though. Jesse is standing in the middle of the foyer, the new concierge is still speaking on the phone, and they are both staring at each other. The new concierge's eyes fall on me, and I almost laugh when I hear a growl emanate from Jesse. Oh good Lord, this poor man is going to get trampled to within an inch of his life. I firm up my grip on Jesse's shoulders and wait for him to take the initiative and walk on, but he's rooted to the spot.

'Where's Clive?' he asks the new guy, disregarding his phone conversation. I wriggle a little to try and free myself, but Jesse flips me a glare and tightens his hold. 'Stay where you are, lady.'

'You're behaving like a caveman.'

'Shut up, Ava.' He returns burning greens of displeasure back to the poor young concierge, who has since ended his call. 'Clive,' Jesse prompts shortly.

The new concierge steps out from behind the desk, and I can't help it when my eyes naturally run the full length of him. He's cute. His blond hair is neatly trimmed, his brown eyes are happy, and his tall frame is lean. He's nowhere near Jesse's league, but he's still a bloke and that makes him a threat – in Jesse's world.

'I'll be working alongside Clive, sir,' he says warily as he walks forward and puts his hand out. 'I'm Casey, sir. I look forward to assisting you with anything you may . . . well, need assistance with.' He shifts awkwardly.

I wriggle again to free myself, feeling like a complete idiot locked in my possessive Lord's grasp while the new concierge introduces himself. He seems sweet and sincere enough, but Jesse isn't letting me go.

'Mr Ward,' Jesse says shortly, ignoring Casey's outstretched hand.

'Nice to meet you, Casey. I'm Ava.' I put my hand out to him, but Jesse steps back. Oh for the love of God! I look at him, noting his eyes planted firmly on the young man in front of us. He's being ridiculous. I force myself from his grip with some effort and step forward, offering my hand again. 'Welcome to Lusso, Casey.' I smile and he takes my hand, shaking it mildly. The poor guy won't come back if I don't intervene. Clive has been here non-stop since the residents moved in. He's no spring chicken. He needs the relief.

'Thank you, Ava.' He smiles, and it's a cute smile, but I don't miss the cautious look he directs over my shoulder. 'Oh, you're in the penthouse?'

'Yes, that's us.'

'Maintenance called to say your new front door has arrived from Italy.'

'That's great, thank you.'

'Have maintenance fit it without delay,' Jesse snorts.

'Already done, sir.' Casey smiles proudly, grabbing some keys from his desk and holding them up.

Jesse swipes them from the poor guy's hand before virtually throwing his car keys at him. 'Bring the cases up.' I'm pulled towards the elevator in an amused daze, and as I knew I would be, I'm pushed inside and thrust up against the mirrored wall. 'He fancies you,' Jesse growls.

'You think everyone fancies me.'

'You're mine.' He slams our lips together and takes me fiercely, pushing me up the wall with the pressure of his body. I'm delighted. This is not gentle Jesse. This is powerful, forceful, dominant Jesse, and I'm bracing myself for a fuck to make up for all those I've been missing out on. I throw my arms around his shoulders and tackle him with as much force – probably more.

'I'm yours,' I pant between hard lashes of his tongue.

'You don't need to reassure me.' His hand feels up my leg and cups me harshly, triggering hot wetness to invade me and an excited thud to attack my core. I really need this. His finger slips past the seam of my lace. 'Wet,' he purrs into my mouth. 'Just for me. Understand?'

'I understand.' My muscles grip his finger as he enters me. 'More,' I beg unashamedly. I need more.

He separates our mouths and withdraws his finger, re-entering with two. He pushes hard and high. 'Like that, Ava?'

My head falls back against the mirror, my mouth gaped, my eyes closed. 'Just like that.'

'Or would you prefer my cock slamming into you?' His voice is carnal and a massive surprise, given his delicate approach to my body in recent weeks. If this is the effect that Casey will have on my Lord, then I hope he stays for ever. I'm being claimed and reminded of who I belong to – not that I ever need a reminder, but I'll always take it. I drop my head and find his greens, then reach forward and slip the buttons of his fly free, before sliding my hand into his boxers and wrapping my palm around his hot, throbbing cock. He pulls in a short breath. 'You haven't answered my question.'

'I want this.' I squeeze his base and draw a long stroke to the tip. He sweeps one last circle with his fingers before removing them and lifting me to his body, my legs wrapping around his waist, my hands seeking out his nape.

'I knew you were a sensible girl.' The elevator doors open, I'm carried out into the penthouse foyer, where the door is opened without delay, and we're quickly on our way upstairs to the master suite. 'You make me a desperate fucking mess, Ava.' I'm placed on the edge of the bed and my dress is pulled up over my head quickly before he yanks his T-shirt off, kicks his Converses to the side and pushes his jeans down his legs, taking his white boxers with them. He really is desperate, and I'm all the more delighted for it. He's going to fuck me.

I'm pushed back onto the bed and my knickers are pulled down my legs, my bra disposed of just as quickly. He's working fast, but it's still not quick enough. My impatience is my undoing – that and his glorious nakedness looming over me. I need to touch him. I sit up and slide my hands around his solid arse and pull him forward so he's standing between my spread thighs, his lower stomach at my eye level. Placing my lips gently over his abdomen, I trail kisses across to his scar, but it doesn't make me wince any more. It's a massive imperfection, a mar on his beautiful body, but it makes him all the more perfect to me. My perfect imperfect Adonis. My god. My husband.

I feel his fingers thread through my hair, and my eyes creep up the firmness of his abs, then his chest, until I'm staring into green eyes filled with . . . love. Not hunger or carnal want – it's love.

He's not going to fuck me. He's going to make sweet love,

and he does it so well, but I'm desperate for his ferocity, desperate for him to stop treating me like I'm breakable. My hands flow back down his torso until my palms are resting on the edges of his perfect V. I lean in and kiss his stomach again before working my way up, standing as I go until I'm feeling his neck out and pulling him down to meet my lips. I lift myself gracefully to his body and link my legs around his waist as he accepts my demand for mouth contact.

Heavy mouth contact.

Indulgent mouth contact.

All-consuming mouth contact.

He doesn't lower me to the bed. He walks me into the bathroom and straddles the chaise longue, standing me over him. He looks up at me. 'We need to make friends.' I'm yanked down and our mouths crash together. 'Mine,' he says around our lips' relentless colliding and tongue battling.

I pull at his hair, trying to draw out his animalistic traits. He knows what I want and need right now, he damn well knows it, and he's going to give it to me.

'My girl wants it hard.' He breaks away, and I'm the one growling this time. He stares up at me, panting and sweating. He wants to give it to me as well; I can see it in the glaze of his green stare. They're smoking out, darkening with desperation.

I'm gently tugged down as he holds himself upright, ready to enter me, but I stiffen, preventing him from seizing me. I might be desperate for him, but I still have to maintain my sensibility, just like I've done over the past few weeks. He's not wearing a condom, and judging by the sharper tug on my arm, he knows exactly why I'm holding back.

'Jesse.' My breathlessness is completely giving away my pent-up lust.

'Ava, I'm taking you now, and you're not going to stop me with trivial fucking requests.' He yanks me down and seals our lips, working into my mouth with deadly determination. I don't try to resist, and I really don't want to. This might be the hard fuck I've been waiting for.

He keeps our mouths locked, and then levels himself up and slides straight in. My legs naturally snake around his waist and lock at the ankles, pulling us closer together.

'Oh Jesus,' he pants against my mouth. 'Fucking perfect.'

It does feel perfect. I'm swiftly reminded of the perfection that is no barrier between us. Just flesh on flesh. Me on him. I'm gasping into his shoulder and digging my nails into his biceps.

'Move,' I demand. 'Please move.'

'In time, baby. Just let me feel you for a moment.' He takes my hands and guides them around the back of his neck where my fingers naturally feel out his hair and tug gently. Then his big hands slowly skate down my sides, over my breasts and onto my waist. He holds me still. The only sounds in the air around us are our strained breaths. They are heavy and desperate.

Tightening his grip on my waist, he lifts me on a deep moan before letting me slide gently back down onto him. My eyes close in pure, comforted bliss, and I gasp, removing my hands from his hair so I can get them onto the firm warmth of his chest. I marvel at his solid, bunched muscles, just flawless hardness before me, screaming to be touched, begging me to feel his perfection. My insatiable hands wander all over him as I'm lifted from his body again and grinded down, slowly and meticulously.

'Don't try to tell me it doesn't feel right,' he moans. 'Don't try to tell me this isn't how we're supposed to be.' He works me, circling his groin firmly. 'Not ever.'

'Don't come inside me.' I might be overwhelmed by his potency, but a small part of me is still aware of what I'm doing.

'Don't tell me what to do with your body, Ava. Kiss me.'

I'm blinded by his carnal words and his claim over me, my body refusing to deny him. He's holding the power, and he knows it. My mouth drops to his and my body presses into him, a clear invitation to take me how he pleases. His head tilts back to maintain our mouth contact as I'm raised again and plunged back onto him. I groan into his mouth – a low, alluring message of submittal. I'm not thinking straight. My mind is scrambled by his energy, the painfully accurate momentum and strikes of his hips, sending me into delirious indulgence.

I hum as I'm slowly and easily lifted, time and time again. The pressure of him pushing into the deepest part of me is pleasure embodied.

'You feel so good,' I pant. 'Jesse, fuck me.' I need this harder.

'Mouth, Ava,' he warns me. 'Just like this. We stay just like this.' His eyes clench shut. He's being too gentle with me. I need shock and awe. I need him to take me hard. It has been like this for weeks. And I know why.

'Why are you being so gentle with me?' I nuzzle into his neck, sucking and biting at him.

'Sleepy sex,' he moans.

'I don't want sleepy sex.' That won't have the desired effect. Yes, I'll come, I'll moan in pleasure and shake all over him, but I need to scream a release. I need scrubbing, not dabbing. 'Fuck me, Jesse.'

He sucks in a sharp breath as I force myself down, hard. 'Mouth, Ava. Jesus!'

'Yes!' I lift and smash back down.

'Ava!' He holds me still above him. 'No, damn it.'

I can feel him throbbing inside me, his heaving chest pushing against my torso. I'm panting into his neck, my fists clenched in his hair. I tighten my grasp. 'Stop treating me like glass.'

'You are glass to me, baby. Delicate.'

'But I'm not breakable. I wasn't two weeks ago, and I'm not now.' I try to lift myself, I need movement, but he's got a harsh hold on me. This is another reason why I hope to God I'm not pregnant. I can't stand this. I pull out of his neck and look into his eyes. 'Hard. I need you hard.'

He shakes his head. 'Sleepy.'

'Why?' I ask. Will he admit to what I already know?

'Because I don't want to hurt you,' he whispers.

I try to keep a hold of my temper. Doesn't want to hurt me, or doesn't want to hurt his baby, who may not even exist? 'You won't.' I feel him relax slightly, so I take the opportunity to whip myself up and right back down on a sharp, satisfied shout. He shouts, too. I know he wants to smash into me, wants to take me hard, rule me and indulge me, but he won't and it's driving me fucking insane.

'Fuck!' he yelps. 'Fucking hell, Ava! No!'

'Do it.' I grasp his face and take his mouth hungrily. If I keep on, I'll have him. 'Own me,' I demand, skating my lips across his cheek.

He catches them as they pass his mouth again, and his tongue enters, frantic and rushed. I've nearly got him.

I wickedly rise and collide with him again, prompting a sharp bark. 'It feels good, doesn't it? Tell me it feels good.'

'Jesus, Ava. Please don't.'

Up and down I go, harder, heavier. I'm driving him crazy, and I know he wants this because he could easily stop my teasing moves. 'I need you.'

Those words are his undoing, as I knew they would be. He releases a frustrated yell and takes over my movements, squeezing my waist and wrenching me up and down on him. 'Like that,' he shouts, almost angry, and I know it's because he can't resist me.

'Yes!' I scream.

He's suddenly standing, my legs still wrapped around his waist as he walks across the bathroom and thrusts me up against the wall. 'You want it hard, baby?'

'Fuck me!' I shout, frenziedly, tightening my legs and moving my hands to his dark-blond mass of hair.

'Damn it, Ava. Stop swearing!' He withdraws and hammers

back in, over and over, my screams of satisfaction ringing through the air. 'Better?' he grunts, hitting me hard and deep. 'You wanted it, Ava. Is that fucking better?' He's really mad.

I'm pinned against the wall, absorbing his ferocious attack, and I want it even harder. I've had two weeks of gentle Jesse. I've had enough of gentle Jesse, but I can't speak. I bear down on every advance, my signal that I *do* want it harder. I want it so much harder.

'Answer the fucking question!'

'Harder!' I scream, grappling at his hair.

'Fuck!' His hips piston forward repeatedly, his momentum and stamina staggering, and I'm loving every hard, forceful strike.

The pit of my stomach starts to burn, and I'm knocked out by a climax that rushes forward so fast, I don't have a chance to prepare myself for it. I explode, my eyes clenching shut, my head thrown back on a desperate scream.

'I'm not done yet, Ava!' he shouts, shifting his hands under my thighs and powering forward.

Neither am I. That orgasm has sent me dizzy, but there is another on the way, assisted rapidly by his relentless power. I find his lips and kiss him deeply, tightening my legs around his hips to the point of pain, my screams and his yells colliding between our mouths. I throw my head back. 'Oh God!'

'Eyes!' he shouts severely.

I obey immediately and fist my hands in his hair as he stops dead, heaving and sweating. The fire at my core recedes immediately, but then he groans and rears back, and I brace myself for more power. He strikes, really hard. My back smashes against the wall on a shocked yell, but he doesn't give me time to gather myself. He pulls straight back and hits me with another forceful pound. He's lost any control he had. This is going to be *really* hard. I strengthen my grip on his hair and try to flex my legs, giving him the access his body's demanding.

'Hard enough for you, Ava?' he shouts, thrashing into me again.

'Yes!' I scream. He's unforgiving. He repeatedly drives into me, each hit getting harder. My mind is blanking out, my body has gone lax, and I'm sky-high on pleasure. But then I feel my back leaving the wall as I'm yanked forward and taken to the bed. He practically throws me down and flips me onto my hands and knees before taking a standing position behind me and grabbing my hips. He re-enters me on a brutal pound and a frenzied bark, yanking me back to meet him with each advance of his powerful hips. My face goes straight into the sheets, my hands grasping at the material, a full-on sweat breaking out. I'm soaking wet.

'Jesse!' I scream his name in delirious, delightful despair.

'You wanted it, Ava. Don't fucking complain.' He bangs into me again, harder still. He's releasing all of the pent-up, animalistic power he's been suppressing for way too long. He's really lost control, and a small part of me is wondering if he's doing this on purpose – trying to shock me or scare me back into the realms of sleepy sex. He's going to fail miserably if that's his plan. My body needs this. I need this.

I drag my twisted mind back to now and focus on meeting his power with acceptance. I accept all of it, the violent accumulation of pressure in my belly working its way straight to my core, ready for detonation. This is going to blow my brain clean out of my head.

'Harder!' I shout, grasping at the sheets.

'Ava!' His fingers flex on my hips and clamp down, the unforgiving hold on my sensitive area not bothering me in the slightest. I'm too busy concentrating on the body-splitting orgasm that's looming.

And then it hits me, taking me by surprise again and sending me out of this world on pleasure. I scream. He yells. Then I collapse on the bed, Jesse following me down, his leanness completely covering me. His breathing is harsh in my ear and our sweat-ridden bodies are flush and heaving severely. I feel completely replete. I'm utterly exhausted, but I feel so much better. It feels like us again.

He groans, his groin circling deeply, the fire of his release heating me and putting me back together again. 'Thank you,' I pant, closing my eyes and finding immense comfort in his strong, frantic heartbeat clattering against my back. He doesn't say anything. The only sound in the colossal master suite is our collective, erratic breathing. It's loud, it's heavy and it's satisfied. But then he breaks away from me, and the absence of his warmth coating my body makes me immediately turn over to see what he's doing. He's walking away, his hands clenching his head as I watch his naked back disappear into the bathroom. I'm still fighting to get my heartbeat steady and my breathing paced, but instead of feeling sated and blissful, I feel uncertain and guilty. I've made him lose his restraint. I've pushed him, tempted him and sent him over the edge of self-control, and now, even though I got my way, I feel guilt-ridden. He's been struggling to rein in his command over my body, although *why* is what I should be worried about. I've accepted that I'll never completely understand him. I've accepted all of his flaws and challenging ways. They are all part of the man I love deeply – the man I share a connection with that is so potent, it's sent us both crazy. We share an intensity that cripples us both.

He appears in the bathroom doorway, still naked, still wet and with his chest still rising and falling noticeably. I'm staring at him. He's staring at me.

Sitting up and pulling my knees to my chest, I feel small and awkward. It shouldn't be like this between us.

'I've been taking your pills.' His jaw ticks and his neck muscles bulge.

The words, spoken with no remorse or regret, widen my eyes and straighten my back. His face is expressionless, and even though I knew, I'm shocked. Hearing him say it aloud, confessing to it, is increasing my already speeding heart rate.

'I said I've been taking your pills.' He sounds angry.

This can't be ignored any longer. I can feel the dormant anger sizzling inside me, pushing me to release it. My period is due tomorrow, and I'm certain it's not going to arrive. This man, my crazy husband, has just completely and unashamedly confessed to stealing my birth control pills, and now my denial is converting into blood-boiling fury.

'Ava, for fuck's sake, woman!' His hands fly to his head in frustration. 'I've been taking your fucking pills!'

I don't even try to reason because there is absolutely nothing reasonable about this.

I snap.

My naked body flies up from the bed and as I pace toward him, he watches me closely, cautiously, until I'm standing before him. Then I slap him clean across his face. My palm is instantly on fire, but I'm too angry to focus on the pain. His head has turned to the side, his eyes are down, and I can still only hear our fitful breathing, except now they're not sated, heavy breaths, they're anger-fuelled gasps. He brings his face back up and before I'm aware of what I'm doing, my hand is flying out again, but this time he catches my wrist in front of his face. I yank myself free and proceed to thump his chest with both fists in a frenzied lash out of anger. And he lets me. He just stands there and takes my deranged beating, my fists persistently striking him as I scream and wail, and when I think I might collapse with exhaustion, I step back and lose control of my tears.

'Why?' I shout at him.

He doesn't try to touch me or come towards me. He just remains standing in the doorway, still with no emotion on his face. His frown line isn't even there, but I know he must be concerned, and he must be really concentrating on not restraining his deranged wife.

'You were ignoring it, Ava. I need you to acknowledge this.' His voice is soft and even. 'I needed to spike a reaction from you.'

I thought I just needed to hear him say it – to admit that he's been underhanded and deceitful. I was wrong. Now I want to know why, and the burning anger inside me is telling me that no excuse is going to calm me.

'Tell me why the fucking hell you did this to me!'

'Because I wanted to keep you for ever,' he whispers.

It's not good enough.

I turn and head for the wardrobe, wasting no time grabbing my jeans and yanking them on once I'm there.

'What are you doing?' His voice is full of the fear I knew it would be. He'll never cope with this, but neither will I if I stay. This has suddenly hit me very hard.

I don't answer him, instead focusing on getting my bra and T-shirt on before I tug down an overnight bag.

'Ava, what the hell are you doing?' The bag is snatched from my hand. 'You're not leaving me.' His words are somewhere between a demand and a plea.

'I need some space.' I seize the bag back and start stuffing my clothes in.

He grips my arm but I pull myself free. 'Ava, please.'

'Please what?' My clothes are being yanked and rammed into my bag viciously, but I worry I might turn on Jesse again if I don't focus on this, and I can't bring myself to look at him. I know what I'll see.

Fear.

'Please, Ava, don't go.'

I turn and storm past him, heading for the bathroom to collect my toiletries. He's not restraining me, and I know why. It's the same reason he's been delicate with me for weeks. Because he thinks he'll hurt his baby.

He's behind me, I know he is, but I continue gathering my

things, fighting the overwhelming need to lash out, but at the same time fighting the need to comfort him. I'm so confused.

'Ava, please, let's talk about this.'

I swing around in shock. 'Talk?'

He nods sheepishly. 'Please.'

'What is there to talk about? You've done the most under-handed thing possible. Nothing you could say will make me understand this. This is my life!'

'But you knew I was taking them.'

'Yes, I did! But perhaps because of all the other shit you've thrown on me since I've met you, I didn't consider how fucked up this really is. Wanting to keep me isn't good enough. That's not a decision you get to make on your own!' I try to calm myself, but I'm fighting a losing battle. 'What about me?' I scream in his face. 'What about what I want?'

'But I love you.'

My grip on my bag tightens until my fingers are numb. I'm seriously losing the plot. I walk past him and quickly make my way downstairs.

'Ava!'

I ignore him and keep going. The anger bubbling inside me has shocked me as much as it's shocked Jesse. This is past con-trolling. This is unforgivable. I don't want a baby.

'Ava, stay. I'll do anything.' His heavy footsteps are close behind me, but he's nude, and as much as I know that he has no shame, I know he wouldn't run out in public completely naked.

When I reach the door, I turn to face him. 'You'll do anything?'

'Yes. You know that.' His terrified face nearly makes me throw my arms around his big shoulders. But if I let this one go, then I'm setting myself up for a lifetime of manipulating. I can't do that. We need some time apart. This is too intense, and perhaps I should have thought about that before I married him, but it's too late now. I might have made the biggest mistake of my life.

'Then you'll give me some space.'

I walk out.

Chapter 7

Kate's not at home, so I let myself in and make my way upstairs to my old room. After sitting on the bed for an eternity ignoring Massive Attack's 'Angel', I finally drag myself up and have a long shower. Under the hot spray, I soap everywhere, running the sponge absent-mindedly over my body and pausing when I reach my stomach. I feel devoid of any emotion. There are no natural motherly instincts in me that make me want to caress my tummy. I've never given motherhood a second thought. I'm too young, and I have a flourishing career to concentrate on. He had no right to do this. He had no right to claim me so aggressively, yet he did. He has no right to dictate what I wear, but he does. And he has no right to trample all over my life with his overbearing, unreasonable and challenging ways . . . but he does. And I let him. I fight him on many things, but he mostly gets his way. Not on this, though. I have accepted many things where Jesse is concerned, but I absolutely cannot accept this. And I won't.

I remove myself from the shower and dry myself off before crossing the landing to my room and throwing on a baggy T-shirt and some sweatpants. Then I crawl into the cold sheets of my old bed. It's hard, it's lumpy and it hasn't got Jesse in it, but I'm on my own, and it's where I need to be right now.

I wake up to shouting – very loud shouting. Pulling the sheets back, I slip out of bed and pad across my room, opening the door quietly.

'I said it's over!' Kate screams. 'This isn't going anywhere!'

Oh shit, I shouldn't be listening to this, but my curiosity is getting the better of me. I can see Kate's back down the hallway, and I pray the next person I'm going to see will be Dan. But it's not. It's Sam. My already aching heart takes a further nosedive for my troubled best friend.

'Kate, come on.' Sam's voice is beseeching and a little confused.

'Just go, Sam.' She stomps off across the landing, straight into the kitchen where she's obviously opening and slamming every cupboard door in sight. Sam follows her in.

'What's brought all this on?' he asks. 'What's changed?'

'Nothing!' There's a further collection of bangs before she comes back out of the kitchen and marches into the lounge. I catch a glimpse of her pale face, looking no brighter than this morning. I know that expression. That's her stubborn, I'm-not-being-honest face. I could throttle the stupid cow.

'Obviously something has!' Sam almost laughs, but it's a nervous laugh. It's a laugh that clearly indicates worry. Sam really does like Kate. A lot.

'Just go,' she spits shortly.

'No! Not until you tell me what the fuck is going on!'

I can't see them, so I creep out quietly, scolding myself for being so nosy, but I need to hear this because I'm just as intrigued as Sam. I suspect I know, which is just spiking my already fraying patience.

'I don't owe you an explanation.'

He laughs properly this time. 'Yes, I think you do!'

I catch a glimpse of Sam trying to hold Kate in place, but the stubborn cow just shrugs him off. 'No, I don't. We were fucking, nothing more. It was fun while it lasted.' Her cold words slice through me, so I can only imagine what they've done to Sam.

He doesn't say anything, but I see the slight shake of his head. 'Fun?' he repeats. 'Just fun?'

'Yes. Not any more, though. I've had all the fun I'm going to have with you.'

My mouth gapes: just when I thought she couldn't be any colder. She's on fire. Sam's body shifts, and I know he's leaving, so I creep slowly and quietly back to my room and push the door shut.

I hear the front door slam, and then the unmistakable sound of sobbing. Kate's crying. She never cries. I'm infuriated with her, but feeling incredibly sorry for my stupid best friend. I can't help but think that this never would have happened if Dan wasn't here.

I could stay in my room and let her have her tears, but instead of letting Kate grieve in peace, I step out and walk across the landing to the lounge. I'm not letting her brush this off later. If I witness her turmoil, then she has to admit that she is, in fact, in turmoil. She's not evading me this time.

I lean up against the doorframe and watch for an eternity as her shoulders jerk and she cries relentlessly. My instincts tell me to sit beside her and cuddle her, but I don't, and after a good ten minutes she harshly brushes her cheeks and stands, turning and immediately clocking me in the doorway. As I knew she would, she plasters on an unaffected face and tries to smile. It's insulting to my intelligence and our friendship.

'Hey,' she chirps on a suppressed sniffle.

'All right?' I ask, not removing myself from the doorway.

'Sure I am. What are you doing here?' She straightens her T-shirt out, diverting her glazed eyes all over her body instead of facing me.

'My car's outside. You didn't see it?'

She still doesn't look at me. 'No. What are you doing here?'

I ignore her repeated question. I'm not going to allow her to change the subject. And what would I tell her, anyway? I've been married for less than a day and I've turned up at her flat with a packed bag. 'You probably didn't take much notice. You know, as you were fighting with Sam.'

Her eyes whip to mine. 'Oh,' she says quietly, then insults me further by smiling brightly. 'Tea?'

'No,' I answer coolly. 'An explanation would be good, though.' I know my eyebrows have just risen expectantly, and I must sound like a nagging parent, but I'm not caving in.

She laughs a little. 'An explanation to what?'

'Well, we could start with your little performance last night with my brother, then you could try explaining why you've just finished with Sam.'

'There was nothing to finish.'

'What about my brother?'

'It's none of your business.' She goes to walk past me, but I shift, blocking her escape. 'Move, Ava.'

'No. You'll sit and talk to me. We're supposed to be friends.' I grab her arm and drag her over to the couch, pushing her reluctant body down onto the soft cushion. 'What's going on, Kate?'

She flops back irritably. 'Nothing.'

'Oh, you make me mad,' I spit. 'Start talking, Matthews.'

She bursts into tears. I'm so relieved. I was on the cusp on slapping her for being so tenacious, but now my arm is around her and she's sobbing into my chest. I don't know about Kate, but I feel so much better for this. She *does* care.

I try to soothe her. 'Let's start with Sam.'

'I told you, it was only meant to be fun.' Her words jerk with her fitful breathing.

'Was?' I ask. 'So it's more than fun?'

'Yes . . . no . . . I don't know!' She sounds so confused, just like me.

'I knew this would happen with Dan arriving.' I sigh. If I was talking to my brother, I'd be shouting down the phone at him. 'Kate, you need to remember every reason why you and Dan called it quits.'

'I know. We're so bad for each other, but we connect, Ava. When we're together, we connect so well.'

'You mean the sex.' I wince and screw my face up a little. I can't think of my brother like that.

'Yes, but everything else fails so horribly.'

'It does,' I agree. I've witnessed the violent rows, the incessant need to rile each other and the unhealthy flow of their doomed relationship. They had no respect for each other – not mentally or physically. It was all just about the sex. At the time, I ignored it all, simply because the thought of my best friend and my brother being in love was so ideal. That was the problem, though. They weren't in love. It was just lust.

She shifts in my embrace and sits up, taking a few calming breaths. 'I hate men,' she declares.

'You shouldn't, especially when there's one who obviously thinks the world of you.'

She looks at me curiously. 'Sam?'

I almost slap her for her blindness. 'Yes, Sam.'

'Ava,' she laughs, 'Sam doesn't think the world of me. I make the world *move* for him, that's all – in the bedroom.'

'You mean you connect so well?' I raise my eyebrows at her. 'Except with Sam, you also get the mental connection.'

She scowls at me. She knows I'm right. 'It was just fun.'

It's me who flops back on the couch in irritation this time. 'You're unbelievable.'

'No, I'm a realist,' she argues. 'It was sex.'

'So why the hell were you blubbering like a baby?'

'I don't know.' She stands up. 'I feel like shit. It gets the emotions going. You want tea?'

'Yes,' I huff, standing to join her before following her into the kitchen.

She reaches up to the cupboard and grabs a couple of mugs. 'Why are you here, anyway?'

The question makes me falter mid-lowering of my bum to

the chair. Should I tell her? A brush-off here is not going to suffice, but she openly admits to her fondness of Jesse, and this could change her opinion dramatically. Even though I'm seething with him, I hate divulging any information that'll have my loved ones questioning him. And questioning me, for that matter. Questioning my sanity.

I decide that I *do* need my best friend on this. I bite the bullet. 'You know my pills that mysteriously kept disappearing?'

She turns and frowns before stuffing a teabag in each of the mugs. 'Yes, you and your ridiculously unorganised life.'

'Hmm, that's what I thought.' I stare at her back, waiting for her to click, but she's happily topping up the mugs with water, and then milk. 'At first, anyway.'

She stirs the tea and brings it over to the table, plonking herself down into one of the mismatching chairs. 'At first?' Her confused face tells me that she really isn't copping on. Maybe it's the hangover.

'Jesse has been taking them.' I blurt it out quickly, before I can change my mind.

Now her confused face is frowning heavily over the rim of her mug. 'He what?'

'He's been taking my pills. He wants me pregnant.'

Eyes wide and with a slightly gaped jaw, she puts her mug down carefully. 'He told you that?'

'Yes,' I breathe. 'Although I kind of already knew.'

'You knew he was taking them? When you replaced them that time and lost them again?'

'I was distracted.'

'Why the hell would he do that? And didn't you use any protection?'

'No, not always,' I mutter indignantly, bracing myself for a lecture on carelessness. I was pretty careless, but I'm now blaming Jesse for the *whole* diabolical situation, not for just lifting my pills. Yes, I should've made him wear protection every time, but

I forgot. Lame excuse, but I did, and that is because my crazy man distracts me far too well.

Kate still looks shocked. I'm not surprised; it's shocking. 'So if you knew all along, then why didn't you take him to task on it?'

'He would never have admitted it, Kate. He's a madcap,' I sigh. It's probably me who's the insane one – insane and stupid.

'But only with you,' Kate says.

'Yes, only with me.' I take a sip of my tea. She's watching me, but not expressing her thoughts. She must have some.

'Why would you ignore it?' she asks.

I was dreading that question, but completely expecting it, and I'm wondering the same thing myself. 'I have no idea.' I feel so frustrated. I have no decent excuse.

Kate shakes her head, making me feel smaller. 'I don't understand you, and I certainly don't understand him.'

'He was scared I'd run away,' I mumble quietly. What's my excuse for being so dim?

'You've married him!' She laughs. 'Fuck me, Ava. What is wrong with that man? Hey, I know he's a bit crazy but—'

'A bit?' I scoff.

'Yeah, okay, understatement of the fucking century, but his way with you has always been so endearing to me. How much he loves you, frets, and protects you. We all know his behaviour is way past unreasonable, but stealing your pills? I didn't think that man could shock me, but he's outdone himself this time.'

'He has,' I muse, swirling my tea in slow, careful circling motions.

'So if you knew, and he knew you knew, then why the big bust up now?'

'He may have succeeded in his attempts.'

Kate chokes on her tea. 'You're pregnant?' She coughs.

The words spike the dormant lump in my throat to swell,

and before I can even think about controlling them, tears start streaming down my cheeks. I drop my tea to the table and cover my face with my palms ... and I sob.

'Oh, fuck! Oh shit!' Kate's chair scrapes across the kitchen floor and the next thing I know, she's standing behind me with her arms wrapped around my shoulders, hushing me quietly. I feel so stupid all of a sudden. Really, really stupid. Stupid for ignoring my suspicions for so long, stupid for not allowing the pieces to click sooner, and stupid for letting Jesse distract me from the enormity of his actions.

'My period is due tomorrow. I know it's not coming, and so does Jesse.' I sniffle and Kate leaves me, hurrying over to a unit of drawers. 'I've been ignoring it, which has frustrated Jesse, but I'm not ready for this, Kate. And now I just feel furious with myself and even more incensed with him. I let things pass sometimes, but this is taking control to a whole new level. I can't let him do this.'

She hands me a tissue and I set about wiping my nose as she takes a seat next to me. 'I completely agree,' she says. I can't believe how relieved I am to hear her say that. I know she's very fond of Jesse, and generally nothing fazes her, not even my husband in all of his challenging ways, but this has shocked her. And I'm so glad. 'What are you going to do?' she asks. 'Make him sweat?'

'Have an abortion.'

Kate's mouth hits the table. It doesn't help.

'Kate, can you imagine what he'll be like? He already smothers me, and I like it to a certain extent, but being pregnant?'

She scoops her chin up. 'Oh God, Ava. You'll send him to the loony bin.'

'That's not a good enough reason,' I reply quietly. I know what this will do to him, but he hasn't considered what any of his actions will do to me. I'm not ready for this, and he hasn't stopped once to contemplate how I might feel. 'It's not just that. I have a career. I'm twenty-six years old. I don't want a baby, Kate.'

'I don't even know what to say.'

'Just say I'm doing the right thing.'

She shakes her head a little. I need her to understand. 'Okay,' she says reluctantly. She doesn't think it's okay at all, but her willingness to halt any guilt trip is enough for me. I feel guilty enough already. I need to regain control.

'Thank you,' I whisper, picking up my tea and taking a shaky sip.

Chapter 8

It's Monday. I wake at the crack of dawn and cry silently to myself. I'm only delaying the inevitable. I need to see Dr Monroe.

I exit Green Park tube station onto Piccadilly and stop for a few moments, absorbing the frantic rush hour blur of people. I miss this. I miss the chaos of the Tube and walking the few blocks to my office – all of the hectic scrambling, the dodging of bodies and the loud voices, mostly shouting down a mobile phone. That, coupled with the screeching of cars and buses, the honking of impatient horns and the ringing of cyclist bells, all strangely bring a small smile to my face, until I get nudged in the back, and then ridiculed for keeping the frantic stream of pedestrian traffic from flowing. I snap out of my daydream and shift my feet into gear, heading for Berkeley Square.

'Morning, flower.' Patrick's big body strides out of his office towards my desk.

I take my seat and swivel to face him. 'Good morning.' I fake chirpiness on a stupidly over-the-top level.

He perches on my desk, prompting the usual shriek of strained wood and my usual tensing in anticipation. It's going to give one day. 'How's the blushing bride?' He clucks my cheek affectionately and winks.

'Perfect.' I smile, laughing at myself and my ability to choose the most inaccurate word to describe how I'm really feeling. Perfectly distraught, that's what I am.

'It was a wonderful reception. Thank you.'

'Oh, you're welcome.' I brush off my boss's appreciation. 'Where is everyone?' I ask, desperate to divert the conversation from my shambolic wedding, and probably shambolic marriage, too.

'Sal's in the stationery cupboard having a tidy up, and Tom and Victoria should be here by now.' He looks at his watch. 'Van Der Haus.' He returns his eyes to mine, and I struggle to look relaxed at the mention of my Danish client's name. 'Has he been in touch yet?'

'No,' I load my computer up and jiggle my mouse to get the screen on. It doesn't escape my thoughts that I've been given a deadline of today to inform my boss of Mikael's revenge mission, but given my current state of affairs and the fact that I've left Jesse, I'm thinking my Lord will not be pressing me on this issue. 'He said he'd be in touch once he's back in the UK.'

'Fair enough.' Patrick shifts on my desk, and I will him to at least be still if he insists on torturing the poor thing. 'And anything to report on your other clients? The Kents, Miss Quinn . . . Mr Ward.' He chuckles at his own little joke, and although I'm in turmoil with my new husband, I'm grateful for Patrick's acceptance of mine and Jesse's relationship. If there will even be a relationship after the next few days.

'All great. The Kents are in full swing, Miss Quinn's work starts tomorrow, and Mr Ward would like me to commission the beds as soon as possible.'

Patrick laughs. 'Ava, flower, you don't have to call your husband Mr Ward.'

'Habit,' I grumble. I could think of a lot of things I could call him at the moment.

'You mean those lovely lattice-style beds?'

'Yes.' I pull out the design from my drawer and present it to Patrick.

'Stunning,' he says simply. 'Bet these will cost a few quid.'

Stunning? Yes. Expensive? Ridiculously. But Patrick doesn't

realise the benefits of these beds in a place like The Manor. To my big cuddly bear of a boss, The Manor is still just a lovely country retreat. 'He can afford it.' I shrug and take the design back when he hands it to me.

I'm happily filing the drawing away when the sharp cracking of splintering wood rings out through the quiet of our office, and I watch in shock as Patrick crashes to the floor with a look of alarm on his face.

'Bloody hell!' he shouts, rolling around among the many pieces of broken wood and stationery that graced my desk, including my flat computer screen. A rip-roaring giggle is bubbling in my throat, and it's taking every modicum of power to hold it back. This is just too funny.

I lose the battle. A burst of laughter flies from my mouth. 'I'm sorry!' I chuckle, regaining control of my twitching body. 'Here.' I put my hand out to him and he reaches up to take it, his stretch straining his shirt buttons. It flies open, scattering buttons all over the office floor and revealing Patrick's pot belly. This does me no favours, and my earlier laughter returns full force.

'Drat!' he curses, keeping a tight hold of my hand. 'Double drat!'

'Oh God!' I cry, bending over to stop myself from peeing my knickers. 'Patrick, are you okay?' I know he is. He wouldn't be rolling around and cursing if he was seriously injured.

'No I'm bloody not. Will you control yourself and help me out?' He tugs at my hand.

'I'm sorry!' It's no good. I'm crying, mascara probably pouring down my cheeks. I throw all of my strength into heaving Patrick up from the floor, making quick work so I can get to the toilet. And I do just that when I've finally got him to his feet. 'Excuse me!' I laugh, running to the Ladies, passing a shocked-looking Sal as I fly past the stationery cupboard.

When I've sorted myself out and composed my jerking body,

I walk back into the office to find Tom and Victoria have arrived and Sal's on her knees collecting up a million paperclips.

'What happened?' Victoria whispers.

'My desk finally gave in.' I smile, and try my hardest to keep the giggling fit from returning again. If I start, I won't stop.

'I missed it!' Tom cries incredulously. 'Damn it.' He hangs his man-bag on the back of his chair. 'Darling! How is the bride?'

'Fine,' I answer.

'Oh yes!' Victoria pipes up. 'When I get married, it'll be just like your wedding, except perhaps not at a se—'

I dart warning eyes to my ditsy work colleague, and she acknowledges her near error by snapping her mouth shut.

I kneel down to help Sal. 'It was beautiful, Ava,' she muses dreamily. 'You're so lucky.'

Sal's sweet words only enhance my gloom – until my phone starts singing 'Angel' from my bag. I glance across at it, sitting amid the chaos of broken desk. I can't speak to him. I'm a little surprised that it's taken him until now to call me, and even more surprised he wasn't so persistent last night. These signs are all an indication of one thing and one thing alone. He knows he's pushed the boundaries. I can't even imagine what he's doing with himself, besides running continuous laps of the royal parks.

Sal looks at me expectantly, but I just smile and continue picking up paperclips and popping them in a pot. It's only now I wonder why, out of all the things we could be clearing up, we're collecting the smallest things of all. 'I'll call him back,' I say to Sal, while thinking how therapeutic this actually is.

When we're done, Sal gets up and heads to the kitchen to make coffee, while I pull myself up and head for Patrick's office. I knock on the door and poke my head around. He's sitting at his desk, a little red-faced, combing his hair. 'Are you okay, Patrick?' I ask, biting my lip furiously to contain my grin.

'I'm fine,' he huffs. 'I think Irene might see this as a sign to lose some weight.' He grins a little, making me feel a whole lot better about laughing at him. 'I'm glad I've made your day, flower.'

'I'm sorry, but you must have heard the creaks every time you sat there.'

'Yes, I did. Stupid cheap tat!'

'I'm sure,' I agree with a serious face. There was nothing cheap about my desk. 'Would you like a coffee?'

'No,' he grumbles. 'I need to go home and change.'

'Okay.' I slip out of his office and return to my pile of wood, rummaging around the loose parts until I find my bag. I locate my phone, clear the missed call from Jesse, then dial my doctor.

'Is he okay?' Tom asks on a chuckle, Victoria joining him.

'He's fine, but keep a straight face when he leaves to go and change out of his burst shirt.' I grin.

'He popped his buttons?' Victoria laughs, flopping back in her chair.

Tom looks over at Victoria and joins her laughter. 'Oh flipping heck!'

I manage to hold my giggles and slip into the stationery cupboard when my call connects, and after getting past the guard dog of a receptionist, I finally get an appointment for four o'clock.

The day passes swiftly, with only a few missed calls from my Lord. The calls were expected, but what wasn't expected was his lack of persistence. He didn't call the office, he didn't stop by and he didn't ring off the hook. I'm not sure if I should be satisfied that he seems to accept my request for space, or worried that he's uncharacteristically giving it to me. I miss him, but I need to override this. I need to stick to my guns and the only way I can ensure that happens is if I don't see or speak to him. It's frightening what he can do to me when I'm determined to hold my own.

I collect my bag and get up from my makeshift desk, which happens to be a paste table. 'I'm off. See you tomorrow,' I say as I pass all three of my colleagues. 'I've cleared it with Patrick.'

A chorus of goodbyes ring out as I shut the door behind me and make my way to the Tube, 'Angel' sounding from my bag the whole way there. So much for his lack of persistence.

As I'm approaching the station, I jump on a shocked gasp when a tall, lean, green-eyed wall lands in front of me. My hand flies up to my chest, resting on my heart as I breathe heavily. Then I get mighty irritated. 'What are you doing?' I ask shortly.

'You wouldn't answer your phone.' He points to my bag. 'Maybe you didn't hear it.'

I look up at him and find an accusing stare. He knows damn well I could hear it. 'You were following me.' I can be accusing too.

'Where are you going?' He steps in closer, but I move back. I can't let him touch me. And shit, where *am* I going?

'A client,' I blurt.

'I'll take you.'

'I told you. I need space, Jesse.' I'm aware of fellow pedestrians stepping around us, some moaning, some throwing filthy glares, but I'm not concerned and neither is Jesse. He's just staring at me, looking shockingly spectacular in a grey suit and blue shirt.

'How much space and for how long? I married you on Saturday and you left me on Sunday.' He reaches forward and grasps my upper arm before sliding his touch down until he's holding my hand. As always, my hairs stand up on end and a shiver reverberates through me. I watch him just stare at our joined hands, his fingers weaving through mine slowly. 'I'm struggling, Ava.' He looks up at me and lands me with a green-glazed stare. 'Without you, I'm really struggling.'

My heart breaks for him, and I clench my eyes shut, desperately fighting my natural instinct to step into him and hold him. If he's not getting his way with fuckings of various degrees or a Jesse-style countdown, then he's breaking me down with heart-wrenching words.

'I really need to go.' I turn, fully expecting to be held back, but he releases my hand and I'm walking away, shocked and actually quite worried.

'Baby, please. I'll do anything. Please, don't leave me.' His pleading voice halts me dead in my tracks, pain slicing through me. 'Let me at least drive you. I don't want you on the train. Just ten minutes, that's all I'm asking.'

'It'll be quicker on the Tube,' I say quietly amid the roaring crowds. I turn to face him.

'But I want to take you.'

I can't tell him where I'm going. He'll have a seizure. I quickly wrack my tired brain and come up with only one option. I'll ask him to drop me off around the corner from the doctor. There are some residential properties close by. He won't know any different.

I sigh. 'Where's your car?'

The relief that washes over his face is obvious, and it emphasises my guilt. Why I'm feeling guilty is beyond me, though. He lifts his arm and takes my hand gently, then slowly leads me back towards a hotel car park. The valet produces the keys from his cabin and hands them to Jesse, and he releases me only when we get to the car so I can get in.

Pulling out onto Piccadilly, he drives with consideration for the other road users and shifts gears gently, too. His driving style is matching his mood; subdued.

'Where am I going?' he asks as he turns the music system on and The XX's 'Islands' filters through the speakers. Even the music is passive and soft.

I scan my brain for a road name around the surgery, and only one comes to mind. 'Luxemburg Gardens. Hammersmith,' I say, looking out of the window.

'Okay,' he answers quietly. I know he's looking at me. I should turn and challenge him, prompt him to explain himself better, but my despondency is getting the better of me. He'd better not mistake it for submission. I'm not surrendering on this. I just need to get myself to the doctor, minus one Jesse, and get my awful situation remedied.

He pulls into Luxemburg Gardens and drives slowly down the tree-lined street. 'Here will do.' I indicate to the left, and he pulls over. 'Thank you.' I open the door.

'You're welcome,' he murmurs. I know if I turn and look at him, I'll see cogs whirling and a concerned frown set in place on his handsome head, so I don't. I step out of the car. 'Will you have dinner with me tonight?' he asks urgently, like he knows his chance is slipping.

I take a deep breath. 'You just asked for ten minutes, and I gave them to you. You said nothing.' I leave a despairing face of hurt and make my way across the road, but suddenly come to an abrupt halt when it occurs to me that I have no *client's* house in which to disappear. I need to back-track at least half a mile, and I can't do that with Jesse sitting at the kerb in his car, so I pull my bag open and feign searching for something while mentally praying for him to leave. I listen for the roar, or possible purr, of the DBS and after what seems like for ever, it finally reaches my ears. It's a purr. I look over my shoulder and watch his car disappear down the street before I head back the way we came. I feel nauseous. I'm not sure how I'm going to approach this. After my numerous visits to our family doctor, seeking replacement pills and the lectures I received from her each time, I'm facing a grilling and an even sterner talk on carelessness. She'll think I'm a glutton for punishment. I think I probably am.

I check myself in and pick up a magazine from the waiting room table, then spend twenty minutes pretending to read it.

I'm fidgeting and pulling at my clothes to try and cool myself down. I really do feel sick, and my nauseous state only worsens when, like an omen, I come across an article expressing the arguments for and against termination. A despairing laugh falls from my lips.

'Something funny?'

I freeze as Jesse's familiar brogue washes over me, then I snap the magazine shut. 'You followed me?' I ask, completely stunned as I turn to face him.

'You're a rubbish liar, baby,' he states factually, but softly. He's right; I'm shit at it. 'Are you going to tell me why you're at the doctor's and why you lied to me about it?' He rests his hand on my bare knee and circles it slowly as he watches me intently.

I throw the magazine back on the table. There is no escaping this man. 'Just a check-up,' I mutter to my knee, trying to shift it from his grasp.

'A check-up?' His tone has altered significantly. He's not soft and soothing any more. There's an edge of anger to it.

He cannot dictate this. 'Yes.'

'Don't you think we should be doing this together?'

Together? My shock makes my angry eyes swing straight to his, finding curious greens greeting me. His hand eases up on my knee and I yank my leg away. 'Like the decision you made to try and get me knocked up? Did we do that together?'

'No,' he answers quietly, turning away from me.

I stare at his perfect profile, unwilling to relent and turn away. He has some nerve and my despondency has been thoroughly chased away and replaced with my earlier anger, only now it's amplified. 'You can't even look at me, can you?' I ask tightly. 'I pray to God I'm not pregnant, Jesse, because I wouldn't inflict the shit you put me through on my worst enemy, let alone my baby.'

It's him who looks shocked now. His eyes are narrowed, his hair starting to dampen at his temples from a stressed sweat. 'I know you're pregnant, and I know how it'll be.'

'Oh?' I don't bother restraining my laugh. 'How's that, then?'

His face softens and he makes my heart slow when he reaches for my cheek and gently strokes it. 'Perfect,' he whispers, flicking his eyes to mine.

Our gazes are locked for a short time, but I'm snapped from the spell that he places me under when my name is called, and I'm swiftly brought back to where I am and why. My anger swiftly returns, too. It wouldn't be perfect. Maybe for him, but for me it would be torture. I stand up, causing his hand to fall from my knee and his other from my face, but to my utter shock, Jesse quickly rises, too. Oh no! He is not coming in with me. This is going to be mortifying enough, without my neurotic Lord trampling all over my doctor's office. Anyway, if I am pregnant, I need Jesse *not* to know. He would never let me terminate his baby, and I hate to think of what lengths he'd go to in order to stop me.

'Don't you dare!' I grate, and he recoils. 'Sit!' I point to the chair and flash him the most threatening face I can muster. It's hard. I could vomit at any moment.

Much to my utter shock, he wisely lowers himself down to the chair gingerly, his expression truly dazed by my outburst. I turn and leave him looking like he's been slapped in the face, and take a deep, encouraging breath before entering my doctor's office.

'Ava! Good to see you.' Dr Monroe is probably one of the nicest women I have ever met – early fifties, a little bit of middle-age spread and a sharp blond bob.

'And you, doctor,' I reply nervously as I perch myself on the end of a chair.

She looks concerned. 'Are you okay? You look a bit green.'

'I'm fine; I just feel a bit icky. It's probably the heat.' I fan my face. It's even hotter in here.

'Are you sure?'

I feel my chin start to tremble, only serving to increase the concern on her round features. 'I'm pregnant!' I blurt. 'I know you'll give me a hard time about the pills, but please don't make me feel any worse. I know I'm a fool.'

Her concern transforms into sympathy immediately. 'Oh, Ava.' She reaches for my hand, her empathy only making me feel like even more of a hopeless fool. 'Here.' She hands me a tissue. 'When was your period due?'

'Today,' I answer swiftly.

Her eyes widen. 'Only today?' she asks. I nod. 'Ava, what makes you so certain? Your period can be a few days late, just as it can be early.'

'Trust me, I know,' I sniffle. I'm no longer in denial, and I'm facing this head-on.

She frowns and reaches into her drawer. 'Take this to the toilet,' she says, handing me a pregnancy test.

I waste no time. Leaving Dr Monroe's office, I peek down the corridor and spy Jesse's back. He's still sitting down, but he's leaning forward, elbows braced on his knees with his head in his hands. I don't dwell on his obvious despair and walk quickly into the Ladies.

Five minutes later, I'm back with my doctor and staring at the test, which is neatly positioned at the other end of her desk. She taps away on her keyboard while I frantically tap my foot on the floor, and then hold my breath when she reaches over and picks the test up, looking down at it briefly before turning her eyes to me.

'Positive,' she says simply, holding it up for me to see myself. I knew it would be, but the confirmation makes it even more of a reality, and it also enflames the hurt and madness that has brought me to this point in my life.

'I want a termination,' I say clearly, looking straight into Dr Monroe's eyes.

I watch as she visibly sags in her chair. 'Ava, of course, this is your decision, but it's my job to give you the options.'

'Which are?'

'Adoption, support. There are many single mothers out there who manage just fine, and with your parents' support, I'm certain you'll be well looked after.'

I cringe. 'I want a termination,' I repeat, ignoring all of her advice and sincerity. She's absolutely right, though. I would be looked after by my parents . . . if I was single. But I'm not. I'm married.

'Right,' she sighs. 'Okay, you'll need a scan to determine how far gone you are.' She starts re-tapping away on her keyboard, while I sit feeling small and stupid. 'I'm prescribing some more pills so once you've sorted yourself out you can make sure you keep protected. The hospital will give you plenty of information with regards to aftercare and side effects.'

'Thank you,' I murmur, taking the prescription from her. She doesn't release it immediately, and I look up at her.

'You know where I am, Ava.' She looks at me questioningly, obviously doubting my decision, so I offer a small smile to reinforce that I really am fine, that I'm making the right choice.

'Thank you,' I repeat, because I don't know what else to say. I leave her office and prop myself up against the wall outside, feeling sicker and hotter.

'Ava! What's the matter?' He's at my side in a heartbeat, his voice spiked with panic. He hunkers down to get to my eye level. 'Jesus, Ava.'

A sweat breaks out across my forehead and my mouth is suddenly invaded with saliva. I'm going to throw up. I dart across the corridor and crash into the Ladies, then proceed to eject the contents of my stomach in the first toilet I find. Jesse's big, warm palm is gently circling my back as I heave.

'I'm fi—' My stomach convulses again, and I let rip another evacuation as I crouch and slump in front of the toilet. Why the hell do they call it morning sickness when it hits you randomly throughout the day?

The door to the Ladies opens.

'Oh dear, should I get you some water?' It's Dr Monroe.

'Please,' Jesse replies.

I hear the door close again and Jesse squats down behind me, cradling me from behind. 'Are you done?' he asks softly.

'I don't know.' I still feel terrible.

'We can stay. Are you okay?'

'I'm fine,' I say haughtily.

He doesn't say anything. He takes the water from Dr Monroe when she returns and assures her that I'm in good hands. I don't doubt him. I always feel safe in his hands. If it wasn't for the small problem of him being so sly and underhanded, he would be perfect. We would be perfect.

He remains crouched behind me, holding my hair back and offering me water every now and then whilst I compose myself. 'I'm good,' I assure him as I wipe my mouth with tissue. I know there's no more to come up. I feel empty.

'Here.' He pulls me to my feet and settles my hair down my back. 'Do you want some more water?'

I take the glass from him and walk over to the sinks to wash my hands. I sip, swill and spit to clean my mouth out, and as I look up into the mirror, I see Jesse standing behind me. He looks worried. I brush my cheeks and ruffle my hair.

'Let me take you home,' he says as he comes to stand closer.

'Jesse, I'm fine.'

He reaches around me and strokes his hand down my cheek. 'Let me look after you.'

'I'm okay.' I step back and pick my bag up.

'You're not okay, Ava.'

'Something hasn't agreed with me, that's all.' My hand is twitching by my side.

'For fuck's sake, lady! You're at the fucking doctor's, so don't tell me you're fine!' He clutches at his hair and shouts as he swings his body away from me in frustration.

'I'm not pregnant,' I blurt quickly, but then suddenly contemplate the horrific thought of him not wanting me if he thinks that. My heart constricts painfully in my chest. I feel sick again.

'What?' He's quickly facing me, his eyes shocked, his body twitching. He really *does* want this badly.

I fight my natural reflex, trying desperately to keep my hands by my side. 'I've had it confirmed, Jesse.'

'Then why are you throwing up all over the place?'

'I have a bug.' My excuse is feeble, but by the look on his face, which I'm definitely not mistaking as devastation, he believes me. 'You failed. My period came.'

He doesn't know what to say. His eyes are flicking all over the bathroom, and he's still twitching. My fear is only strengthened by his reaction to my lie. I'm confused, exhausted and utterly heartbroken. No baby equals no Jesse. It's all very clear now.

'I'm not happy about this. I'm taking you home where I can keep an eye on you.' He takes my hand, but I pull it away, bristling immediately at his words.

'You're never happy with me.' I look him square in the eyes. 'I'm always doing something to upset you. Have you thought that perhaps you would be *less* not happy without me around?'

'No!' He looks horrified. 'I'm worried, that's all.'

'Well, don't be. I'm fine,' I snap, leaving the loo in a complete haze.

I walk out of the doctor's, straight into the pharmacy and hand my prescription over the counter, then plonk myself in a chair and watch as Jesse paces up and down outside with his hands shoved into his trouser pockets. Sitting up again, I notice the pharmacist glancing up at me every now and again, and it's then I realise that he's probably wondering what I'm doing with all of these pills. The temptation to explain myself nearly makes me stand and approach the counter, but he calls my name, and

I'm approaching to take the paper bag from him instead.

'Thank you,' I smile before making my escape, but only to go and face my brooding man.

'What's that?' His eyes are fixed on the bag.

'Back-up pills,' I hiss in his face. 'Now that we know I'm not pregnant, I want to stay that way.'

His shoulders slump and his head drops. I'm battling consuming guilt at his reaction to my news, but I have to ignore it. Sidestepping him, I start walking away, my legs a little shaky, my heart pounding relentlessly in my chest.

'You're not coming home, are you?' he calls after me.

I squeeze the bulge back in my throat and march on. His words carry an air of finality, and, more worryingly, he's not demanding that I stay with him. If I remove this baby from my life, it's becoming quite obvious that I'll be removing Jesse, too. I walk against the breeze, my face wet with tears.

Chapter 9

The empty feeling was inevitable. The hollow, desolate, miserable feeling was inevitable. But the overwhelming guilt that has swamped me was not so expected. I fought off twinges here and there, but now I'm consumed by it. And I'm furious for feeling like this. The lack of urgency to chase my scan appointment is also screwing with my mind.

It's Friday. It's day number four without Jesse. My week has been a steady torture, and I know it's never going to get better. My heart is slowly splitting, each day widening the crack, until I know I'll probably cease functioning. I'm close already. What hurts the most, though, is the lack of contact, leaving me wondering if Jesse is drowning in vodka, which also means he's probably drowning in women.

I jump up from my desk and run to the toilets, throwing up immediately, but I don't think this is morning sickness. This is grief.

'Ava, you really should go home. You've not been right all week.' Sally's concerned voice comes through the cubicle door. I heave myself up on a sigh and flush the chain before exiting to splash my face and wash my hands.

'Stupid bug hanging around,' I mutter, glancing at Sal and admiring her grey pencil skirt and black blouse. The dowdy A-line skirts and high-necked shirts are a distant memory. I haven't asked, but with this consistent new attire, I assume dating is going well. 'Are you still seeing that Internet bloke?' I ask. I would refer to him by name, but I have no idea what he's called.

'Mick?' She giggles. 'Yes, I am.'

'And it's going well?' I turn and lean against the sink, watching as she starts brushing down her skirt, then proceeds to smooth her high ponytail.

'Yes!' she squeals, making me jump. 'He really is perfect, Ava.'

I smile. 'What does he do?'

'Oh, some professional nonsense. I don't pretend to understand.'

I laugh. 'Good.' I was just about to say *be yourself*, but I think it's too late for that. I hear my phone shouting from my new desk. 'Excuse me, Sal.' I leave her in the mirror, reapplying her red lipstick.

Approaching my new L-shaped desk, I ignore the deep-seated disappointment because I'm not hearing 'Angel', but I can't ignore my exasperation when I see the caller is Ruth Quinn, my tiresome but infectiously enthusiastic client.

'Hi, Ruth.'

'Ava, you sound terrible.'

I know, and I probably look terrible, too. 'I'm fine, Ruth.' That's because I've just emptied my stomach again.

'Oh good. Can we arrange a meeting?'

'Is there a problem?' I ask, hoping to God there isn't. I'm trying to keep this project as smooth as possible because even though Ruth seems pleasant enough, I predict a tricky customer if things don't go her way.

'No problem. I just want to clarify a few details.'

'We can do that over the phone,' I prompt.

'I would prefer to see you,' she informs me, and I sag in my chair. Of course she would. 'Today,' she adds.

I sag further on an audible groan. I am *not* ending my shitty week with Ruth Quinn. I practically started it with Ruth on Tuesday, and I've had a mid-week interlude on Wednesday. Anyway, it's three in the afternoon. Does she think she's my only client?

'Ruth, I really can't do today.'

'You can't?' She sounds irritated.

'Monday?' Why did I say that? I'll be starting my week with Ruth Quinn again.

'Monday. Yes. Eleven okay?'

'Great.' I flick through my diary and pencil her in.

'Lovely.' She's back to chirpy Ruth. 'Have you anything nice planned for the weekend?'

I stop writing, suddenly feeling very uncomfortable. I don't have anything nice planned for the weekend, apart from nursing my breaking heart, but before I can really consider what I'm about to say, I come right out and say it. 'No, nothing much.'

'Me neither!' She's going to do it again, I know it. 'We should do drinks!'

My forehead hits the desk. She either can't, or simply won't, take a hint. I pull my heavy head up. 'Actually, Ruth. I said nothing much, but I'm visiting my parents in Cornwall. It's not much really, not fun, anyway.'

She laughs. 'Don't let your parents hear you say that!'

I force myself to laugh along with her. 'I won't.'

'Well, have a nice weekend doing nothing much with your parents. I'll see you on Monday.'

'Thanks, Ruth.' I hang up and glance at the clock. Another hour and I can escape.

I drag my exhausted body up the stairs to Kate's flat and head straight for the kitchen, opening the fridge and being immediately confronted with a bottle of wine. I just stare at it. I don't know for how long, but my eyes are fixed on the damn thing. It takes the sound of a very familiar voice to pull my eyes away, and I turn, seeing Kate, but hers wasn't the familiar voice that caught my attention. Dan walks in, and they both look as guilty as sin.

'What's going on?' I ask, slamming the fridge door. Kate

flinches, but remains quiet. My brother doesn't, though.

'None of your business,' he snipes, slipping his hand around Kate's waist and kissing her cheek. This is the first time I've seen or spoken to him since my wedding, and it's not playing out to be a happy reunion, either. He frowns at me. 'Maybe I should ask *you* what's going on. Why are you here?'

I freeze in position and flick wide eyes to Kate, catching her very faint head shake. She's not told him. 'Just swinging by after work.' I return my eyes to Dan. 'When are you going back to Australia?'

'Dunno.' He shrugs, brushing off my question rapidly. 'I'm off.'

'Bye,' I spit, turning and reopening the fridge to grab that bottle of wine. Kate is asking for trouble, and I'm liking my brother less and less by the day. I never thought I'd be glad to see the back of him. I ignore the exchange of goodbyes going on behind me and focus my attention on pouring a big glass of wine.

By the time I've sipped half, I hear footsteps going down the stairs, and I turn to face my stupid, redhead friend. 'Are you fucking mad?' I wave my wine glass at her.

'Probably,' she grumbles, sitting herself down on a chair and signalling for some wine. 'How are you feeling?'

'Fine!' I grab another glass and pour some, passing it over the table to her. 'You really are getting yourself in a mess.'

She scoffs and takes a quick slurp. 'Ava, shall we re-evaluate the situation here? You're the one who's been married for less than a week, left your husband, and is knocked up.'

I recoil at her harshness as she eyes up the glass I'm clenching. I'm instantly on the defence. 'I'm a few weeks. Some women don't find out until they're three months.' I'm trying to dampen down the burning guilt that's smouldering in my gut.

She gets up, climbs onto the worktop and lights a cigarette. 'A few drinks won't hurt you, not that it matters,' she says, opening the kitchen window and draping her arm over the ledge.

'Not that what matters?' I frown, and take a more reluctant sip.

'Well, you're getting rid of it, aren't you?'

The insensitive words spike at my conscience, but it doesn't stop me slurping more wine. I think I'm more in denial now than I ever was. 'Yes,' I mutter, sinking onto a chair, my thoughts wandering off somewhere.

'Right!' Kate's assertive tone snaps me from my reverie. 'We're going out.'

'Are we?'

'Yes. I'm not letting you mope around any longer. Has he called?' She takes a drag of her cigarette and looks at me expectantly.

I wish I could say yes. 'No.'

Her lips purse, and I know she's thinking it's strange, too. 'Get showered. We're going for a quiet drink. Not too much, though.' She looks at my glass. 'But like I said, not that it matters.'

'I don't think so.' I shake my head, her further blasé words eating me up inside.

She sighs and flicks her cigarette butt from the window before lowering herself down. 'Come on, Ava. Just a sensible glass and a chat, not about Jesse or Sam or Dan, just us two like old times.' By old times, she means post-Matt and pre-Jesse. We did have some laughs in those four weeks, before The Lord of the Sex Manor trampled my life.

'Okay.' I get up from the table. 'You're right. I'll get ready.'

'Fab!'

'Thank you for not telling Dan why I'm here.'

She smiles as we leave the kitchen together to get ready for a quiet drink and a chat.

He's constantly on my mind, and I'm trying my hardest to put him to the back, but when we walk into Baroque and the first person I see is Jay, the doorman, I give in. He frowns at me as I walk past, dropping all conversation with a fellow guard, but I proceed to the bar without a word.

'Wine?' Kate asks, as she muscles in at the bar.

'Please.' Casting my eyes around, I immediately spot Tom and Victoria. I tap Kate on the shoulder and she turns her head slightly. 'Did you know they would be here?'

'Who?'

I nod in the direction of Tom and Victoria, who are dancing over. They have no idea what's happening in my life. 'Barbie and Ken,' I quip drily. I can tell by Kate's eye roll that she didn't.

'Love the dress!' Tom croons, stroking my midriff.

I look down at the tight black dress that I borrowed from Kate. 'Thanks.' I take the glass being handed over Kate's shoulder.

'You okay?' I ask Victoria.

She fluffs her hair and sweeps it over her shoulder. 'Amazing.'

Oh? Not good or great, but amazing? 'That good?' I ask, wishing she could transfer some of that *amazing* over to me.

'Yes, that good.' She giggles.

'She's in love again.' Tom nudges Victoria in the side, spiking a heavy scowl from the pretty blonde.

'I'm not, and that's rich, coming from the man-whore here!'

Tom looks genuinely shocked, and for the first time in days, I laugh. It feels good. Kate joins us, and with a lack of free tables, we just stand near the bar, chatting. He's still floating around in my mind, of course, but my cunning best friend is doing a great job of distracting me for a while.

That is, until I look up and see him.

My heart doesn't speed up . . . it stops. I've not seen him since Monday, and if it's even possible, he looks more devastating than ever. I know immediately that Jay has called him, and I also know I'm probably going to be hauled from the bar, but that doesn't stop my eyes from slowly dragging up his jean-clad legs, onto his white shirt, up his neck and finally onto his face – the one that sends my eyes delirious with pleasure, even when I'm mad with him. He doesn't look mad, though, and he doesn't look like he's been drinking. He looks fresh, healthy, and as spectacular as ever. And every other woman in the bar thinks so, too. They have noticed this breathtaking male, who's striding across the bar, some even following him. His sparkling greens land on me briefly and my heart resumes beating . . . very *very* fast. His face is expressionless as he stares at me for a few seconds before he slowly pulls his gaze away without so much as an acknowledgment to my presence. Then he continues to the bar with a flurry of women in tow.

I'm crushed; my racing mind thinking up all sorts of explanations for his quiet absence over the last four days – where he's been, what he's been doing. He's clearly not mourning his loss. He looks arrogant, confident, and sickeningly handsome – just like he did on the day I met him. They are all familiar traits to me, but right now, they are all enhanced.

Uncertainty and raging jealousy are strangling me, and I'm still staring at him, watching as he assaults the women surrounding him with that fucking face, making them disintegrate on the spot.

Oh yes, there he is, my husband, looking like he's just landed from planet fucking perfect. My eyes narrow as I watch a woman in a red dress stroke his arm, and I literally hold myself back from physically removing her. I'm very aware of the silence in our group, so I drag my eyes away from my bastard of a husband and see Kate watching me closely, Tom dribbling along with the other hussies, and Victoria scuffing her ridiculous heels on the bar floor. I shake my head on a little laugh and take a massive swig of the wine I've been carefully sipping, flicking my eyes briefly over in his direction. He knows I'm watching. If he wants to play games, then I'm willing, and I don't plan on settling for anything less than gold.

'Let's dance.' I down the rest of my wine and slam the glass on the bar before pushing my way through the small crowds until I find myself on the dance floor. When I turn around, I find my three loyal friends have all joined me.

Kate looks nervous. I make a snatch for her wine, but she swipes it away. 'Don't be stupid, Ava,' she warns in my ear. 'I know you're still pregnant.'

I'm trying to piece together something to strike back with, but nothing is coming to me, so in an act of complete stupidity, I turn and stomp over to the bar. I know he's watching me, and I know Kate is, too, but it doesn't stop me from ordering and downing a fresh glass of wine before returning to the floor.

'What are you trying to prove?' Kate yells at me. 'Because if it's that you're a fucking twat, then you're succeeding.' Her words would probably hit a nerve if the alcohol wasn't getting in the way. I don't care.

I'm distracted from Kate's wrath by Tom's squeal, his eyes lighting up when the DJ launches Rob D 'Clubbed to Death'. He pounces on me. 'Get me a whistle, shove me in some hot pants and put me on that podium! *Ibiza!*'

I shut my mind down, cancelling out all thoughts of my infuriating man, and let the music take me, my body falling into sync with the track, my arms rising above my head and my eyes closing. I'm in a world of my own. My only awareness is of the loud music and me at the centre of it.

I'm lost.

Numb.

Silently devastated.

But he's near.

I can sense him. I can smell his fresh-water scent closing in, and then there's his touch. My arms slowly fall as I feel his palm slide across my stomach, his groin pressing into my lower back, his hot breath in my ear. I'm surrounded by him, and even though I should be pushing him away, I can't. My blank mind remains blank, and I start moving with him as he kisses my neck, his hardness pushing into my back. I'm powerless to stop my head from falling to the side, giving him better access. My throat's taut, making me hypersensitive to his firm tongue, which is trailing straight up my vein until he's at my ear, breathing heavy, hot, controlled breaths. The music seems to get louder, his handling of me more severe, and before I can open my eyes, I'm being dragged from the dance floor. I could try to stop him, but I don't. I follow his lead until I'm being pulled through the corridor towards the toilets, everything around me seeming slow and slurred as I focus only on his broad back in front of me. As we approach the end of the passageway, I glance back and see Jay watching us, then I look to Jesse and see him give the doorman a nod before opening the door to a disabled toilet and pushing me inside. The door is swiftly shut, the lock flipped and within a second I'm pushed up against the wall by his body. The music is louder, and I look up, seeing integrated speakers in the ceiling, but my face is soon yanked back down. Our eyes meet. His greens are dark, completely smoked out, and his lips are slightly parted. I'm panting as he takes my wrists and pulls them up, pinning them on either side of my head before he leans in and takes my bottom lip between his teeth and bites down, then pulls away, dragging it between his grip. I've lost all control of my bodily reactions. My belly is turning, shifting the thump that's hammering away inside me straight down to my core. I'm desperate for him, but the placing of my hands and his hard body compressed to mine is preventing me from moving anything but my head, so I reach forward with my lips. He ducks my aim. This is going to be on his terms. His lips hover over mine, only millimetres from my reach, his hot, minty breath heating my face, but then he pulls away. He's teasing me.

My husky voice breaks. 'Kiss me.' I'm begging, I'm aware of it, but I don't care. I want and need him all over me.

His face is completely impassive as he flexes his grip on my wrists and increases the pressure of his body against mine. He slowly moves his face forward, his green orbs penetrating me completely, and tickles my lips with his. I moan and try to capture them, but he pulls away again, still poker-faced, still completely controlled. Not me, though. I'm about to go crazy with desperation.

'Kiss me,' I demand harshly.

He ignores me and shifts one of my arms across to meet the other, then takes both of my wrists in one grasp. With his other hand, he reaches down and places his fingertip on my knee, and slowly, lightly, starts a painfully tormenting trail up my thigh, over my hip, across my ribs, my breast and up, up, up, until he has my neck completely encased by his palm, his thumb resting on the hollow of my throat, his fingers splayed at my nape. My pulse has accelerated, my heart is bucking wildly in my chest and my knees could give at any moment. And all of the time, he is burning holes through me with his addictive eyes. I could scream with frustration, which is no doubt his plan. I lean forward again, but he dodges my lips stealthily and homes straight in on my chest, nudging my dress down with his chin and latching onto my breast. He's freshening up his mark.

My head falls back against the wall and my eyes close in hopelessness. The continuous buzzing between my thighs is excruciating, and I fear he's going to leave me like this. He's done it more than once. He's trampling me. He has no right to, but I'm craving this touch, and now it has started, I never want it to stop.

With the music pumping loudly around us, you would think all other sounds would be drowned out, but they're not. My feverish breaths are thick and piercing. Jesse's breathing, though, is slow, shallow and controlled. He is in complete control. He knows what he's doing.

I'm about to shout in frustration but I'm spun around and

pushed back into the wall, my body crashing harshly against the tiles. I turn my face and rest my hot cheek on the coldness, and his knee comes up, separating my thighs. He takes my hands and places them, palms flat, against the shiny surface. He doesn't need to tell me to keep them there. His firm placing and the slow removal of his grip tell me what's expected of me. That and his lips pushed to my ear. When his palms rest on the outside of my thighs and clutch the hem of my dress, my breathing hitches further, and I begin to physically shake. He slowly pulls it up to my waist, and then I hear the fly of his jeans being pulled down. Impatient, I push my arse out invitingly, only to have his hand collide with my cheek, the instant sting on my bareness spiking a scream.

'Fuck!' I pant, earning myself another swift slap. 'Jesse!' I turn my face to the wall, resting my forehead against the tiles, my scorching breath steaming up the black, shiny surface. How long is he going to do this? How long will he make me suffer? But then my hips are pulled back, my knickers yanked to the side and he slams into me. I yell at the shock, fast invasion, but he's silent, not even panting, not even shaking. He slowly pulls back, holding himself steady for a few moments, before he powers forward again. My stomach twists and my head is whirling. I don't know what to do with myself. I'm struck again, hard and fast, and I scream, but the music drowns me out. Slowly, he pulls out, and I feel a hand leave my hip, sliding up my body until he's holding the back of my neck. His grip twists, prompting my head to turn out to the side, and then his lips are on mine. I moan, accepting his hard mouth and delighting in the familiarity. I don't get nearly enough, just a little teaser of what I've been missing out on, before he leaves me craving so much more.

Keeping deadly still for a few seconds, he then shifts his feet and rears back before letting go of his control. I'm yanked back to meet him over and over again, each forceful, punishing blow assisting me in achieving my main aim: ultimate detonation. And just when I think I'm there, he pulls out and spins me around, lifting me up to straddle him. He slips straight back in, my arms fall around his neck and he charges forward, quickly recapturing my bubbling orgasm. My head falls back and the warmth of his mouth is straight on my throat, biting, sucking and licking. I start trembling as the pulses riddling my entire body all collect together and find their way to the tip of my clitoris. I'm screaming before I've even climaxed, but then the rush of pressure soars and flings me into an abyss of intoxicating pleasure and I shatter, screaming louder, and I know he's come too, even though he remains silent. My head drops, finding a sweat-covered face, glazed greens and still a straight, unemotional, unaffected face. It completely baffles me. I shift my hands to his hair and pull him forward, but he resists, instead moving his hands to my legs and pushing them down from his body. I find my feet, keeping myself relatively stable by leaning against the wall while I watch him slide his hand into my knickers to collect the wetness, and then run his palm all over my chest before he wipes his brow, refastens his trousers, turns and walks out.

Chapter 10

After standing in a stunned silence for a while, the music suddenly unbearable, I straighten myself out and do my best to compose my ruffled state. It's no good. I'm shocked. He never said one word from finding me on the dance floor to leaving me alone in the disabled toilet of a bar, where he's just fucked me. Not made love or even had wild sex. He just fucked his wife, like I'm some whore he picked up. I'm injured, my uncertainties even stronger than ever before. What do I do now?

I fly around when the door swings open and Kate barrels in. 'There you are! We're leaving!'

'Why?'

She looks panicked. 'Sam's here.'

Is that all? 'You can cope with that, can't you?'

'And your brother,' she adds drily.

'Oh . . .'

'Yes, *oh*. Come on.' She grabs my hand and pulls me from the toilet. 'Where's Jesse?' she asks as we pass the bar entrance.

I glance through and see him standing at the bar, a glass of clear liquid in one hand, and in his other . . . a woman's arse.

I see red.

I yank my hand from Kate's and steam toward my fucked-up, fucking twat of a husband.

'Hey, Ava! I need to leave!' Kate calls.

I ignore her and fight my way through the crowd. He looks up and clocks me, but his eyes don't widen, he doesn't look guilty or like he's been caught out. Why would he? I catch a glimpse of Sam, who looks more fearful than Jesse at my determined approach, and the first thing I do when I reach him is snatch the glass from his hand and down it. It's water. I drop it to the floor, the smashing of glass only just breaking the loud roar of music and chatting. Then I pivot toward the woman, who now has *her* hand on my neurotic Lord's tight arse.

'Fuck off,' I yell in her face, physically removing her hand from Jesse. I don't need to repeat the move when it comes to Jesse's palm on her backside. That has already been wisely removed, and there is no need for me to repeat my words, either. The woman's eyes widen and she backs away cautiously. It's probably the most sensible move she's ever made. I feel lethal. 'What the fuck are you doing?' I scream.

His eyebrows slowly raise, a hint of a smirk breaking the corner of his lush mouth. It's the first emotional reaction I've gotten from him since he walked into the bar. But he doesn't say anything.

'Answer me!'

He shakes his head and turns away from me, signalling the barman over. Oh, he asked for this. I turn and see all three of my friends, plus Sam and my brother, all standing in shocked silence. I'm shocked myself, but I'm far from silent.

'Move!' I shout and push my way between them, striding determinedly towards the dance floor. It doesn't take me long to find what I'm looking for; I get plenty of offers when I hitch the hem of my dress up. I take a few brief seconds to scan the selection and home straight in on a tall, dark-haired, blue-eyed man. A hot man. I don't give myself time to consider rejection. I walk straight up to him, let him drink me in for a few moments, before I slip my hand around his neck and move in. He accepts willingly, pushing his tongue into my mouth without delay and slipping his arm around my waist. I scorn myself for thinking how good he is, and I soon fall into his steady rhythm, until he is suddenly gone.

I open my eyes and see the strange man scowling at Jesse. 'What the fuck?' he shouts incredulously, to which Jesse replies by drawing his fist back and punching the poor guy straight in the face ... hard. I watch in horror as his nose shatters and blood sprays everywhere. It doesn't stop him, though. He goes straight back at Jesse, tackling him to the floor, fists flying, throats being squeezed and everyone moving back to give the two big men room to fight.

'Ava, what the fuck were you thinking?' Sam's angry voice stabs at my ears from the side, and I look up to find an accusing stare. I don't know what I was thinking. I don't think I was thinking at all.

I follow Sam's gaze back to the floor, just as Jesse takes a clean swipe of a fist to his jaw. I wince. 'Sam, please stop them.' All I can see is Jesse's white shirt smothered in red and the other guy's face mangled, his nose clearly broken.

'Are you fucking mad?' Sam laughs.

I'm just about to start begging when Jesse gets to his feet and drags the man up, pinning him against a pillar before bringing his knee up and striking with a full-on, hard blow to the ribs. The man crumbles to the floor with his arms wrapped around his torso. I feel horrible, and not because I'm watching my husband rub his sore jaw. I feel responsible for the poor stranger, who I targeted to get the crap beaten out of him. What the hell is wrong with me?

I gasp as I'm shoved out the way and Jay charges through, doing a quick assessment of the situation before practically diving on Jesse and manhandling him out of the bar. I move back as they pass me, but Jesse fights against the skinhead and grabs hold of me. 'Get your fucking arse outside,' he growls.

I'm suddenly very aware that I've made a grave mistake, and not wanting to face the music that will be a raging beast of a man outside, I decide my safest option is to remain in the bar. I struggle against Jesse, and he struggles against Jay.

I can hear the doorman cursing as he battles with us. 'Out!' he shouts, and I'm abruptly lifted from my feet and secured against the doorman's chest. 'I'll carry her out if you remove your stubborn fucking arse from the bar!' he yells at Jesse.

It works, but not before Jesse snarls at the doorman, 'Keep your fucking hands exactly where they are.'

In my crazed state, I register exactly where Jay's hands are – one holding me around my waist and the other clenching my forearm. I defiantly wriggle. 'Get the hell off me!'

'Ward, how the fuck do you put up with this?' Jay asks as he paces out of the bar.

What?

'She drives me fucking crazy,' Jesse answers, flicking me a critical stare before refocusing his attention and rubbing his jaw. 'Be careful with her.'

I'm gently placed on my feet and given a disapproving head-shake by Jay while he claps hands with Jesse and leaves us on the pavement. We're both glowering at each other when everyone comes rushing out of the bar, including Dan. I don't need him seeing this.

'Fuck off, all of you!' Jesse roars.

Dan steps forward. 'You think I'm leaving her with you?' he laughs. I pray for Dan to just shut the hell up because after what I've just witnessed, there is absolutely no question that Jesse will annihilate my brother. I turn slowly back to face Kate with a *help* face, but all I get is Kate's pursed lips and the rest of them frantically flicking eyes from Dan to Jesse. They have seen madman Jesse. They're not going to help.

Jesse takes my elbow and points his glare at Dan. 'You don't mind if I take my wife home.' It's a statement, not a question.

'Yes, actually, I do.' Dan's not going to back down here. I can see it in the steely sheen of his dark eyes.

'Dan, it's fine. I'm fine. Just go.' I turn to face the rest of the group. 'All of you, please, just go.'

But no one makes the first move to leave.

Jesse's grip on me increases. 'What the fuck do you think I'm going to do?' he bellows. 'This woman is my fucking life!'

I recoil at his fierce declaration, and so do the others, including Dan. If I'm his life, then where has he been for the last four days? Why did he take me like I'm nothing more than an object? And why did he have his hands on that woman at the bar? I wrench my arm from him and step back, taking a quick glance at my friend. I'm not sure what for – guidance, maybe, because I don't know what to do. She gives me a subtle shake of her head. It's a don't-kick-up-a-stink shake.

With the encouragement of Kate's reassuring look, I walk over to her while pulling the hem of my dress down and, stupidly or not, in one last act of defiance, I grab her wine and down the lot.

'Ava!' She tries to stop me, but I'm on a mission now.

'See you later,' I say as I grab my clutch from her other hand and turn towards Jesse. His lip is curled in warning, but I couldn't care less. Everything he has done tonight is playing on repeat in my head and, with each replay, I'm getting angrier. 'Don't bother following me.'

He looks down at me, the fury in his expression more than evident. I hope my displeasure is obvious, too, but just in case it's not, I throw him a contemptuous look before I push past him and use all of my concentration not to stagger. I shouldn't have drunk that wine, for more reasons than one.

I haphazardly step into the road to hail a cab, but I don't even get my arm in the air. 'Don't step out into the fucking road!' he growls, slinging me over his shoulder. 'You stupid woman!'

'Fucking hell, Jesse!' I'm taken from the road, back to the pavement. 'Put me down!'

'No!'

'Jesse, you're hurting me!'

I'm immediately lowered and instantly have concerned

greens running all over my body. 'You're hurt? Where?'

I smack my palm on my chest. 'Here!' I scream in his face.

He recoils, but then performs the same little rendition, thumping his own chest over his bloodstained shirt. 'Join the fucking club, Ava!' he roars.

I flinch before turning on my slightly drunken heels and storming off.

'The car is this way,' he shouts from behind me. I stop and carefully carry out an about turn before marching back in the other direction. There is little point in trying to get away. I'm tipsy, and he's determined. 'I don't like your dress,' I hear him snarl from behind me.

'I do,' I counter, walking on.

'And why is that?'

I stop and swing to face him. 'Because I knew you wouldn't!' I shout, drawing a little attention from passers-by.

'You're right!' he yells back at me.

'Good! Is that the only reason you're pissed off, or is it because I'm drunk, or is it because I kissed another man?'

'All of the above but kissing another man gets the fucking gold!' He's shaking with anger.

'You had your hand on another woman's arse!'

'I know!' He glares at me, and I glare right back.

'Why? Getting bored of keeping it for just one woman?' I screech, and then tense, looking around to see who has heard my little outburst. I'm relieved to see our friends have all escaped the scene.

He narrows his dark-green eyes on me, his lips forming a straight line. 'You fucking asked for it, woman!'

'Me? How?'

'You left me! You promised you would never leave me!'

We stand opposite each other, staring each other down like a pair of circling wolves, neither one of us backing down.

'You shouldn't have taken it upon yourself to decide my

future,' I say more calmly and carry on to the car, staggering slightly towards the kerb. I've no idea where it is parked, but I've no doubt some directions will be barked at me soon enough.

'You're a fucking pain in the arse,' he snaps. 'And I was thinking about *our* future.' He scoops me up from behind and carries me in his arms.

'Jesse, put me down,' I complain weakly. My meagre attempt to wriggle free is pathetic.

'I'm not putting you down, lady.'

I give in. My body is weak, my mind even weaker and my throat sore and raspy from too much shouting. I let him carry me to the car and deposit me in the passenger seat, not even kicking up a stink when he leans over to buckle me in. He mumbles incoherently as he pulls the hem of my dress down and then slams the door. I'm aware of him getting in the car, and I'm vaguely aware of the pleasant sounds of Ed Sheeran, but then mental exhaustion overwhelms me and my forehead hits the passenger window. I stare blankly at the bright lights of London by night, flashing past the window.

'Oh dear!' I hear Clive's disapproving tone as I come round, bobbing up and down in time to Jesse's strides. 'Should I get the elevator for you, Mr Ward?'

'No, I've got it.' Jesse's voice vibrates through me. 'Fucking dress is ridiculous,' he mumbles as he steps in the elevator.

I come to in his arms and writhe to free myself. 'I can walk,' I snap.

He scoffs and lowers me to my feet, but only because there's nowhere for me to escape and there are no cars that I can walk in front of. The elevator door opens, and I'm the first to exit whilst fishing around in my clutch for my keys. I find them remarkably quickly, considering my disorientated hands, but getting it in the lock is another matter entirely. I close one eye to try and focus as I slowly guide the key to the lock, hearing him grumbling under his breath behind me, but I ignore him and carry on trying to insert the key. He must get fed up with waiting because suddenly there is a hand wrapped around my wrist, holding it steady and guiding it to the lock successfully.

The door opens. I kick my shoes off and trample through the colossal open space, taking the stairs carefully. When I reach the top, I don't veer left to the master suite, instead taking a right and letting myself into my favourite spare room. I collapse in the bed fully dressed and without taking off my make-up, a clear indication of thorough exhaustion and drunkenness. I don't let it concern me for long, though. My eyes close of their own accord, and I feel myself slipping into a drunken slumber.

'Let's get rid of that.'

I feel my dress being peeled from my body. I'm half asleep; I know I'm still slightly drunk and my eyes are semi-stuck together with mascara. 'Are you going to cut it to pieces?' I mumble irritably.

'No,' he says calmly, his strong, familiar arms wrapping around me and lifting me from the bed. 'I might not be talking to you, lady,' he whispers, 'but I want to be not talking to you in *our* bed.'

My arms automatically reach up and around him to hold on, and my face buries in his neck. I might be a little drunk and massively pissed off, but I recognise my favour- ite place. He lowers me to the bed and a few moments later, he's lying the full length of my back and pulling me into his chest.

'Ava?' he whispers in my ear.

'Hmmm?'

'You make me crazy, lady.'

'Crazy in love?' I mumble sleepily.

I feel him squeeze me closer. 'That too.'

*

'I love you.'

What is that? I splutter and rip my mascara-clogged eyes open.

'Drink,' he commands softly.

I groan and roll over into my pillow. 'Leave me alone,' I whine, hearing him chuckle. My head is banging. I've not even lifted it off the pillow and it already feels like Black Sabbath are having their practice session in my skull.

'Hey, come here.' He curls his forearm around my waist, and then drags me across the bed, onto his lap. I feel his palm smooth my hair and pull it from my face, and I peek through my eyes to see a glass of fizzing water being held to my lips. 'Drink,' he presses. I let him tip the glass to my mouth, and I sip the welcome cool, fizzing liquid.

I finish the whole glass and then collapse against his bare chest.

'How bad is it?' he asks.

'Bad,' I croak. My eyes are heavy, and I'm far too comfortable to open my mind to the events that have united me and this stinking hangover – united me with this maddening man.

I feel him shift on the bed and then lean back, taking me with him. At least he's talking to me enough to look after me in my pitiful state. What sort of person punishes the alcoholic love of her life by going out and getting drunk? And when she's pregnant, not that he's aware. What sort of person torments her crazily possessive husband by shoving her tongue down another man's throat? The same sort of person who hides the love of his life's pills to try and get her pregnant on the sly, that's who. We're made for each other.

'I'm sorry-ish,' I say quietly.

He kisses my hair. 'Me too.'

I lie in a sorry heap across him, drifting in and out of sleep and in and out of thought.

'What are you thinking?' he asks quietly, almost apprehensively.

'I'm thinking we can't go on like this,' I answer honestly. 'It's
not good for you.' I leave out the fact that it's not good for me,
either.

He sighs. 'I don't care about me.'

'What are we going to do?' I press.

He's silent for a few moments, and then he shifts me onto
my back and nudges my thighs apart to cradle himself between
them. He takes a deep breath and drops his forehead to my
chest. 'I don't know, but I do know how much I love you.'

I sag and look up at the ceiling. I know that as well but the
saying *love conquers all* is being tested to its limit here. He plays
the love card every time, like it's an acceptable excuse for his
neurotic ways.

'Why did you do it?' I ask. I don't have to elaborate further.
He knows what I'm referring to.

He looks up at me, his frown line crawling across his forehead. 'Because I love you,' he says defensively. "Everything is
because I love you.'

'You treat me like trash, fuck me in the toilet of a bar, and
then walk out to go and feel up another woman? Did you do
that because you love me, too?'

'I was trying to prove a point,' he argues quietly. 'And watch
your mouth.'

'No, Jesse, you were trying to be a wanker.' I shift slightly
under him, and he looks up at me anxiously. 'I need a shower.'

He searches my eyes but eventually rolls off to let me up. I
drag myself from the bed and into the bathroom, closing the
door behind me before brushing my teeth and getting in the
shower. I feel completely deflated and want to crawl back into
bed and forget about everything, but my racing mind is venturing into frightening territory, making my head ache further.
I've not seen him for four days. I'm trying my hardest not to

go there, but I really can't help it, especially in light of his last disappearing act.

I jump when I feel his hand slide around my stomach and his lips rest on my shoulder. 'Let me,' he whispers, taking the sponge and turning me around. He kneels in front of me and takes my foot, resting it on his thigh, before starting to sweep the soapy sponge up my leg.

His frown line is nowhere to be seen. He looks content, peaceful and relaxed, just how I like him to be. 'Where have you been since Monday?' I ask as I watch him closely. He doesn't tense or flick me cautious eyes; he just continues slowly washing me as the water beats down around us.

'In hell,' he answers softly. 'You left me, Ava.' He doesn't look at me, and he's not using an accusing tone, but I know he's pointing out that I broke my promise.

'Where were you?' I push, dropping my foot back to the shower floor and lifting my other when he taps my ankle.

'I was trying to give you space. I realise how I am with you, Ava, and I wish I could stop myself, I really do.'

He still hasn't answered me. I know all of that. 'Where were you, Jesse?'

'Following you,' he whispers. 'Everywhere.'

'For four whole days?'

He looks up at me and stops with the sponge sweeps. 'My only comfort was seeing how lost you were, too.' He reaches up and takes my hand, pulling me down to him so I'm kneeling, too, mirroring him. He pushes my wet hair from my face and leans in to softly kiss my lips. 'We're not conventional, baby. But we're special. What we have is really special. You belong to me, and I belong to you. It just is. It's not natural for us to be apart, Ava.'

'We drive each other crazy. It's not healthy.'

'Not healthy would be my life without you in it.' He encourages me up onto his lap and links my arms around his neck before circling my waist with his big hands. 'This is where you're supposed to be.' He squeezes my waist to reinforce his point. 'Right here, always with me. Don't ever kiss another man again, Ava. They'll be locking me away for a long time.'

I reach up and caress his jaw. There's no bruising or marks. 'You need to stop with the crazy shit.'

He clenches my cheeks and pushes his lips to mine. 'And you need to stop with the defiant shit.' He's grinning around my lips.

'Never.' I soak him right up, there in the soaking shower.

Chapter 11

We spend most of Saturday making friends. I've relished in the sleepy sex, and I've disagreed with almost everything Jesse has said, just to get some sense fucked into me. I then swiftly forgot what I'd agreed to during the sense fucking, instigating a reminder fuck. We had an alfresco fuck right after we ate on the terrace, followed by a retribution fuck when Jesse decided that breaking my promise warranted one. I've been fucked in every way, shape and form, and I've loved every single second of it. I'm back to relaxing sweetly on Central Jesse Cloud Nine. With the absence of a pregnancy, he's back to taking me how and when he wants and any which way, too. Yesterday has more than made up for my lack of dominant Jesse in recent weeks. I couldn't be happier. But there is really no lack of a pregnancy.

Kate checked in, and I'm sure I heard my brother in the background, but she denied it, proceeding to ask me if Jesse and I had made friends. Yes. She also asked if I'd told Jesse that I'm pregnant. No. After a full day of being indulged in him and having things completely back to normal, just how they should be, I'm sure this is the right decision.

'Are you going to lie there all day, or are you getting dressed so we can shoot to The Manor?' He stands in the bathroom doorway gloriously naked, rubbing a towel over his dark-blond locks.

I push myself up and crawl to the bottom of the bed, then flop down on my front, propping myself up on my elbows and resting my chin in my palm. I know what I'm doing, and so does he by the look in his twinkling greens. Not that I don't want to go to The Manor. With the absence of a certain whip-wielding witch, Jesse's country estate is a far more pleasant place to be.

'I might.' My voice is inviting and low, just how I intended it to be. 'You're hard.' I nod at his groin and flick my eyes back up to him, struggling to hold back my grin. I bite my lip and watch him closely.

'That would be because I'm looking at you.' He drapes the towel over his shoulders and leans on the door frame.

I drool at the mass of pure, tempting gorgeousness. 'You're hard everywhere.'

'Except here,' he says, all deep and coarse, tapping his chest. 'Here, I'm as soft as shit. But only for you.'

I smile seductively. 'You can be hard-hearted sometimes,' I muse, rolling over onto my back, my head hanging off the end of the bed.

'You're a temptress, Mrs Ward.'

I watch his upside-down body approach slowly until he's standing looking down at me, his steel shaft brushing my top lip.

'You want it?' he asks, clasping the base and guiding himself from side-to-side across my lips. The hot dampness has my tongue darting out to taste, but he pulls back, his lips tipping at the corners. 'Say please.'

'Please.' I reach up and run my fingertips down the centre of his chest, and he moans, guiding his cock back to my lips. I open slowly while watching as his face contorts with anticipation, then close my lips around him.

'Ava, that damn fucking mouth of yours,' he groans, clenching his eyes shut.

'Should I stop?' I bite down lightly and drag my teeth across his smooth flesh. 'Do you want me to stop?'

'I want you to shut the fuck up and concentrate on what you're doing.'

I smile and release him before flipping myself over and sitting on the end of the bed between his thighs. I grab his cock and squeeze . . . hard.

'Stop teasing me, lady.' His hands find my hair, his fists clenching, and he pushes me onto him.

I don't put up any resistance. I love taking him like this. My head drifts forward and my fingernails grip onto his firm arse.

'Oh fuck!' he barks, holding my head in place. 'Just stay there.'

He's brushing the back of my throat, and I'm struggling to stop my stomach from convulsing, but I keep quiet while he spasms against me, his head dropped back and his fists tightening in my hair. I need to keep control here. I can't be throwing up, I'll never explain it; so instead of concentrating on my mouthful of solid cock, I focus solely on keeping myself from retching. I close my eyes and inhale through my nose. What is wrong with me? If pregnancy brings aversions and mine is a sudden intolerance of Jesse's manhood in my mouth, then I *never* want to be pregnant again.

I relax a little when he withdraws and quickly drop him from my mouth before crawling up his body and wrapping my legs around him. I need to play this perfectly, especially judging by the incredulous look on his handsome face. He doesn't like me halting things. That's his call. I lean in and bite his lip. 'I want you inside me.'

'I was quite happy where I was,' he splutters in disbelief. It makes me laugh. 'I'm glad you find it funny, Ava.'

'I don't, I'm sorry.' Pushing my lips to his, I wave the *need* card. It's my only option. 'I need you inside me now.'

He pulls back and narrows his eyes. It worries me, but then he knocks me out with his smile, reserved only for me. 'You'll never have to ask me twice, baby.' He lowers me to the bed and comes down with me. 'Get rid of the towel.'

I yank the bath sheet from around his neck and fling it across the room.

'Put your hands in my hair,' he orders. I comply immediately, lacing my fingers though his mass of wet, dirty blond. 'Pull it.' He leans down and licks my lips as I tug at his hair on a moan. 'Kiss me hard, Ava.' His stern tone just spikes my need further. I tackle his mouth with desperation and conviction. 'Stop,' he orders, and I do, even though I really don't want to. 'Kiss me softly,' he whispers, and I sigh, gently sweeping my tongue through his mouth, so very lazily. It's heaven. 'Enough,' he says harshly, and again I stop. He pulls back and drops a loving kiss on my lips. 'Why can't you do everything I ask that quickly?'

I grin and pull him in closer, reclaiming his mouth. 'Because your power-hungry persona is rubbing off on your wife.'

He laughs and rolls over so I'm astride his hips. 'Take the power, baby.'

'Okay,' I agree quickly, lifting myself from his groin. He reaches down, and I slap his hand away. 'Excuse me.'

'Oh, sorry.' He grins sheepishly. 'Don't fuck about, though, will you?'

'You're forgetting, God.' I grab his erection and guide him to me. 'You've just relinquished the power.' I lower gently, his grin soon disappearing, being replaced with thorough appreciation.

He moans and grabs the tops of my legs. 'I might give you the power more often.'

I lift and slowly sink back down, running my hands all over his chest. 'You like?'

'Oh, I love.' He looks up at me and starts smoothing his hands over the tops of my thighs.

'You're so handsome.' I lift and lower gently again on a sigh.

'I know,' he says simply.

'You're arrogant.'

'I know. Up you go.'

I raise my eyebrows. 'Who has the power?'

'You do, but you won't for long if you abuse it. Up.' He's

restraining a smile, and I scowl, but lift myself anyway. 'Good girl,' he pants. 'Faster.'

Sinking back down, I grind gently. 'But I like it like this.'

'Faster, Ava.'

'No. I have the power.' I work my way back up, but don't get the chance to tease my way down. I'm flipped onto my back and pinned down.

'You lost your chance, lady.' He drives straight in with purpose. 'I'm taking the power back.'

Bang!

I yell, my legs falling open.

Bang!

'Fuck!' I scream as he hits my womb.

'Mouth!'

Bang!

'Jesse!'

'You pushed your luck, baby,' he grunts, flexing his grip of my wrists and hitting me over and over and over. My eyes close. 'Eyes!' I rip them open on a shocked yelp. 'Better.' Sweat is pouring down his face, dripping onto my cheeks. I need to hold onto him, scratch him and bite him, but I'm completely powerless, just as he likes me.

'Let me hold you,' I cry, pulling at his grip as he thunders on.

'Who has the power?'

'You do, you fucking control freak!'

'Watch,' *Bang!* 'your,' *Bang!* 'mouth!'

I scream.

'Fuck!' he yells. 'Come for me, Ava!'

I can't. I'm trying to focus on the climax that's lingering somewhere deep, but every time I think I've captured it, he hits me again with those punishing hips and knocks it back. My eyes close and I can do nothing more than accept the assault my body is under.

'Jesus, Ava. I'm going to come!'

And with that he shouts, grinds and collapses on top of me, releasing my hands from his fierce grip. His breathing is chaotic, his body twitching, and his skin wet. I'm all of those things, too, minus one satisfying climax.

'You didn't come,' he pants into my neck. I can't talk, so I hum and shake my head, my arms flopped limply at the side of my head. 'Baby, I'm sorry.'

I hum again and attempt to lift my arms to cuddle him so he knows that I'm fine, but my muscles are on shut down. Our sweaty chests are compressed together and our erratic breathing is loud. We're both completely shattered. I want to stay in bed, but then I feel the absence of his weight, and I'm being lifted into his arms. I mumble an audible protest as I'm carried to the bathroom. He turns the spray on, grabs a towel from the shelf and chucks it on the floor of the shower before laying me down on it. I just about muster up the strength to frown up at him as he lowers himself to the floor and spreads my legs.

'Let's bring you back to life.' He flicks the shower to cool and settles between my thighs before *really* waking me up with a stretched out, agonisingly soft stroke of his tongue, right up the centre of my core.

My back arches, my lifeless arms spring to life and my voice comes back. 'Ohhhhh Godddd!' I grab his wet hair and push him further into me, the previously deep, misplaced orgasm now gushing forward. I don't even try to control it. I start panting, my stomach muscles tensing, my head lifting, as the cool, fresh water rains all over me. He's everywhere, licking, biting, sucking, trailing kisses down the insides of my thighs and slowly back up again to plunge his tongue in deep.

'Awake yet?' he mumbles around my flesh, then bites lightly on my clit.

'More!' I demand, yanking at his hair. I hear him laugh a little before he follows through on my order and seals his mouth completely around me and sucks me gently to climax.

I burst. I see stars. I moan and throw my hands over my head. Way too good. Just way, way too bloody good. I'm pulsing against him and completely limp, and the cool spray is divine, the constant purring of the shower relaxing.

'I love, love, love feeling you throb.' He kisses his way up my body until he finds my lips, giving me more special attention. I only respond with my mouth, unable to convince my muscles to move, and not bothering to make much effort of it, either. 'Am I redeemed?'

I nod against his kiss and he laughs, pulling back to study me. My eyes are still working fine. He's just beyond fucking beautiful. 'I love you.' I just about manage to squeeze the words past my fitful breaths.

He dazzles me with that smile . . . my smile. 'I know you do, baby.' He gets up, far too spritely for my liking. 'Come on. Now that I've fulfilled my godly obligation, we need to go to The Manor.'

He takes my hand and heaves me up with absolutely no effort at all, then spends some quiet time rinsing me down and washing my hair.

'You're done, lady. Out.' He slaps my arse and sends me on my way, while he finishes his shower.

We have lots to catch up on. We've broke the back of it, and this is all the more reason for me to remedy the situation that will undoubtedly take me back to being treated like I'm break-able if I remain pregnant.

I walk into the kitchen and find Jesse rummaging frantically through the cupboards. With his arms raised, his broad back is accentuated by the pull of his white polo shirt, the vast expanse of firmness making my hands twitch at my sides and my eyes blink to confirm he's real. I smile. He's real all right, and he's also mine.

'What are you doing?' I ask, pulling my hair up into a messy mass of wildness on top of my head.

He turns around and looks at me in alarm. 'I've run out of Sun-Pat.'

'What?' I laugh at his genuine distress. 'You've run out of peanut butter?'

'It's not fucking funny!' He slams the cupboard door shut before stalking over to the fridge, yanking it open, and shifting endless bottles of water. 'What the fuck is Cathy playing at?' he barks to himself.

I can't help it. I double over with laughter. This is not the normal behaviour for someone who merely *likes* something. He's addicted to it. My Lord is addicted to peanut butter and, quite possibly, is going to have a seizure if he doesn't get his fix soon. I'm happily tittering away when I hear the fridge door slam. I bolt upright and do a rubbish job of re-straining my grin. I'm clamping down painfully on my lip to prevent it.

'What are you grinning at?' He scowls at me, good and proper.

'Why the compulsion for peanut butter?' I ask quickly, before re-clamping down on my lip.

He folds his arms across his chest, still scowling. 'I like it.'

'You like it?'

'Yes, I like it.'

'You're in a bit of a pickle, considering you just *like* it.' My lip drags through my teeth as I completely lose the battle to keep back my smirk.

'I'm not in a pickle,' he argues on a small laugh. 'It's no big deal.'

'Okay,' I shrug, still grinning. It is *such* a big deal.

He walks across the kitchen and around the island toward me, his eyes widening as my lower body comes into view. 'What the hell are they?' he blurts.

I look down at myself and back up to shocked green eyes. 'Shorts.'

'You mean knickers?'

I'm grinning again. 'No, I mean shorts.' I grab the hem on each leg of my denim shorts and pull them up. 'If they were knickers, they'd look like this.'

He gasps a little, still studying the offending garment. 'Ava, come on, be reasonable.'

'Jesse,' I sigh. 'I've told you. If you want long skirts and roll-neck jumpers, then go find someone your own age.' I pull my shorts back down and kneel to tie the laces of my Converses, ignoring the grumbling and bristling emanating from every delicious fibre of my unreasonable man. 'I might go for a swim at The Manor.' I look up at him, finding his grumpy face is back to horror.

'In a bikini?'

I laugh. 'No, in a snowsuit. Of course in a bikini.' I'm really pushing my luck here, and I know it.

'You're doing this on purpose, aren't you?'

'I'd like to go for a swim.'

'I'd like to strangle you,' he snaps. 'Why do you do this to me?'

'Because you're an unreasonable arse and you need to loosen up. You may be an old man, but I'm only twenty-six. Stop acting like a caveman. What'll happen if we go on a beach holiday?'

'I thought we could go skiing.' He's the one smirking now. 'I'll show you how good I am at *very* extreme sports.'

I grin and jump up to his body, my nose diving straight into his neck. 'You smell luscious.' I inhale his yummy scent as he carries me out to the car, still wearing the short shorts.

We pull up at The Manor, and I'm quickly collected from my side of the car before being pulled up the steps and into the entrance hall. I hear the distant hum of chatting from the bar and smile when I see John approaching, looking ever the frightening mountain of a man.

'Ava would like to go swimming,' Jesse grumbles as John joins us.

The big guy looks down at me, his eyebrows peeking above his wraparounds. 'You do, girl?'

I nod. 'It's hot out there.'

The small smile flashing across John's face is an indication that he knows damn well what I'm doing. Yes, I'm trying to bash all unreasonableness out of my husband.

We pass the bar, and I spot Sam. I can't see his face, but his body slumped on a stool is a clear indication of how he's feeling. My best friend is an idiot. She's running away from something good, just to reignite something that's terribly bad.

As soon as we enter Jesse's office, he drops my hand and goes straight to the integrated fridge. He pulls out a jar of peanut butter, immediately unscrews the lid and plunges his finger in. John doesn't bat an eyelid, instead taking a seat on the other side of Jesse's desk while I look on with a smile. Jesse walks casually over to his chair and takes his seat, slipping his finger into his mouth and sighing. 'What's happening?' he asks John around his finger.

'Camera three is out. The surveillance company is scheduled to come and sort it out.' John shifts in his seat and pulls his phone from his pocket. 'I'll chase them up.' He dials and puts his phone to his ear before standing and walking over to the window.

'Baby, you okay?'

I flick my eyes from John's back to Jesse, finding a concerned look on his face. 'Yes, fine.' I start toward his desk and sit myself down in the chair next to John's. 'Daydreaming. Sorry.'

His finger slips into his mouth again. 'What about?'

I smile. 'Nothing. Just watching you settle now that you have your peanut butter.'

He looks down at the jar and rolls his eyes. 'Want some?'

'No.' My nose wrinkles in distaste, and he laughs, his eyes twinkling, his soft lines springing from his greens as he screws the lid on and slides the jar onto his desk. 'How's Sam?' I ask.

'Shit. He won't talk about it. How's Kate?'

'Not good.'

'What do you know? Why did she end it?'

I shrug as casually as possible. 'Who knows.' I dare not even mention my brother. 'It's probably for the best.'

He nods thoughtfully. 'Do you want to swim or stay with me?'

'What are *you* going to do?' I ask, eyeing up the piles of paperwork on his desk. I've never seen it so messy, and I know why. No Sarah. But I'm not feeling in the slightest bit guilty about it, even if it means Jesse's desk looks like a bomb's gone off on it.

He looks at the paperwork, too, and sighs. 'This is what I'll be doing.' He flicks through one of the piles.

'Why don't you employ someone else?'

'Ava, it's not that straightforward in this line of work. You have to know someone, trust them. I can't just call the job centre and ask them to send along someone who can type.'

Okay, now I *am* feeling a little guilty. He's right. We're talking about people of high society, people with high-powered jobs. Jesse has told me that they delve into the history of these people to determine their financial status and medical history, including any criminal convictions. I suppose there is a confidentiality issue. 'I could help,' I offer reluctantly, even though I wouldn't have the first idea where to start, but his overwhelmed expression as he scans the masses of paper on his desk is really nudging the guilt.

His eyes fly up. 'You would?'

I shrug and grab the first piece of paper I can lay my hands on. 'An hour here and there, I suppose.' I scan the text in my hands. It's a bank statement. At least I think it is. The figures look more like international telephone numbers. I glance up at him. He's grinning.

'We're very rich, Mrs Ward.'

'Fucking hell!'

'Ava . . .'

'I'm sorry, but . . .' I try to focus on all of the digits but lose my place. 'This sort of stuff shouldn't be lying on your desk, Jesse.' It has his account numbers on it and everything. 'Wait . . . Did Sarah look after your finances?'

'Yes,' he says quietly.

I bristle. I don't trust the woman. 'Do you have any idea where your money is? How *much* there is?' I place the paper back on his desk.

'Yes, look.' He takes the piece and points at it. 'I have this much and it's in this bank.'

'You have just one account? What about business accounts, savings, pensions?'

He looks a little alarmed, and almost irritated. 'I don't know.'

I gape at him. 'She did everything? All of your accounts?' I don't like that thought at all.

'Not any more,' he grumbles, throwing the paper back down. 'But you'll help?' He's smiling again.

How can I not? This man is stinking rich and has no idea where and how any of his money is stored. 'Yes, I'll help.' I grab a pile and start sifting through, but then I have a very worrying moment of realisation. My head snaps up, finding a contented face staring straight at me. 'I said I'd help; that's all. A few hours here and there, Jesse.'

He visibly sags at my words. 'But it's the perfect solution.'

'For you! The perfect solution for you! I have a career. I am not giving it up to come here every day and file paperwork!' The cheeky swine. He wants me to replace Sarah as his office girl. Not a chance. 'And anyway,' – I dump the pile back on the desk and stand – 'I don't know how to lash a whip, so I think I'm a little underqualified.' I don't know why I said that. It was unnecessary and really quite spiteful.

He's shocked. He's sitting far back in his chair with a mixture of disbelief and anger on his face. 'That was a little childish, don't you think?'

'I'm sorry. I didn't mean it.'

John joins us again and breaks the uncomfortable silence. 'They'll be an hour.' He slips his phone back in his pocket. 'Before I forget, we've had a further three memberships cancelled.'

Jesse's eyebrows raise in curiosity. 'Three?'

'Three,' John confirms as he walks toward the door. 'All female,' he adds, leaving the office.

I watch as Jesse's elbows hit his desk and his face falls straight into his palms. I feel rotten. I make my way around his desk and push him back in his chair before sitting on his desk in front of him. He watches me as he chews that lip. 'I'll sort all of this out,' I indicate the paperwork everywhere, 'but you need to get someone on this. It's a full-time job.'

'I know.' He clasps my ankles and pulls them up so my feet are sitting on his knees. 'Go for a swim. I'll make a start on this, okay?'

'Okay.' I study him closely and he studies me studying him.

'Go on, beautiful girl. Spit it out.' He's smiling a little.

'They're withdrawing their memberships because you're no longer available to fu—' I bite my tongue. 'To have sex with.' That makes me immensely happy and it's obvious.

'It would seem so, wouldn't it?' He narrows his eyes on me. 'I can see this pleases my wife.'

I shrug, but I can't hide my pleasure at this news. 'What's the ratio of women to men?'

'Members?' he asks.

'Yes.'

'Seventy–thirty.'

My mouth drops open. I remember Jesse saying there were roughly fifteen hundred members. That's a thousand women who are potentially after my Lord. 'Well,' I brush off my shock. 'You might have to turn The Manor into a gay club.'

He laughs and dangles my feet back off the desk. 'Go take a swim.'

The changing rooms are empty. I wriggle into my bikini, remove my diamond, retie my hair high on my head and stuff my things in one of the wooden lockers. In all of the time I've been with Jesse, I've never used the spa and sports facilities, but I'm reliably informed that there's no skinny-dipping allowed, so I'll brave it and put Jesse to the test at the same time. I wander through the area, looking for any sign of life, but it's completely deserted. It's lunchtime on a Sunday. I would have thought it would be a peak time for members to utilise this part of The Manor.

Stepping into the huge glass building, I scan the area, finding all of the Jacuzzis, the huge pool, and the sun loungers are empty. It's eerily quiet, the only sound a distant hum of water pumps. Laying my towel on a wooden lounger, I gingerly take the first step into the water and sigh. It's tepid. Lovely. I wade down the rest of the steps, push myself into the water, and start a breaststroke to the other end of the pool.

I'm relishing in the calmness and quiet as I swim length after length, no one joining me, no one venturing in to use the Jacuzzis, and no one coming to relax on a sun lounger. But then I hear movement, and I stop mid-length to see who appears from the entrance that leads to the changing areas. Jesse emerges, wearing a loose pair of black swimming shorts. I sigh in appreciation, and he blasts me with his smile, before diving straight in, his body stretching out, making minimal noise or splashing as he slips below the surface. I float in the middle of the pool and watch the shadow of his tall body approaching me under the water until he's right in front of me, but he remains submerged beneath me.

Then I feel his palm wrap around my ankle, and I squeal as I'm yanked under the water, just catching a lungful of air before I disappear, my eyes naturally clenching shut. His lips meet mine, his arms surround me, and he rolls us around, our skin slipping all over each other, our tongues dancing wildly.

My lungs scream a thank you when we surface, my legs clenching around his waist and my arms around his shoulders. I try to grab hold of my bearings and attempt to open my eyes, and when I do, I'm greeted by a dirty great big grin. I know he can't touch the bottom himself, so he must be treading water frantically with my dead weight clinging to him. You would never know it, though. He looks like he's just floating effortlessly in front of me.

I push his wet hair from his face and match his grin. 'You closed the pool, didn't you?'

'I don't know what you're talking about.' He shifts me around to his back and starts swimming to the side.

'I don't believe you.' I rest my chin on his shoulder. 'You couldn't stand the thought of me in a bikini and others seeing. Admit I'm right.' I've got my Lord worked out.

He reaches the edge of the pool and pulls me from his back, pushing me up against the side. 'I love the thought of you in a bikini.'

'But for your eyes only?'

'I've told you before, Ava. I don't share you with anyone or anything, not even their eyes.' He slides his hands down my sides and onto my thighs. 'Just for my touch,' he whispers. It makes me immediately clench my thighs as he leans in and kisses me gently before scanning my face. 'Just for my eyes.' His finger slips into the side of my bikini bottoms, and I hold my breath as he strokes me softly. 'Just for my pleasure, baby. I know you understand me, don't you?'

'I do.' I shift in front of him and drape my arms over his shoulders.

'Good. Kiss me.'

I dive right in and show my appreciation with a long, hot, passionate kiss that draws a low moan from each of us. His hands shift to my waist, his big palms circling me completely as he holds me tight, and we kiss for the longest time – there in the middle of the pool, just me and him, drowning in each other, consuming each other, loving each other.

Everything that happens between us is a result of the potent, sometimes poisonous, love we share. It pushes us to behave erratically and unreasonably. In reality, we're probably level pegging in the crazy department, or maybe I've overtaken him. What I'm planning definitely qualifies me as crazy. And if my crazy husband finds out, then I've no doubt I will see him tip over the edge of craziness.

Chapter 12

'I love you.'

The low whisper makes me smile as I roll over and blindly grab at him. 'Hmmm,' I hum, pulling his body down to mine.

'Ava, it's seven-thirty.'

'Sleepy sex,' I demand, my hand drifting down his thigh until I find what I'm looking for. I grasp him loosely.

'Baby, I'd love to, but when you wake up properly, you're going to fly into panic and leave me halfway finished.' He grabs my hand and pulls it up to his face, kissing my fingers sweetly. 'It's Monday morning. It's seven-thirty.'

My eyes open, seeing his wet face suspended over mine. He's had a shower, which means he's been for a run, which means it's late. I bolt upright, and he quickly moves to avoid being headbutted. 'What time is it?'

He smiles fondly. 'It's seven-thirty.'

'Jesse!' I jump up and run into the bathroom. 'Why didn't you wake me?' I flick the shower on and turn to the sink, loading my toothbrush with toothpaste.

'I didn't want to disturb you.' He leans on the door frame and watches me frantically scrubbing my teeth. He's grinning, no doubt at my little fluster.

'Never … bother … 'fore.' I spit around my mouthful of paste.

His grin widens. 'Pardon?'

I shake my head on an eye roll and return to the mirror, finishing up and rinsing out. 'I said it never bothered you before.'

I step in the shower and make a quick job of washing my hair and shaving before stepping out and practically running into the walk-in wardrobe. I stand and stare at the rails and rails of clothes, mostly all with tags still attached. It's too much like hard work trying to choose; there's way too much, so I yank down my old red shift dress.

By the time I've rough dried my hair, haphazardly slapped on my make-up, and landed downstairs, Jesse is suited up and collecting his car keys.

'I'll take you.'

'Where's Cathy?' I eye him up. All of him. That's my husband.

He frowns a little. 'I don't know. It's not like her to be late.' Grabbing my hand, he starts leading me from the penthouse.

We make our way down to the foyer of Lusso and as we approach the concierge desk, I see Cathy leaning on it, chatting with Clive. I grin and look up to Jesse, but he ignores me, even though he knows damn well I'm looking at him and probably what I'm thinking, too. 'That would explain,' I say on a little laugh.

'They're just talking,' Jesse grumbles, leading on.

'They look very friendly.' I watch Cathy fidget and giggle as Clive entertains her with words and hand gestures.

She spots us. 'Oh! I was just on my way up!'

'No problem.' Jesse doesn't sound impressed, and he doesn't stop. I, however, would love to hang around and see the developments. My grin widens as I pass, and Cathy and Clive both blush profusely. 'I'm out of peanut butter,' Jesse calls back crossly.

'There's a whole box of it in the cupboard, my boy. Do you think I'd let that run dry?' Cathy sounds irritated by Jesse's critical comment. It makes me laugh, especially when Jesse starts grumbling under his breath.

'Don't be so moody. They're only talking,' I rebuke him as we emerge into the sunshine and Jesse slips his Wayfarers on.

'It's not right.' He shudders and releases my hand.

I start rummaging through my bag for my own shades. 'Ooh, she might be inviting him up when we're not there. I did notice the sheets in the spare room were a little . . . ruffled.'

'Ava!' he yells as he points a screwed-up face of displeasure to the heavens. 'Don't!'

I laugh. 'Stop being ageist.'

'I'm not.' His disgusted face disappears immediately. He's grinning now.

'What are you smirking at?' I ask.

He removes his shades and closes the distance between us, stooping down so our noses touch. 'I've bought you a wedding present.'

'You have?' I rest my lips on his. 'What?'

'Turn around.'

I pull back and watch his delighted eyes as he nods over my shoulder, so I slowly pivot and stand for a few moments, scanning the car park for whatever I should be looking for. His arm appears over my shoulder and dangles a set of car keys in my face. It's then I spot a dirty great big, bright-white, sparkly-wheeled Range Rover Sport. Or tank – whichever.

Oh no!

I can't even think of any words. I squint as the keys are jangled in front of me, like he doesn't realise that I've clocked my present and he's trying to hint further. No need. I can see it. And I hate it!

'Over there,' he prompts, jangling the keys again.

'You mean that spaceship?' I ask drily. I'm not driving that thing, no matter how many countdowns or sense fucks I get as a consequence.

'You don't like it?' He sounds hurt.

Oh shit, what do I say? 'I like my Mini.'

'It's not safe.' Now he sounds affronted. He makes his way around me and looks down at my shocked face. 'This is safer.'

I can't help the incredulous look my face is naturally morphing into. 'Jesse, that's a man's car – a John car. It's fucking huge!'

'Ava! Watch your fucking mouth!' He scowls at me. 'I got it in white. That's a lady's colour. Come on, I'll show you.' He takes my reluctant shoulders and leads me over to the giant snowball. The closer I get, the more I hate it. It's far too showy. I love my Mini. 'Look.' He opens the door . . . and I gasp.

It gets worse.

White . . . everywhere. White leather steering wheel; white leather gearstick; white leather seats. Even the carpets are white.

I look up at him, my deluded husband, and shake my head, but I can't be ungrateful. He looks so pleased with himself. 'I don't know what to say.' I really don't. 'You could've just bought me a watch or a necklace or something.' I wish he had bought me a watch or necklace or something.

'Jump in.' He ushers me forward.

I gasp. Oh no! Stitched in the headrest of the front seat is 'Mrs Ward'.

Now that's going too far. 'I am not driving this!' I blurt, before my brain filters the insulting declaration.

'You fucking are!'

Well, that just got rid of any guilt I had and now I'm really digging my heels in. 'I am not! Jesse, it's way too big for me!'

'It's safe.' He picks me up and places me on the driver's seat. I feel small. 'Look.' Reaching in, he presses a button and a compartment pops open, revealing a computer screen. 'Everything you'll need. I've loaded all of your favourite music.' He grins, pressing a button, and Massive Attack seeps through all of the millions of speakers. 'You can think of me.'

'I think of you every time you call and I hear that track.' I jump out. 'I want your car. You can have this.' I signal to the gleaming heap of metal.

'Me?' A worried looks passes over his face. 'But it's a bit . . .' he runs his eyes over my present, 'girly.'

'It is, and I know your game, Ward.' I look inside and my mind conjures up images of baby seats and child booster seats . . . and a pram in the boot. I turn and storm off towards my lovely little Mini, in which there is no chance of squeezing a pram in the boot.

I'm stunned when I make it into my car without any Jesse-style intervention. I look in the rear-view mirror as I settle in my seat and see him leaning against his own car with his arms folded over his chest. I ignore the heavy glower on his stunning face and start my Mini, quickly reversing out of the space and heading for the gates. 'Impossible man,' I mutter to myself, reaching up to smash the button on the little black device that will open the gates.

It's not there.

'What!' I yell disbelievingly to absolutely no one. 'Fucking hell!' I slam my brakes on and jump out, finding the glower has morphed into a dazzling smile.

'Planning on going somewhere?'

'Oh, fuck off!' I yell across the car park, grabbing my bag from the front seat and leaving my car exactly where it is, driver's door open. I stomp my angry heels towards the pedestrian gate, but I'm not lucky enough to avoid a Jesse-style intervention this time. I'm swiftly grabbed and hoofed back to my shiny new wedding present.

'Will you watch your fucking mouth!' He places me in the driver's seat and puts the seatbelt on me before whipping the keys to my Mini from my hand. 'Why do you have to defy me on absolutely everything?' He starts transferring all of my keys onto my new car key.

'Because you're an unreasonable arse!' I shift irritably in my seat. 'Why can't *you* take me to work?'

'I'm already late for a meeting because my wife won't do as

she's told.' He grabs the back of my neck and yanks me forward. 'Anyone would think you're after a retribution fuck.'

'I'm not!'

He grins and hits me with a full-on, hot, meltworthy kiss. A long one – one of those kisses that bashes all of the obstinacy right out of me. 'Hmmm, you taste delicious, baby. What time are you finishing work?'

I'm released and, as ever, breathless. 'Six.'

'Come straight to The Manor and bring your files so we can finalise the orders for the new rooms.' He pushes another button, lowering the driver's window before shutting the door and leaning in. He looks so smug. 'I love you.'

'I know,' I mutter, turning the key in the ignition.

'Have you spoken to Patrick yet?' he asks, halting my strop and reminding me that I have yet to fulfil his request.

'Move my car!' I snap, not knowing what else to say.

'I'll take that as a no. You'll speak to him today.' It's not a question.

'Move my car,' I repeat touchily.

'Anything you want, lady.' His eyes are giving me a thorough warning, but I ignore it.

'Where the hell am I going to park this thing?'

He starts laughing and strolls off to move my car before jumping in his DBS and screeching out of the car park.

After driving around the nearest car park for an age, I finally find two spaces to straddle. Bursting through the office door, the first thing I see is a bunch of Calla lilies spread on my desk and as I get nearer, a little box.

'Darling!' Tom's croon doesn't distract me from the small box.

'Morning,' I greet, taking a seat and picking it up. 'You okay?'

'Chirpy, chirpy. You?' Tom sounds curious now and that *does* have my eyes dragging away from the box as I remember the last time I saw him.

'I'm good.' I brush it off and watch as his face spreads into a cheeky grin.

'I've said it before and I'll say it again. God, that man can do a sexy brood!' He starts fanning his face with a coffee coaster. 'Hot!'

I scoff and turn my attention back to the box. What's he bought me now? 'Who delivered this?' I ask, holding the box up.

'Flower girl.' Tom shrugs and returns to his computer, leaving me to unwrap the neatly covered gift box. I sigh when I open it up and come face to face with a graphite and gold Rolex. It's the women's equivalent to Jesse's and stunning, but more responsibility.

'Wow!' Sally gushes as she catches sight of the contents. 'Wow, wow, wow! That's beautiful!'

I smile at her enthusiasm and take it from the box, slipping it over my wrist. It really is. 'I know,' I say quietly. 'Thanks, Sal.' I move the flowers from my desk and slip the box into my bag.

'Would you like a coffee, Ava?' Sal heads for the kitchen.

'Please. Where are Patrick and Victoria?'

'Patrick has a personal meeting and Victoria is on a site visit.'

'Oh, okay.'

After putting my flowers in water, I get stuck into my work, preparing my file to take to Ruth Quinn's, and then printing off all of the details for the obscenely expensive beds that Jesse wants made for The Manor.

At ten o'clock, I abruptly come over all queasy and disappear into the toilet to try and throw up, but it's just not happening. I slump on the toilet, feeling hot, bothered and tearful. I need to chase up my hospital appointment. Suddenly a little determined, probably because of how crap I feel, I exit the toilets to do exactly that, but I'm soon halted mid-resolute march when the main office comes into view and I clock someone sitting in one of the tub chairs opposite my desk.

Sarah.

I don't feel ill any more. I feel angry. What the fucking hell is she doing here?

'Ava?'

I bristle further at her voice. 'Sarah,' I say flatly. She's looking rather understated, her hair softer than usual and her boobs tucked neatly behind a substantial cropped jacket, the short dresses sidelined for a respectful knee-length matching skirt. 'Why are you here?' I ask.

'I was hoping we could talk.' She shifts in the chair uncomfortably, her usual cocky demeanour nowhere in sight.

'Talk?' I ask cautiously. 'About what?' I've got nothing to say to this woman.

She glances around the office, as do I. Tom is looking curiously across at the strange woman who's sitting at my desk. 'Perhaps I could buy you a coffee?' she asks, returning her eyes to mine.

While I should be telling her where to go, curiosity is getting the better of me. I walk over to my desk and grab my bag. 'I have half an hour,' I say curtly, leaving her behind and walking out of my office. My heart is pumping too fast for my liking. I thought I'd seen the back of this whip-wielding witch, and now that I've clapped eyes on her again, all of the torment and drama she's caused is fresh and clear in my mind. All I can see are lash marks on Jesse, his tortured face, and my pitiful body draped over him. She has a nerve.

I walk into the nearby Starbucks and settle in a chair. I know my face is plastered in a look of contempt as she approaches the table, but I can't help it. I don't want to help it. I want her to know how much I hate her.

'Would you like a drink?' she asks politely. This is not the Sarah I know and despise.

'I'm fine.'

She smiles a little. 'Well, I think I'll get one. I don't think the management would be very happy about us taking up a table otherwise. Are you sure?'

'Yes.' I watch her go to the counter, ensuring she's busy ordering before I pull my phone from my bag to text Kate.

The cheeky bitch has turned up at my office!

She replies immediately. Granted, it wasn't the sort of text that you could cast aside with the intention to reply soon.

No!!!!! Really? Ava, stop talking in fucking code! Who's the cheeky bitch?

I almost let an exasperated curse fall from my lips.

Sarah!

Her reply is instant again.

Nooooooooooooo!!!!!!!!!!!!!!!!!

My fingers work fast across the pad as I look up to check that Sarah's still being served.

Fucking yes!!!!! Will call u.

I shove my phone back in my bag when Sarah approaches with a coffee, crossing my legs and maintaining a look of complete hatred. I do hate her. I hate everything she represents, but most of all, I hate her for inflicting pain on Jesse. I should stop thinking. I'm getting angrier.

She lowers herself and stirs her coffee gingerly, looking down at her cup. 'I wanted to apologise for everything that's happened.'

'You do?' I laugh.

She pauses and looks up at me nervously. 'Ava, I'm so sorry. I guess I was a little shocked at your arrival.'

'Oh?' I say on a frown.

'I've behaved dreadfully. I have no excuse.'

'Except that you're in love with him,' I say frankly, and her eyes widen in surprise. 'Why else would you behave like that, Sarah?'

She looks away, and I think I detect tears in her eyes. Oh, she's *really* in love with him. Have I underestimated this *issue*? 'I'm not going to fob you off, Ava. I've been in love with Jesse for as long as I can remember.' She returns her eyes to mine. 'It doesn't excuse me, though.'

'But you whipped him.' I don't get it. 'Why would you do that to someone you love?'

She laughs mildly. 'That's what I do. I dress in leathers, hold a whip, and thrash men before I fuck them.'

I wince. 'Okay.'

'Jesse was never interested in that.'

'But you've still fucked him,' I say candidly. Jesse has admitted that to me, and I know he was never whipped before that horrible day when I found them in his office. She must have been in her element, especially when she managed to entice me to The Manor to witness the whole horror scene.

She looks surprised. 'Yes, but just once.' She's definitely holding back tears. I've *really* misjudged this issue. 'Funny, isn't it? Even when he was smashed he didn't want me. He'd take them all, but never me.'

I'm beginning to understand this now, even if I'm not overly happy about the reminder of Jesse's history. He screwed all over the place, took anything, anytime . . . except Sarah. The Manor is full of willing women, none more so than Sarah, and he never wanted her. 'You were hoping he'd fuck you after you thrashed him?' The words turn my stomach. I feel sick again.

She shakes her head. 'No, I knew he wouldn't. He was too screwed up over you. I never thought I'd see the day when Jesse Ward would fall to his knees for a woman.'

'You mean you *hoped* you would never see the day.'

'Yes, I hoped. I also hoped that you'd run a mile when you found out about The Manor.'

I did run a mile, but I went back. I look at the woman across the table from me, and I feel sorry for her. I hate myself for it, but I do.

She frowns and returns to stirring her coffee. 'After what you did, and seeing how he reacted to that, it made me realise how stupid I'd been. He deserves happiness. He deserves you. You love him despite The Manor, what he did, and his problem with alcohol. You love him in his entirety.' She smiles. 'You've made him feel. I should never have tried to take that away from him.'

I'm sitting in a stunned silence, just staring at her, with not a clue of what to say in response. What do I say to that? 'You want your job back.' So I say that.

Her eyes widen. 'I don't think that can happen, do you?'

No, it couldn't. Despite her confession, I could never trust her or even like her. I can feel a little sorry for her, but I could never invite her back into our lives. 'You must have seen him with many women. Why target me?' I ask, although I already know the answer to that question.

'You were different; that was obvious. Jesse Ward doesn't pursue women. Jesse Ward doesn't take women back to his home. Jesse Ward doesn't *not* drink. You've changed that man. You've done what many women have tried and failed to do for many years, Ava. You've won The Lord.' She stands up. 'Congratulations, Mrs Ward. Take care of him. Make him happy. He deserves it.'

She leaves.

As I watch her back disappear out of Starbucks, I feel tearful again. I've won The Lord. I've changed him. I've made him stop drinking and fucking around. I've made him feel and love. And he does love. He loves really hard. Fiercely. I need to see him. I really need to see him. Damn Ruth Quinn and her demanding arse.

I jump up and race to the car park to collect my present, calling Kate on the way.

'What did she say?' she screeches down the phone before it's even rung.

'Apologised.' I'm a little breathless. 'Anyway, I'm keeping the baby.'

She laughs at me. 'Of course you are, you stupid cow.'

I smile as I run to my car, keen to get my appointment with Ruth out of the way so I can get to Jesse.

'Ava!' Her smiley face almost irritates me.

'Hi, Ruth.' I practically push past her into the shell of a kitchen, doing a quick analysis. Everything looks like it's on track. Nothing is jumping out as being a problem. 'I can't stay long. I have another meeting.' I turn to face her.

'Oh? Coffee?' She looks hopeful.

'No, really. What's the problem?' I ask, trying to prompt her along, but she doesn't look like she's in a hurry as she meanders over to a makeshift table and starts faffing with a mug.

'I'll just make myself one, and we can go and sit in the lounge where it's less dusty.'

I screw my face up in frustration. 'I'm sorry, Ruth. Can we rearrange?' I'm feeling panicky.

'Oh. It won't take long.' She carries on about her slow business, while I shift impatiently behind her. 'Did you have a good weekend with your parents?'

The question throws me, but I quickly engage my brain before I drop myself in it. 'Oh. Yes, thank you.'

She lazily strolls over to the fridge to get the milk. 'It's funny. I was sure I saw you on Friday evening,' she says casually. 'In a bar. What's it called?' She pours the milk leisurely and stirs even slower. 'That's it. Baroque on Piccadilly.'

'Oh?' Shit! 'Yes, I joined a few work friends. Nothing much. I left Saturday morning to visit my parents.' My fingers are twisting wildly in my hair. Why am I even lying to her? What I do and when I do it is none of her business.

She turns with a smile, but then her eyes fall on my left hand and there is no mistaking the eye bulge. I look at my diamond-adorned ring finger and suddenly feel uneasy. 'You've never said you're married,' she laughs. 'I feel so stupid! There's me, telling you to steer clear of all men, and all along you were married!' She actually starts blushing, and a horrible realisation kicks in.

She's gay! Oh no! That would explain it – all of the invitations to drinks, the persistent calling and meetings, and now her eyes bulging at my rings. She fancies me. Now I really do feel uncomfortable.

'Wait there.' She frowns. 'I remember you saying you had a boyfriend.' Her frown deepens. 'And you didn't have any rings on last week.'

I shift on my heels. 'I only recently got married.' I'm not going into this. 'My rings were being resized.' I can't look at her. She's attractive, but not like that.

'Why didn't you say?' She sounds offended.

Why didn't I say? Lots of reasons! 'It was a low-key affair. Just family.' Would she have expected an invite, or would she have tried to stop me? All this talk is making me want to get to Jesse even more. Should I tell her that I'm pregnant, too? By the look on her face, it would probably finish her off. 'Ruth, I really must get going. I'm sorry to do this.'

She makes an obviously bad job of hiding her alarm and giving me a fake smile. 'No, you go. It can wait.'

I'm relieved. Maybe this was the best thing that could've happened. Will she ease off on the persistent offers of drinks and meetings? I can't believe I didn't see this before. I don't dwell on it for long, though. I'm itching to escape, and not just because I have a female admirer.

'Thank you, Ruth. We'll rearrange.' I don't hang around. I exit hastily and wave my arm over my shoulder as I do, running down the path and jumping into my shiny new car, nearly breaking down in tears when 'Angel' hits my eardrums.

I frantically stab at the button on the intercom, but after a few agonising minutes, the gates still aren't opening, so I dive into my bag and retrieve my phone to dial him. It rings once.

'Ava?'

'The gates won't open!' I sound distressed and crazy, but I'm going out of my mind with the need to see him.

'Hey, calm down.' He sounds equally anxious. 'Where are you?'

'I'm at the gates! I've been pressing the button, but no one's opening them!'

'Ava, stop it. You're worrying me.'

'I need you,' I sob, finally giving in to the overwhelming guilt that's been looming deep inside of me for days. 'Jesse, I need you.'

I can hear his laboured breathing down the phone. He's running. 'Pull down the sun visor, baby.'

I look up through my tears and yank down the white leather, finding two small black devices. I don't wait for his instruction. I press them both and the gates start to swing open. I throw my phone on the passenger seat and bang my foot down on the accelerator, immediately zooming forward. I'm crying hard now, painful, aching, heavy tears as I weave up the tree-lined driveway in a blur until I see Jesse's Aston Martin come speeding from the other direction. I slam my brakes on and jump out, running at full pelt towards him.

He looks absolutely terrified as he flies from his car, leaving the door open, and sprints toward his crazy, hysterical wife. I can't help it, I'm freaking him out, but this sudden clarity has sent me into a panic attack. I've lost control of my emotions. The cold-hearted bitch I've been is suddenly melting and letting me see things clearly.

Our bodies crash together, and I'm immediately engulfed by him, every hard muscle pushed up against me as I'm lifted and held tight to his body. I sob relentlessly into his neck as he paces around the driveway just holding me. I'm so stupid. I'm such a stupid, selfish, heartless cow.

'Jesus, Ava,' he pants into my neck.

'I'm sorry.' I still sound frantic, even now when I'm in his arms.

'What's happened?'

'Nothing. I just needed to see you.' I grip him tighter. I can't get him close enough.

'Fucking hell, Ava! Please, explain!' He tries to release me, but I firm up my already iron hold, refusing to let him put me down. 'Ava?'

'Can we go home?'

'No! Not until you tell me why the fuck you're in such a state,' he shouts, battling with my clutching arms. I'm no match for him. He soon detaches me from his body and stands me in front of him, scanning every square inch of my figure as he holds the tops of my arms. 'What's going on?'

'I'm pregnant,' I sob. 'I lied to you. I'm sorry.'

He physically starts twitching and drops me, stepping back, his eyes wide, his frown line deep. 'What?'

I brush my rolling tears away and drop my eyes to the floor. I feel so ashamed of myself. He's no saint, but while he was trying to make life, I was thinking about destroying it.

'You make me so mad,' I whisper pitifully. 'You make me mad and then you make me so happy. I didn't know what to do.' It's a feeble and pathetic excuse.

When a few silent moments have passed, and he still hasn't spoken, I chance a glance at him. He looks in shock.

'Fuck! Ava, are you trying to get me sectioned?' His hands delve into his hair, and he looks up to the sky. 'Are you fucking with my mind because I really don't need this, lady. I've just got my head around you *not* being pregnant, and now you are?'

'I always have been.'

His head drops and so do his hands. They just dangle by his sides as he studies me closely, a disbelieving look on his face. 'When were you going to tell me?'

'I don't know. When I accepted it myself.' Maybe I was trying to make the most of dominant Jesse before he started treating me like glass again. I don't even know. I've been so stupid.

'We're having a baby?' He barely whispers the words. I nod my confirmation, and his eyes fall from mine to my stomach, lingering for a while. Then I see a tear trickle down his cheek. It enflames the guilt further, but when he drops to his knees, I lose complete control of my own weeping. I'm just standing and crying, watching his slumped body silently shedding tears in front of me. My natural response to my beautiful, neurotic man's reaction is to walk straight to him and join him on the floor. My arms creep over his shoulders and hold him tight to me as he sobs into my neck, his hands drifting all over my back, like he's checking that I'm really here.

'I'm so sorry,' I say quietly.

He doesn't speak. He stands and lifts me with him before taking me to his car and depositing me in the passenger seat, remaining silent as he buckles me in. Taking his phone from the inside pocket of his suit jacket, he shuts the door before walking off and making a call while he moves my new car to the side of the driveway.

He returns and puts my bag between my feet before driving us home in complete silence.

Chapter 13

He still hasn't said a word by the time we pull up at Lusso. He gets out and collects me, walking me straight past a cautious-looking Casey and putting me in the penthouse elevator. I glance up at him, but he's keeping his gaze pointed forward, not even meeting my eyes when I look at him in the reflection of the doors. When he opens the door into the penthouse, Cathy appears from the kitchen, her happy smile dropping away as soon as she notices her cheerfulness isn't being reciprocated.

'Is everything okay?' She assesses us both, then looks to Jesse for an answer, but he just hands me my bag and nods towards the stairs. I look at him, silently begging for some words. He doesn't indulge me. He nods again.

'Boy?' Cathy prompts warily.

'Ava's not feeling too well.' He lightly pushes into my back with his hand, urging me forward.

'Are you coming?' I ask.

'I'll be up in a minute. Go.' He reinforces his words with a firmer push of his hand, and I leave him with Cathy.

As I'm passing Jesse's sweet housekeeper, she reaches out and gently strokes my shoulder, giving me a small smile. 'I'm glad you're home, Ava.'

I return her smile. It's a feeble smile. I feel uncertain and a little concerned by Jesse's despondent state. 'Thank you.' I make my way upstairs, entering the master suite and settling on the end of the bed.

My eyes are brimming with tears again as I clutch my knees

to my chest and wait for him. I know that right now is when we'll talk about this, now that we have *both* acknowledged what is happening; but in order to have a talk, both of us need to be speaking, and Jesse doesn't look like he plans on saying anything. I have no idea what is going through that crazy mind of his and the strained atmosphere is pushing doubts back into me. I need reassurance, not silence, not time to talk my way back out of this.

My head snaps up when he enters the bedroom, but he doesn't look at me. Instead, he goes straight to the bathroom. I hear the waterfall tap of the bath start pouring and his movements as he follows through on his usual bath-time routine. We're having a bath?

After way too long just sitting on the bed, listening to the water running and Jesse's quiet activities, he eventually walks soundlessly into the bedroom. Taking my hand and pulling me up from the bed, he strips me down, removes my diamond and my Rolex before picking me up and carrying me into the bathroom.

He lowers me gently into the bath. 'Is the water okay?' he asks softly, releasing me and kneeling by the side of the tub.

'It's fine,' I answer, watching as he removes his suit jacket and unbuttons the cuffs of his shirt before pushing them up his arms. He collects the sponge and dips, then squeezes some soap on it and turns me away from him. He starts gliding it across my back in gentle, steady strokes.

I'm confused. 'Aren't you getting in?' I ask quietly. I want him to lie behind me so I can feel him, take comfort in him. I need that.

'Let me look after you.' His voice is low and unsure. I don't like it.

I turn myself around to face him, finding glazed green eyes and a stoic expression. It pulls at my heart. I've really fucked with his mind this time. 'I need you closer than this.' I reach up with my wet hand and lay my palm on his cheek. 'Please.'

He watches me carefully for a few moments, like he's deciding whether he should, but he eventually sighs and drops the sponge, then stands and slowly removes his clothes. Stepping in behind me, he lowers himself to cocoon me completely. I feel immediately better with his warm hardness cradling me, but I can't see him, so I turn over and sit on his lap, encouraging his knees up so I can lean back and look at him. I take his hands and interlace our fingers, and we both watch in silence as we play with each other's hands, our tangled fingers glimmering now and then when our rings catch the reflections of the water. It's not a difficult silence any more.

'Why did you lie to me, Ava?' he whispers, still watching our snaking fingers working together.

My movements falter for a few moments but don't stop completely. 'I'm scared.' He needs to know that this whole situation terrifies me.

'Of me,' he says simply. 'You're scared of me.'

'I'm scared of how you'll be.'

'You mean more crazy,' he confirms, keeping his eyes on our entwined fingers.

'It wasn't even definite and you were treating me like a priceless object.'

He exhales softly and takes both of our hands to his chest, resting them over his heart, but he still doesn't look at me. 'You also think that I might love our child more than you.'

The words make me go rigid. They're the words I have refused to acknowledge every time they've whirled around in my head. I *am* worried that he'll love our child more than me. Selfishly, yes; it frightens me to death.

'Would you?' I ask quietly. I'm not sure how he'll answer. All I've got to go on is how desperate he is for a baby.

His eyes lift slowly, revealing a sadness I've never seen before.

'Do you feel that?' He flattens my palms on his chest and holds them there firmly. 'It was made to love you, Ava. For too long it was useless, redundant, not required. Now it's gone into overdrive. It swells with happiness when I look at you. It splinters with pain when we fight. And it beats wildly when I make love to you. Maybe I go overboard with my love, but that's never going to change. I'll love you this fiercely until the day I die, baby. Children or not.'

I'm crippled more than ever before. It really isn't possible for me to love this man more. 'I never want to be without your fierce love.'

He reaches up and slides his hand around the base of my neck, pulling me down so our foreheads meet. 'You won't be. I'll never stop loving you hard. It'll only get harder because every day that passes we create more memories. Memories I'll treasure, not memories I want to forget. My mind is being filled with beautiful images of us, and they are replacing a history that lingers. They're chasing away my past, Ava. I need them. I need you.'

'You have me,' I breathe, shifting my hands up to his shoulders.

'Don't ever leave me again.' He kisses me gently. 'It hurt so badly.'

I sit up on his lap and pull him up with me, wrapping my arms tightly around him and pushing my mouth to his ear. 'I'm crazy in love with you,' I whisper. 'Fiercely, too. That's never going to stop.' I kiss his ear. 'End of.'

His head turns into me, catching my lips. 'My heart's swelling.'

I smile a little as he reinforces his happiness with his kiss, drifting back down in the tub until I'm sprawled across his chest. We just kiss, for a long, long time. It's gentle and sweet, but it's what we both need right now. Pure, unapologetic, powerful love. It's potent. It cripples us both.

He pulls back and encases my face with his hands. 'Let me bathe you.'

'But I'm comfy.' I just want to lie on his chest and stay until the water cools and I'm forced to vacate the giant tub.

'We can be comfy in bed and you can fall asleep in my arms where you're supposed to be.'

I frown. 'It's not even mid-aft—' I halt. 'I've not gone back to work!' I start to scramble off him to call Patrick, but I'm swiftly restrained and pulled back down to his chest.

'I took care of it. Unravel your knickers, lady.'

He turns me around in his lap and retrieves the sponge from the water.

'What did you tell him?'

'That you're ill.'

'He'll be sacking me soon.' I sigh and lean forward, dropping my heavy head between my propped up knees and letting Jesse soak me all over with lazy rubs and squeezes of the sponge. The silence is comfortable, my mind serene. I close my eyes and absorb the love that's flowing into me from our contact through the sponge. That's how powerful it is. It can battle through any obstacle that's placed between us, be it an inanimate object, such as a simple sponge, or a living, breathing person, such as a Coral or a Sarah . . . or a Mikael. Nothing can tear us apart . . . only us.

When he's looked after me for a while, he wraps me in a towel and sits me on the vanity unit. 'Stay there,' he orders gently before dropping a chaste kiss on my lips and leaving me with a furrowed brow.

'Where are you going?' I call after him.

'Just wait.'

I hear him rummaging and the crumpling of paper, and he's soon standing in front of me again, holding up a paper bag with slightly raised brows. 'What's that?' I ask, pulling my towel in a little more.

He takes a deep breath and opens it up, thrusting it at me so I can take a peek. I throw him inquisitive eyes and lean forward to look in the bag, quickly bolting upright on a shocked gasp when I register the contents. 'You don't believe me?'

He rolls his eyes and reaches in, pulling out a pregnancy test. 'Of course I do.'

'Then why do you have a paper bag with—' I grab it and tip it upside down, emptying the little boxes into the sink next to me. I start picking them up and chucking them on the counter. 'One, two, three ... eight! Why do you have eight pregnancy tests?' I wave one of the boxes under his nose.

He shrugs sheepishly and bats the box away. 'There are two in a box.'

'Sixteen?' I blurt.

He starts opening one of the boxes. 'Sometimes they don't work properly. They're just back-ups.' He slides a stick out and takes it to his mouth, ripping off the plastic packaging before he thrusts it at me. 'You have to pee on this bit here, look.'

I watch him pull the cap off and point to the only non-plastic part of the stick. 'I did one at the doctor's, Jesse. Why won't you take my word for it?'

His lip slides straight between his teeth and starts to receive a nervous chew. 'I do take your word for it, but I need to see for myself.'

I feel a little offended, although I have no right to be. 'How long have you had these?'

He pouts and shrugs guiltily, dropping his eyes. He doesn't need to say. I put my hand out and his eyes lift. They are sparkling again.

'Give.' I nod at the stick and watch as his lip slips through his bite and he smiles. He really, *really* smiles. I think this smile even tops his one reserved only for me. I quickly bat away the silly pang of jealousy that stabs at me because of it and jump down from the unit. 'Some privacy, please.'

He recoils, a look of disbelief on his face. 'I'm staying!'

'I'm not peeing on a stick in front of you!'

He sits down on the floor in front of me, his towel gaping open and revealing ... everything. 'Move me.' He's fighting a smug grin from his lush lips.

'I'll use another bathroom,' I retort haughtily as I sidestep him to exit the bathroom, but I yelp as my ankle is grasped and I'm suddenly trying to pull a dead weight to escape. 'Jesse!' I tug my leg, but it's completely hopeless. I turn to find him lying on his stomach, now with both palms wrapped around my one ankle.

He's looking up at me with adorable, shimmering eyes, and he's pouting. 'Humour me, baby. Please.' He actually bats his long lashes at me.

I try my hardest to restrain my smile. 'Can you at least turn around?'

'No.' He jumps up and whips his towel off, his beauty hitting me like a sledgehammer. 'Does this make you feel better?' He holds his arms to the sides, and I can't stop my appreciative gaze dragging down his solid loveliness.

I sigh happily. 'No, that just distracts me,' I muse, continuing to drink him in – all of him. Every wondrous, magnificent, sickeningly perfect inch of him. I reach his face. His eyes have smoked out, and I know mine have, too. 'You wield that physique unfairly.'

'Of course I do. It's one of my best assets.' He reaches forward and yanks my towel off. 'It comes a close second to this one.' His eyes leisurely skate down my nakedness, and he sighs to himself. 'Just perfect.'

'You won't say that when I'm fat and swollen,' I grumble, suddenly realising that I will, in fact, get fat and swollen. 'And if you say there will be more of me to love, then I might divorce you.' I snatch the towel up and rewrap myself, ignoring his obvious annoyance at my concealing his best asset.

'Don't say the word "divorce",' he threatens, taking my hand and leading me to the toilet. 'If it makes you feel better, I'll eat for two, too.' He's looking down at me with a smirk.

'Promise you won't leave me when I'm unable to reach your cock with my mouth because my belly is in the way.'

He throws his head back on a laugh. 'I promise, baby.' I'm turned around and positioned in front of the toilet. 'Now, let's pee on some sticks.'

I hitch up my towel and reluctantly lower myself to the toilet, while Jesse crouches in front of me. I hold the stick between my thighs and empty my bladder.

'There.' I pull my hand out and hand him the test, and he takes it, immediately giving me another. 'What?' I ask, frowning at the new stick.

'I told you, sometimes they don't work. Quick.' He thrusts it forward.

My head rolls back in complete exasperation, but I take the stupid stick and repeat the same routine, only to finish and have another one shoved at me. 'Jesse, come on!'

'One more.' He removes the lid.

'For God's sake.' I snatch it on a scowl and shove it between my thighs. 'That's it!' I drain the rest of my bladder, making sure it's completely empty so I physically *can't* pee on any more sticks. 'There.' I yank some tissue from the roll and sort myself out while he takes all three tests to the unit and places them neatly in a row.

Despite my irritation, I can't help smiling as I watch him standing there, naked and bent slightly, bracing his hands on his knees and getting his face up close and personal with the tests.

'Are you okay there?' I ask, joining him and copying his position in front of the unit.

'I think they're broken. We should do some more.' He makes to shift, but I grab his arm.

'It's been thirty seconds.' I laugh. 'Here, wash your hands.' I take his hands and hold them under the tap while he keeps his eyes on the test.

'It's been longer than that,' he scoffs. 'Much longer.'

'No it hasn't. Stop being neurotic.' I resume knee brace pose in front of the unit, as does he.

Peeking out of the corner of my eye, I meet his sideways glance, my lips curving at the corner. He raises defensive eyebrows at me.

'Are you taking the piss out of me, lady?'

'Not at all.'

The silence falls again, and we both remain motionless, braced and waiting. Time seems to slow slightly while we both stare in silence as some faint letters appear on the first test. My heart picks up pace as my eyes drift over to the next test and find the slow development of the same letters. My heart is now trying to break free from my chest and our heads inch to the left a little to watch as the very same letters form on the third and final test. I realise I'm holding my breath, and I let it gush out as I sense Jesse next to me twitching. I turn my face to his, feeling completely overwhelmed with emotion. His head turns, too, until he's facing me. We're still bent over the unit, we're still both bracing our arms on our knees and we're both completely expressionless.

'Hi, Daddy,' I whisper, my voice quivering slightly as I watch him scanning my face.

'Fuck me,' he whispers back. 'I can't breathe.' He collapses to the floor on his back and stares up at the ceiling.

I straighten myself out and roll my shoulder blades a little. I feel all stiff. 'Are you okay?' I ask, looking down at him. This wasn't what I expected, but then his mouth starts twitching and his greens land on me. He jumps up and seizes me in his arms, lifting me clean from my feet on a shocked squeal. 'What's the matter with you?'

He paces quickly into the bedroom and places me on the bed way too gently, yanking my towel away before crawling up above me and settling his body between my thighs and resting his chin on my stomach. He looks up at me with the most incredible amount of contentment in his eyes. They are twinkling madly; his damp hair is all over the place and his frown line and chewed lip are nowhere to be seen. How could I have ever doubted this when he's looking so relaxed, like I've just given him life? Well, I have, I suppose. Or he has given life to me. Either or, my husband is one happy man, and now that I have got my own head around this, I can see clearly – very, *very* clearly. He has more than enough love to share. This devastating man, this ex-playboy, will be an amazing daddy, if a little overprotective. I've not just given him life, a life revived and worthy, by giving him me, I've given him new life, too – a part of him and a part of me combined. And seeing him so unbelievably euphoric has chased away every single doubt. I can have a baby with this man.

'I love you,' he says quietly. 'So much.'

I smile. 'I know.'

He presses his lips to my stomach tenderly, and then strokes it softly. 'And I love you, too,' he whispers to my flat belly. He circles his nose around my belly button before he works his way up the bed and lays himself all over me. My hair is brushed from my face and he gazes down at me. 'I'll try to be better. With you, I mean. I'll try not to smother you and make you crazy.'

'I like you smothering me. It's the unreasonableness that we need to work on.'

'Give me specifics,' he prompts.

'You want to know exactly what drives me crazy?'

'Yes, tell me. I can't try to control it if I don't know exactly what bothers you.' He drops a chaste kiss on my lips, and I struggle to prevent a laugh. He doesn't know? We could be here for the rest of the year, but I'll focus on my main grievance for now.

'You treated me too gently. When you thought I was pregnant, you stopped being fierce in the bedroom and I didn't like it. I want my dominant Jesse back.'

He pulls back and his eyebrows shoot up. 'What the hell have I done to you?'

'You're addictive, and lately I've been having Jesse withdrawal.' I'm frank and honest with my answer. I need to get this out because another eight-ish months with gentle Jesse might send me crazy.

His frown line flickers straight across his brow. 'I've taken you hard lately.'

'Yes, but only when you thought I wasn't pregnant, and when you thought I *was*, I had to provoke you into it. I want shock and awe.'

His frown deepens further. 'Don't you like sleepy sex?'

I sigh and reach up to grab his cheeks. 'You won't hurt it, you know.'

'It?' he laughs. 'Let's get one thing straight, lady. We will not be calling my baby *it*.'

'It's hardly a baby at the moment.'

'What is it, then?'

'Well, it's probably more like a peanut.' I watch as his eyes sparkle delightedly and a cheeky grin spreads across that otherworldly face. 'Oh no, Ward!' I laugh.

'What?' He leans down and rubs his nose up my cheek. 'It's perfect.'

'I am not referring to our baby as *peanut*! End of!' I yelp as I'm grabbed on my sensitive hipbone, and I start bucking under him, somewhere between delight and torture – the torture for obvious reasons and the delight because this is normal. This is us. 'Stop!' I cry.

And he does. 'Shit!' he curses.

'What are you doing?' I shout angrily. He looks down at my stomach and then back up at me, his expression shamed. 'See?' I hit him with critical eyes. 'That is what I mean! If you don't reinstate some of your normal behaviour soon, then I'll be moving to my parents' for the rest of this pregnancy.' I'm not even being dramatic. I absolutely will. 'I mean it, Ward. All of the fierceness, the rough, the countdowns and fuckings of various degrees, I want them back, and I want them now.'

He's just looking at his wife like she's a complete nutcase. I think she is. 'Calmed down yet?' he asks seriously.

'That depends on whether any of this is sinking into this thick skull of yours.' I reach for his hair and yank it.

'Ouch!' He laughs a little and then sighs, rolling over onto his back and taking me with him. His knees come up to support my back, and he studies me thoughtfully. I let him. I sit and wait for him to piece together what he wants to say until he inhales deeply. 'Do you remember when I found you at the bar, when I showed you how to dance?'

I smile as I relax against his thighs behind me. 'That was the night I realised I'd fallen in love with you.'

'I know, because you told me.'

'Hmm. Must have been the dancing.'

'I know.' His shoulders jump up casually. 'I'm good.'

I shake my head at his impertinence. 'You're arrogant.'

'It would seem that I'm a little brighter than my beautiful wife,' he says, wrapping his palms around my ankles.

'You're *really* arrogant.'

'No, not this time. This time I'm just honest. You see, I realised that I was in love with you way before then.'

I pout. 'Does that make you cleverer than me?'

'Yes, it does. The whole time you were running, I was so frustrated. I was thinking there must've been something wrong with you.' He smiles shyly. 'You know, because you wouldn't submit to me.'

'Like the others did.'

He nods, and I sigh.

'It was only because I knew I'd get hurt. Even though I didn't know you, it was obvious you . . .' I pause briefly, 'were experienced.' I was going to say a womaniser, but I don't think Jesse could be labelled that at all. Women threw themselves at his feet, made it easy for him, so he didn't need to resort to chasing. Until he met me.

His fingertips start tracing up my shins, and he watches their path. 'When I left you for those four days . . .'

'Don't!' I blurt. 'Please don't talk about that.'

'Just let me explain something. It's important.' He reaches up and pulls me down so we're nose to nose. 'I was so confused by what I was feeling. It took that time away from you to piece together exactly what it was. I couldn't work out why I was behaving like a madman. I really did think I was going fucking crazy, Ava.'

I absolutely do not relish these reminders. I already know why he left me. I don't need to hear it all again.

He has a little nibble of his lip, right under my nose, and then presses on. 'I spent day three and four reliving every single moment with you. I replayed them repeatedly until I was torturing myself, so I came to find you. Then you fucking ran again.'

Of course I ran again. My instincts didn't fail me. Even if I wasn't wholly sure of why I should be running, I knew I had to.

'Ava, the night you told me you loved me, everything became so fucking clear, but at the same time it was a massive blur. I wanted you to love me, but I knew you didn't really know me. I knew there were things that would make you run again, but I also knew that I belonged to you, and it scared me to fucking death to think that once you started unravelling it all, you'd be off again. I couldn't risk it, not after it took me so long to find you.' His eyes close and he takes a further deep breath of confidence. 'I took your pills that night.'

I'm not even shocked. He's confessed, not only to stealing them, but why he did. It makes sense to him in his crazy world and, worryingly, it kind of does to me.

His lips press to mine softly. 'I sat there all night and watched you sleeping, and all I thought about was every reason for you not to want me. I knew it was wrong to take them, but I saw it as collateral. That's how desperate I was.'

I relax into him, my face falling into his neck. 'So you don't want a baby? You just want to keep me?'

He pulls me out of his neck and hits me with his smile, reserved only for me. 'I want everything in the world with you, baby, and I want it all yesterday.'

Deep down, I think I knew that, too. 'Thank you for my watch.'

He smiles and reaches up to drag his finger across my bottom lip. 'You're more than welcome.'

I fall to his lips and lose myself in him. It's slow, it's soft, it's exquisite. It's just how it's supposed to be in this moment.

Chapter 14

The familiar sound of whirring and banging wakes me, and knowing where to find him, I take myself down to the gym. I stand on the other side of the glass door and watch his sweat-drenched back flexing and rippling as he pounds the treadmill. Opening the door quietly, I wander in and take myself around the front of the machine, sitting my naked arse on the weight bench in front of him.

He's running very fast, and when I lean back on my arms, he slams his fist on the slow button, and starts a steady pace down until he's stopped completely. My sleepy eyes are beside them-selves, watching as he grabs a towel and runs it through his hair and over his face. He's a mass of pure, solid, shimmering sweatiness. I could eat him.

I'm being watched very closely as he bends forward and rests his forearms on the front of the machine. 'Morning.' His eyes run down my front and all the way back up again until he's back at my eyes.

'Morning yourself. Why are you running in here?'

'I fancied a change.'

I throw him a questioning look, but don't bother challeng-ing him on it. If pregnancy stops him from dragging me out of bed at sunrise for a trek around London, then I'm looking more forward to the next eight months. 'I don't remember fall-ing asleep.'

'You went out like a light. You're sleeping for England, baby.'

At that comment, I yawn and stretch my arms over my head.

'What time is it?' Just as the words leave my lips, I hear the front door open and shut, and then the cheerful calling of Cathy. If Cathy's here, then I must be late, and I'm stark bollock naked! I jump up. 'I'm naked!'

He smirks and steps down from the treadmill. 'So you are,' he laughs, walking over to me. 'Whatever will Cathy think?'

I do a quick scan of the gym, looking for a towel or anything to conceal my naked form so I can escape upstairs with my dignity still intact. I laugh to myself. I lost my dignity the morning Cathy walked in on us *both* naked. My eyes land on the towel in Jesse's hand, and I quickly snatch it from his grasp to flap it out.

'I don't think that'll quite cover it,' he muses smugly.

He's right. It's little more than a facecloth. 'Help me.' I lift pleading eyes to him and find a soft smile.

'Come here.' He opens his arms, and I walk right into them, lifting myself up in my usual chimp-ish manner. His damp skin is slippery and smells delicious.

Walking to the gym door, he opens it and sticks his head out. 'Cathy?' he calls.

'Yes, boy?'

'Where are you?'

'In the kitchen.'

With that confirmation, he slips out and takes the stairs quickly. I watch over his shoulder as we rise, praying that Cathy doesn't come to investigate. She doesn't. I make it to the safety of the master suite with my dignity still whole.

'There.' He places me on my feet and drops a kiss on my forehead.

'What time is it?'

'Ten to eight.'

I roll my eyes and point an accusing glare at him. 'Why didn't you wake me?' I walk off to the bathroom.

'You needed to sleep.'

'Not for fifteen hours.' I flip the shower on and step straight into the water, not bothering to wait for it to warm. I need waking up.

'You obviously do need it,' he mumbles from the other side of the glass as he removes his running shoes.

I slip past him, dry my hair, apply my make-up, *and* get dressed in ten minutes flat, then head downstairs.

'Morning, Cathy.' I take my phone off the charger and slip it in my bag.

'Ava, you look a little brighter.' Cathy dries her hands on the front of her apron and does a little assessment of me. 'Yes, much brighter.'

'I feel it.'

'What would you like for breakfast?'

'Oh, I'm late, Cathy. I'll grab something at work.' I throw my bag over my shoulder.

'You'll eat!' Jesse's stern, take-no-shit voice hits me from behind, and I turn to find a scowl fixed to his face as he fastens his tie. 'She'll have a bagel, Cathy. With eggs.' He seems to consider something for a second. 'Actually, no eggs.'

My eyes widen. 'Cathy, thank you, but I'll eat at work.' I walk out of the kitchen, leaving Jesse with his jaw slightly gaping.

I slam the penthouse door behind me. No run. I *will* eat. No eggs. My contentment was short-lived. I stab at the elevator keypad, but it doesn't open, so I re-stab, getting myself more and more worked up. 'No eggs?' I yell at the row of numbers when the door still doesn't shift.

'You okay?'

I swing around and find my neurotic control freak with his hands draped loosely in his trouser pockets, watching me lose my temper with the innocent keypad.

'I can eat eggs!' I yell at him. 'What's the new code?'

'Excuse me?'

'You heard.' I bash the pad with the side of my fist.

'Yes, I heard. But I'm giving you a chance to retract that tone.'

He's completely straight-faced and unaffected by my little out-burst, while my eyes have just bulged at his insolence.

I walk up to him, calm and composed, and reach up on my tiptoes so I'm as near as possible to his nauseatingly splendid face – the one I want to smash in at this particular moment in time. 'Fuck ... off,' I breathe on him before stomping off towards the stairwell, praying he hasn't taken the initiative to change the code on this door yet. He hasn't. I smile smugly as I push my way through. Thirteen floors is going to kill me, but I start tackling them anyway.

By floor seven, I've removed my heels and by floor four, I have to stop and take a breather. I'm hot, sweaty and I feel sick. 'Fucking man,' I grumble, taking a deep breath and carrying on my way. I push my way through the fire door and walk straight into that damn chest, before being pushed back into the stair-well. I don't even try to battle free from his grasp. I'm absolutely beat.

I'm lifted from my feet and held in place against the con-crete wall. I'm damp with sweat and panting heavy, exhausted breaths in his face.

'You're not getting an apology fuck,' I practically wheeze all over him. I'm struggling to fight off his potency, but I'm not yielding to this. It's no eggs today, but it'll be something more extreme tomorrow.

His lips form a straight line and his green eyes narrow. 'Mouth!'

'No! You are not—' That's as far as I get before his mouth hits mine, attacking me full force. I know exactly what he's doing, but that doesn't stop my bag from dropping to the ground and my hands from grappling at his suit-covered back. This is the Jesse I know and love. I couldn't be happier. I moan, I yank at his jacket, I pull his hair and bite at his lip.

'Stubborn woman.' He works up to my ear and bites down. 'Someone's gagging for it.' He kisses the sensitive void under my lobe, and I shudder from top to toe. 'Shall I make you scream in the stairwell, Ava?'

Oh good Lord, I want him to fuck me in the stairwell. 'Yes.'

He pulls away, letting me slide down the wall to my feet, and then rearranges his groin area while observing my shocked face under hooded eyes. 'Would love to, but I'm late.'

'You bastard,' I spit, trying desperately to compose myself. I stoop and grab my bag before pushing the door open and clinking on my frustrated heels through the foyer.

'Good morning, Ava.' Clive's fresh, happy tone irritates me.

I just about manage a low grunt as I pass, walking out into the sunshine and putting my sunglasses on, immediately loving the fact that my present isn't here, but my Mini is. He'll have to let me out, and he'd better. I jump in and start her up, and there's an immediate tap on my window. 'Yes?' I ask as the glass pane lowers.

'I'll take you to work.' It's that tone.

I do the window back up. 'No, thank you.' I reverse out of the space before pulling my phone from my bag and dialling Lusso. 'Morning, Clive.' My greeting is a million miles away from the grunt that I've just given the old boy.

'Ava?'

'Could you open the gates?'

'Of course. I'll do it now.'

'Thank you, Clive.' A smug, private smile breaks the corners of my lips, and I chuck my phone on the passenger's seat as the gates start to open. I don't hang around. I drive straight out of the car park, catching Jesse's arms waving around above his head before he stalks back into the foyer.

I fall through the office doors a whole half an hour late. I'm still slightly sweaty, I'm even more out of breath, and my frustration is obvious, especially when I throw my bag across my desk and it takes my pen pot with it, the loud clatter attracting the attention of my work colleagues.

'Feeling better?' Tom asks, his inquisitive gaze running the length of my clammy form.

'Yes!' I bark, wrenching my bag to the floor and collapsing into my chair. I take a few calming breaths and turn my swivel chair, finding three sets of raised eyebrows. 'What?'

'You look terrible,' Victoria pipes up. 'Maybe you should've stayed off work.'

'I can pick you a Starbucks up,' Sally offers sweetly.

I soften my scowling face at the expressions all pointed at me, which have now turned from curious to concerned. I forgot that I was supposedly ill yesterday. 'Thanks, Sal. That would be lovely.'

She walks over to her desk and pulls some money from the petty cash tin. 'Anyone else?'

Tom and Victoria both shout their orders at Sal, who barely holds back to hear them before leaving the office promptly. I turn my computer on and load up my e-mail account. Tom and Victoria are standing at the end of my desk in a blink of an eye.

'You look pasty,' Tom observes, twirling a pen in his fingers, his turquoise shirt and yellow tie playing havoc with my tired eyes.

'Really pale, Ava. Are you sure you're okay?' Victoria sounds and looks more concerned than Tom, who just looks downright suspicious.

I start flicking through my e-mail, highlighting and deleting the mass of junk. 'I'm fine. Where's Patrick?' It's only now I've noticed my boss hasn't come to investigate the noise.

'Personal meetings,' they chant in unison, and I look up on a frown.

'Wasn't he in private meetings yesterday?'

'He'll be in tomorrow,' Tom tells me as he strolls off to his desk, Victoria following.

The office door opens and a woman with a basket draped

over her arm walks in. 'Ava Ward?' She looks at Tom, and then follows his pointed pen over to me.

'Hi,' I say as she makes it to my desk and rests her hamper on the edge. 'Can I help you?'

She pulls the gingham towel from the top of the carrier and my eyes naturally follow her hand into it. 'Breakfast,' she smiles, placing a paper bag in front of me, and then reaches back in, she pulls out a takeaway coffee cup. 'My coffee wasn't good enough, so he had me pick one up from Starbucks. Cappuccino, extra shot, no chocolate or sugar. Enjoy.' And with that she turns and walks out.

I sigh and push the bag to the side. I'm not in the least bit hungry, but I'm dying for some coffee. I take a sip and immediately screw my face up at the bitter taste. 'Ewww.'

'All right?' Tom frowns across the office at me.

'Fine.' I stand and take myself into the kitchen, removing the lid from my coffee and tipping sugar into the cup before giving it a good stir and taking another sip. I hum in sweet satisfaction.

'Coffee for Ava!' Sally walks into the kitchen, waving a Starbucks cup at me. 'Oh?' A look of complete confusion invades her face as she watches me gulping down the hot, sweet liquid.

I exhale happily. 'Delivered, courtesy of my husband.'

She melts. 'That's so sweet.'

'No, actually, it wasn't, but I added a few myself.' I walk past a puzzled Sal, back to my desk. I'm digging through my bag when I hear my phone shout the arrival of a text.

Are you eating your breakfast?

I take another swig of my coffee and text back:

Yummy.

I don't get a chance to put my phone down before it chimes again.

I'm so glad our marriage is based on honesty.

My eyes instinctively lift and there he is, holding a bunch of calla lilies and with an annoyed glare drilling into me. I can't prevent the long, drawn-out exhale of air that rushes from my mouth as I lower myself to my chair. He strides over, giving Tom and Victoria a nod in greeting, before sinking his tall leanness into a chair on the other side of my desk, placing the flowers in front of me. 'Eat,' he orders flatly, nodding at the paper bag that's been shoved to the side.

'I'm not hungry, Jesse.'

He leans forward, looking worried, his eyes evaluating my face. 'Baby, you look pale.'

'I feel rubbish,' I admit. Finally, morning sickness at the correct time of day. There is no point in feigning *fine* because I absolutely don't feel it and I clearly don't look it.

He rises and comes to stand behind my chair, leaning down and placing his palm across my brow and his lips to my ear. 'You're hot.'

'I know,' I sigh, pushing my cheek to his mouth, my eyes closing with no instruction from my brain. 'I hope you feel guilty,' I say quietly. I'm feeling sorry for myself.

I'm released and he swivels my chair around to face him. He crouches in front of me and takes my hands. 'Let me take you home.'

'It'll pass.'

'You're impossible sometimes.' He reaches up to cup my cheek. 'Pregnancy is making you moody and even more defiant.'

I force a small smile. 'I like keeping you on your toes.'

'You mean you like keeping me crazy.'

'That, too.'

Sighing, he leans in and kisses me sweetly. 'Please eat.' He's begging, not demanding. 'It might make you feel better.'

'Okay,' I agree. I'm willing to try because even though the thought of swallowing food makes me want to gag, I couldn't possibly feel any worse than I already do.

He looks a little surprised at my lack of disobedience. 'Good girl.'

I'm turned back toward my desk and presented with the paper bag. As I open it, the waft of bacon hits my nose and I *do* actually gag. 'I don't think I can.' I snap the bag shut again, but it's soon whipped from my hand, the bagel unpacked and placed on a napkin in front of me. As I gingerly pick at a corner and bring it to my lips, I'm fighting the overwhelming desire to run to the toilets and shove my fingers down my throat. I chew slowly for an age, under the watchful eye of my worried husband, then swallow. I don't retch.

He smiles. 'Do you see how happy you make me when you do what you're told?'

I ignore him and pop the bread in my mouth, each chew becoming easier, each swallow instigating less stomach turning. He just stands and watches me until I've worked my way through most of my breakfast. 'Happy?' I ask. I know *I* am. I feel better already.

'Your colour's back. Yes, I'm happy.' He scoops up the remains and throws it in the bin, and then bends down, getting nose to nose with me. 'My work here is done.' He pushes his lips to mine. 'Now I'll leave my wife to work in peace.'

I scoff. 'No you won't.'

Pulling back, he hits me with a cheeky grin. 'I might check in once or twice.'

I scoff again. 'No you won't!'

'I won't make a promise I can't keep. Is Patrick here?' His question reminds me that I still haven't spoken to my boss about Mikael.

'No. He's in meetings all day.'

He straightens, flicking his eyes to my hair, clearly looking for signs of my fiddling fingers. 'You've made me late,' he says, looking down at his Rolex.

'You make yourself late.' I shoo him away and pick up my flowers to put them in water. 'Go.'

He holds his hands up and starts backing away from me. 'Feeling better?'

'I do. Thank you.'

Blessing me with his smile, reserved only for me, he winks, blows a kiss and walks out, leaving me with a little grin on my non-pale face. Victoria and Sal are smiling fondly and Tom's swooning at my Lord's back.

They're all still so affected.

I make it to the end of the day with my breakfast still in my stomach. I feel so much better. Jesse has texted me five times, each time asking how I feel. My answer is the same for every reply. Better.

The final message asks a different question, though.

I'm still at The Manor. Come? We'll have steak.

The last bit gets me.

On my way x

I pack my desk up and wave a goodbye to all of my colleagues, meeting a woman holding a bunch of flowers at the door.

'Ava O'Shea?' she asks. It's not the usual florist, and she called me by my maiden name. Jesse would absolutely never do that.

'That's me.' I sound cautious, which is fine because I am. I've just noticed the flowers are not calla lilies and they are far from fresh. In fact, they're dead. She places the flowers in my arms and thrusts the clipboard under my nose. She wants a signature for dead flowers? I shift my full arms and manage a rough scribble across the paper.

'Thanks,' she says casually as she turns to walk away.

I look down at the flowers a little puzzled. 'They're dead,' I call to her back.

'I know,' she replies, not in the least bit troubled by that.

'You think it's okay to deliver dead flowers?'

She turns and laughs. 'I've had stranger requests.'

I flinch. Like what? I find the card and remove it from the tiny envelope.

HE SAYS HE NEEDS YOU. HE DOESN'T. YOU THINK YOU KNOW HIM. YOU DON'T.

I DO. LEAVE HIM.

Chapter 15

My heart stops beating in my chest and one name springs to mind immediately.

Coral.

I should feel concerned, but I don't. I feel deadly possessive at the suggestion. A lightning bolt of Jesse's famous attribute flies through me, leaving me dropping everything in my arms to the floor and tearing the malicious warning up slowly. Who the hell does she think she is? A fuck, that's what she was, nothing more than a convenient fuck. Has she been in touch with Jesse again? Should I ask him and prick his curiosity? I don't want him to know about this. I don't want anything tipping him over the edge. I can deal with empty threats. Leave him, or what? After gathering my things from the ground, I make my way to the car park, the desperate urge to be with him suddenly overwhelming me.

I come to an abrupt halt when I see the parking space where I left my Mini this morning is empty. No car. I glance up at the board displaying the floor number and note that I'm in the exact right place. So where the hell is my car?

"S'all good, girl.' John's low rumble pulls my body around to find him leaning out of the window of his Range Rover. 'In you get.'

'My car's been stolen.' I wave my arm at the empty space and turn back to check that I'm not imagining things.

'It's not been stolen, girl. Get in.'

'What?' I turn startled eyes back to the mountain of a man. 'Where is it, then?'

John has a clear look of embarrassment on his mean face. 'Your motherfucking husband had it picked up.' He nods his head to the passenger side.

'Are you winding me up?' I laugh.

His eyebrows appear over his wraparounds. 'What do you think?'

I take a deep, calming breath and make my way around to the passenger side and climb in. Yes, he needs me all right. He needs me to drive me fucking crazy! 'I might strangle him,' I mutter, yanking my seatbelt around and clipping it in place.

'Take it easy on him, girl.' John commences strumming on the steering wheel as he drives out of the car park, back into the daylight.

'John,' I start in a matter-of-fact tone, 'I like you, I really do, but unless you can enlighten me on an acceptable reason for my husband's neurotic ways, then I won't be taking any notice of your request to take it easy on him.'

He laughs a deep, rolling belly laugh, his neck retracting and revealing those chins he keeps hidden. 'I like you, too, girl,' he chuckles, reaching under his glasses and wiping under his eyes. I've never seen this big, menacing beast so vivacious. It makes me smile, thoughts of challenging husbands and threatening notes soon making way for the giggles. But then John's face straightens all too quickly, and I'm left laughing alone with wraparounds pointed at me. The sudden change in his expression snaps me right from my hysterical state.

'He might get worse. I believe congratulations are in order.' His face dips, an indication that he's looking at my stomach, before he returns to face the road.

'He's told you?' I ask disbelievingly. I don't want anyone to know yet. It's way too soon.

'Girl, he didn't need to.'

'He didn't?'

'No, when I found Harrods baby department on the screen

of his computer, it kind of let the cat out the bag. That and the smile on the motherfucker's face all day.'

I sink into my seat, wondering what people might think. Shotgun, that's what. A rush job because he's knocked me up. My contentment wavers. And what about my parents and Dan?

John pulls up at The Manor, and I waste no time jumping down from his Range Rover and making my way up the steps.

'He's in his office,' John calls.

'Thanks, John.' I head straight for the back of The Manor, passing through the summer room and smiling to myself at the sudden silence that falls. I cast my eyes across the gathering of women, all with drinks in their hands and all with sour faces. 'Evening,' I smile brightly and receive a chorus of mumbles in return for my trouble. My smile widens at the thought of those faces souring further when they learn of my pregnancy.

As I approach Jesse's office, the door opens and a man exits, looking tense but relieved all at once. It's Steve. He looks different, fully clothed and without a whip in his grasp. I halt dead in my tracks, completely shocked, mainly because he's in one piece. 'Hi,' I stammer, the surprise clear in my tone.

His eyes lift and he smiles, a little embarrassed. 'Ava.'

I'm staring at him, and I realise it's rude, but I'm not sure what to say. There are no bruises or black eyes; he's not limping and he doesn't look like he's just been offered burial or cremation. 'How are you?' I ask, when my brain fails to give me anything better to say.

'I'm good.' He slips his hands into his jacket pockets, looking no less uncomfortable. 'You?'

'Yes, I'm fine.' This is so awkward. The last time I saw him, he had me trussed up and was whipping the crap out of me. He was cocky and smarmy, but there is no trace of that man now. 'You've been to see Jesse?'

'I have.' He laughs. 'I've avoided it for long enough. I needed to apologise.'

'Oh.' My brain is failing me. He looks sincere enough, but if I was a man and I had Jesse vying for my blood, I think I would face the shame of grovelling, too.

'I should apologise to you, too.' He stammers through his words, Yeah . . . urm . . . I'm . . . I'm sorry.'

I shake my head. I'm the one who's embarrassed now. I asked him to whip me. It's me who should be feeling remorseful for setting him up for certain annihilation. 'Steve, I shouldn't have asked you. It was wrong of me.'

'No,' he smiles, but this time it's a sweet offering. 'I'd been walking a fine line for too long, getting carried away, losing respect for the women trusting me. You actually did me a favour but, of course, I wish I'd never hurt you.'

I smile back. 'I'll accept yours, if you accept mine.'

He pulls his car keys from his pocket and starts to pass me. 'Accepted. I'll see you.'

'See you,' I call, watching his back disappear down the corridor.

I push through Jesse's office door and find him on his knees in the middle of the floor, my mind suddenly awash with painful memories. But he's fully dressed in his suit and there are piles and piles of paperwork spread on the carpet in front of him. He looks up, and my heart constricts at the exasperated look on his beautiful face.

'Hey.' I shut the door behind me, and his look changes from mentally exhausted to contented in a split second.

'Here's my beautiful girl.' He sits on his arse, knees bent and with his feet flat on the floor, opening his arms. 'Come here. I need you.'

I walk slowly over. 'Need *me*, or need me to sort all of this out for you?'

He pouts and waves his arms impatiently. 'Both.'

I sit myself between his thighs and shuffle back until my back is pressed to his front. His arms wrap around my shoulders and his nose goes straight into my hair, taking a long, loud inhale. 'How are you feeling?'

'Better.'

'Good, I don't like seeing you poorly.'

'Then you shouldn't have been underhanded and knocked me up,' I retort drily, earning myself a nudge of his leg. 'I saw Steve leaving.'

'Hmm,' he hums in my ear, nibbling at my lobe.

'Did you offer burial or cremation?' I grin to myself when I'm nudged again.

'I offered him an olive branch, actually. Sarcasm doesn't suit you, lady.'

I'm pretty speechless. I would've put my life on the imminent demise of the poor Steve. 'What's made you so reasonable?'

'I'm always reasonable. It is you, beautiful girl, who's the unreasonable one.'

I don't bother challenging him. I don't even bother scoffing or laughing, but his little comment has just reminded me of something. 'What's so reasonable about having my car stolen? And how did you manage it without any key?'

'Tow truck,' he replies with absolutely no shame or further explanation.

I reach forward and pick up a few pieces of paper, anything to stop myself from countering his ridiculous claim of not being unreasonable, or shouting at him for stealing my car.

'How was your day?' he asks.

I try to prevent the slight tensing of my body. 'Productive. Shall we make a start?'

He groans but releases me. 'Suppose so.'

Over the next hour, we sort through endless papers, bills, contracts and invoices. I've collated them all in date order, stacked them in neat piles, and secured them with elastic bands.

Jesse slumps in his office chair and starts fiddling with his computer, and I watch as I finish binding the final pile of papers. He's guiding his mouse around, his frown a perfect line on his brow. Curious, I get up to go and see what he's so rapt with, and as I walk around his desk, he flicks his eyes quickly to me, and then hastily shuts his screen down.

'Dinner?' He stands.

I give him suspicious eyes and lean past him, turning the screen back on. It's as I thought: baby paraphernalia everywhere. I turn my face to his with a questioning look, but I can't possibly be cranky with him, especially when he shrugs sheepishly and starts biting at his bottom lip.

'Just doing a bit of research.' He actually looks down and starts scuffing his shoes on the office carpet. I melt at his feet. I could hug him. So I do. Tightly.

'I know you're excited, but could we hold off telling people?'

'I want to shout about it,' he complains. 'Tell everyone!'

'I know, but I'm only a few weeks. Women usually wait until their first scan, at least.'

'When's the first scan? I'll pay. We'll get one tomorrow.'

I laugh and pull away. 'It's far too early for a scan, and anyway, the hospital will do it.'

He looks at me like I've just grown another head. 'You are *not* having my baby in an NHS hospital!'

'I—'

'No, Ava. This is not up for discussion. End of.' It's that tone – the one I know for absolutely sure never to challenge. 'Never, no way.' He shakes his head. He's horrified at the thought, clearly.

'What do you think they'll do?'

'I don't know, but I'm not giving them the chance.' He takes my hand and starts leading me from his office.

'You pay your taxes and so do I. It's a privilege to have the National Health Service. You should be grateful.'

'I am, it's wonderful, but we won't be utilising it. End of.'

'Neurotic,' I mutter, looking up at him on a grin.

My grin is returned, even though I can see he's trying to remain serious. '-*ish*,' he replies. 'I like your dress.' His eyes wander down the front of my nude structured pencil dress, as do mine.

'Thank you.'

'I want to show you something. Come on.' He opens the door and places his hand on the small of my back to guide me.

'What?' I ask, letting my body be gently pushed from his office.

I shiver when I feel his mouth at my ear. 'You'll see.'

I'm curious, and I'm also feeling a little breathless. From just a few whispered words and his hand on my body, I'm mentally begging for him. Pregnancy might be responsible, or it could just be him. No, it's the latter, for sure, but combined I could be in a whole heap of sexual trouble.

We pass the members of The Manor in the summer room, Jesse nodding, me smiling, and make our way up the stairs until we're walking down the corridor to the extension.

He opens the door to the very last room, the one I fled from, the one I sat on my arse sketching drafts in, and the one in which I received my warning from Sarah. I don't particularly like this room, but as I'm pushed through and the whole area comes into view, I gasp.

It's no longer an empty shell of raw plaster with a rough wooden floor. It's now a palatial space, garnished in sumptuous materials, all in black and gold. I gingerly wander in, gazing around, drinking in the stunning space. The huge bed that I sketched has come to life and dominates the room, dressed in pale-gold satin. The windows are adorned with heavy gold drapes of the same material, and the floor is soft and squidgy under my heels. I trail my eyes across the walls, finding the paper I picked on one wall and the three remaining walls painted in a dull gold to match the bedding and curtains. It's almost an exact replica of my rough drawing.

I turn to face Jesse. 'You did this?'

He shuts the door quietly. 'I gave someone your drawing and told them to create it. Is it close?'

'It is. When?' I ask.

'It doesn't matter when. What matters is if you like it.' He's trying to gauge my reaction, looking a little cautious and maybe even a little nervous, too.

'It's perfect.'

'It's ours.'

My eyes widen a little. 'Ours?' What does he mean by that? Does he want us to live here?

He must catch the worry on my face because he smiles mildly. 'No one has ever *been* in this room. This is our room. If I'm working and you're with me, maybe you'll want a sleep or some rest.'

'You mean when I have swollen ankles or am exhausted from carrying too much weight?' I'm suddenly contemplating the awful thought that we're having a baby, we are starting a family, and The Manor will be a huge presence in our lives. My baby's daddy owns a sex club. Once I have this baby, I'll never want to bring it here, and with Jesse working I'll hardly see him. He'll hardly see *us*. The terrifying, unsure feelings are still lying dormant, but with this realisation, they are threatening to rear their ugly heads and send me back a few paces. He'll never sell this place. He's already confirmed that. It was Carmichael's baby.

'I mean if we need it, it will be here,' he says quietly.

I don't want to need it, although I don't say that. He's gone to all of this trouble for me, so instead I break my eyes away from Jesse's thoughtful greens and cast them around the pale-gold walls. There's no wall art, no pictures or decorative pieces.

Except the cross.

My eyes remain fixed on the giant, dark wooden crucifix, and I notice at each end of the horizontal piece of wood spanning two thirds of the way up, there are manacles – shiny, gold, intricately carved pieces of metal bolted to the far edges to hold something in place.

To hold a person in place.

I slowly turn my eyes back to Jesse's and find his are still on me, watching carefully, assessing my reaction to the piece of art. 'Why is that here?' I ask quietly.

'Because I had it put in here.' He's just as quiet, and his hands are draped loosely in his pockets, his legs slightly spread.

'Why?'

'I think it might . . . help.' His eyes are smoking out, his lip chewed.

Help? Jesse just stands there with rapt intention written all over that heart-stopping face, and it's playing havoc with my vital signs. 'What do we need help with?' My voice is a husky murmur, full of want and longing, and all of those vital signs escalate further when he slowly starts walking toward me.

'You want it hard,' he says quietly, 'and I'm not very comfortable with that when you're carrying my baby.' He removes his Grensons and socks, then slides his jacket off his shoulders and drapes it on the bed. 'So I thought carefully and came up with the compromise fuck.'

My exhale falters in my throat and for some reason unbeknown to me, I step back. I don't know why: I trust him, but I'm a little shocked by his obvious intention. 'I don't understand.'

He reaches up and pulls at his tie before slowly unfastening his shirt buttons. 'You will.' He leaves his shirt draping open, teasing my eyes with only a sliver of his flesh, and walks across the room, opening a cupboard door and fiddling with something. Then the whole room is swamped with a slow-building hum of spiritual, tingle-provoking music.

I go rigid. 'What is this?' I ask as he walks slowly back to me, reaching my body and breathing down on me.

'This is Amber "Sexual",' he says gently. '"Afterlife". Appropriate, don't you think?'

I couldn't agree more, but my mouth refuses to speak and tell him so.

'It doesn't always have to be hard, Ava. I hold the power, no matter how I take you.' He pushes me back gently until I'm positioned in front of the cross. 'It's not the hard you love, anyway. It's me taking you so unapologetically.' His voice is low and sure. It should be. He's totally right. It's the power he has over me, not just the power of his body.

'You'll never fuck any sense into me again?' I ask, just as low, but not so sure.

His lips break into a concealed smile. 'Will you defy me again?'

'Probably,' I breathe.

'Then I've absolutely no doubt I will, my temptress.' He rests his finger under my chin and brings my face up to his. 'If I want to fuck you hard and make you scream, then I will. If I want to make love to you, Ava, and make you purr, then I will.' He places his lips gently over mine, and my eyes close, my breathing hitching quietly. 'If I want to bind you on this cross, then I will.' He reaches around my back and lazily draws the zipper of my dress down before pulling it away and lowering himself with it so I can step out. Working his way back up my body, he takes my hand and kisses my wedding ring. 'And you are mine, so I'll do what I like with you.'

My eyes are still closed, my head dropped low. My breathing is weak and shallow, too, and my ears are saturated by the sensual tones of the calm music. My flesh screams for his touch. However he wants to do it. However he wants to take me.

I feel my bra being removed, and the slow lift of my hand to meet the gold manacle. It clips into place and he kisses me again before slowly guiding my free hand to the other gold shackle.

I'm bound, spread on the cross and at his mercy. But I'm one hundred per cent safe, and I'm one hundred per cent comfortable.

'Look at me, baby,' he whispers, stroking my cheek.

My heavy lids lift and I'm crippled by dark-green pools of pure love. Sliding his hand around the nape of my neck, he pulls me forward slightly so our faces are as close as can be without touching. 'Better.' His mouth meets mine tenderly, and I close my eyes, opening to his soft lips willingly, but not frenzied. I feel calm and serene as he leisurely works his tongue through my mouth, rolling, lapping and withdrawing before evenly plunging back inside to continue lazily seducing me. He's holding my neck firmly, kissing me like I'm glass, and I have no physical hold of him. His mouth is giving me everything I need. Trailing his lips to my ear, he runs his tongue up the edge of my lobe, my cheek pushing into his jaw, his light stubble comforting and so familiar. I'm riddled with tingles, every scrap of my form buzzing to the erotic routine of his lips. And then they leave my ear and he pulls away. 'Eyes, baby.'

I rip them open with some determined effort and watch as he shrugs off his shirt, the revealing of toned, smooth flesh attacking my eyes. My gaze drifts all over the hard vastness of his chest, over his pecs, over his abdomen, over his scar. The sight makes me shift in my heels and wish that I wasn't bound. But I'm quickly distracted from my need to lay my hands on him when his belt is unfastened, along with his button and zip, and he's pushing his trousers down his robust thighs.

He's standing before me, uncovered and unforgivingly phenomenal. I'm not serene any longer. I'm fighting the instinct to wrestle with my restraints and shout a demand for contact. He must catch my pending loss of control because he's pressed up to my body in a split second and looking down into my desperate eyes.

'Let the music sink back in, Ava. Control it.'

I try, but with his naked muscles spread all over my restrained frame, it's just way too hard. 'I can't,' I admit unashamedly. I'm not ashamed. I'm consumed. I close my eyes again, willing some strength from my weakness to obey him. My hands are suddenly warm from his palms encasing the fists I have formed and I flex them silently, showing my cooperation. He releases me before lightly dragging his fingers up the insides of my arms, a flurry of goose pimples tracking their path, until he's on my chest and cupping both of my breasts. My eyes are still closed, but I know his mouth is moving in. I can feel his breath spreading further over my skin the closer he's getting. And then there is the unmistakable heat of his mouth completely closed around my right breast. His tactic is exact. He sucks deeply, rolls his tongue slowly and pulls back to kiss my nipple sweetly before repeating, sucking, rolling and kissing. My head falls back, and I moan, a low, raspy noise of surrender. I soak up the attentive motions as I quietly sigh and let my head go completely limp. A buzzing has developed between my thighs and is beating a steady, consistent thrum.

I feel his teeth clamp painfully onto my nipple and my head flies up on a small cry. He doesn't release me, even though it obviously hurts. He just gazes up through his long lashes at me struggling to deal with the pressure. He smiles a little around my breast, and my nipple is released, the blood rushing back in as he sucks it back to life. I release a quiet gasp.

'My beautiful girl is learning to control it,' he muses, drawing my knickers down my thighs and tapping each ankle to lift. Pecking his way between my breasts, up my throat and back to my lips, he cups me delicately and then slowly pushes two fingers inside me. I'm panting immediately.

'Shhhh,' he whispers. 'Soak it up, Ava. Feel every single bit of pleasure that I bless you with.' His fingers pull free and firmly drive forward again, deep and high. He might be measured and soft, but my muscles are gripping him harshly. And then the fingers are gone, but before I can voice a frustrated complaint, I feel the soaking wet head of his cock meet the very tip of my clit. I don't miss the slight, sharp intake of breath from him, but I'm too drunk on his heated touch to tell him to control it. He guides himself around, rolling the steel, slippery head across me, getting his face up close to mine and breathing heavily all over my lips. Our eyes lock, complete adoration clashing between them, and he slowly lowers his lips to mine. It's a kiss of passion and it's full of heat and devotion.

This time, we both groan, we both lose our breath and we both shift on the spot to steady ourselves.

'Are your arms okay?' he murmurs into my mouth.

'Yes.'

'Are you ready for me to take you, Ava?'

'I'm ready.'

He stoops and hovers at my entrance, then releases my lips. 'Open your eyes for me, baby.'

I instantly comply, the magnetism of his own pulling me straight to where they should be, and I watch him as he unhurriedly breaches my opening and slides into me. 'Oh God,' I breathe, maintaining our eye contact, refusing to break this incredible intimacy.

'Jesus.' His cheeks puff slightly; he shakes his head very mildly and a shimmer of sweat materialises across his brow as he reaches down and takes the backs of my thighs and lifts them to his narrow hips before drawing back and pushing forward on a low, throaty moan, dipping his head and latching onto my throat. My head naturally falls to the side, my eyes close as he lazily licks up the column, finishing with a tender kiss under my ear. 'I set the pace,' he murmurs, 'and you follow.'

His words make me swallow hard and turn into his mouth,

capturing his lips and worshipping him while he truly blesses me with the consistent, calm and controlled advances of his hips.

In and out. In and out. In and out.

We're surrounded by this calming music, gliding against each other's bodies and completely out of our mind on pleasure. Out he pulls, and in he goes again. He's filling me wholly and not just with each and every perfect stroke. My heart is full, too. It's full of fierce, powerful, undying love.

He pushes forward, but this time I hear a clear, harsh pull of breath. 'You're going to come.' My words come out on a quiet rush of breath.

'Not yet.' I watch as his eyes clench shut and his frown line trails the entire width of his brow, but he still maintains his steady pace. He is remarkably controlled, but I'm moving fast to where I need to be. Just looking at that face has sent the spiralling rush of pressure descending downwards, and now I'm worried that I'll break before Jesse.

I pant and rest my lips on his again, and he eagerly accepts, his tongue darting into my mouth and mimicking my big sweeping circles. His fingers dig into the backs of my thighs, lifting me higher so he can get more leverage, and then he hits me firmly and yells into my mouth. I free his lips and take refuge in the crook of his neck on a suppressed cry as I'm attacked by feverish spasms. He's grinding firmly, retreating slowly, and flowing back in, so controlled.

'Jesus fucking Christ,' he mumbles quietly, drawing back and striking precisely and expertly one last mind-splitting time.

'Jesse!' I latch onto his shoulder and bite down hard, while I ride out the violent pulsations firing off all over my body. He bucks, yells, and squeezes my thighs as he comes, the feeling of his scorching essence filling me, warming me, completing me. I'm lightheaded and limp.

His face is buried in my neck, mine in his, and despite the

calmness of that whole lovemaking session, the ending wasn't a calm roll over into orgasm, and it wasn't a frenzied rush to explosion. We just found our middle ground – a mixture of pure, gentle Jesse, and the dominant sex Lord I love.

'That was perfect,' I whisper in his ear. I really need to hold him, but I don't need to ask. He's already grasping me with one arm and reaching across with the other to undo me. He then swaps arms and releases my other hand. In spite of the slight ache and lack of life in my limbs, they still find their way around Jesse's strong shoulders. I smother him completely, my thighs tightening and my cheek resting on his shoulders as he carries me to the bed and takes us down, me beneath him. The cool satin is a welcome sensation across my hot, clammy back, and it doesn't escape my notice that he isn't spreading his full weight all over me, instead opting to hold himself up slightly across my tummy.

'Do you like our room?' he asks into my hair.

I smile up at the ceiling. 'Are we going to have a cradle put in here? You know, for when we bring our baby to The Manor.' My question is enough to plant the seed, and judging by the stilling of his heaving body, my seed has settled well.

He slowly pulls himself up and shifts to my side, resting the side of his head in his palm on his propped elbow. His fingertip starts circling around my belly button while he studies me. 'Sarcasm doesn't suit you, lady.'

I put on my most innocent face. I know it won't make a jot of difference. He's cottoned right on to my little dig. 'Just a question.'

His eyebrows slowly rise and serious eyes skate down my body to watch the slow rotations of his finger. 'You have a bump.'

I shrink into the mattress on an offended snort. 'Don't be stupid! I'm barely pregnant.'

'I'm not being stupid.' His hand flattens and strokes softly.

'It's faint, but it's there.' He leans down and kisses my belly before propping his head on his bent arm again. 'I know this body, and I know it's changing.'

I frown and look down at my stomach, but it looks perfectly flat to me. He's seeing things now. 'Whatever you say, Jesse.' I'm not arguing after that perfect moment, even if I do want to slap him for insinuating that I've put on weight.

He leans down again and gets his mouth up close to my abdomen. 'See, peanut? Your mother's learning who has the power.'

'No peanut!' I throw my head up and lob him a mighty scowl. He's grinning at me. 'Think of another name. You're not referring to our child as something disgusting that you obsess about and devour daily.'

'I obsess about you. I also devour *you* daily. But I can't call our baby a defiant little temptress.'

'No, that would be wrong.'

He jumps up and straddles my hips, pinning my wrists down, but still not resting himself on my stomach. 'Let me call our baby peanut.'

'Never.'

'Sense fuck?'

'Yes please,' I reply way too hopefully, grinning.

He laughs and kisses me chastely. 'Pregnancy's making you a monster. Come on. My wife and peanut must be hungry.'

'Your wife and *baby* are very hungry.'

His greens twinkle and he pulls me up from the bed, dressing me first before he pulls on his own clothes. I step into his chest and remove his hands from his collar, taking over the fastening of his buttons while he watches me quietly. Reaching around his back to tuck his shirt into his trousers, my cheek rests on his chest as I take my time making him look presentable.

'Belt?' I ask, as I pull away from him. He stoops down and retrieves it from the floor, handing it to me with an amused smile. I take it, returning his smile, and start feeding it through the loops of his trousers and buckling it up. 'You're done.'

'No I'm not.' He nods at his shoes. 'If you're going to do a job, do it properly.'

I ignore his insolence, instead pushing him down so he's sitting on the end of the bed. I kneel in front of him, resting my bum on my heels, and start putting his socks on. 'Is this okay for you, Lord?' I yank at a few of the dark-blond hairs at the bottom of his shins.

'Fuck!' he reaches down and rubs his shin. 'There was no need for that.'

He slips his feet in his shoes and stands, grabbing his jacket and stuffing his tie in the pocket, all the time frowning at me. 'You really are a monster.'

I smile sweetly, prompting his frown to iron out and his lips to twitch. 'Ready?' I ask.

He shakes his head and takes my hand, leading me from our room, down to the bar. I'm placed on my usual stool, and Mario is with us in a heartbeat.

'Mrs Ward!' His cheerful accented voice draws the usual response from me.

I smile. 'Mario, it's Ava,' I scold him lightly. 'How are you?'

'Ah!' He flips a bar towel over his shoulder and leans forward. 'Very well. What would you like?'

'Two waters,' Jesse interjects swiftly. 'Just two waters please, Mario.'

I flip critical eyes straight to my husband, who has seated himself on the stool next to me. 'I might like some wine with my dinner.'

He's not at all perturbed by my reproachful glare. In fact, he doesn't even look at me. 'You might, but you're not having any.' Mario scoots straight off, while I glare at Jesse, but he still refuses to face me, instead signalling Pete over. 'Two steaks, Pete. One medium, one well done. No blood whatsoever.'

The confusion in Pete's face is obvious, and the disbelieving look on mine must be clear, too. 'Urhh . . . yes, Mr Ward. Salad and new potatoes?' he asks. His puzzled eyes have drifted across to my dumbstruck face, I can feel them on me, but I'm too busy staring at my impossible husband to acknowledge him.

'Yes, just make sure one steak is thoroughly cooked.' Jesse accepts the bottled water from Mario and starts pouring mine into a glass. 'Is there egg in that salad dressing?'

I actually choke on a cough, not that it makes a bit of difference. Poor Pete has no idea what's going on. 'I'm not sure. Should I check?'

'Yes. If there is, leave the salad with the well-cooked steak un-dressed.'

'Okay, Mr Ward.'

Mario backs away, as does Pete, and we're alone at the bar, me in a stunned silence and Jesse busying himself with water-pouring duties to avoid facing his astonished wife. He knows that I'm gawking at him; he damn well knows it.

I turn myself back to the bar, all calm and unruffled, but I'm quietly raging. He just can't help himself. 'If you don't go to that kitchen, change my order and get me a glass of wine, then I'm one step closer to moving in with my parents for the rest of this pregnancy.' I know he's looking at me now. I can feel his shocked greens burning a hole in my profile. I take my glass of water and slowly turn my face to his. 'You are not trampling my diet, Ward.'

'You've already got yourself pissed while you were pregnant,' he spits quietly. He's not happy, but neither am I.

'I was mad with you.' I still sound calm, but now I feel guilty, too.

His eyebrows shoot up. 'So you thought you would take it out on my baby?'

I soak up the resentment pouring from him. 'You keep saying *my* baby. It's ours.'

'That's what I meant!'

'Then say it!' I snap.

I've shocked him because he's not coming at me with a counter-attack. He's just severely chomping on that bottom lip. His mind's cogs are racing at a million miles per hour, and he finally sags, swinging away from me on his stool, his hands diving straight into his messy array of dark blond. 'Fucking hell,' he curses quietly. 'Fucking, fuck, fuck, fuck!'

'I mean it, Jesse.' I reinforce my threat. I was wrong to go out and get myself pissed, aware that I'm pregnant, but it was only a result of what this man does to me – what this man spikes in me. I won't be getting pissed again, but a small glass of red wine won't hurt and a half-cooked steak is harmless. Don't even get me started on the eggs.

I see his eyes clench shut and he takes a deep breath before turning towards my calm face. He takes my water and places it on the bar, and then holds my hands in his. 'I'm sorry.'

I very nearly fall off my stool. 'You are?' There's no escaping the shock in my voice. Even if I was threatening him with con-fidence, I had absolutely no faith that he would take any notice of me.

'I am. I'm sorry. This is going to take some getting used to.'

'Jesse, this is hard enough to cope with without dealing with an enhanced control freak.' I let out an almighty sigh and stand up, positioning myself between his legs. 'I want my baby to have a daddy. Please, try to reduce the risk of a stress-induced heart attack by chilling out a little.' I kiss every part of his face that I can lay my lips on, and he lets me.

'Hmmm. I'll work on it, baby. I'm really trying, but can we at least compromise?'

'Compromise how?'

I feel his hand slide onto my head and grasp my hair, pulling my busy lips away from him. He pouts. 'Please don't drink.' His eyes are pleading with me, and I realise all too quickly how important it is to him. He's a recovering alcoholic, even if he won't admit it. For me to drink in normal circumstances would be thoughtless. While I'm carrying his baby would be way past that. It would be cruel.

'I won't,' I agree, and the relieved look that washes over his face makes me feel awful. Really, really awful. 'Go and get me a medium-cooked steak.' I peck his lips and pull out of his hold, placing myself back on my stool. 'And I'd like that dressing on my salad.' I nod past him.

He gives my cheek a quick stroke and leaves me at the bar to go and fulfil his obligation of getting his pregnant wife a medium-cooked steak.

As my eyes wander around the bar, I immediately notice that it's busy. Did they hear anything? Oh God, have we just revealed to a bar full of members that I'm expecting? My eyes flick across various groups, all drinking and chatting. The curious interest that always surrounds me when I'm here is ever-present. I spot Natasha in the corner with voice one and voice three, and I'm mortified when her eyes drop to my stomach. My face heats, and I swing back to the bar, hastily escaping her inquisitive look. It's so easy to forget there's a world happening around us when we're so wrapped up in each other, whether we're arguing, making friends or just plain getting our fix of each other.

'Evening, Ava.' Drew's reserved tone pulls my attention away, and I'm more than thrown to find him in jeans. He has a formal shirt tucked in and his black hair is perfectly placed, as usual, but jeans?

'Hi.' I can't help my eyes roving repeatedly up and down his body, and when he shifts uncomfortably, I realise that he's caught me at it. I quickly snap myself out of my rude observations. 'How are you?'

'I'm good.' He nods at Mario, who promptly collects a beer from a fridge and delivers it to Drew. 'Oh, congratulations.' He raises his bottle and takes a swing.

I gape at him. He knows, too?

'Never thought I'd see the day.' He shakes his head.

'Yes!' Mario sings. 'A baby!'

My exhale of exasperation is loud, just as I intended it to be. I hope it reached the ears of my husband in the kitchen. 'Thank you,' is all I can think to say. That is until Jesse walks back into the bar, and I start mentally preparing my words as he walks toward me.

He gets in first, though. 'Just remember, none of our business.'

'What?' I frown at him as he gives me a warning look, which would be fine if I knew why I was receiving a warning. 'What are you talking about?'

He rolls his eyes and grabs his water from the bar, and then I see them.

Sam and Kate.

Chapter 16

'What the hell?' I jump up from my stool, only to be placed back on it before I can launch into my rant.

'Ava.' His tone is clipped and stern, not that I'll take any notice, but then it very quickly occurs to me that Sam is oblivious to Kate's straying ways, as is Jesse, so I aim my aggravation at my husband instead. 'Who else have you told?'

His warning face soon drops. 'A few.'

My lips purse. 'You've told everyone, haven't you?' I can't believe this man. My poor parents don't even know that they're going to be grandparents yet.

'I might have.'

'Jesse,' I moan, completely deflated.

His adorable face takes the edge off my irritation slightly, and then he shrugs guiltily, completely diminishing the rest of my exasperation. 'Can we visit my in-laws this weekend?' he asks quietly.

'Well, yes. We'd better before news travels and makes it to Cornwall before we do.'

He grins at me and stoops down to seal our mouths, his hand landing on my stomach and caressing my non-bump, while his tongue caresses my mouth. 'You make me a very happy man, Mrs Ward.'

'That's because I'm letting you trample all over me at the moment.'

'No, it's because you're beautiful, spirited, and all mine.'

'My man!' Sam's happy greeting distracts us from our

moment. He claps Jesse's shoulder and stands me up, looking me up and down. 'I can tell,' he says, staring at my tummy before lifting his sparkling blues. 'You've got that healthy glow about you.'

I actually laugh, and I'm dying to ask if any of these happy well-wishers know of the circumstances surrounding my pregnancy. 'That's funny because I mostly feel like shit,' I quip.

'Mouth, Ava!' Jesse snaps, but I snub him and move past Sam to take Kate's hand. 'Let's sit in the corner.' I smile sweetly and lead her away from the bar. Her pale face is cautious, and it bloody well should be, but she doesn't resist, letting me direct her away from the men to a little table in the quietest part of the busy bar.

I practically push her into a chair. 'Okay, Matthews. Spill.' We've got way past the *fun* excuses, so she'd better not even try. Not now that my brother is involved.

'So,' she begins, all chirpy and unfazed by my sharp order. 'It's official, then?'

'What?' I sit down opposite her.

'The baby.' She nods at my stomach. 'You're not getting rid of it.'

'Kate!' I blurt on a shocked whisper, her hard-hearted words hitting a nerve, and for the first time since all of this sank in, my hand rests on my tummy protectively. I feel untold guilt.

She smiles. 'Ava, I knew you'd never see that through.'

I'm a little speechless. 'Why didn't you tell me?'

'You needed to figure it out.' She looks across to the men, who are all chatting at the bar. 'I don't get him, but look at that face,' she says, smiling fondly at Jesse. 'I was a breath away from telling him, Ava.'

I knew she would be. I follow her eyes and see a very happy man, but he's always happy when we're together, or he's always happy when I'm conceding to him and his impossible ways. Jesse catches my eye and flips me a wink, sending a comforting, warm shot of contentment deep into my heart, but then I remember that I have a friend with some explaining to do.

'Hey!' I blurt across the table. 'It's time to explain.'

Kate gives me a tired look. I don't appreciate it. 'I've told your brother to go back to Australia.'

'Oh?' I lean forward, utterly rapt by this news. 'And will he?'

She shrugs. 'I don't know, but I haven't heard from him since Saturday.'

'I knew he was there.' I'm scowling. 'What happened?'

'Sam happened,' she answers quietly. 'We're only going to have sex with each other from now on.' Her face is somewhere between amusement and complete seriousness – amusement because I know my mouth has just fallen open, and seriousness because I know that despite her open-mindedness and blasé approach to her relationship with Sam, she really likes him, and that has never happened.

I close my gaping mouth. 'I'm happy for you.' I'm ecstatic, in fact. 'So why are you here then?'

'There are private suites.' She grins.

'Your bedroom is private!'

'It is, but it's not . . .' her grin widens, 'furnished suitably.'

My lips clamp shut, my eyes widen . . . and I laugh. Holy shit, the filthy little minx! I'm really laughing, tears and all. 'I can't believe you,' I snort. 'And who have you and Sam invited to play? Before you made this new rule, I mean.'

Her blue eyes dance in delight. 'A certain dashing, black-haired moody type.'

'No!'

She nods with wide eyes. 'Just as moody in the bedroom. It's hot!'

'Fuck off!'

'I will not!' She measures out at least eight inches between her palms. 'And he's fucking brilliant with it.'

'Oh God! Stop!' I blurt on a hushed snort.

She falls back in her chair and fights to keep her laughter under control. 'He might be good, but he can't match Sam for stamina and skill.' She sighs on a smile. 'And he doesn't make me laugh like that adorable twat.'

I can't help the huge smile invading my face. We have a breakthrough, and I'm so happy. 'You don't know how pleased I am to finally hear you say that.'

'Yes, I do,' Kate retorts drily, leaning across the table. 'Let me just tell you one more thing, and then we speak no more of Mr Moody, okay?'

'Ooh, this sounds interesting.' I mirror her pose, leaning in so our faces are only a few inches away from each other. 'Dish.'

'He has a piercing.'

'Nipple?' I ask, far too enthralled, but she shakes her head. I sit up straight and measure roughly eight inches between my palms. She nods. 'No!' I look over to the reserved, stand-offish Drew, my eyes automatically dropping to his crotch.

'You won't see it through his jeans, Ava,' Kate chuckles, and I'm off again, too. Uncontrollable, belly-clenching, might-pee-my-knickers laughter. Through my tears, I see Kate stick her tongue in her cheek. 'I nearly cracked a tooth.'

'Please!' I'm falling all over my chair. I'm helpless.

'Something funny?'

I battle to pull myself together and wipe my eyes, looking up at my Lord of the Sex Manor, who's staring down at his giggling wife with a bemused look plastered all over his face. 'No, nothing.' I bet he knew about this, which was why he persistently told me to mind my own business.

Jesse sits down next to me. 'Here's your dinner.' He signals to Pete, who's wandering over with a tray.

'Ooh, I'm starving.' I get myself comfy in my chair and smile a thanks when my steak is placed in front of me. 'Medium?' I ask.

Pete smiles fondly. 'Just to your liking, Ava.' He hands me a knife and fork, and then sets Jesse's plate down. 'Can I get you anything else, sir?'

'No, thanks, Pete.'

'I'll leave you to eat.' Kate makes to stand, but I wave my knife at her.

'It's fine. Sit down.'

She lowers to the chair again. 'Okay, you don't have to get all violent on me.'

Jesse's hand is suddenly wrapped around my wrist and pulling it down to the table.

I look at my knife, which is now safely set on the side of my plate. 'Sorry.' I start carving my way through my steak and sigh, long and satisfied, as I plunge a piece into my mouth.

'Good?' Jesse asks, and I look at him, finding a pleased beam around his fork.

'As always,' I confirm before returning my attention to Kate. But I quickly realise that our new company is preventing any further questioning. In fact, I can't think of anything to talk about now. All of the interesting stuff is now off the cards, even more so when Sam *and* Drew join us.

My chewing slows down, and I watch as Drew sits on one side of Kate, Sam on the other. I'll never look at them the same again, and damn if my eyes won't stop wandering into Drew's lap. A piercing? And a piercing there? I fail to prevent the small chuckle that spurts from my mouth around my mouthful of steak. Kate catches my eyes and sticks her tongue back in her cheek.

I choke.

I'm coughing and spluttering all over the place. Jesse's cutlery hits his plate and his hand lands on my back. He starts smacking me. 'Fucking hell, woman. Slow down.'

This doesn't help me in the slightest. I'm gasping for breath, trying to swallow down my half-chewed piece of meat and through the tears that have sprung into my eyes, I can see Sam and Drew staring at me with perplexed looks on their faces, and my delinquent best friend with the biggest smirk spread across her pale features. 'I'm okay,' I wheeze, coughing again to clear my throat. 'Went down the wrong way.'

'Here.' Jesse takes my knife and fork and replaces them with a glass of water. 'Drink.'

'Thank you.' I accept the glass and gulp it all down, striving to avoid Kate's gaze across the table, but failing miserably. Her mischievous mood is like a magnet to my vulnerable state. This time she's mimicking a blowjob, her fist casually wanking thin air in front of her mouth. I spit my water across the table, all over Drew and Sam, and I aim well because I catch Kate, too. Sam and Drew fly up from their chairs, but Kate stays exactly where she is, laughing.

'Fucking hell, Ava.' Jesse grabs a napkin. 'What the hell is wrong with you?' He starts dabbing at my mouth while I fall apart all over the place, hearing Sam and Drew cursing to themselves and Kate's continued giggles.

'I'm sorry,' I laugh. 'I'm so sorry.' I look at Sam and Drew, both patting themselves down with napkins. I refuse to look at Kate.

'Are you okay?' Jesse's concerned voice drags my attention back to him.

'I'm sorry,' I repeat. 'I don't know what's wrong with me.' I do, and the wicked cow is sitting opposite me, silently willing me to look at her. I don't. I take my cutlery back and turn my eyes down to my plate, and that's where I'll be keeping them until I've finished my dinner.

'Is this what pregnancy does to women?' Sam asks on a chuckle.

'It's better than mood swings,' Kate snickers.

'Yeah, let me know when they start,' Drew pipes up. 'I can handle being spat at, but I'm not up for a tongue lashing.'

Oh, good Lord! I can feel my shoulders starting to jerk up and down, and I know Kate is grinning at me again, but this time I control it. I keep my head down and work my way through the rest of my dinner.

'I take it you're done?' Jesse says to my empty plate.

'Hmm.' I fall back in my chair. 'That was heaven.'

'We can see.' Drew's eyebrows are raised as he watches Pete clear the table.

'Say your goodbyes, lady. It's getting late.' Jesse leans over the table and shakes hands with the boys before standing and giving Kate a peck on the cheek.

'Ring me,' I whisper to Kate as I lean in to kiss her, too.

'I will,' she sings.

As we exit the bar, Jesse looks down at me with enquiring eyes. 'Gathered yourself together now, Mrs Ward?'

I meet his stare with a questioning look. 'You knew, didn't you?'

'About what?'

'About Kate, Sam, and Drew.' I let him guide me through the entrance hall, but keep my eyes on him.

There's no denying the flash of surprise that flies across his face. 'Is that what you were laughing about? She told you?'

'Yes,' I confirm, wanting to add that she actually told me a lot more – a lot, *lot* more. 'Why didn't you tell me?'

'And give you something to get your knickers in a twist over?'

'I wouldn't have,' I announce confidently, as we crunch our way across the gravel. 'Shall I take my giant snowball?'

'No, you're coming with me.' I'm directed into the passenger seat of the DBS, but I don't complain.

He starts the engine and cruises sensibly down the driveway, and it's not until I feel his hand rest over mine that I realise mine is laid flat on my stomach. I don't need visual validation that he's looking at me, so I continue to watch the trees slowly passing the passenger window as I feel his fingers lace through mine and squeeze gently.

I smile to myself. This is just so right.

Chapter 17

There's that familiar whirring again as I come awake. I sit up and immediately feel gut-wrenchingly sick. Flopping back to my pillow on an enormous groan, I soon appreciate my error when my stomach turns, indicating that I haven't got time to lie here and determine just how crap I feel. I'm going to be sick.

I dive from the bed, straight into the bathroom, where I just about make it to the toilet before I decorate it with last night's dinner. 'No,' I whine to myself. It doesn't feel so right now. My body is completely rejecting my contented thoughts. I hug the toilet for an age, my head resting on my arms as I fight off the sweats and moan under my breath. 'Rubbish,' I grumble. 'Why are you doing this to me?' I look down at my stomach. 'You're going to be challenging like your father, aren't you?'

On a long, drawn-out sigh, I pull myself up and go to the bedroom, tugging on Jesse's discarded shirt from last night. I don't bother to try and make myself look better. I want him to see me suffering. I go downstairs and meet him as he rounds the corner from the gym, looking all spectacular in his running shorts with a towel draped across his naked shoulders and his hair a mess of damp loveliness. It makes me feel sicker.

'Oh, baby,' he mumbles sympathetically. 'Crap?'

'Terrible.' I try to pout, but my exhausted body won't allow it. I'm just standing in front of him lifelessly, my arms hanging limply by my sides.

He picks me up and carries me into the kitchen. 'I was going to ask why you're not naked.'

'Don't bother,' I grumble. 'I'll throw up on you.'

He laughs and sits me on the worktop, brushing my wild mane from my pasty face. 'You look beautiful.'

'Don't lie to me, Ward. I look like shit.'

'Ava,' he scorns me gently. I hear the front door open and close, and then the chirpy sounds of Cathy singing. All I have on is Jesse's shirt, but I can't even find the strength to be concerned by that, so I remain exactly where I am, unbothered and very unwell.

'Morning!' she sings at us as she places her huge carpet bag on the worktop. 'Oh dear. Whatever's the matter?'

'Ava's not feeling too good,' Jesse answers for me.

I scoff at his understatement and direct my forehead straight to his chest. I feel positively dull – dead, even.

'Oh, the dreaded morning sickness? It'll pass,' Cathy declares. She knows, too, then. I shouldn't be surprised and I'm not.

'Will it?' I garble into Jesse's chest. 'When?' I feel his hand stroking my back and his mouth in my hair, kissing me dotingly, but he remains silent.

'It depends. Boy, girl, mum, dad.' I hear her flick the kettle on. 'Some women have a few weeks of it, some struggle throughout the whole of their pregnancy.'

'Oh God,' I howl. 'Don't say that.'

'Shhh,' Jesse hushes me and increases the rubs of my back.

'Ginger!'

That one random word drags my splattered face from Jesse's wet torso. 'What?'

'Ginger!' she repeats, rooting through her bag. I look at Jesse, but he looks equally confused. 'You need ginger, dear.' She pulls out a pack of ginger biscuits. 'I came prepared.' She pushes Jesse from in front of me and opens the packet, presenting me with a biscuit. 'Have one every morning when you wake up. Works wonders! Eat.'

I wisely note that with Jesse hovering in the background, there's little point in refusing, so I take the biscuit and have a little nibble.

'It'll settle your stomach.' She gives me one of her warm smiles and cups my cheek with her hand. 'I'm so excited.'

I can't match her enthusiasm, not when I'm feeling like this, so I smile weakly and let Jesse place me gently on a barstool.

'The new boy gave me these.' She hands Jesse a pile of mail. 'Cute little bugger, isn't he?'

That makes me laugh, especially when Jesse lets out a disgusted snort and snatches the envelopes from Cathy's wrinkled fingers. 'He's very sweet,' I confirm, suddenly finding the energy to form a whole sentence.

I'm happily chatting away to Cathy, eating my breakfast and filling her in on my recent bouts of sickness, when it strikes me that Jesse has been silent for an eternity. He also hasn't moved. And his bagel is sitting untouched in front of him.

I push his plate towards him. 'Eat your breakfast.'

He doesn't move, nor does he acknowledge me.

'Jesse?' He looks like he's in a trance. 'Jesse, are you okay?'

He flips an envelope over and runs his eyes across it. So do I.

Jesse Ward
Private and Confidential

'What is that?' I ask.

He turns his eyes to mine. They are glazed and wary. I don't like it. 'Go upstairs.'

I frown. 'Why?'

'Don't make me ask you again, Ava.'

I recoil at his harsh tone, but this is one of those times when I know not to argue. He's starting to shake and though I have no idea what about, I'm certain it's not for Cathy's ears. I excuse myself, leaving the kitchen and walking quietly up the stairs, all of the time wondering what on earth is wrong with him. I don't get long to ponder it. He strides into the room, still holding the paper and envelope.

He's bubbling with anger. I can see it in the slight shaking of his hands and in the flash of black in his eyes. 'What the fuck is this?'

My eyes fall naturally to the paper that he's holding up. 'What is it?' I ask nervously.

He chucks the papers into the space between us. 'You were going to kill our baby?' He says it so calmly.

The ground falls away from under me, and I feel like I'm free-falling into a black hole of nothing. I can't face him. My eyes are burning up with hot tears as they trace every square inch of the floor at his feet. My brain has failed me, but even if it did give me some inspiration and load my mouth with the right words, I would be lying and he would know.

'Answer me!' he roars, and I jump, but I still can't bring myself to face him. I'm completely ashamed of myself, and having spent the last few days with Jesse and seeing how truly blissful he is, how caring and attentive he's being, the guilt couldn't get any worse. I thought about terminating this pregnancy. I thought about ridding my body of this baby. His baby. Our baby. I'm inexcusable. 'Ava, for fuck's sake!' He grasps the tops of my arms and bends to get his face in my line of sight, but I still evade his greens, not being able to bear facing what I know will be there. Contempt . . . disgust . . . disbelief. 'Damn it, look at me.'

I shake my head faintly, like the pathetic coward I am. He deserves an explanation, but I don't know where to begin. My mind has completely shut down, like I'm protecting myself from the inevitable that will be Jesse flying off the handle. He's pretty much there already.

My jaw is grasped harshly and pulled up so I'm forced to acknowledge him. My eyes are glassy with red-hot tears, but I can see with one hundred per cent clarity the hurt on his face. 'I'm sorry,' I sob. It's the only thing I can think to say. It's the only thing I should say. I *am* sorry for having such horrid thoughts.

His face crumbles before me, enflaming the guilt further. 'You've broken my fucking heart, Ava.' He drops me and stalks into the wardrobe, leaving me a pathetic form of shaking body parts. Sickness has moved aside and made way for crippling shame.

He appears again with a handful of clothes, but he doesn't stuff them in a bag or go to the bathroom to get anything else. He just walks out. My throat has closed off on me, so I can't even scream for him to stay. I'm paralysed on the spot, nothing working, except my eyes, which are releasing a relentless flow of tears. Then I hear the front door slam, and I find myself in a heap on the floor, silently sobbing to myself.

'Ava, dear?' Cathy's soft, warm voice is only just detectable through my heaving. 'Ava, my goodness, whatever is the matter?'

I feel her squidgy body against me, and I instinctively turn into her apron-coated body, wrapping my arms around her back.

'Oh dear, oh no.' She starts rocking me gently, shushing me and whispering quiet words in my ears. 'Oh, Ava, come on, dear. Tell me what's happened.'

I try to form some words, but it just results in me crying even harder. My compulsion to spill my guilt, to share my remorse, is just emphasising how incredibly selfishly I was thinking.

'Come on. Let me make you a cup of tea,' Cathy soothes, hauling her round body up from the floor before tugging on my arm, encouraging me to stand. I just about manage it, and then I'm cradled under her arm and guided down to the kitchen.

She hands me a hanky from the front of her apron, then sets about making a pot of tea. I watch her in silence, except for the odd judder of breath that escapes as I try to gain control of my shaky body and erratic breathing. I'm trying my very hardest, but it's inevitable for me to think about all of the other times

I've sent him crazy mad, except this time he *really* looked unhinged. This time I've really sent him over the edge.

Cathy sets a pot of tea down on the island and pours two cups, putting a few sugars in mine. 'You need the energy,' she says as she stirs, then picks it up and places it between both of my palms. 'Drink up, dear.' She takes her own, blows across the top, and a wave of steam streams through mid-air and disintegrates in front of me. I stare at it until it's gone, and I'm left gazing blankly at nothing. 'Now, tell me what's got my boy in such a pickle and you in this state?'

'I was thinking about having an abortion.' I don't want to see the look of horror that will have undoubtedly jumped onto the face of Jesse's sweet, innocent, wholesome housekeeper.

Her silence and the mug of tea that I can see in my peripheral vision, hovering at her lips, only confirms my thoughts. She's shocked, and having heard the words aloud, so am I. 'Oh,' she says simply. What else can she say?

I know what *I* should be saying. I should be explaining myself and the reasons, but not only do I feel like I've let Jesse down and trampled all over his happiness, I feel protective of him. I don't want Cathy to judge him if I tell her how I ended up pregnant, which is ludicrous. It's the only reason I considered a termination, and the fact that I didn't think I was ready, but the last few days have proved me wrong. Jesse has unearthed a deep feeling of hope, happiness and love for this baby growing inside me. Now the thought of ridding it from my body is absolutely abhorrent. I'm disgusted with myself.

I turn to Cathy. 'I would never have seen it through. I soon realised I was being stupid. I was just so shocked. I don't know how he's found out.' Now that I've calmed slightly, I'm wondering how he *does* actually know.

That paper. The envelope.

'Ava, he's obviously shocked. Give him time to come round. You're still pregnant and that's all that matters.'

I smile, but Cathy's words haven't made me feel any better. She doesn't know what happened the last time he walked out on me. 'Thank you for the tea, Cathy,' I say, getting down from the stool. 'I'd better get ready for work.'

Her wrinkled brow furrows, and she looks at my mug. 'But you've hardly touched it.'

I quickly scoop it up and take a few hot sips, eager to get upstairs where there's a piece of paper lying on the floor of the master suite, screaming for me to read it. I give Cathy a quick peck on the cheek before I escape the kitchen.

I run upstairs fast and pick the paper straight up. The letter is a scan appointment and stapled to it are pamphlets with information on abortion. As I lift my eyes to the top of the letter, I notice my name and address. No, not my address. It's Matt's address.

I gasp, throwing the paper at the wall on an infuriated yell. I'm so fucking stupid. I've not changed my address with the surgery. I've not changed my address with anyone. He must've been in his element to find this. At the risk of lashing out on the door or the wall or anything I can lay my hands on, I throw myself in the shower instead.

I'm still shaking with anger when I walk out of Lusso. John's here. He shrugs, and I shake my head. 'I'm not coming with you, John.' I fire my key fob at my Mini and start across the car park.

'Come on, girl. Let's not push it.' His voice is a low rumble, even though he's pleading with me.

'John, I'm sorry, but I'm driving myself today,' I insist in the firmest tone I can find. I stop and swing around to face the big friendly giant. He's standing at the hood of his Range Rover, holding his big arms out to me pleadingly. 'Is he okay?'

'No, he's gone motherfucking crazy, girl. What's going on?'

'Nothing,' I say quietly, feeling so thankful that John

is unaware of why Jesse has lost the plot. He's probably too ashamed of me to admit it to anyone, and he has every right to be.

'Nothing?' He laughs, but then his frightening face turns deadly serious. 'It's nothing to do with that Danish motherfucker?'

'No.' I shake my head.

'Are you okay?' His wraparounds are still firmly in place, but I know he's looking at my stomach. He thinks something has happened to the baby.

I nod, my hand naturally sliding across my dress and onto my navel. 'Fine, John.'

'Ava, girl, let me take you to work so I can at least tell him I got you there safely.' He gestures toward his shining heap of black metal.

It's hard for me to refuse John. He's thinking about Jesse, and I know that he cares about me. Under any other circumstances, I would, but I have an ex to deal with, and I can't wait to rip him to shreds. 'I'm sorry, John.' I jump in my car and dial Casey to open the gates. No code, no gate device. Anyone would think that he was trying to keep me prisoner. I leave a clearly exasperated John in the car park of Lusso and drive myself to work.

The look I flash all of my work colleagues the second I walk into the office makes them cautiously put their heads back down to work. I'm left to get on in peace, until Patrick perches on the edge of my new desk. 'Flower, update me. We've not spoken for a few days. My fault, I know.'

I don't need this. My brain is awash with everything except work, and I'm dreading the Mikael question. I'm living on borrowed time here, I realise that, but I can't broach this now. 'There's not a lot to report, really.' I continue composing the email that I've been working on for the last hour.

'Oh, everything's in order, then?'

'Yes, everything.' I sound short and terse, but I'm trying my best not to be.

'Are you okay, flower?' My boss's concern is clear, when he should actually be telling me to buck up and answer him properly.

I stop typing and turn to face my cuddly bear of an employer. 'I'm sorry. Yes, I'm fine, but I've got a heap of things I want to get done before the day's out.' I mentally applaud myself for blagging my way through that whole little speech.

'Excellent!' He laughs. 'I'll leave you to it, then. I'll be in my office.' He lifts from the desk and for the first time in four years it doesn't creak, but I still wince anyway.

'Ava, I'm sorry to bother you,' Sal says, sounding apprehensive.

'What's up, Sal?' I look up at our plain-Jane-turned-office-siren, and force a smile, until I see the plaid skirt. It's back, and I was so busy throwing cautionary looks at everyone when I arrived this morning that I hadn't noticed. I also hadn't noticed the lack of polished nails or scoop-neck top. Or the face that looks like it's just been dealt the most dreadful news. She's been dumped.

'Patrick has asked me to run through all of the invoices due for payment. Here's a list.' She hands me a printout of clients. 'He'd like you to gently remind your clients so we get the payments on time.'

I frown and cast my eyes over the spreadsheet. 'But they're not due yet. I can't remind them when they've not even forgotten.'

She shrugs. 'I'm just the messenger.'

'He's never asked us to do this before.'

'I'm just the messenger!' she snaps, and I recoil in my chair. Then she bursts into tears. I should be jumping up and soothing her, but I'm just sitting here, watching her wail all over my desk. She's snorting and sniffling, attracting the attention of everyone, including Patrick, who has ventured from his office to see what the commotion is all about, but he retreats hastily when he spots Sal in tears. Tom and Victoria sit tapping their pens, neither one of them rushing over to comfort Sal, so it's down to me to sort her out. I stand, taking Sal's elbow, and lead her into the toilets, where I stuff her hands full of tissue and wait silently for her to pull herself together.

After a good five minutes, she finally speaks. 'I hate men.'

My heart breaks a little for her. 'Things not too good between you and—'

'Don't say his name!' she blurts. 'I never want to hear it again.'

It's a good job because I can't remember it. 'Do you want to talk about it?'

She rubs away at her cheeks. There is no make-up transferring onto the tissue. She has well and truly returned to boring Sal.

'He's here, then he's not. He calls, then he doesn't. What does that mean?' She looks at me expectantly, like I might know the answer.

'You mean he's messing you around?'

'I'm on call when he wants, so yes. I sit around waiting for him to ring me, and when he does want to see me, it's lovely, but all he wants to talk about is me. My friends. My job.' She sniffles a bit more. 'When will he want to have sex?'

I cough on a laugh. 'You're worried because he hasn't tried to get you into bed?'

'Yes!' She collapses against the wall. 'I don't know how much more we can *talk*.'

'It's nice that he wants to get to know you, Sal. Too many men are after one thing.' Is she sexually frustrated? Or is she sexually clueless? Has she ever even had sex? I can't imagine it, and if I go by the deepening red of her cheeks, then I think I might have my answer. Sal's a virgin? Fucking hell! How old is she, anyway?

Victoria's head pops around the door, halting my intended

interrogation tactics. 'Ava, your phone's ringing off the hook.' She can't resist a quick inspection of herself in the mirror before she leaves.

'Sal, I'd better get that.' It might be Jesse, and he'll be beside himself. 'Will you be okay?'

She nods, sniffles and blows her nose before running her teary eyes all over me. 'Are you feeling better?' she asks.

'Yes,' I frown, forgetting my recent absences from work. I'm not ready to share my news yet.

'You don't look it. What's wrong, anyway?'

I search my brain for a feasible reason for my constant dashing to the toilet and bad moods. 'Tummy bug' is the best that I come up with.

'And married life? Good? Honeymoon?'

I stand for a few silent moments, wondering how this turned around on me and where her usual genuine tone has gone. 'All great,' I lie. 'Maybe we'll catch a holiday soon. Jesse's busy,' I lie again, but Sal is one of the few people in my life who hasn't worked out my bad habit, so I'm confident that I've not been rumbled. I leave her before she can pry any further and rush back to my desk, hoping to find a mass of missed calls from Jesse. I'm sorely disappointed. It's Ruth Quinn. I haven't spoken to her since I abandoned our meeting, and I'm not sure I want to, but the phone starts wailing again in my hand. I don't need to call her back. She's going to call me until I answer, and I can't avoid her for ever.

'Hello, Ruth.' I sound normal enough.

'Ava, how are you?' She sounds normal, too.

'Good, thank you.'

'I was waiting for you to call. Did you forget about me?' She laughs.

Actually, I did. Her lesbian crush has made way for other, more important, things. 'Not at all, Ruth. I was going to call you later.' I'm lying through my teeth.

'Oh, well I beat you to it. Can we meet tomorrow?'

I sink into my chair, my mind whizzing through a million excuses to put her off, but I know I have to face this head on. I can be professional. 'Sure. How about one-ish?'

'Perfect. I look forward to it. Bye!' She hangs up, and I hang my head, but soon snap it back up when Tom coughs.

He lowers his fashion specs to the end of his nose. 'She's been dumped?' he asks.

'It's complicated.' I brush him off and start to mark up some drawings, but something catches my attention outside the office.

My brother.

He's standing on the pavement looking into the office and after what seems like an age of us staring at each other, he pushes his way through the door. 'Hi,' he smiles.

My hand comes up in a little wave. 'Hi,' I whisper. We're in that awkward place again.

'Lunch?' he asks hopefully.

I smile and collect my bag, joining him at the front of the office. My simmering anger has cooled, but I'll re-stoke it later. Right now, I want to fix things with Dan, get things on track before he goes back to Australia. He's been a complete arsehole, but I can't hold grudges, not with my brother. 'Tom, I'll be back in an hour.'

'Hmmm,' he replies. I look back and see him staring dreamily at Dan. 'Bye, Ava's brother,' he croons, waving a limp wrist. I purse my lips and shake my head, especially when Dan's eyes widen in alarm and he starts walking backwards.

'Urm, yeah.' He coughs and straightens his shoulders in an obvious attempt to make himself look more manly. 'See ya.' His voice has gone deeper, too.

I laugh. 'Come on.' I push Dan through the door. 'You have an admirer.'

'Great,' he quips. 'Not that I'm homophobic or anything. You know, whatever tickles your fancy.'

'I think Tom wants to tickle *your* fancy.'

'Ava!' He looks at me in horror, but then breaks out in a grin. We're going to be okay.

Dan sets down the coffees and his sandwich, and I immediately tip three sachets of sugar into my cup, momentarily unaware that what I'm doing is completely out of character, until I look up and see Dan's brow all knitted as he watches me stir it in. 'Since when have you taken sugar in your coffee?'

I freeze mid-stir, frantically searching my brain for a viable excuse. We've not talked, but things are comfortable. Advising him that I'm pregnant will catapult us straight back to awkwardness. 'I'm knackered. I need a sugar hit.' It's the best I come up with.

'You look tired.' He sits down, eyeing me suspiciously.

'I am tired,' I admit. No hair twiddling needed.

'Why?'

'Work stress.' Half true, but now I'm fighting my hands to keep them on the table. 'So, you're okay?'

'Kate told me to take a leap, but I'm sure you know that already.' He unwraps his sandwich and takes a bite.

'You should never have gone there, and you really shouldn't have gone there on my wedding day.'

'Yeah, I was out of line. I'm sorry.' He reaches over and places his hand over mine. 'We've never had cross words.'

'I know. It was horrible.'

'It was my fault.'

'It was,' I grin, and he dips his finger in the froth of my coffee and flicks it at my nose. 'Hey!'

'Congratulations, anyway.' He smiles.

'What?' I blurt.

'I never congratulated you on your actual wedding day. I was too busy being an arsehole.'

'Oh, thanks.' The relief that takes hold makes me sag in my

chair, but just as quickly, I'm stiff as a board. Matt knows, and he has been doing a fantastic job of keeping my parents informed and up-to-date on my love life. He'll be like a pig in shit over this. That cooling fury has just boiled over into the realms of panic. I quickly disregard the possibility that he's called my parents already because if he had, then Dan would know, and he wouldn't be sitting opposite me happily chomping his way through a tuna melt. I need to get to Matt before he gets to my parents. Or I could just ring my parents and tell them myself. But I want to see them with Jesse. I want to do this bit right, make it special.

'You okay?' Dan's worried tone pulls me from yet more mental meltdown.

'Yeah, so when are you going back?'

'I need to check flights.' He dabs his mouth with his napkin and proceeds to launch into a proper apology speech.

I spend the next half-hour listening, nodding, yes-ing and no-ing, but I'm a million miles away from the conversation, my head struggling to decide on what to do for the best. Why hasn't Matt called them already?

'You'll get sacked.'

'Huh?' I glance down at my Rolex, noting it's two-fifteen. I'm already late, but I feel no sense of urgency to hurry back to the office. The only urgency I have is to resolve my little Matt issue once and for all. 'Yeah, I'd better shoot.'

'Nice watch.' He nods at my wrist.

'Wedding present.' I stand and brush myself down. 'Which way are you headed?'

'Back to Harvey's.'

'Okay, will you call me? I mean, you won't just leave, will you?'

His eyes warm and he stands before pulling me into him and giving me the biggest cuddle. 'Of course not.' He kisses my head. 'Let's not fall out again, okay?'

'Okay. Keep it in your trousers then.'

'I promise,' he assures me. 'Take care.'

'You, too.' I leave Dan, but instead of going to the office, I call in sick again and go to get my car. I'm walking on thin ice, but this really cannot wait. Matt won't be home, but he'll be at his office, and I really don't care where I verbally bash him.

Chapter 18

But he's not at his office, and he hasn't been for weeks. After driving across the city in mid-afternoon traffic, I pulled up at the firm where he works, only to be told that Matt lost his job a few weeks ago.

Despite his misfortune, though, I don't feel pity or concern. Nothing is going to damp down my resentment and contempt. I sit in my car and pull my phone from my bag, full of determination. I'll track him down.

It rings once. 'Ava?'

I was expecting a voice laced with smugness and deep satisfaction, so when I hear this one, which is broken and strained, I'm thrown completely. It takes me a few moments to piece a sentence together and when I do, it's not at all what I had intended to say. 'Are you okay?'

He laughs, but it's weak. 'Why don't you ask your husband?'

The back of my head hits the headrest of my seat, and I stare up at the ceiling of my car. I should have predicted this. 'How bad?'

'Oh, just a couple of broken ribs and a black eye. Your husband knows how to do a job properly, I'll give him that.'

'Why did you do it?'

'Because I want everything he has with you. Or I did. Kate took great pleasure in telling me you were marrying him, and then that letter fell on my doormat and I wondered why you would be seeking an abortion if you were married, so I guessed he didn't know. I took a chance. Why are you having an abortion?'

'I'm not.'

'Then why—'

'Because I was shocked!' I shout defensively. I'm not explaining myself to him. An uncomfortable silence falls down the line, but I'm the first to break it. 'I think this is where you give up, Matt.'

'Well I won't be setting myself up for another beating from your unhinged husband. Not even *you* are worth the pain I'm in right now. Oh, and don't worry about Elizabeth and Joseph. I've been given a little taste of what will happen if I share your news. Can I suggest that you get your address changed so I don't receive any of your shit in the future?' He hangs up, and I stare down at my phone in disbelief. I didn't blast him with half of the words I've been mentally preparing throughout the day. I didn't get to spit my hatred at him, or even slap his face. Despite that, though, it's one more thing ticked off my list of *issues*. Sarah has apologised, for what it's worth, but she's gone and that's all that matters. Kate and Sam are together, and Kate and Dan are not. I've made friends with my brother, and Matt has been trampled. But what I really need to be doing is finding my husband and making friends with him. I chuck my phone on the passenger seat and make my way back to the city.

I feel like I'm on a cleansing mission, and it's right now that I decide to tackle the final issue tomorrow. Mikael. I've still not heard from him, but I'll call him. I'll beat him to the punch. I'm full of determination to eradicate this final *issue*. There's nothing he can say, nothing he can tell me, so I don't know what the point of our *meeting* will be.

As I'm driving over London Bridge, I glance up to my rear-view mirror and spot a familiar car. Jesse's car. He's dipping in and out of the traffic in his usual haphazard style, overtaking and generally causing mayhem in his wake. I spend a few moments flicking my eyes between the road and my rear-view mirror, the potential of what I'm about to face slowly settling in the pit of my stomach. He's been following me, which means he has followed me to Matt's office, which means he is going to hit the fucking roof. I'm not going to try and convince myself that Jesse wouldn't know where Matt worked.

I know it's him, but that doesn't stop me taking a right, and then a right, and then a right again, bringing me back to where I started, and as I knew it would be, the DBS is still tailing me a few cars behind. I feel around on the seat for my phone and stab at the buttons.

'Yes?' he spits, curt and clipped.

'Nice drive?' I ask.

'What?'

'Are you having a nice drive?' I repeat myself, this time the words pushed through clenched teeth.

'Ava, what the fuck are you talking about? And when I send John to fetch you, get in his fucking car.'

I glance back up to my rear-view mirror, just to check I'm not imagining things. I'm not. 'I'm talking about you following me.'

'What?' he yells impatiently. 'Ava, I haven't got time for fuck-ing riddles.'

'I'm not talking in riddles, Jesse. Why the hell are you fol-lowing me?'

'I'm not following you, Ava.'

'So I suppose there are hundreds of Aston Martins driving around London, and one just *happens* to be following me.'

Silence falls down the phone line, then his heavy breathing starts. 'You're driving?'

'Yes!' I shriek. 'I'm driving around in bloody circles, and you're following me. You'd make a shit detective!'

'My car's following you?'

'Yes!' I actually hit my steering wheel in a temper.

'Ava, baby, I'm not driving my car. I'm at Lusso.' He doesn't sound impatient any more. He sounds concerned.

I take another look in my mirror and find the DBS is now only one car behind me, drifting in and out of my sight. 'But it's your car,' I say quietly.

'Fuck!' he roars, and I instinctively pull the phone away from my ear. 'John!'

'Jesse? What's going on?' My stomach is suddenly a knot of panic at his reaction.

'My car's been stolen.'

'Stolen?'

'Where are you?' he asks.

Frantically looking around, I search for something familiar. 'I'm on the Embankment, driving towards the city.'

'John! The Embankment. City bound. Call her in two.' I hear car doors closing. 'Baby, listen to me. Just keep driving, okay?'

'Okay,' I agree, my earlier anger giving way to pure fear.

'I've got to put the phone down now.'

'I don't want you to,' I murmur. 'Stay on the phone, please.'

'Ava, I've got to put the phone down. John's going to call you as soon as I hang up. Put it on loudspeaker and place it in your lap so you can concentrate. Understand?'

He's trying to stay calm, but he's failing to conceal his distress. It's thick in his husky voice, and I'm frightened by it.

'Ava, baby. Tell me you understand!'

'I understand,' I whisper, and then the distinctive roar of a motorbike pours down the line. One of Jesse's bikes. The phone goes dead.

My heart has gone berserk and is punching its way through my chest, my hand is visibly shaking on the wheel and my eyes are glazing over with panic-fuelled tears. When my phone starts ringing, I fumble with the keypad until I manage to connect the call.

'John?'

'Hey, girl. Are you on hands-free?'

'No, wait.' I quickly place the call on loudspeaker before dropping my phone into my lap and replacing my hand on the wheel, gripping harder to try and stop the shakes. 'I'm done. I've done it.'

"S'all good, girl.' He sounds so calm. 'Just take a quick peek and tell me how far back Jesse's car is.'

I do as I'm told. 'It's only one car behind.'

He hums a little. 'I want you to drive as slowly as possible, without looking suspicious. Just below the limit, you got it?'

I instantly ease off the accelerator a little. 'Okay.'

'Good girl. Now, tell me exactly where you are.'

I glance to my left. 'I'm approaching Millennium Bridge.'

'That's good,' he muses. 'Concentrate on the road now.'

'Okay. Why are you so calm?' An air of serenity is travelling down the line and calming me, which is crazy, considering the source of it – a giant, mean-looking, wraparound-wearing black man, who oozes terror.

'One crazy motherfucker is enough, don't you think?'

I manage a small smile through my growing fear. 'Yes.'

'Now, tell me how you've been today.' He asks it like we're having a perfectly normal conversation.

'Fine. I've been fine.' What sort of question is that when I'm being chased down in a car?

'He'll be an extraordinary daddy, Ava.' John's softly spoken words seep from the phone and seem to linger in the closed air around me, briefly pulling me away from this awful situation and putting a smile on my face.

'I know.' I can't see John, but if I could, I know I would see that gold tooth.

'So you two are going to stop fucking about and sort this shit out?' He sounds like a father, and my fondness grows for the burly beast of a man.

'Yes,' I agree. 'Oh!' I'm suddenly thrust forward in my seat and my seatbelt locks, pulling straight across my collarbone and burning the skin beneath my dress.

'Ava?' John's voice is distant and muffled, and I can't work out why. 'Ava, girl!'

'John?' I feel around on my lap, but there's nothing. 'John!'

Bang!

I'm jolted forward again, my arms instinctively locking on the wheel and sending a sharp flash of pain straight up to my shoulders. 'Shit!' I look in the rear-view mirror and freeze when I see the DBS now directly behind me, but it's quite a way back. 'John?' I yell. 'John, can you hear me?' My eyes are moving constantly from the road ahead to the mirror, back and forth, and each time they're back on the mirror, Jesse's car is closer. I attempt to step on the accelerator, but all body functions are failing me, except my eyes which are watching in horror as the DBS gains on me.

Bang!

'No!' I cry, as I swerve and struggle to regain control of my Mini. I don't stand a chance. My brain is being inundated by a million different orders, but I can't gather any cognitive thought to establish my best move. I straighten up my car to be immediately hit again. Now I'm crying. My emotions are taking hold, telling me that I should be crying, that I should be frightened. And I am. I'm terrified.

Crash!

This time I lose complete control. I scream as the wheel starts spinning of its own accord, and I'm suddenly travelling sideways down the carriageway. Then I'm hit again and facing forward once more. I frantically grapple with the steering wheel, but it's got a mind of its own and in a total panic, I yank at the handbrake. I'm not sure what happens next, but I'm thrown forward and back again, and dizzy, blurred images whirl past the windows – buildings, people and cars all spinning around me until eventually a loud crash rings through my ears, my body jolts violently, and my eyes close. I don't know where I am. But I'm still. I'm not moving any more.

I flex my neck on a groan and open my eyes to look out of the window. The traffic has stopped. All of it. And people are getting out of their cars and wandering over to me. I shuffle my legs and move my arms, quickly noting that I have feeling in all of them, before I unclip my belt and let myself out of my car. People are walking towards me, but I'm walking away. I'm walking towards the DBS, which is sitting a few yards away, the engine still purring. I should be running in the other direction, but I'm not. I'm running towards it. The desperate need to know who would do this has suddenly flattened my fear. Drugged, threatened, and now this? I'm only a few yards away when the engine starts revving, like some sort of eerie fucked-up threat. It doesn't stop me. What does, though, is the sound of a high-powered machine getting louder and louder. I halt and stand rooted to the spot as I watch the DBS screech off, and then John's Range Rover go sailing past in pursuit. This isn't happening to me. I want to pinch myself, slap myself across the face, or, at the very least, wake up. I slowly turn when that high-powered machine sounds like it's speeding around in my head. He skids to a stop and throws his bike down before sprinting towards me, no leathers, no helmet, just some faded jeans and a plain black T-shirt protecting his body. I can't move. All I can do is wait for him to reach me, and he soon does, his hands starting to work fast strokes all over my stunned face as I stare blankly into his green eyes, which are drowned in pure terror.

'Ava? Jesus, baby.' I'm pulled into his chest, one hand cradling the back of my head, the other wrapped around my waist to hold me tight. I want to hold him, I need to hold him, but nothing is happening when I tell it to happen. I hear Jesse's phone ringing and he releases my head to fish around in his pocket. 'John?'

Being buried under Jesse's chin, I can hear the low rumble of John's pissed-off voice, and I distinctly hear him asking why the fuck he has to own such a stupidly fast motherfucking car.

'Where are you?' Jesse asks, kissing my head between words.

This time I can't hear him. All I can hear are sirens – coming from every direction are sirens. I pull out of Jesse's chest and find a mass of police cars and two ambulances. Just for me? But then I notice a crumpled heap of a car, and it's not mine. Neither is the one wrapped around a lamp-post nearby. I search through the chaos of people and abandoned cars and spot my Mini crunched up against some railings that are separating the road from the pavement. I shudder.

'John, don't stop until you've found out who's in my fucking car.' Jesse hangs up and stuffs his phone back in his pocket. He pulls at my chin. 'Look at me, baby.'

I gaze up at him. 'Where's your helmet?'

He takes a deep breath and claps my cheeks in his palms. 'Fucking hell.' He kisses me hard on the lips. 'Why do you refuse to play ball?' He kisses my nose, my lips, my eyes, my cheeks. 'I sent John to get you, Ava. Why didn't you let him take you to work?'

'Because I wanted to shred Matt,' I admit. 'But you beat me to it.'

'I was so angry, Ava.'

'I would never have seen it through. I wouldn't have killed our baby.' I know I need to say this, at the very least.

'Shhh.' He continues placing his lips all over my face and my arms finally lift to hold him tightly. I never want to let go.

'Excuse me, sir.' The strange voice pulls our attention to the side, where a policeman is standing. 'Is the young lady okay?'

Jesse looks back at me and starts doing an all over visual assessment. 'I don't know. Are you okay?'

'I'm fine.' I smile awkwardly.

'You're very lucky. Shall we get you checked over before we

run through some questions?' The copper smiles and signals over to an ambulance.

I feel all dramatic and a bit of a bother. 'I feel fine, honestly.'

Jesse growls and tosses me a fierce scowl. 'I'm going to take that *fine* in my palm and slap you all over the arse with it.'

'I *am* fine.' My car's not, though. It looks terrible.

Jesse makes a meal of exhaling and flopping his head back. 'Ava, don't defy me on this, please. I have no problem with pinning you down in the ambulance so they can confirm you're okay.' His head drops back down. 'Are you going the easy way, or the hard way?'

'I'll go,' I agree quietly. I'll do anything he says. I free myself from his chest. 'My bag.'

'I'll get it.' He sprints away.

'My phone's on the floor!' I call after him, but he just waves his arm over his head to acknowledge that he's heard. He's back in seconds, and the policeman leads us to the ambulance, pushing his way through the growing crowds of pedestrians.

A paramedic on the back puts his hand out to me, but I don't get the chance to grasp it. I'm lifted and placed in the white van. 'Thank you.' I smile down at Jesse and watch as the copper gets a pad and pen from his pocket.

'Sir, while she's being taken care of, do you mind answering a few questions?'

'Yes, I do. You'll have to wait.'

'Sir, I'd like to ask you a few questions.' The policeman isn't asking nicely this time.

Jesse turns his full body into him, the edge of threat clear in his stance. 'My wife and child are in the back of that ambulance and the only way you're going to stop me from seeing to them is if I'm dead.' He steps back and holds his hands out to the side. 'So fucking shoot me.'

The policeman looks up at me, and I smile apologetically. The last thing I need is Jesse being arrested. I don't know whether it's put down to emotions running high, but the copper nods and gestures for Jesse to join me. My trampling Lord's glower is still fixed to his face as he turns back towards me, but it soon falls away. His face is level with my stomach, but his eyes are currently dropped and looking at my bare legs.

Reaching forward, he runs his finger up the inside of my calf. 'Baby, you're cut.'

I glance down. 'Where?' I can't feel anything. I pull at my dress, hitching it higher, but there is no sign of any cut. Higher it goes; still more blood but no cut. I look at Jesse in confusion, but he's frozen as he watches me searching for the source of the blood. His eyes lift to mine. They are wide and uneasy. It doesn't sit well. I start shaking my head as he moves forward, taking my dress up as far as it can go.

There is no cut.

The blood is coming from my knickers.

'No!' I cry out, realisation crashing into me like a tornado.

'Oh Jesus.' He yanks the hem of my dress back down and jumps up to the ambulance, engulfing me in his arms. 'Fucking hell, no.'

'Sir?'

'Hospital. Now!'

I'm placed on a gurney gently and hear the slamming of metal doors, making me jump. I turn into his chest, clutching at his T-shirt and hiding my face from him. 'I'm sorry.'

'Shut up, Ava.' He grabs the back of my hair and pulls me out. His eyes are a cloud of green. 'Please, just shut up.' His thumb drags under my eye, collecting some tears. 'I love you.'

This is my punishment. This is my penance for having such toxic thoughts. I deserve it, but Jesse doesn't. He deserves the happiness I know this baby would've given him. It's an extension of me. I've destroyed his dream. I should have seen things clearer sooner. I should have changed my address at the surgery. I should have let John take me to work. I shouldn't have gone to

Matt's office. There are so many things I have and haven't done that could have changed how things are playing out.

My shame is eating away at me and it will for the rest of my life. It hasn't happened how I had stupidly first thought, but the end result is the same. I've killed our baby.

Chapter 19

The silence surrounding us is painful. The whole way in the ambulance, I sobbed and Jesse constantly told me how much he loves me. I can't help but think it's simply because he doesn't know what else to say. There's no comfort or reassurance coming from those three words. He hasn't said it doesn't matter because I know it does. He hasn't said it's not my fault because I know it is. He hasn't said that we'll be fine, either, and I don't know if we will be. Just when I was beginning to see light at the end of the never-ending tunnel of issues, we're hit with the worst kind of devastation – a damage that can't be fixed. He'll resent me for ever.

He carries me from the ambulance, rejecting the wheelchair that's brought out by a nurse, and silently follows the doctor down the busy corridor, all of the time looking straight ahead and flipping one word answers to anyone who asks him questions. I can't feel anything except Jesse's thundering heartbeat pulsing into me.

After what seems like an eternity of gently bobbing up and down in Jesse's arms, I'm lowered onto a huge hospital bed in a private room. He's gentle and all of his actions are tender and loving as he strokes my hair, props my head up slightly, and covers my legs with the thin sheet that's lying at the foot of the bed. But there are still no comforting or reassuring words.

We're closed in from every direction by machines and medical equipment. A nurse stays, but the ambulance men leave after giving a brief rundown on me, what has happened, and the observations they have already performed on the way to the hospital. The nurse takes notes, sticks things in my ear and holds things to my chest. She asks questions, and I answer quietly, but the whole time, I keep my eyes on Jesse, who's sitting in a chair with his face in his palms.

The nurse pulls my reluctant eyes away from my grieving husband when she hands me a gown. She smiles. It's a sympathetic smile. Then she leaves the room. I just hold it for a while, until so much time has passed, I think it could be next week, or even next year. I want it to be next year. Will this crippling pain and guilt be gone by next year?

I finally slide myself to the side of the bed, my back to Jesse, and reach around to unzip my dress and stand. In the quiet, I hear him move.

'Let me,' he says softly. He's in front of me, but my stinging eyes remain on the floor.

'It's okay. I can manage.'

'You probably can.' He pulls my dress up over my head. 'But it's my job and I'd like to keep it.'

My chin starts to tremble as I fight to restrain the persistent tears. 'Thank you,' I whisper, still keeping my welling eyes from his line of sight.

It's an impossible task, especially when he bends and pushes his face up into my neck, forcing my face up to his. 'Don't thank me for looking after you, Ava. It's what I've been put on this earth to do. It's what keeps me here.'

'I've ruined everything. I've lost your dream.'

He pushes me down onto the bed and kneels in front of me. 'My dream is you, Ava. Day and night, just you.' My vision is hazy and blurred, but I can clearly see the tears trickling from his green eyes. 'I can manage without anything, but never you. Not ever. Don't look like this, please. Don't look like you think it's the end. It's never the end for us. Nothing will break us, Ava. Do you understand me?'

I nod through my quiet weeping, unable to form words or even say them if I could.

He brushes the back of his hand roughly across his cheeks. 'We let these people tell us you're going to be okay, and then we go home to be together.'

I nod again.

'Tell me you love me.'

A loud sob spills from my mouth and my arms find his shoulders and pull him into me. 'I need you.'

'I need you, too,' he whispers. His hands all over my back, despite being cool and a little shaky, give me all of the comfort I need. We'll be okay. Heartbroken, but okay. 'Let me get you into this gown.'

I'm pulled up from the bed, but he remains kneeling and starts peeling my bloodstained underwear away from my body. I can't look. I clench my eyes shut and feel instead of see my knickers being slowly drawn down my thighs. The familiar feel of his fingertip tapping my ankle prompts me to step out, but all of the time I keep my eyes clenched shut. For the briefest of moments, I know he has moved from in front of me, and then I hear a tap running before he's back and gently sweeping a wet cloth up the inside of my thigh. My heart constricts painfully in my chest.

'Arms.' Jesse's soft instruction encourages me to open my eyes. I find him holding the gown in front of me. My arms thread through, and I'm turned so he can fasten it. 'Up you get,' he orders. I shift myself back into position just as there's a knock on the door. Jesse calls an okay.

The same nurse has returned, but this time she has a male doctor with her. He shuts the door softly and nods at Jesse, who is suddenly more alert, and I know why.

The doctor has a fiddle with the machine at the side of me, and then perches on the edge of the bed. 'How are you feeling, Ava?' he asks.

'Fine.' The one word that Jesse has threatened to spank my arse with just slips right out. 'I'm okay, thank you.'

'Okay. No aches or pains, cuts or bruises?'

'No, nothing.'

He smiles mildly and folds back the sheet that's covering my stomach. 'Let's see what's going on. Would you like to pull the gown up so I can feel your tummy?'

Even now, when we are in the darkest most desperate place, I can feel Jesse's tension at the prospect of another man laying his hands on me. I glance over to him and give pleading eyes, but he just shakes his head. 'I might step outside,' he says quietly, stepping back towards the door.

'Don't you dare!' I cry. 'Don't you dare leave me!' I know he's struggling, but he can overcome that now. He *has* to overcome that now.

The doctor looks between us, a little baffled, and waits for Jesse to take the initiative and join me at the bed. It feels like an eternity, but then he inhales a long, controlled gathering of strength and comes to sit next to me. My hand is picked up and encased in both of his before he brings the bundle to his chest and drops his head to it. He can't watch.

I'm flanked on both sides, one man pushing my gown up and feeling around on my stomach, the other breathing deeply and squeezing my hand. I just rest my head back and stare up at the ceiling, wishing this could be over so Jesse can take me home and we can start painfully processing what has happened.

'This will be a little chilly,' the doctor says as he squirts some gel on my abdomen. He rolls the device around while he watches the screen, and the small room is instantly filled with a wishy-washy distortion of crackling and whirring. He hums and makes odd noises as he flicks switches with his spare hand and pushes the grey contraption firmly into my stomach. It doesn't hurt. Nothing hurts because I'm still totally numb. And then he stops moving his hand and stops flicking buttons on the huge machine. I sneak a peek at the doctor, finding him looking intently at the screen. He eventually looks at me. 'Everything is okay, Ava.'

'I'm sorry?' I whisper. My dying heart has suddenly roused and is climbing up to my throat, set on choking me with shock.

'Everything is okay. Light bleeding in early pregnancy can be perfectly normal, but given the circumstances, it's wise for us to be cautious.'

I can feel Jesse's hands tightening around mine, slowly constricting until I hiss a little with pain. He eases off immediately and slowly raises his head until his eyes find mine. They are wide green pools of shock and his cheeks are drenched. I shake my head mildly, like out of all the horror today had brought, it's this bit that I must be dreaming about. We're both just staring at each other, neither one of us knowing how to handle this news. He goes to speak, but nothing comes out. I go to say something, too, but no words materialise.

He stands up, sits back down, and then stands again, letting go of my hand. 'Ava's still pregnant? She's ... she's ... there's ... we're ...'

The doctor laughs a little. 'Yes, Ava is still pregnant, Mr Ward. Sit down, I'll show you.'

Jesse turns stunned eyes to me briefly before directing them towards the monitor of the machine. 'I'll stand, if you don't mind. I need to feel my legs.' He leans over the bed slightly, his eyes squinting. 'I don't see anything.'

It's hard, but I pull my eyes away from my dazed husband and take a look myself, but all I can see is a black and white jumble of fuzz. The doctor points at the screen. 'There, look. Two perfect heartbeats.'

I frown to myself. Two heartbeats?

Jesse recoils and almost scowls at the doctor. 'My baby has two hearts?'

The doctor laughs and turns amused eyes onto us. 'No, Mr

Ward. Each of your babies has one heart, and both are beating just fine.'

Jesse's mouth falls open and he starts walking backwards until the backs of his legs hit a chair and he collapses, his arse colliding loudly with the seat. 'I'm sorry, say that again,' he murmurs.

The doctor chuckles. He finds this funny? I don't. I've gone from having one baby, to having no baby, to having two babies? At least, that's what I think he's saying. The doctor turns his body fully to Jesse. 'Mr Ward. Let me put this into plain English, if it will help.'

'Please,' Jesse whispers.

'Your wife is expecting twins.'

'Oh fuck,' he gulps. 'I had a feeling you were going to say that.' He looks at me, but if he's expecting any words, a facial expression, or anything, then he's looking in vain. Twins?

'About six weeks, I would say.'

Yes, I'm stunned, but I know damn well that *that's* impossible. I had a period five or so weeks ago. I can't be any more than four weeks. 'I'm sorry, that can't be right. I've had a period within that time and was on the pill previous to that.' He doesn't need to know that I missed a few here and there. It's irrelevant now.

'You had a period?' he asks.

'Yes!'

'That's not unusual,' he flips casually. 'Let me do some measurements.'

It's not? I glance across at Jesse warily, seeing nothing but a lean physique frozen in place. He looks like he's been fossilised. Is he so excited now? I don't know, but he had better get used to it. This is revenge at its best. He didn't bargain on this, and if I wasn't so shell-shocked, then I think I'd be smug. My challenging, neurotic ex-playboy has a challenge on his hands, and it's called a hormone-frenzied wife and two screaming babies. I actually smile to myself as I lie back on the pillow and drift off to a fantasyland of chaos, where Jesse is pulling his hair out while I look on, smiling as our two toddlers run around his ankles, vying for his attention – a fantasyland that's going to be all too real very soon. My Lord is going to have some stiff competition in the demanding department because one thing I wholeheartedly wish for most is that both of these babies have every irritating trait that he does. I hope they take after their father, and I hope they challenge him every day for the rest of his life. I look at his motionless frame and smile on the inside. I also hope they are just like him because he's beautiful and bursting at the seams with pure, intense love. Love for me, and love for our babies. I've just landed softly on Central Jesse Cloud Nine.

After he told me to take it easy for a day or two, the doctor printed off a picture and sent us on our way. We strolled out of the hospital hand in hand, with Jesse holding the little black and white scan picture gently at the corner. I guided him the whole way because he was too rapt by the photo to look where he was going. John picked us up and dropped us at Lusso, and laughed the hardest I'd ever seen when I told him the news that we'd just received. I told him because Jesse still wasn't talking, not even to ask John if he caught the DBS. So I did. He lost the motherfucking thing.

We passed Casey, who looked a little shocked that he wasn't growled at, and I directed Jesse into the elevator and just about coaxed the new code from him. He didn't tell me it. He just absent-mindedly punched in the four digits.

3,2,1,0.

We're now in the kitchen, Jesse slumped on the stool, still staring at the picture, and me sipping a glass of water, waiting for him to spring back to life. I'll give him half an hour, then I'll chuck some cold water over him.

I go upstairs, call Kate, and listen to her gasp in shock – first at the news of my dramatic car chase, then at the news of twins. I take a shower and dry my hair, then throw on my Thai fisherman pants, smiling when I realise that these will grow with my belly.

When I get back downstairs, Jesse is still sitting motionless at the island, staring at the scan picture.

Feeling a little frustrated, I sit next to him and pull his face to mine. 'Are you going to speak anytime soon?'

His eyes roam all over my face for so long, until they eventually land on mine. 'I can't fucking breathe, Ava.'

'I'm shocked, too,' I admit, although clearly not as shocked as he is.

His lip slowly slips through his teeth, which seem to clamp down severely, his cogs firing into action in his head. It makes me immediately wary.

He speaks in a near whisper. 'I was a twin.'

Chapter 20

I shrink back on my stool and drop his chin, and for the millionth time in one day, I can't form any words. Nothing. Absolutely zero inspiration is coming to me. I'm more shocked now than at any other point during this long day.

He smiles mildly. 'My spirited girl is speechless.'

I am. Well and truly floored, in fact. You would think I'd be used to shock and surprise from this man, but no, he gets me every bloody time.

Reaching up, he strokes my cheek gently and slides his hand onto my neck, circling his thumb on my throat softly. 'Have a bath with me,' he says quietly, rising from the stool and pulling me up. 'I need to be with you.'

I'm lifted up to his body, my arms sliding around his shoulders and my legs finding their favourite place as he walks us upstairs. It takes no thought or any mental encouragement for my lips to find his neck and kiss him. Just kiss him and smell him and feel him, all of his minty freshness and all of his hard edges comforting me deeply. I'm not going to press him for information. He could've easily used our recent news as the reason for his shock and I would have believed him, but he didn't. He's shared something, a part of himself. He's confessed that he *was* a twin, not that he *is* a twin. And now his wife is pregnant with twins, and it has clearly unearthed something from deep within him.

He places me on the vanity unit in the bathroom and sets about his usual bath-time routine of testing the temperature, pouring in the bath soak and swishing to instigate some bubbles. Then he returns to me once he's done and the bath is full. He reaches to pull my vest top up, resting his lips on mine as he does, and we fall straight into a slow massaging of each other's tongues as he works my clothing, only pulling away briefly to get my top past my face before we find ourselves again and continue with our sweet, lingering kiss. It's a special kiss. A really special one, and I delay pulling off his T-shirt, just so I don't have to leave his lips. This kiss is not leading to an intense lovemaking session. This kiss is leading to him sharing something painful. Right now, when he's pouring his love into me through our kiss, it's his way of finding the strength to tell me his story. It's his way of ensuring that I'm real before he offloads a past of pain.

My hands find their way under his T-shirt and to the hard, rippling waves of his stomach. 'Take it off,' he says between our mouths. 'Please, take away everything between us.'

His request makes me falter slightly, but when his lips press a little harder, I find my flow again. That wasn't just a plea to remove his clothes. I work fast. The urgency to get his bare skin on mine is very quickly my top priority, so I drop his mouth and pull his shirt up, then start on his jeans, pushing them down his legs so he can kick them off. I'm pulled down from the unit, my Thai pants are removed and my lace knickers are drawn down my thighs. I don't miss the quick check for blood. There is none. Our babies are okay. I'm lifted to him, my hands sliding straight into his hair and my lips falling straight to his mouth as he steps into the bath with me wrapped around him and lowers to his knees.

'Is the water okay?' he mumbles as I settle on his thighs.

'Fine.' I press my body into his, my breasts flattening against his chest, my elbows resting on his shoulders while my hands roam all over his head and my lips work relentlessly but softly.

'Always fine,' he whispers.

'Always perfect if I have you.'

'You have me.' His fingers thread through my hair and grip before he pulls me back. 'You do know that, don't you?'

'You married me. Of course I know.'

He shakes his head and grabs my hand, pulling off my wedding ring and holding it up. 'Do you think *this* signifies my love for you?'

'Yes,' I admit quietly.

He smiles a little, as if I just don't get it. I don't. 'Then we should get these diamonds removed and have it re-encrusted with my heart.' He slowly slides it back onto my finger, and I dissolve in his lap, reaching forward and resting my palm on his chest.

'I like your heart exactly where it is.' Leaning down, I place my lips on his skin. 'I like how it swells when you look at me.'

'Just for you, baby.' He pushes our mouths together and spends a few moments reinforcing exactly that. 'Let me bathe you,' he mumbles, working his lips down to my throat. 'Turn around for me.'

I begrudgingly let him shift me from his lap so he can come off his knees and sit back before he arranges me between his thighs and starts with his bathing routine. I sigh contentedly but say nothing. And I don't plan on instigating tub-talk, either. Not this time. This is for him to lead. Of course, my curious mind has gone into overdrive, but I won't be the first one to break the comfortable silence. My Lord's past holds no significance to our future. He has said that before and now, more than ever, I know just what he meant.

'Are you fine?' he asks, working the sponge around the base of my neck.

I smile down into the water. 'I'm okay.'

I watch the water ripple, the little waves lapping around me as he moves in closer and rests his mouth at my ear. 'I'm a little worried about my defiant temptress,' he whispers.

I don't want to come over all hot and tingly, but it's something I'll never prevent when he's near, let alone breathing in my ear. I push my cheek into him. 'Why?'

'Because she's too quiet when there's information to be had.' He kisses my temple and lies back, taking me with him.

'If you want to tell me, then you will.'

His chest jolts beneath me on a silent laugh. 'I'm not sure I like what pregnancy is doing to my girl.' His hands rest on my stomach. 'First of all, she's developed a phobia of my cock in her mouth.' He lifts his hips into my lower back, as if demonstrating what I'm missing. I know exactly what I'm missing, and I'm not liking it. 'And secondly, she's not blessing me with her forceful demands for intelligence.'

I shrug nonchalantly. 'My Lord isn't blessing me with his wide range of expert fuckings, so we're even, aren't we?'

He laughs, and I'm a little annoyed that I'm not facing him because if I was, I know I'd see the sparkle in his eyes and the light fans at the corners. 'But she's still blessing me with her filthy mouth.' He gives me a tweak above my hipbone, and I perform a jerk and a yelp before he lets me settle again. The silence settles, too.

He eventually sighs and starts circling tiny rings with his fingertips on each side of my belly button. 'His name was Jake.' He doesn't say any more than that, so I lie quietly on him, waiting for him to elaborate. 'He idolised me. He wanted to be me. I'll never understand it.' He sounds angry, and I'm suddenly moving, being turned around to face him. I'm now on my stomach, spread all over him and looking up into green grief. 'I can't do this on my own, baby. Help me.'

My instincts kick in and I push myself up his body, settling higher so I can get my face in the crook of his neck. 'Were you not alike?'

'We were the furthest away from alike you could get. In looks *and* personality.'

'He wasn't a god?'

His hands caress my back gently. 'He was a genius.'

'How is that far away from you?' I ask.

'Jake had his brain to get him by; I had my looks and I used them, as you well know. Jake didn't use his brain. If he did, he wouldn't be dead.'

Questions are popping into my mind left, right and centre, and I can't hold them back. 'How did he die?'

'He got hit by a car.'

'How would that be not using his brain?'

'Because he was pissed when he staggered into the road.'

Realisation is dawning, and it's dawning very fast. 'Carmichael isn't the only reason you don't talk to your parents, is he?'

'No, the fact that I'm responsible for my brother's death is a major contributing factor.' He says it with no emotion at all, almost sarcastically. 'Carmichael and The Manor came after and kind of put the nail in the coffin.'

'Jake was their favourite?' I hate saying that. It makes me angry to think it, but I'm slowly working this out. I don't know Jesse's family, and I have no desire to after he told me that they're ashamed of him.

'Jake was everything they wanted from a son. I wasn't. I tried to be. I studied, but it didn't come as naturally to me as it did to Jake.'

'But he wanted to be like you?'

'He wanted the small piece of freedom I gained through being considered the one with the least potential. All of their attention was focused on Jake the genius – the one they could be proud of. Jake would go to Oxford. Jake would make his first million before he was twenty-one. Jake would marry a well-bred English girl and breed well-spoken, polite, clever children.' He pauses. 'Except Jake didn't want any of that. He wanted to choose the direction of his own life and the tragic thing is, he would've chosen well on his own.'

'So what happened?'

'There was a house party. You know, full of drink, girls and . . . opportunities.'

Yes, I know, and I bet Jesse was a regular at these house parties.

'We were coming up to our seventeenth. Of course, it was my idea.'

'What?' I'm not sure I like where this tale is heading, but I know I'm going to find out.

'To go out and be teenagers, get away from the constant grind of studying and to stop trying to live up to our parents' expectations. I knew I'd pay for it, but I was prepared to face my parents' wrath. We were going to have a few drinks together, like brothers. It was just one night. I never expected to pay so severely.'

My heart is breaking for him. I pull myself from my snug place in his neck and sit up. I need to see his face. 'You got carried away?'

His eyebrows shoot up. 'Me? No! I'd had a few, but Jake was throwing back shots like he'd never drink again. I virtually carried him out of that house, then it all came out. How much he hated the suffocation, how he didn't want to go to Oxford. We made a pact.' He smiles fondly. 'We agreed to tell our parents together that we didn't want to do it any more. We wanted to make our own decisions based on our dreams, not based on what would impress the snotty fuckers our parents socialised with.' Now he really smiles. 'He wanted to race motorbikes, but that was considered uncouth and common. Reckless.' His eyes clench shut and reopen, and he loses his beam. 'I'd never seen him so happy at the thought of rebelling with me, doing what we wanted for once, not what we were told to do. And then he walked out into the road.' He keeps his eyes on mine, gauging my reaction. He wants to know if I think it's his fault.

'You can't be held responsible.' I'm feeling a bit mad.

He smiles and brushes my hair from my face. 'I'm held responsible because I *am* responsible. I shouldn't have dragged Jake off the perfect path. The stupid idiot shouldn't have listened to me.'

'It doesn't sound like you dragged him anywhere.'

'He wouldn't be dead, Ava. What if—'

'No, Jesse. Don't think like that. Life is full of *what ifs*. What if your parents hadn't suffocated you? What if you stood up sooner and said "enough"?'

'What if I had played ball?' His face is straight. This is a question he has asked himself repeatedly and never found the answer to.

I'm about to give it to him.

'You would never have found me.' I can feel my emotions squeezing at my vocal cords. 'And I would never have found you,' I whisper, the very thought finishing me. Tears start streaming down my face. It's unthinkable. Unbearable. Everything happens for a reason and if Jake was still alive, then I've no doubt that Jesse's life would have taken a different direction, and then we would never have found each other.

His head rests back, and he looks at my tummy. 'Everything that's happened in my life has led me to you, Ava. It's taken for ever, but I've finally found where I belong.'

I grab his hand and hold it against my stomach. 'With me and these two little people.'

His eyes drift up my body and his other hand grabs my waist, pulling me down so I'm sprawled on his chest. 'With you and those two little people,' he confirms. 'Our little people.'

Jesse's reaction to our news is understandable now, and the more he speaks of his parents, the more I dislike them. The unreasonable need to keep up appearances tore their family apart. 'What about Amalie?' I ask.

'Amalie would marry well and be a good wife and mother,

and I believe she might have fulfilled her obligation. It said *Doctor* David, didn't it?'

'It did.'

'There you are, then.' His tone carries an air of bitterness which I can't help but feel too.

He really did go all out after Jake died, like he was on a defiance mission to make up for Jake's absence; like, in a weird kind of way, he was avenging his brother's death. He was doubling up on the delinquencies, ensuring he didn't break the pact. 'You started spending more time with Carmichael after Jake's death?'

'I did. Carmichael knew the score. He'd been through it himself with my granddad.' His hands slip all over my back. 'Are you comfy?'

'Yes, I'm fine.' I brush off his concern quickly, wanting him to continue.

'It was a relief. I escaped the daily reminder that Jake wasn't with me any more, and I distracted myself with jobs that my uncle gave me around The Manor.' He shifts a little. 'Are you sure you're comfy?'

'I'm bloody comfy!' I tweak his nipple, and he laughs. This is good. He's at ease sharing this with me.

'She's comfy,' he muses.

'She is. What jobs did you do?'

'Everything. I'd collect the glasses in the bar, mow the lawns. Dad went through the roof, but I didn't let him stop me. Then they announced that we were moving to Spain.'

'And you refused to go.'

'Yes. I hadn't ventured into the rooms of The Manor at that point. I was still a Manor virgin.' He's grinning. I know he is. 'But on my eighteenth birthday, Carmichael let me loose in the bar. Worst thing he could've done. I slipped right in. It came naturally. Too naturally.' I shift and look up at him. The grin has gone. 'If simply being at The Manor took my mind away from all of my troubles, then being drunk and having sex at The Manor eliminated them completely.'

'Escapism,' I whisper. He escaped the guilt that his parents landed on him by drinking excessively and dabbling with too many women. 'What did Carmichael think of all this?'

He smiles. 'He thought it was a phase, that it would pass. Then he went and died on me, too.'

'And your parents tried to make you sell The Manor.' I already know all of this.

'Yes, they soon flew home from Spain at the news of my uncle's death. They found me, a younger version of the family black sheep, lording it up, drinking and gorging on women. I'd experienced freedom, without them trying to mould me into suitable son material. I'd grown cocky and confident, and now I was also extremely wealthy.' His lips press into a straight line. He is full to the brim with resentment. 'I told them where to shove their ultimatum. The Manor was Carmichael's life, and then it became mine. End of.'

I thought so much was clear, but today's tub-talk has put all other enlightenment to shame.

'Our children will be whoever they want to be.' I bite his chin. 'As long as they don't want to be playboys.'

My bum cheeks are clenched in his palms and squeezed tightly. 'Sarcasm doesn't suit you, lady.'

'I think it does.'

'You're right; it does.' He slides me up and kisses my nipple. 'My mark is fading.'

'Freshen it up, then.' I push my chest into him, like the little temptress he knows me to be, and he wraps his lips around my puckered bud and laps gently. I moan, long, low and deeply satisfied, my nose rubbing through his wet locks and taking a hit of his delicious scent.

'Nice?' he asks, clamping down with his teeth.

'Hmmm.' I feel peaceful, enlightened.

His lips drift across to the site of my fading mark, and he begins to suck gently, drawing the blood to the surface. 'Ava, I'm not sure how I feel about our babies taking to your breasts.' He releases me and I slide back down, brushing across something very hard. His eyes widen, and he inhales sharply. 'Oh no, we can't.' He shifts me and sits up. 'I won't, Ava. And don't you dare kick into temptress mode, either.'

I scowl at him. 'Cornwall,' I threaten, and he recoils in horror, but soon matches my scowl, his probably fiercer.

'You're not going anywhere!' he asserts on a growl as he stands, his beautiful, smooth iron rod of flesh just at the right level for my kneeling form. I seize it quickly before he can step out of the bath, wrapping my palm around him and clamping down. 'Fuck, you little fucking temptress.'

'Are you going to walk away from me?' I pull a long, slow draw.

He shakes his head. 'Ava, there's not a fucking chance on this planet that I'm taking you.'

'Sit down.' I nod to the side of the bath and flick my tongue across the wet head of his huge cock.

He hisses and looks up to the ceiling. 'Ava, if you leave me hanging to throw up, I'll lose my fucking mind.' He thrusts forward gently.

'I won't.' I don't know that for sure, but there are other ways to do this. 'Sit.' I push him down onto the side of the bath and kneel between his thighs, but I don't get a chance to be creative.

He grabs my arms. 'If I'm sitting on this side, then you're sitting on the other.' He hits me with a hungry kiss and pulls away panting, his eyes completely smoked out. Anticipation is making my tummy clench. 'With your legs wide open.'

I gasp a little, and immediately curse myself for it. He's luring me in to that place where he takes all control. He's goading me with those eyes which are full of promise and pleasure, daring me to refuse. Slipping his hands under my arms, he lifts me to my feet before gently pushing me back. I find my place and rest my bum on the edge of the giant bath. It's hard under my wet flesh, not that I'm particularly concerned. I can't seem to focus on anything, other than this man sitting opposite me, all smouldering and hard. Then he runs his tongue across his bottom lip, and I find myself mimicking him.

'Lick your fingers, Ava,' he orders. He's in dominant Jesse mode. I know there will be no hard fuck to wrap this up, but it's that look, that stance, that commanding tone.

I take my fingers to my mouth and slide them between my lips, slowly and precisely, never removing my eyes from his. I couldn't if I tried. The usual addictiveness is hard enough to pull away from, but when they are all hooded, his lashes fanned and hunger oozing from them . . . impossible.

'Slide your hand down your front,' he says roughly. 'Slowly.'

I comply and lazily drag my palm down my body, brushing my nipples and skimming my stomach until I arrive at the juncture of my thighs.

'Stop.' He rips his eyes from mine and they wander down, taking their time, drinking in his asset before they reach my hand. 'One finger, baby. Slowly slide one finger in.'

Doing as I'm instructed, I insert one finger on a deep inhale of breath.

'Remember, that's mine.' He flicks his eyes to mine. 'So be gentle with it.'

Those words, the way he says them, and the fact that he absolutely means them, pushes me to close my eyes and mentally gather my wits.

'Eyes, Ava.'

Using breathing exercises to try and calm myself down, I follow through on his order.

'Good girl.' He reaches down and takes a loose hold of himself. My heart rate multiplies. 'Taste.'

I don't feel shy. I never have, no matter what he does or

asks me to do. My hand glides back up my body, and then I slowly, seductively, teasingly slide my finger into my mouth and shamelessly moan as I do.

'Good?' He's drawing easy strokes of his arousal as he watches me. It's sending me wild with want, but I know that I'm not moving from this side of the bath. I know who has the power.

I give him heavy, lustful eyes as I lick and suck around my finger, working myself up into a desperate wreck of trembling nerves.

'I'll take that as a yes.' He jerks a little and pauses with his lazy rhythm, seeming to gather his own wits. 'Fucking hell, Ava.'

Knowing his self-control is slipping, I take advantage and drift back down to my entrance, scissoring my fingers and beginning a measured, meticulous caressing of myself. My back arches, my legs spread further and my head rolls on a groan. I'm rippling all over and releasing uncontrolled bursts of breath as my pleasure builds with my own rhythmic touch.

'Damn it, Ava. Look at me,' he hisses. My eyes and head drop at his command. He's tipping the edge, too. His body has solidified and his fist is working firmer and faster. This only encourages me, my own fingers speeding up, my own body tensing. 'You're close, baby.'

'Yes!' I'm losing it.

'Oh Jesus, not yet. Control it.'

'I can't!' I shout, the thought of him stopping this making me panic slightly. I'm brimming. It's coming. 'Oh God!'

'Ava, fuck, control it!' Now his fist is moving urgently, his head is rolling, but he's keeping those greens right on me.

I attempt everything. I tense all over, my legs splashing the water as I jerk and fight the convulsions riding through me. 'Jesse,' I cry desperately. The buzzing at my core is getting out of control.

'Ava, you look fucking amazing.' His unrestrained movements get the better of him and he moans, falling to his knees in the water and letting out a suppressed bark.

I move my hand immediately when his head falls between my thighs and his mouth takes over, while he continues to work himself in front of me. The warmth of his lips all over my sex pushes me that little bit further into ecstasy. I'm yanking at his hair, pushing him further into me. I'm going to burst at the seams with pleasure.

And then I do.

My thighs clamp to the sides of his head as I let go on an elongated shudder of comforting bliss and a heavy rush of air. My lungs burst. I go lax. He rolls and laps gently, softly flicking his tongue, and then works his way up my body until he finds my mouth. He pulls me down to my knees and takes my hand, replacing his with mine around his steel shaft. He hasn't come. 'My turn,' he whispers. 'Hold it against you.'

The wet tip of him meets my clit, pushing against me, taking the edge off the persistent buzz. I take over, holding him lightly and massaging him to climax. His hands are free now, and they are encasing my neck, holding my head firm as he works my mouth with the same care as I'm working him with my hand. This isn't urgent and frenzied. This is controlled and relaxed. He can control it so much better than I can.

'Just keep it like that,' he mumbles into my mouth. 'I could stay like this for ever.'

'I love you.' I don't know why I feel the need to say this now, but I do anyway.

His tongue sweeps gently through my mouth. He pulls back, he plays with my lips, and then he's back in my mouth, flirting with my tongue. And the whole time, I just soak up his attention and keep up my seduction of his velvet hardness against me. It's working me down perfectly and working him up just as well. 'I know,' he murmurs, and with a small whimper and hardening of his kiss, he comes, the hot essence of him pouring all over me as he throbs in my hold and moans around our kiss.

After I've worked him slowly down, he sits on his heels, pulling me onto his lap. 'Are you cold?'

'A little.' I shrug and seek warmth by pushing myself into him.

'My lady's tired.' He kisses my nose. 'Snuggle?'

I nod, and he lifts me from the bath. We dry each other off in silence and find our way to the bed, falling in together and immediately finding our snuggle places – him on his back, me spread all over his chest, my face in his neck and his hands running all over me.

'I'll never love one more than the other,' he proclaims quietly.

I don't answer him. Instead, I kiss his neck and snuggle deeper.

Chapter 21

I could lie here for ever, just watching him sleep, the peaceful streams of air intermittently reaching my face, reinforcing the deep sense of belonging inside of me. The tender placing of his palm on my tummy is strengthening my love for this man. And the close perfection of his body is swelling my desire for his touch. There are a million things about this man that make me despair, but there are endless things that make me adore him. Some of those despairing things I even adore.

Unable to resist, I reach forward and run my thumb down his stubbled cheek and onto his parted lips, smiling as he twitches a little, and then sighs and settles again, his hand on my belly unconsciously starting to circle. The flawlessness of his beautiful face will amaze me until the day I die – his lightly tanned skin, his almost girly long lashes, the faint crease across his brow. It would take me a lifetime to run through all his stunning features. My devastating man, in all of his challenging ways.

My wandering hand floats across his face; my fingertip traces the taut flesh of his throat and my palm skims his solid chest. I sigh, all dreamy and content as I spend this quiet time exploring his body and face.

'Have you finished feeling me up?' His rough voice drags me from my daydreaming, my hand pausing on his scar. His eyes remain closed.

'No, just be still and silent,' I order quietly, carrying on with my fondling.

'Anything you say, lady.'

I grin and lean forward, hovering my lips over his. 'Good boy.'

His closed lids flicker and the corners of his mouth blatantly restrain a smirk. 'What if I want to be a bad boy?' One of his eyes opens cheekily.

Nothing will prevent me from smiling at that face. 'Morning.'

He moves too fast. I'm on my back and pinned under his body in a nanosecond, my arms held over my head. I don't even have time to register his attack or let out a squeal of shock. 'Someone has sleepy sex on their mind.'

'No, I have Jesse Ward on my mind, which means I also have various degrees of fuckings on my mind.'

His eyebrows rise slowly, thoughtfully. 'You're insatiable, my beautiful girl.' He kisses me hard. 'Watch your mouth.'

I quickly return his kiss, but he halts me by pulling away. I scowl. He smiles. It's that smug smile. I scowl harder, but I'm ignored. 'I've been thinking.'

My scowl falls away immediately. Jesse thinking is almost as worrying as him trampling all over the place. 'What about?'

'About how dramatic our married life has been.'

I can't argue with that. 'Okay . . .' I drag the word out slowly, meaning I'm not sure it's okay at all.

'Let me take you away.' His green eyes are pleading with me, and now he's pouting, too. Is he beginning to realise that his face has just as much impact as a sense fuck? 'Just us two on our own.'

'We'll never be alone ever again,' I remind him.

He lifts and glances down at my stomach, and I see him smile and shift down to kiss my tummy before returning those puppy dog eyes to mine. 'Let me love you. Let me have you to myself for a few days.'

'What about my job?' My commitment recently has been really questionable.

'Ava, you were in a car accident yesterday.'

'I know,' I concede. 'But I have appointments and Patrick is—'

'I'll sort Patrick.' He cuts me straight off. 'He'll deal with your appointments.'

My eyes narrow. 'Sort Patrick or trample Patrick?'

He pulls that hurt face. I'm not buying it. 'I'll speak to Patrick.'

'Delicately.'

He grins. '-ish.'

'No, Ward. No "–ish" about it. Delicately. End of!'

'Is that a yes?' he asks hopefully. I could cuddle him, the adorable pain in the arse that he is.

'Yes,' I agree. He needs the break just as much as I do, probably more. Yesterday's events will not help his worrying. 'Where are we going?'

He springs into action, jumping up from the bed like an excited child on Christmas morning. 'Anywhere. I don't care.'

'I do! I'm not skiing!' I sit bolt upright in bed at the very thought of being kitted out in padded skiwear with some giant planks of wood attached to my feet.

'Don't be stupid, woman.' He rolls his eyes and disappears into the wardrobe, appearing moments later with a suitcase. 'You're carrying my babies in there.' He points to my stomach. 'You're lucky I'm not chaining you to the bed for the rest of this pregnancy.'

'You can if you like.' I hold my wrists against the headboard. 'I won't complain.'

'You're a temptress, Mrs Ward. Come pack.' He goes back into the wardrobe, leaving me hanging on the bed. On a grumble loud enough for him to hear, I shuffle to the edge and follow him. He's pulling down clothes haphazardly and chucking them into a pile by the case.

'Where are we going?'

'I don't know. I'll make a few calls.' He continues happily

packing his case, but then he looks up at me, where I'm leaning on the door frame, silently observing him. 'Aren't you going to pack?'

'Well, I don't know where I'm going. Hot, cold? Car, plane?'

'Car,' he asserts firmly, turning to reach for more T-shirts. 'You can't fly.'

'What do you mean, I can't fly?'

'I don't know. Cabin pressure.' His naked shoulders shrug. 'It might squish the babies.'

I laugh because if I don't, I might bash him around the head instead. 'Tell me you're joking.'

He slowly turns to face me. He's not impressed by my humour. It's written all over that bloody perfect face. 'I don't joke when it comes to you, Ava. You should know that.'

'Cabin pressure won't squish our babies, Jesse. If you're taking me away, then you're taking me on a plane.' I very nearly stamp my foot to assert my order.

He looks a little shocked by my demand, and he slips into thought, munching his lip, the cogs slowly starting to kick into action. 'It's not safe for pregnant women to fly,' he says quietly. 'I've read about it.'

'Where have you read about it?' I ask on a laugh, fearing he's about to produce some sort of *Guide to Pregnancy* manual. I stop laughing immediately when he reaches between his suits and produces a *Guide to Pregnancy* manual.

'In here.' He holds it up sheepishly. 'You should also be taking folic acid.'

I gape at the book being dangled in front of me and watch with a mixture of astonishment and amusement as he starts flicking through the pages. There are pages folded over at the corners, and I think I even get a glimpse of a passage highlighted in neon pen. He knows what he's looking for, and I can do nothing more than stand and stare as my beautiful, neurotic control freak finds it.

'Here, look.' He shoves the book under my nose and points to the centre of the page, where a section has been highlighted in neon pink. 'The Department of Health recommends that women should take a daily supplement of four hundred micrograms of folic acid while they are trying to conceive, and should continue taking this dose for the first twelve weeks of pregnancy when the baby's spine is developing.' He frowns. 'But we have two babies, so maybe you should take eight hundred micrograms.'

My heart swells to bursting point. 'I love you,' I say on a smile.

'I know.' He flicks some more pages. 'The flying bit is here somewhere. Just . . .'

I smack the book from his hands and we both follow its fall to the floor, where it bumps around before settling. He looks up at me with narrowed eyes, his lips pressing into a straight line. It just makes me smirk, which makes him scowl harder. I kick the book. He gasps.

'Pick the book up,' he snarls.

'Stupid book.' I kick it again. I'm still grinning.

'Pick the book up, Ava.'

'No,' I snap back petulantly. I know exactly what I'm doing here. My eyes are delighting at the fierceness seeping from his refined physique.

He raises those eyebrows. He's thinking really hard about this. He knows my game. Then three fingers appear in front of my face. 'Three.'

My grin widens as I bat his hand away. 'Two,' I counter.

He's trying his hardest to conceal his own grin. 'One.'

'Zero, baby,' I finish for him and squeal in delight as I'm hoofed up over his shoulder, with conviction but care, and carted into the bedroom. I'm laughing hard as I'm dropped to the bed, with way too much precision, before he blankets me and brushes my hair from my face.

'Lady, when will you learn?' he asks, cupping the back of my head and raising it to meet his nose.

'Never.'

He smiles that smile, reserved only for me. 'I hope you don't. Kiss me.'

'What if I don't?' I ask. I so will. And he knows it.

Reaching down, he rests the tip of his finger on the hollow void above my hipbone. I hold my breath. 'We both know you're going to kiss me, Ava.' His lips tickle mine. 'Let's not waste valuable time when I could be losing myself in you. Kiss me now.'

My tongue slides from my mouth, meeting with his bottom lip, and I perform my own little tease, lightly skimming until he submits and lets his own tongue make an appearance. We meet in the middle and circle sweetly until he moans and attacks my mouth with brute force.

'Hmmm,' I sigh, matching the purposeful lashes of his tongue. This is what we need. We need a few days with each other, loving each other and getting used to our imminent future together. A future that now has two babies in it. I need Jesse to myself for a while, with no distractions, except him, and with no issues, except us.

'It didn't really say I can't fly, did it?' I ask, stupidly or not. I know it couldn't have, because I've seen pregnant women on planes before. This is just another one of Jesse's stupid pregnancy rules.

My lip is bitten and sucked. 'It's logical.'

'No, it's neurotic,' I argue. 'Pregnant women fly all of the time, so you are taking me on a plane to somewhere hot and you're going to let me feast on you the whole time. Constant contact. I want constant contact.' I know this will please him and when he lifts his head, sucking my lip as he does, the wonderful smile on his face confirms it.

'I can't fucking wait.' He kisses my nose and gets up. 'Come on, then. We're wasting valuable feasting time.' He winks, turns, and leaves me wallowing among the white sheets. This really is Central Jesse Cloud Nine.

I pull my case down the stairs and it bumps as it goes.

'Hey!' The shout makes me jump and falter mid-step, causing me to clutch the handrail to steady myself. A loud gasp rings through the air, followed by thundering footsteps up the stairs. I'm grabbed and held still. 'What the fuck are you doing, woman?'

My fright turns to anger. 'For fuck's sake, Jesse. Fucking hell! That was your fucking fault!' I immediately realise my slip-up, the growl coming from Jesse confirming that I have, most definitely, just sworn like a sailor. Three times . . . all in one rant. I brace myself for it, closing one eye on a wince.

'Will you watch your fucking *mouth*!' He takes my case. 'Wait there!' he barks, and I do, but mostly because I've been shocked into stillness and silence by that infuriated yell. He practically throws my case down when he reaches the bottom, muttering and cursing under his breath, before coming back up the stairs and picking me up. 'You'll break your fucking neck.'

'I was carrying a case! It was you who made me jump.' I don't wriggle or try to break free.

'You shouldn't be carrying anything, except my babies.'

'Our babies!'

'That's what I fucking said!' He puts me on my feet. 'No doing stupid shit, lady.'

I rearrange my top, huffing and puffing as I do. 'How is carrying a case stupid?'

'Because you're pregnant!'

Oh, I can't bear this. 'You'd better rein it in, Ward.' I point my finger right in his face. 'Cornwall!'

He actually starts laughing, which only serves to notch my frustration up a few more levels. He should be worried, not laughing. 'How many times are you going to threaten me with fucking Cornwall?' he asks cockily, like he knows I'll never see my threat through. I might do, although I don't relish the thought of spending my whole pregnancy with my parents, but anything has got to be better than this.

'I'll go now!' I shout in his face.

'Come on, then. I'll take you.' He picks my case up and walks to the door, looking back over his shoulder at me standing startled on the spot. 'Are you coming?'

He's pulling my leg. 'Have you called Patrick?' I ask, following behind. There's no way on this earth Jesse will voluntarily take me to my mother's.

'Yes,' he answers short and sharp. 'You need to be back in work by Tuesday.' He shuts the door behind me before calling the elevator.

We travel down in silence, me looking at him in the reflection of the mirrored doors while he makes a call to John. The doors open, and he nods his indication to lead on as he continues his conversation, telling John to get Steve on it before advising him that he's taking me to my parents'. I still don't believe it. And get Steve on what?

'Hi, Ava.' Casey's cheerful tone quickly has a bright smile replacing my fixed furrowed brow.

'Mrs Ward!' Jesse barks, between words with John as we pass the concierge desk.

I ignore him. 'Morning, Casey. Are you okay?'

'Very well, thank you. It's a lovely day.' He nods outside, and I look to find bright sunshine. 'Have a nice day, Ava.'

'Thank you.' I'm all dreamy as I emerge into the muggy air, instantly noticing my wedding present has miraculously made its way back to Lusso, but my bright-white Range Rover is forgotten when I see an Aston Martin.

'Yeah, thanks, big guy.' Jesse hangs up and walks straight to the boot of the strange car, slipping the case in.

'What's this?' I ask, pointing to the DBS.

He shuts the boot and clasps his stubbled chin thoughtfully. 'I think it might be a car.'

'Sarcasm doesn't suit you, God. I mean, where has it come from?'

'It came from a garage to replace mine until it's located.' He takes my elbow and directs me in.

'They've still not found your car?'

'No,' he answers quickly and finally, with no room for pushing on the matter, not that it stops me.

'What's Steve doing?' I ask, and he pulls back, momentarily faltering in his purposeful stride of actions.

'Nothing.' He's lying, and I raise my eyebrows suspiciously. 'He's looking into a few things for me,' he huffs, reaching across to belt me up.

I bat his fussing hands away when he adjusts the lap belt across my tummy. 'Will you just stop?' I push him out and shut the door on him, leaving a brooding mass of male on the other side of the window, glaring at me. I'm beginning to wish he *was* taking me to my mum's. I don't know if I can stand it, and I'm not going to even try and convince myself that he can stop. Double babies looks like double mollycoddling. Jesse mollycoddling. And I know damn well what Steve's looking into. Jesse likely only left Steve intact on the condition that he investigates my drugging, and now the accident, too. I throw my head back against the headrest and turn a little to watch Jesse settle in the driver's seat. 'Why didn't we just take my car?' I ask, nodding across to my shiny snowball.

He freezes and looks at me out of the corner of his eye. 'You can't drive too far.'

I smile on the inside. 'No, but you could.' I should throw a hissy fit and make him drive the damn tank. I wouldn't be surprised if it was bulletproof as well.

'Yes, I could, but I have this now.' He brushes me off and

starts the engine, revving it loudly on a satisfied smile. 'Listen to that,' he sighs, whacking it into gear and pulling off.

I begrudgingly admire the guttural roar of the DBS as I keep my relaxed head facing him, admiring his stunning profile. 'Where are you taking me, then?' I ask, retrieving my phone from my bag.

'I told you, your mother's.'

I roll my eyes dramatically. 'Okay,' I sigh, dialling Kate.

'Give me your phone.' His hand comes toward me, his fingers grasping in the space between us. 'No phone.'

'I need to call Kate.'

My phone is seized and turned off. 'I've called everyone who needs to know that we're going away, including Kate. Unravel your knickers, lady.'

I don't try to reclaim it. I don't want it.

'Ava, baby, wake up.'

I open my eyes and stretch, my hands hitting the ceiling above me. Confused, I look up and see the roof of a car. Then my sleepy eyes fall to the side and come face to face with my lovely control freak. He's smiling brightly at me. 'Where are we?' I rub my eyes.

'Cornwall,' he replies quickly.

'Stop it,' I snap. I'm a little grizzly. 'I need a wee.' I shift in my seat and clasp the handle to get out, catching the first glimpse of our surroundings. I recognise it. The low wall circling the small graveyard, the little hut you can walk through to take the winding path down to the beach and the mixture of sand and leaves that gather in the gutter. It's all familiar. Too familiar.

I swing to face him. 'You weren't kidding!' I double check, but the line of hanging wetsuits in the garden across the road only confirm my fears. 'You're dumping me on my mum?' I sound hurt. I am hurt. Perhaps he can't cope with his ridiculous overprotectiveness either.

I feel his hand slide across my neck and grasp my nape, turning my face to his. 'Don't threaten me with Cornwall.' He's grinning. And I start crying, like a stupid, hormonal pregnant woman. Through my unreasonable tears, I see his grin vanish and a look of anxiety replace it. 'Baby, I'm joking. Anyone would have to slice their way through me to get to you. You know that.' He pulls me over onto his lap, and I burrow into his neck, sobbing stupidly. I'm being completely unreasonable, I know that. He would never leave me. What's the matter with me? 'Ava, look at me.'

I sniffle into him and reluctantly pull my head up so he can see my tearstained mess of a face. 'I'm going to be so fat. Massive! Twins, Jesse!' My smugness from the hospital has long gone. All of the thoughts of torturing him with screaming babies and mood swings have just diminished. I'm going to be stretched to within an inch of my life. I'm twenty-six. I don't want saggy bits and stretch marks. I'll never pull off lace again. 'You won't . . .' I can't think it, let alone say it.

'Desire you.' He finishes for me. I nod my head, feeling guilty for being so selfish, but that look in his eyes when he has me in his arms, or anytime he looks at me, in fact – I don't know what I'd do if I never had it again. He smiles a little and places his hand on my cheek, his thumb brushing gentle circles. 'Baby, that will never happen.'

'You don't know that. You don't know how you'll feel when I've got swollen ankles and I'm walking like I've got a melon wedged between my thighs.'

He laughs, really hard. 'Is that how it'll be?'

'Probably.'

'Let me tell you, lady. I desire you more with every day that passes, and I believe you've been carrying my babies for quite a few weeks.' He gives my tummy a little rub with his spare hand.

'I'm not fat yet,' I mutter.

'You're not going to be fat, Ava. You're pregnant, and let me tell you, the thought of you keeping a piece of me and you warm and safe makes me fucking deliriously happy, and . . .' He slowly thrusts his hips upward. He's solid. 'It makes me desire you even fucking more. Now shut up and kiss me, wife.'

I give him a cynical look, and he gives me an expectant one, delivering another thrust. It catches me perfectly, and I practically dive on him. I decide right here in this moment that I'm not going to *let* it happen. I shall be doing those pelvic floor things until I'm blue in the face. I'll be running, too, and wearing lace when I'm in labour.

'Hmmm, there's my girl,' he hums when I let him up for air. 'Shit, Ava, I would love to rip those lace knickers off and fuck you stupid right now, but I don't want an audience.'

'I don't care.' I assault him again, raiding his mouth with my tongue and pulling at his hair viciously. He just said he'd love to fuck me. I don't care where we are.

'Ava.' He struggles against me on a laugh. 'Cut it out or I won't be responsible for my actions.'

'I won't hold you responsible.' I don't give up. I'm pulling at his T-shirt, grinding myself down on his erection.

'Fucking hell, woman,' he groans.

I've nearly got him, but then there's a hard rapping on the window right next to my head, and I pull back on a gasp, quickly gathering my near-on unquenchable lust. We look at each other for a few seconds, both of us panting, and then slowly turn our heads in unison towards the window.

There's a policeman. And he doesn't look very happy. I'm quickly shifted from Jesse's lap and placed on my seat, where I smooth my hair down and blush a million shades of red. Jesse grins that roguish grin as he watches me sort myself out. 'That'll teach you.' He lets his window down and turns his attention to the copper. 'Sorry about that. Pregnant. Hormones. Can't keep her hands off me.' He's suppressing a laugh, and I gasp, smacking his thigh. He chuckles, grabbing my hand and squeezing. 'See?'

The policeman actually coughs and blushes himself. 'Yes ... well ... urm ... public place.' He signals around in thin air. 'Move on, please.'

'We're visiting.' Jesse does the window back up, blocking any further stuttering and stammering from the red-faced policeman, before turning his mischievous face back to me. This is easy-going Jesse. He's shameless, just like any other time, but adorable and lovable and all roguish. 'Ready?'

'I thought you were taking me on a plane?' I love Newquay, and I can't wait to see my parents, but Jesse all to myself is what I want right now.

'I am, after we've told my delightful mother-in-law that she's going to be a grandmother.' He jumps out of the car and leaves me all horrified and suddenly not so keen on seeing my mum and sharing our news. The door opens next to me. 'Out you get.'

I close my eyes, trying to gather some confidence. 'How did you know where to come?'

'I called and asked for the address, and I believe that's your father's car.' He points to my dad's Mercedes. 'Am I right?'

'Yes.' My parents are obviously expecting us.

As we approach the front door, Jesse lifts my hand and kisses it sweetly, giving me a little wink. I smile at the irritating rogue. Then he snaps a pair of handcuffs over our wrists.

'What are you doing?' I pull against him, but it's too late. He works those cuffs well. 'Jesse!'

The front door swings open and Mum stands there, looking all lovely in a pair of cropped jeans and a cream jumper. 'My girl's home!'

'Hi, Mum,' Jesse chirps, lifting our cuffed hands and waving on a grin. I knew he would do that, and even though my poor mum has just staggered in shock, I can't help breaking out in a huge smile. He's all playful, and I love it.

She gets herself in a fluster and does a quick scan of the outside area before grabbing Jesse and hauling him into the hallway. 'Get those cuffs off my daughter, you menace.'

He laughs and removes them promptly, quickly restoring Elizabeth's smile. 'Happy?'

'Yes.' She knocks his shoulder before moving in and squeezing me to her bosom. 'It's so good to see you, darling. I've got the spare room ready for you.'

'We're staying?' I ask, accepting her hug.

'We fly out in the morning,' Jesse pipes up. 'I thought we'd run a visit in before your mum starts thinking that I'm keeping you from her.'

Mum drops me and takes Jesse in her arms. 'Thank you for bringing her to visit,' she says, squeezing him extra tight.

I smile as I watch him accept her hug, rolling his eyes over her shoulder at me. All of this isn't for him. I know that he'd rather have me to himself any day of the week, but he really is trying, and I love him all the more for it.

'Make the most of it because I'm kidnapping her in the morning.'

'Yes, yes, I know.' She releases him. 'Joseph! They're here! I'll make tea.'

We follow her down to the kitchen, and I gaze around, taking in the ever-perfect neatness and preciseness of my parents' home.

My dad is sitting at the kitchen table, reading a newspaper. 'Hi, Dad!' I lean over his shoulder and kiss his cheek, and, like always, he tenses at my show of affection.

'Ava, how are you?' He closes his paper and puts his hand out to Jesse, who has made himself comfy in the chair next to Dad. 'Is she keeping you on your toes?'

'Of course.' Jesse flicks me a look and I scoff.

After visiting the bathroom, I settle at the table with my dad and husband and watch quietly as they chat at ease while Mum makes tea, throwing little bits into the conversation here and there. It's a wonderful sight. I'm so happy.

'I thought we could go down to The Windmill for dinner tonight.' Mum places the tea on the table. 'We'll stroll down. It's going to be a lovely evening.'

Dad grunts his agreement, no doubt looking forward to a few pints. 'That sounds like a plan.'

'Perfect.' Jesse places his hand on my knee and squeezes.

Yes, perfect.

Chapter 22

'Ladies first.' Jesse holds the door open, and Mum and I slip past. 'Joseph.'

'Thank you, Jesse.' My dad walks ahead, leading us to a table by the fireplace that is lit with an array of candles rather than the usual logs and flames that crackle during the winter months.

'Drinks?' Jesse asks, pulling out a chair for me, but soon stopping me from resting my bum down when he notices it's hard wood and free of anything cushioned. Leaving me standing, he quickly swaps it for a nearby high-backed chair with arms, upholstered in a regal green velvet.

'I'll have a glass of white.' Mum perches neatly down and takes her glasses out to read the menu.

'Pint of Carlsberg for me, please,' Dad says.

'And for my beautiful girl?' Jesse asks, pushing me down onto the soft seat.

'Water, please.' I place my order with absolutely no thought, until my mum's head flies up from the menu.

'No wine?' Her face is shocked as she looks over her glasses at me.

I shift on my seat and feel Jesse fidgeting behind me as he tucks me in closer to the table. 'No, we need to get away early,' I flip casually, picking up a menu.

She still looks surprised, but she doesn't push the matter further, instead pointing out the specials on the menu.

I feel Jesse's hot breath at my ear. 'I love you.' He kisses my cheek, and I reach up to feel his stubbled cheek.

'I know.'

He leaves us at the table to order the drinks, and I watch as Mum reads out everything on the menu to my dad, and then proceeds to recite the daily specials from the various blackboards dotted around the bar.

'Have you heard from Dan?' I ask.

'Yes, he called earlier, darling,' Mum tells me. 'He said that you met for lunch yesterday. How lovely. I told him you were coming down before you go on holiday, but he didn't know. I'm surprised Jesse didn't think to tell him.'

I'm not surprised, but Mum seems to be blissfully unaware of the animosity batting between my brother and my husband. 'This was last minute.' I shake my head dismissively. 'Jesse probably forgot.' I feel a tad guilty. It didn't cost me a thought to let Dan know that I was out of London for a while.

I'm saved from further interrogation when a tray is placed on the table. Everyone takes their drinks, and my parents both gasp appreciatively around the rims of their alcohol-filled glasses. I look at my own clear filled highball with as much enthusiasm as I feel for it, and then at my mum's wine glass on a sigh.

'What are you having, then?' Mum asks. 'I think I'll go for the seafood platter.'

I lean over to Jesse and share his menu, my hand falling to his knee. He picks it up and absent-mindedly kisses it, not taking his eyes from the menu. 'What would you like, baby?'

'I'm not sure.'

'I'm having the mussels in garlic,' Dad declares, pointing at the board, which is displaying a mouthwatering selection of seafood dishes. 'Bloody delicious.' He smacks his lips and takes a swig of his pint.

I'm torn. Seafood is a must, especially being so close to the sea, but what shall I have? The seafood platter, full of cockles, mussels, crab and king prawns, or the mussels drenched in garlic butter with warm, freshly baked bread? My stomach growls, pushing me to hurry and fill it up. 'I can't decide.'

'Tell me what you're thinking, and I'll help you.' Jesse looks over, waiting for me to enlighten him on my quandary.

'Mussels or the seafood platter,' I muse.

His eyes bug. 'Neither!' he blurts, drawing the attention of my parents, who both pause with their drinks halfway to their mouths.

'Why?' I turn a frown on him, but very quickly realise exactly why. He's read something in that bloody book. 'Oh, come on, Jesse!'

He shakes his head. 'No way, lady. Not a chance. There's some sort of mercury in fish that can damage an unborn baby's nervous system. Don't even try to defy me on this one.'

'Are you going to let me eat anything?' My brow is completely furrowed. I love seafood.

'Yes. Chicken, steak. Both are high in protein, and that's good for our babies.'

I let out a frustrated protest and grab my water viciously. I'm going to lose my mind and probably be on Prozac by the time these babies arrive.

I'm so busy having a sulk, it takes me a few moments to register my parents' stunned faces across the table.

Oh shit!

'Do it in style, Ava,' Jesse mutters, placing his menu on the table. I shoot incredulous eyes to him. *Me?*

'You're pregnant?' Mum blurts, the information overload obviously registering.

'Ava?' Dad presses when I remain focused on Jesse, who is remaining focused on the menu that he's just laid down.

I take a deep breath of confidence and bite the bullet. 'Surprise,' I whisper, like a feeble cop-out.

'But you've been married for five minutes!' Mum gasps. 'Five minutes!'

I watch as my dad places a calming hand on her arm, but that isn't going to stop her. I can feel a rant coming on, in which case, I also feel a Jesse-style trample coming on. I can't imagine him taking a critical speech from my mother too well. She's right, though. We *have* only been married for a few short weeks. Not quite five minutes, but it may as well be. I dare not tell her how far pregnant I am. She'll work out the timeframes fast enough and soon calculate just how soon after meeting this man I got myself knocked up. I remain quiet, as does Jesse, as does my father, but not my mother. Oh no, she's only just getting started. I can tell by the flex of her fingers on her wine glass and the drawing of deep breaths.

And then I get really worried because her eyes widen and swing towards Jesse. 'It was a shotgun wedding, wasn't it? You married her because you had to!'

'Thanks!' I laugh, thinking how obscene it is for her to say such a thing.

'Elizabeth.' Jesse sits forward, all stern, his jaw ticking. I fear the worst. 'You know better than that.' He sounds so calm but I can detect the irritation in his tone, and I can hardly blame him. He's insulted, and so am I.

Mum huffs a little but Dad interjects before she can retaliate. 'So you didn't know at the wedding?'

'No,' I answer quickly, taking my glass with both hands to prevent my natural reflex from failing me.

'I see,' Dad sighs.

'I can't believe it,' Mum whines. 'A pregnant bride suggests only one thing.'

'Then don't bloody tell anyone,' I snap, feeling immensely pissed off with my mum and her reaction. I can't blame her, it is shocking, more so than she'll ever know, but to suggest I was rushed down the aisle because of it? That just makes me fuming mad. I don't know how Jesse must be feeling. His twitching, tense frame should be a clue, and when he takes my left hand

and starts twirling my wedding ring, I know that my mum is about to be trampled.

He leans forward, and I close my eyes. 'Elizabeth, I'm not an eighteen-year-old lad being forced to do the right thing after a quick fuck about with a girl.' He's not quite snarling at my mother, but as I open my eyes to gauge exactly how much fierceness we're dealing with, I immediately notice him fighting a curling lip. 'I'm thirty-eight years old. Ava is my wife, and I'm not having her worked up or upset, so you can accept it and give us your blessing, or you can carry on like this and I'll take my girl home now.' He's still twirling my ring, and even though he has just firmly put my melodramatic mother in her place, and quite harshly, I could kiss him. And slap him, too. He doesn't want me worked up? Coming from him, that's bloody hilarious.

'Now, let's all just calm down a little, shall we?' my dad says all calm and softly, ever the mediator. Not only does he avoid affection, he's not all that keen on confrontation, either. I notice he gives my mother a sideways glance in warning, something rare from my father and only delivered to his wife when he thinks it's absolutely necessary. It is definitely necessary right now.

'Ava,' Dad smiles at me across the table, 'how do you feel about this?'

'Fine,' I answer quickly, feeling Jesse squeeze my hand. I need to find a replacement for *fine*. 'Perfect. Couldn't be happier.' I return my dad's smile.

'Well, then. They're married, financially stable,' he laughs, 'and they're bloody adults, Elizabeth. Get a grip. You're going to be a granny.'

I'm feeling pretty mortified. After what has just transpired, you would think we were a pair of teenagers. I smile apologetically at Jesse, who shakes his head in complete exasperation.

'I will not be a granny!' Mum chokes. 'I'm forty-seven years old.' She fluffs her hair. 'I could be a nana, though,' she muses thoughtfully.

'You can be whatever you like, Elizabeth.' Jesse picks the menu back up, clearly fighting to leave it there.

'And you should watch your language, Jesse Ward!' She reaches over the table and flicks the top of his menu, but he doesn't apologise. 'Wait!' she shrieks.

'For what?' Dad asks.

Mum's eyes are passing between me and Jesse, back and forth, again and again, before finally resting on Jesse, who has raised brows, waiting for her to advise us on what we're waiting for. 'You said "babies", plural. You said "our *babies*".'

'Twins.' Jesse smiles brightly, all irritation and trampling signs disappearing in a split second. He rubs my tummy lightly. 'Two babies. Two grandchildren.'

'Well, I'll be damned.' Dad laughs. 'Now that really is very special. Congratulations!' His chest swells a little in pride, making me smile fondly.

'Twins?' Mum jumps in. 'Oh, Ava, darling! You are going to be exhausted. What are—'

'No, she won't.' Jesse cuts her off completely before she can dig herself any further into his trampling pit. 'She's got me. End of.'

Mum sits back vigilantly and shuts her trap, and I melt on a little sigh. Yes, I have him.

'And you have us, darling,' Mum says quietly. 'I'm so sorry. It's just a bit of a shock.' She leans over and puts her hand out. I take it. 'You'll always have us.'

I smile, but realise instantly that I won't actually have them. They live miles away from London, and with Jesse's family well out of the picture, there will be no calling the grandparents to pop over and relieve me for an hour. There will be no popping in to see my mum for a cup of tea and a chat so she can see her grandchildren. I feel Jesse's hand tighten around mine, dragging me from my unexpected, unwelcome thoughts. I look at him, and he gazes straight into my eyes.

'You have me,' he affirms, as if he's read my mind. He probably has.

'Have you decided?'

I look up, finding a waitress armed with a pad and pen, ready to take our order. She's smiling brightly, and she's smiling brightly at Jesse. 'I'll have the steak, please,' I say, my hand slipping onto his knee instinctively, indicating the beginning of my own little trampling session. She makes no attempt to write anything down and doesn't ask how I'd like it cooked. She just hovers, all starry eyed and dreamy as her greedy eyes run continuous trails up and down my god's seated frame. 'I'll have the steak,' I repeat, minus the *please*. 'Medium.'

'Pardon?' She rips her eyes away from Jesse, who is hiding a small smirk as he pretends to read the menu.

'The steak. Medium. Would you like me to write it down for you?' I ask tightly. I hear Jesse chuckle.

'Oh, of course.' Her pen hand kicks into action. 'And for you?' she asks, looking at my parents.

'Mussels for me,' Dad grunts.

'And the seafood platter for me,' Mum sings. 'And I'll have another wine.' She raises her glass.

The waitress scribbles it all down before turning back to Jesse. She's smiling again. 'And for you, sir?'

'What would you recommend?' He blows her back a few metres with his smile, reserved only for women.

I roll my eyes as I watch her pull at her ponytail and blush profusely. 'The lamb is good.'

'He'll have the same as me.' I collect up the menus and shove them at her, smiling sweetly. 'Medium.'

'Oh?' She looks at Jesse for confirmation.

'The wife has spoken.' He leans in and drapes his arm over

my shoulder, but keeps his eyes on the waitress. 'I do as I'm told, so it looks like I'm having the steak.'

I scoff, Mum and Dad laugh, and the waitress swoons all over her pad, almost certainly wishing that she had a god who did what he's told. 'You're impossible,' I say quietly, as my parents chuckle and look across the table fondly at Jesse making a meal of eating my neck.

'Ava, that was really quite rude,' Mum chastises me. 'Jesse can make his own meal choices.'

'It's okay, Elizabeth.' He sucks on my neck a bit more. 'She knows what I like.'

'You like to be impossible,' I quip, rubbing the side of my face into his stubble.

'I love watching you in trampling action,' he whispers in my ear. 'I could bend you over this table and fuck you *really* hard.'

I don't gasp or recoil at his crass words, spoken with no concern for the company we're sharing. They were definitely for my ears only. I turn into him, pushing my mouth to his ear. 'Stop saying the word *fuck*, unless you're going to fuck me.'

'Watch your mouth.'

'No.'

He laughs and bites my neck. 'Cheeky.'

'Let's raise a toast!' Dad's cheerful tone pulls us out of our private moment. 'To twins!'

'To twins!' Mum chants, and we all clink our glasses in acknowledgment to the fact that I'm going to get really fat.

After Jesse pays the bill, we take a slow wander back to my parents' house, Mum pointing out all of the sights to Jesse as we walk and chat. When we get home, Dad takes his usual seat in the window, armed with his remote control, and Mum fills the kettle.

'Bedtime tea?' she asks.

Jesse looks across the kitchen to me, clocking me yawning.

'No, I'm taking Ava to bed. Come on, lady.' He walks over and rests his hands on my shoulders, then proceeds to direct me out of the kitchen. 'Say goodnight to your mother.'

'Goodnight, Mother.'

'Sleep well,' she says, flicking the kettle on.

'Say goodnight to your father,' Jesse instructs as we pass the lounge.

'Goodnight, Dad.'

'Goodnight, you two.' Dad doesn't even crane his neck around from the television.

I'm pushed up the stairs and guided down the hallway until we reach the guest room, where he begins to strip me down. 'That was nice,' I muse as my dress is pulled up over my head.

'It was, but your mum is still a pain in the arse,' Jesse replies drily. 'Give me your wrist.'

I hold my hand up to him and watch while he removes my Rolex and slides it onto the bedside table. 'You trampled her again.' I'm smiling.

Reaching up to my neck, he starts unknotting my cream lace scarf. 'She'll learn eventually.' My scarf is removed, revealing my diamond, and he smiles, straightening it out. 'Are you looking forward to a few days of constant contact?'

'I can't wait,' I answer without a second hesitation, reaching up to unbutton his shirt and pushing it from his shoulders on a sigh. 'You're just too perfect.' I lean in and kiss his chest, leaving my lips lingering.

'I know,' he agrees, with no humour or sarcasm. The arrogant arse.

I drop his shirt and start working the button fly of his jeans before sliding my hands into the back and working them over the solidness of his arse. 'I love this.' I dig my nails in as I pass.

'I know,' he concurs again, making me smile. When I'm down to his thighs, I slip my hand around the front and grasp him loosely. He's solid, as I knew he would be. 'And you know how much I love this.'

He sucks in a hiss of breath through his teeth and pulls his groin away, but I maintain my hold. 'Ava, baby, there is no way in hell I'm taking you under your mother's roof.'

'Why?' I pout. 'I can be quiet.' I'm drifting into temptress mode.

He looks at me doubtfully, and so he should. I can't guarantee that at all. 'I don't think you can.'

I lower to my knees and unlace his shoes, and he lifts each in turn for me to remove them, along with his socks. Taking the waist of his jeans, I slowly pull them down his legs. 'I think you'll be surprised by what I can do. Lift.' I tap his ankle.

'You mean I'll be surprised by what I can *make* you do.' He lifts in turn, so I can remove his jeans and boxers. 'And I'm never surprised. I have that effect on you.'

Instead of stroking his overinflated ego, I stoop down and kiss the top of his foot before moving my lips to his ankle, circling my tongue and kissing my way up his legs. I take my time, flattening my palms on the fronts of his thighs, just feeling him as my lips skim every naked inch of his flesh, but I soon find myself at his neck, despite my determination to drag out the whole episode.

I inhale his scent and lift up on my tiptoes to reach his chin, which is higher than usual because he's looking up at the ceiling. I can't reach. 'What's the matter?'

'I'm trying to control myself.' His voice is all gravelly.

'I don't want you to.'

'Don't say that, Ava.'

'I don't want you to,' I repeat, all low and throaty, biting at his neck.

He moves fast. His arm snakes around my waist, and I'm pushed up against the nearest wall on a growl. I'm ecstatic and trying to play it cool, but my lips are parted and I'm breathing shocked gasps. 'You seem to be making some noise,' he observes quietly, holding one side of my face and pushing his mouth to my ear. I close my lips, clench my eyes shut and rest my head against the wall. I need to focus because he's going to *make* this hard for me, even if he doesn't *give* it to me hard. 'Now, listen very carefully.' He unhooks my bra while keeping a hand on my cheek and his mouth at my ear. 'Your parents seem to like me. Don't fuck it up.'

Oh good Lord, my confidence is diminishing fast. I bite painfully down on my lip, determined to keep quiet, as my lace bra is pulled away from my body and dropped to the floor before he leans down, taking my nipple in his mouth and sucking my nub gently until it's tingling and stiff. I hit my head against the wall, my face distorting as I try urgently to withhold a moan of pleasure.

I fail.

'Ohhhh God,' I groan, banging my head against the wall again.

'Oh *dear*.' He's at my lips immediately. 'You just can't control it, can you?'

I shake my head, unashamedly agreeing with him. 'No.'

'Which just confirms what we both know, doesn't it?' He rolls his naked hips upward, forcing me onto my tiptoes to try and escape the rub that will have me losing further control.

I fail again. 'Yes,' I pant, uncontrolled and grappling at his naked shoulders.

'And what is that, Ava?' He bites my lip and keeps hold while he waits for me to answer.

'You have the power.'

His eyes sparkle in approval, and I reach down to stroke him, but he pulls away from me on a mild head shake.

'I thought we just clarified who has the power.' My hand is pushed away. 'And I need to safeguard my current favourable standing with your parents, so you'll keep quiet.' He's staring at me, obviously waiting for confirmation that I understand. I do, but I absolutely cannot guarantee my silence. 'Can you be quiet, Ava?'

I lie. 'Yes.' I've been ambushed by him and his potency, and I'm not saying *no* if it means he'll tuck me up in bed to snuggle. Pregnancy is doing serious things to me. I'm more desperate than ever, if that's at all possible.

His eyes blink lazily, an almost undetectable smile flashing across his face, as he reaches up and pulls my hand away from my hair. 'It looks like we have a problem,' he whispers. 'Don't move.' He backs away and picks something up, and I'm distracted as he slowly comes towards me again, concealing whatever he's holding behind his back.

I'm fidgeting, squirming and thinking really hard about what the hell he's hiding, but I'm not left suffering for too long. He brings his hands around to the front of him and holds up my lace scarf, then wraps it around his fists and pulls it taut.

'I think we'll call this one the quiet fuck.' He brings the scarf to my mouth and slips it between my lips. 'Keep your tongue relaxed,' he instructs softly, taking it around the back of my head and tying it firmly but not tightly. 'If you feel the need to scream, bite down. Understand?'

I nod, my eyes following him as he leans down and removes my knickers. Soon I feel his hot tongue running up the inside of my leg. I don't want to scream, but I bite down on the scarf anyway, my eyes closing, my drumming heart beating an even pulse in my chest. He makes a point of breathing heavily in my ear as he laces his fingers through mine and pushes my hands up to the wall behind me before kissing down the sensitive flesh of my inside arm, softly and painfully slowly. I quickly fear that the only screaming I'll be doing will be in impatience. 'I think we'll do this lying down.' His low, sure voice has me praying for control as he brings our hands down, fingers still laced, and then starts walking backwards, encouraging me to step with him. Not that I need any encouragement. I'll follow this man wherever he goes, whether it's to a bed or to the end of the earth.

He places me gently on the bed, the tip of my nose is kissed, my hair smoothed from my face, and then I'm turned onto my side slightly, my leg lifted and bent so he can straddle the one still flush with the bed. He edges forward, holding himself with one hand and keeping my leg up with the other, watching what he's doing, getting closer until he skims my opening. If I could, I'd yelp, but I'm resorted to reaching behind me to grab the headboard. My back bows, even though he's just holding himself there. It's torturous.

'Ava,' he kisses my foot, 'nothing can beat this.' He sinks slowly into me, his head falling back. I overcome the overwhelming need to close my eyes in utter bliss, just so I can watch his face. His jaw tenses, his grip of my ankle increases, his free hand rests on my waist and his torso sharpens, the lines of every muscle defined and protruding. I so want to feel him there, but I'm immobilised by pleasure, rendering me incapable of moving. He's right. Nothing can or ever will beat this. It's agonisingly good, and I'm transfixed on him, completely captivated by him. So incredibly in love with him.

'Do you like what you see?' he asks as he withdraws slowly. I'm so fixated on the movement of his muscles, I've not noticed his head has now dropped and he's studying me. He gags me, inflicts this pleasure on me, and then expects the impossible. He wants me to reply? I shouldn't need to, he knows the answer very well, but I nod anyway. He doesn't smile or show any approval of my answer. He just gradually works his way deep inside me, as if rewarding me for my silent response. 'I like what I see, too.' I'm blessed with a precise grinding of his hips. I might not be able to cry out in pleasure, but I can moan. So I do.

Pulling out slowly, he plunges straight back in. He's starting to work up a steady rhythm. It remains controlled, it remains exact and it remains profoundly powerful, but without the force I know he's capable of. He's determined to make his point. I'm being thoroughly indulged. I'm being doted upon. I can live with this for the next few months.

I'm moaning again as he grinds, and when I feel his teeth graze my ankle, my head flies back and I'm unexpectedly overcome with heated tingles stabbing all over my skin, but more intensely between my thighs.

'She's losing control,' he gasps quietly, lifting up higher on his knees, taking my lower body with him. I start shaking my head, tightening my grip on the headboard and twisting my body to try and get onto my back. I'm attempting in vain. I could never overpower him. He has a firm hold on my hip, keeping me where he wants me. 'Don't fight me, Ava.' He strikes firmly but carefully, still denying me his power. But it's still good.

I don't *need* it. I crave it. Big difference, but my insatiable want has been fed good and proper, and now it's expected. In he goes again on a suppressed hiss. I bite down on the scarf and let out a muffled yell.

'Am I making you crazy, baby?' he asks, the tinge of smugness clear as he reverts back to a smooth, even pace.

I don't look at him. I close my eyes and turn my attention to catching the booming beat at my core before he tells me to control it. He's ruling me, and even though it's slow and almost effortless, it's still very deep and it's still very pleasurable, and I'm still going to erupt.

'You're doing well, Ava.' In he sinks, around he grinds, out he comes. 'My temptress is getting stronger.' Back in, back around, back out.

I whimper, flexing my hands on the headboard. The flowing of his body into mine is inconceivably good. So good. Holy shit! I try to shout his name, but all I achieve is a stifled, inaudible howl.

'Ava!' he whispers loudly. 'Shut the fuck up!' With that harsh demand comes a less controlled buck of his hips. It just pushes another yell from me, but it's no more decipherable. That cusp of pleasure is teasing me as he turns his mouth into my leg and bites down, and then reaches down to circle his thumb over my clitoris. That does it. I gulp, my body being yanked into a rigid arch as every muscle starts to spasm and I bite down on the lace scarf. If I could talk, I would be firing *fucks* off all over the place, so it is undoubtedly a good job that I can't. I'm shaking, moaning, and Jesse is still plunging into me, still solid and still biting on my ankle. I'm riding out the pleasure, but it's just going on and on and on.

I'm immensely grateful when my leg is released and I'm allowed to roll onto my back. I'm wrecked, and still relentlessly contracting around Jesse as he keeps himself buried deep and arranges my legs so he can settle between my thighs.

'Good?' he asks, his brows raised confidently as he looks down at me. I nod, my eyes closing, no matter how desperate I am to keep them on his damp, handsome face. I also want to feel his hair and give it a little yank, but my arms are welded to the headboard. 'You'll never know how much satisfaction I get from watching you fall apart under my touch,' he whispers, and I flick my eyes open briefly, seeing him raising his torso so he's braced on two muscle-swelling arms. He doesn't make any attempt to get any friction, instead seeming quietly content to just hover above me, and after a few moments have passed and he's unmoved but still twitching within me, I force my eyes open properly. He's gazing down at me, waiting for my eyes. 'She's back.'

Yes, only just, and she's still pulsating around his throbbing cock. I attempt to say something, my exhausted mind having forgotten that I'm gagged, but as soon as I realise my limitation,

I convince my arms to lift and sandwich his face between my palms. His stubble is nearly two days' worth. I love it.

He turns his head and kisses my palm before lowering himself onto his elbows and tucking his fingers under the scarf, pulling it down over my chin so it rests on my neck. I can talk, but funnily enough, I don't want to say anything now. I'm holding Jesse's face, soaking up the happiness oozing from his beautiful greens, and I'm happy to do just that.

'I want to kiss you,' he declares, but while his little proclamation is sweet, it's also light years away from the usual *kiss me* demand. That is probably why my brow is completely furrowed and Jesse's eyes are sparkling in amusement.

'You do?'

'Hmm.' He drags his thumb across my bottom lip and watches intently. 'I really do.'

'You can kiss me.' Being gagged has dried my throat out, making my voice rough and low.

His thumb reaches the corner of my mouth, and then sets off again, back across my lips. 'I'm not asking permission.' His eyes close and reopen, landing directly on mine. 'I'm just thinking out loud.'

'Why don't you stop thinking and do.' I raise my hips, signalling that kissing me is not the only thing I'd like him to do. Jesse working himself up is *really* going to work me down. I'm still buzzing, his arousal still held snugly inside me.

'Are you demanding, Mrs Ward?'

'Are you denying, Mr Ward?'

'No, but you do—'

'I know who has the power,' I interrupt, and he gives me that roguish grin as he slowly dips, his lips finding mine and taking what I'm so willing to give.

'I've never tasted anything so good.' His hips swivel, sweeping through my remnants of pleasure.

'Not even an Ava éclair?' I ask around his lush, wet mouth.

'Not even an Ava éclair,' he confirms, nibbling his way up to my ear. 'Not even peanut butter,' he murmurs, reaching down and hooking his arm under my knee. He pulls my bent leg upward and plants his fist in the mattress so my leg is draped over his arm. 'Just pure,' he sucks my earlobe, 'raw,' he bites down, 'naked,' and then drags it teasingly through his teeth. I shudder as he skims across my cheek and plunges his tongue into my mouth. 'Ava,' he finishes on a whisper. 'Pure, raw, naked, Ava. And I've got her for three whole days . . . all . . . to . . . myself.'

I smile around his lips and find his hair, unable to resist a playful yank as he moans and pleasures me with those damn delectable, wonderfully talented hips. Deep grinds. Firm dives. Easy retreats. I sigh, and when I feel the rolling waves of his muscles tensing around my body, I know that he's tipping the edge, so I harden my kiss, yank at his hair a little more and moan. He's blazing, and he pulls away on a gasp. My hands move straight to his neck. The throbbing in his neck vein is matching his laboured breaths, and our eyes lock, his full of hunger, mine full of surrender.

'My heart's bucking wildly,' he murmurs, pushing into me one last, deep, steady time and just holding himself there as he inhales severely and begins to shake. 'Fuck, that feels good.'

I'm not joining him in his climax, but it doesn't stop me from whimpering shallowly and sucking in my own sharp breath, my thighs finding his waist and my arms moving to his shoulders to pull him down. I kiss him deeply, invading his mouth forcefully, helping him through the twitching and jerking of his body.

'Good?' I ask around his mouth.

He keeps our kiss up and bites my tongue lightly. 'Don't ask stupid fucking questions.' He rolls onto his back and lifts his arm for me to find my happy place. My fingertips find his scar and start their usual trailing from side to side as he pulls me in snugly and breathes into my hair. 'Okay?'

'Don't ask stupid fucking questions.' I grin into the side of his chest.

'Ava, one day I'm going to shove a bar of soap in your mouth.'

He probably would. 'What time are we leaving?'

'Sevenish. We're flying at noon from Heathrow.'

'Heathrow? We've got to drive all the way back to London?' Is he kidding me?

'Yes. It was the only place where I could get a flight at such short notice.'

'You could've got something from Bristol, at least.' I just can't help myself.

'Shut up. Let's talk about our plans for the weekend.'

'Have you made plans?'

'Yes, it involves lots of lace and even more naked flesh.'

Just me, Jesse and lots of naked flesh, after lots of lace has been removed . . . slowly. I smile, snuggle deeper and let my sleepy mind wander to all things Jesse-ish.

Chapter 23

'Have you got everything?' Mum's still in her dressing gown as she faffs all over the driveway.

'Yes,' I sigh with optimum exasperation, for the tenth time.

'It was brief, but I'm so happy you came to see us.' She clasps my cheeks and kisses me. 'You must take care.'

I roll my eyes, but hug her.

'Are you insinuating that I can't look after my wife?' Jesse asks seriously as he shuts the boot of the car.

She throws a small scowl over to him. 'I would never insinuate that you couldn't look after *my* daughter.' She's poking him. It's like the O'Shea women have a compulsion to goad Jesse Ward.

Jesse strolls over, leaving my dad browsing around the loaned DBS. 'She doesn't need to take care because I do that for her.' He pulls me from my mum's grasp. 'Mine.' He grins and smothers me to make his point.

'Menace,' Mum huffs, trying not to smile. 'Joseph! Don't get any ideas.'

We all turn to see my dad running his palm down the gleaming bonnet of the Aston Martin. 'Just admiring,' he says. 'I thought yours had black leather?'

I glance at Jesse and send a telepathic message to think of something fast to explain why the interior has gone from black leather to cream. 'Mine's in for a service. It's a courtesy car.' He reels off the explanation with complete ease.

Dad laughs. 'I don't get courtesy cars like this from my garage.'

Jesse smiles and leads me to the passenger side, pushing me down gently and buckling me in before adjusting the lap belt. I bat his hands away, earning myself a growl. 'I'm not incapable.'

'No, you're very capable,' he narrows annoyed eyes on me, 'of driving me fucking nuts!'

'You drive yourself nuts,' I retort, pushing him away and shutting the door. I let the window down. 'Bye!' I blow my parents a kiss and watch as Jesse shakes hands with my dad and kisses my mum chastely on the cheek before making his way around the front of the car, drilling holes into me through the window as he does.

He slips in and starts the engine. 'This weekend will be a lot more pleasant if you do as you're told,' he grumbles, pulling away from my parents' house. He starts flicking a few switches on the steering wheel. 'No sickness this morning?'

'No,' I sigh. 'You shoving a ginger biscuit in my mouth the second I woke up took care of that,' I quip, bolting upright when the car stereo kicks in and Mr JT himself joins us. I turn eyes mixed with surprise and amusement to Jesse. He knows that I'm looking at him, but he's ignoring it. 'You had them put this CD in, didn't you?' I'm using every ounce of willpower not to grin.

He frowns at the road. 'Don't be stupid.'

'You did. On the special request part of the form that you completed, you wrote: "Please load the disc player with Justin."' I pause. 'Did you put a love heart and a few kisses on it, too?' I'm most certainly grinning now.

He slowly turns unamused eyes to me. 'Do you think you're funny?'

'Yes.' I reach forward and crank the volume up, and then start jigging in my seat, singing along and generally taking the piss out of my JT fanatical god. 'Hey!' I yelp when his fingers squeeze my hipbone and the music is suddenly low again. 'I was enjoying that.'

'You should. He's a very talented man.'

'*You're* a very talented man.'

'I know.' He shrugs. 'We have a lot in common. He's a great guy.'

'You've met him?'

'No, he keeps putting his requests in, but I'm too busy.' It's him concealing a grin now.

I laugh, and he slips his Wayfarers on, but not before giving me a wink and a little jiggle of his shoulders.

Laid-back Jesse. God, I love this man.

Jesse takes us on an adventure around the airport, dipping in and weaving past cars, taking turns in the wrong direction and generally just seeming like he has no idea where he's going. I watch the sign for the airport car park go sailing past my window and frown to myself. Then I look at the clock. It's eleven-thirty and we're supposed to be flying in half an hour. We haven't checked in, done security or anything.

'Shit!' I blurt, grabbing my bag up from the floor.

'Ava, mouth! What's up?' He takes a corner too hard, and my hand shoots out to steady myself on the door.

'Will you take it easy?' I snap irritably.

'Ava, there's no place you're safer than in a car with me. What's the matter?'

'My passport,' I say, diving into my bag, looking in vain because I know it's not in here. I didn't put it in here, and my rummaging slows when I realise exactly where my passport is. He'll go spare. 'I've left my passport in my box of junk,' I tell him, mentally cursing myself for not sorting that box out yet.

He reaches forward and flips the glove compartment open. 'No you haven't, but you have forgotten to get your name changed, Miss O'Shea.' He drops it on my lap and tosses me a reproachful look.

'So I'm travelling a single?' I ask, opening it up and admiring my maiden name.

'Shut up, Ava.' He screeches to a stop and jumps out, making quick work of getting around to my side and opening my door. I would have done it myself, but I'm just staring out of the windscreen with my mouth slightly agape. 'Come on.'

I look up as a well-suited and booted man approaches with another in a captain's uniform. My passport is whipped from my grasp, hands are shaken, paperwork and signatures are exchanged, and then our luggage is removed from the boot.

'Are you going to sit there all day, lady?' He holds his hand out to me, and I take it automatically, letting him pull me from the car.

'What's that?' I ask, nodding at the toy-like plane sitting a few yards away from us.

'That's a plane.' There is humour in his voice. I'm pulled towards the jet, not feeling any more enthusiastic as we get closer because it's not getting any bigger, and I'm not filled with any further confidence when Jesse has to dip to enter the damn thing to avoid smacking his head. I halt on the ridiculously small number of steps that will have me boarding.

'I'm not getting on this thing.' I'm attacked by an unreasonable bout of fear. I've never been afraid of flying, but this little plane is really pumping the anxiety through my veins.

Jesse smiles, but frowns at the same time. 'Of course you are.'

My arm is tugged gently, encouragingly, but I'm not shifting. In fact, I'm backing away.

'Ava, you've never said you're scared of flying.' He dips again and stands up straight, back on the outside of the jet.

'I'm not in big planes. Why are we not going on a big plane?' I look behind me and see heaps of big planes. 'Why can't we go on one of those?'

'Because they're probably not going where we need them to,' he says softly. I feel my arm go lax in front of me from where he's getting closer, and then his palm is on my cheek. 'It's perfectly safe,' he assures me, pulling my gaze away from all of the big planes that I'd like to board instead.

'It doesn't look safe.' I glance past him and see a perfectly positioned woman with perfectly styled hair, perfect make-up and a perfect smile. 'It looks too small.'

'Ava.' His soft voice pulls my eyes back to his. He's smiling down at me. 'This is me, your possessive, unreasonable, overprotective control freak.' He kisses me gently. 'Do you really think I'd willingly put you in danger?'

I shake my head, fully aware that I'm being a complete baby.

'Answer my question.'

'No, I don't.'

'Good.' He rounds me and clasps my shoulders, pushing me gently up the steps. 'You'll love it; trust me.'

'Good morning!' The perfect woman, who's still standing perfectly in place, greets us, holding her arm out in a signal of where to go. It's really not necessary. There are one of two ways, and I'm not going anywhere near the cockpit.

Peering inside, I notice just a few chairs, all massive, all leather, all reclining, and just two rows of them – one on each side of the jet. I'm directed to the middle, turned around and eased down into the soft plumpness. I keep quiet and resist the urge to bolt as Jesse secures my seatbelt and takes a seat opposite me. He immediately lifts my feet to his lap.

'Champagne, sir?' Perfect lady is back, and I spy her beaming at my god, but I'm too busy gathering my pathetic anxiousness to trample.

'Just water,' Jesse answers shortly, with no smile, no acknowledgment and no please. She beats a hasty retreat, and Jesse slips my ballet pumps from my feet, dropping them carelessly to the floor before getting comfy and repositioning my feet so they're at a good angle for him to massage. 'Okay?' he asks.

'Not really.' I wiggle my toes. 'I haven't got swollen feet yet, you know.'

His thumbs are working delicious, firm circles into the insteps of my feet. 'Close your eyes and make yourself comfy, baby,' he orders tenderly, and I do. My eyes slowly shut, and the last image I see is of my god lovingly massaging my feet, trying to ease me out of my unwarranted fit of nervousness.

I let my mind shut down and drift into a semi-conscious state of bliss. It's not a difficult task to achieve when he's touching me, even if it is just my feet. It's the usual scenario of Jesse drawing all of my troubles out of me, whether it's justified troubles, or completely trivial, unnecessary troubles, like a sudden fear of flying. My subliminal state only barely notes that regardless of trivial or justified troubles, Jesse is the maker.

And then my mind moseys through all things Jesse-ish – the lace, the calla lilies, the peanut butter, the dislike of swearing – and I mentally smile. All of the various degrees of Jesse-style fuckings, the temper, the playfulness, the gentleness. I might really be smiling now. The handcuffs, the lace gag, the crucifix, the rowing machine, the Ava éclair. My heart has speeded up. The dirty blond, the addictive, sludgy but bright eyes, the sculptured perfection, the one and two days' worth of stubble. The way he flicks the collar up on his polo shirts, his various smiles – for women, for me, and now for my tummy, too. His fierceness, his protectiveness, his dominant ways. The way he walks and the way he tramples, and all of the ways in which he loves me, with unapologetic, raw adoration. The way I return that love.

I shift in my seat and in my subconscious, I hear his laugh. The soft, low one. Then I feel the wet warmth of his tongue on my toe. I smile, being snapped from all of my mental assessments of my beautiful husband. Then I open one eye, and I'm greeted by his smile, reserved only for me.

'Dreaming?' he asks, biting down on my little toe.

'Of you,' I sigh. 'Tell me when we take off so I can put my head between my legs.'

'I'll put my head between your legs.' He sucks my toe, and I shudder.

'Just tell me.'

'Look out the window, baby.'

I frown and gaze out, expecting to find runways and planes, but instead, I find clouds. My relaxed state falters, just for a split second, before I register no movement. There is hardly any sound, either. It's really peaceful. I look to the side and see our waters placed on a highly polished table, and then I peek down the aisle and see the perfect woman pottering around at the other end of the jet. 'Why didn't you tell me?'

He kisses my toe. 'And miss the sounds and looks you were making?' He drops my foot. 'Come here.' I don't stall for a second. I unclip my belt and virtually dive onto his lap, nestling my head under his chin and wrapping my arms around his neck. 'Go back to sleep and dream of me, lady.'

He doesn't need to ask twice.

I come to, still tucked into Jesse's body. I can hear him quietly speaking, but it's all muffled. A little groggy, I pull myself up and find the perfect woman hovering over us. 'Welcome to Malaga, Mrs Ward.' She blasts me with a part-of-the-job smile.

'Thank you.' I return her smile, although mine is weaker. Malaga? Like Spain Malaga? Like near to Marbella Malaga?

'My beautiful girl's back.' He kisses my cheek. 'Enjoy your flight?'

I look at him through my fog of sleepiness and note a stubbled, hazy, smiling face, and a dishevelled mop of dark blond. 'Do I yank your hair in my sleep?' I croak, reaching up to pat it down.

'You do a lot in your sleep. I could watch you for ever.'

I make to move, but get absolutely nowhere. 'I need to stretch,' I complain, wriggling.

I hear a click, and I'm instantly free. 'I needed to belt you in.' He helps me to my feet and watches as my arms rise, nearly touching the ceiling of the plane. 'Aren't I supposed to be belted into my own seat for landing?' I ask. 'With my seat in the upright position, my table stowed away, and all of my belongings tucked neatly under the seat in front?'

He raises a sardonic eyebrow. 'Yes. I very nearly had to trample the lovely lady.' He stands himself and pulls my blouse down, which is riding up my navel from my stretched position. He holds it in place until I've finished. 'Done?'

'Yes,' I yawn, as he releases the hem of my top. I know this is probably a sign of things to come over the next couple of days, but he'd better lighten up and fast because I've packed my bikinis, and I'll be wearing them.

As we emerge into the bright sunlight, I smile, the heat hitting my face and warming me to the core. Or warming me further. I already have a lovely, peaceful warmth coursing through me, and that's only going to increase over the next few days. Taking the steps down to the Tarmac, we're immediately greeted by a smart Spanish man, who hands Jesse a set of keys. Then I spot the DBS.

'Really?' I blurt. 'We couldn't have taken a taxi?'

He scoffs and signs the paperwork presented to him. 'I don't do public transport, Ava.'

'You should. It'll save you a fortune.'

Handing back the paperwork, he makes quick work of putting me in the wrong side of the car, throwing me off a little. Once he's buckled me in and I've gathered my bearings, I settle in the familiar, if a little warmer, softness of the leather seat and listen to the bumping and banging of the luggage being loaded into the boot.

Jesse jumps in and slips his shades on. 'Are you ready to be binged on for the next three days?'

'No, take me home.' I grin and lean across, planting a kiss on his lips.

'Not a chance, lady. You're all mine, and I'm going to make the most of it.' He returns my kiss, palming the back of my head to pull me closer.

'I'm always yours.'

'Correct. Get used to it.' I'm released before he hastily rams the Aston in gear and screeches away from the jet.

'I am used to it,' I muse, resting my elbow on the door and settling my head so I can watch the unfamiliar world go by. It's all very boring and concrete-like for a while as we make our way out of the airport and away from the hustle and bustle of central Malaga, but then we hit a coast road, and the sight of the Mediterranean meeting the sky holds my attention for the rest of the journey. Mansun sing about a 'Wide Open Space', and the smell of heat mixed with the kicked-up dust of the well-worn road overpowers the usual lingering scent of fresh water, leaving me resentful of its intrusion on my nose. We cruise along in a comfortable silence, the stereo in the background keeping us company, Jesse's hand resting on my knee, and mine clutching it. I sneak a peek of his profile and smile before I close my eyes, relax further into the leather and think of the tranquil, undisturbed time ahead of us.

I'm not asleep, but my eyes come open when the road beneath the tyres becomes bumpy and the car starts jolting all over the place. I look to the road ahead and the first thing that strikes me is the appalling condition of it. There's rubble all over the rut-riddled surface, leaving Jesse negotiating the prestigious car with care. 'Where are we?'

'This is paradise, baby,' Jesse says, deadly serious. I almost laugh, but worry is preventing it. I've seen paradise, in pictures mainly, and this couldn't be any further removed. There is nothing, only this dusty shambles of a road and a few houses – if you can call the ramshackle structures that.

I'm starting to feel nauseous from being tossed around in this lovely car when a colossal set of wooden gates come into view and my attention is captured by the high, whitewashed wall stemming from each side and stretching out into the distance. And then I see it.

Paradise.

There is a sign on the wall next to the gate and it says 'Paradise'. He cannot be serious. My tranquil mind isn't feeling so tranquil, not now that I'm surrounded by this most untranquil vista. Yes, it's quiet, but the whole deadness of our surroundings is just making it feel eerie, rather than peaceful.

'Jesse . . .' I'm not sure what to say. He doesn't seem in the least bit perturbed by all of this, which leaves me thinking that he's been here before. If he has, then why would he return? I'm not given any explanation, he just flips a switch and smiles fondly as the wooden gates start to creak open.

We breach the gates and we're immediately closed in by darkness, a canopy of the greenest green I've ever seen draping over us and the driveway ahead. Clusters of white flowers are spotted here and there among the foliage and the most potent fragrance is seeping into the car, even with all of the windows closed.

'That smell.' I sniff deeply and exhale on a sigh.

'This is nothing. At nightfall it's pungent.' Jesse breathes in deeply himself, humming in pleasure as he exhales.

The sunlight flickers towards the end of the concealed driveway and makes me squint, even through my shades. It's like a light has been abruptly switched on and, all of a sudden, I've been transported to . . .

Paradise.

My breath catches in my throat, and I unclip my belt to sit

forward, blinking to ensure that I'm not imagining this. The grimy concrete and wasteland jungle is no more, and in its place is an idyllic haven, bursting with greenery, neatly trimmed lawns and pergolas dripping in pompoms of red flowers. We're suddenly not moving any more, and I waste no time ejecting myself from the car, shutting the door and absorbing my new, improved surroundings. I start walking across the uneven, cobbled driveway toward the terracotta villa up ahead, not bothering to wait for Jesse, or even to check that he's following. I take the steps up to the veranda that circles the entire property and turn to get the full view of the grounds.

Paradise.

When I think that I've taken it all in, I turn my attention back to Jesse, finding him sitting on the bonnet of the DBS, legs stretched and crossed at the ankles. His arms are folded over his chest, too. And he's smiling. 'What's my beautiful girl thinking?'

My hand reaches out and pulls a stray leaf from the shrubbery hanging from some trellis on the veranda. I smell it and sigh. 'I'm thinking that I've just officially arrived on Central Jesse Cloud Nine.'

'Where?' The confusion and amusement in his tone is clear.

I grin, drop the leaf, and start running towards him, only vaguely registering his increased amusement as he stands and readies himself for my attack. I launch myself at him, my body taking up the usual baby-monkey-style hold, and I tackle his mouth, full of enthusiasm. He doesn't stop me. He holds me under my bum and smiles around my brute force.

'It's my most favourite place in the world,' I say, easing up on his lips and looking down at him, noticing immediately that his Wayfarers are still fixed to his face. I pull them off so I can see all of him.

'Are you happy?' he asks.

'Delirious.' I thread my fingers through his hair and give it my usual little tug.

'Then my work here is done.' His mouth goes to my neck and bites lightly before he disconnects me from his body. 'Let me get the cases.'

'I'll help,' I say, automatically following him to the rear of the car but immediately backing off when he turns and flashes me a cautionary look. 'Okay, I won't help.' I hold my hands up and fetch my bag from the car instead, then follow Jesse to the single-storey villa.

He drops the cases briefly while he unlocks the door, then I'm ushered in to complete darkness, with only slices of light penetrating the gaps between the closed shutters. I can't see much, but I can smell, and that perfume is rife inside, too, the potency incredible and lingering everywhere.

'Wait here,' Jesse instructs, dumping the cases by the door and disappearing outside again. I stand, gazing around the walls for a light switch, but I can't see a thing, even with the faint light pouring in from the doorway. And then it's like a spotlight has hit a blackened stage when a sudden gush of sunlight shoots across the room and collides with the wall opposite. Then there's another, and another, then another. I watch as the space transforms into a busy crossroads of light lines until there's no more darkness, just sunlight streaming in from every window and door. My sensitive eyes want to close, but it's impossible when there is so much to focus on. The walls are smooth and white, the floor is laid in giant honey-coloured flagstones, with cream rugs scattered randomly and a giant U-shaped couch facing the doors that lead to a pool surrounded by bright-green grass. And beyond that, a beach.

'Oh wow,' I breathe, walking tentatively forward, my excitement building the closer I get. Before I know it, I've crossed the terrace, padded my way over the lawn, and I'm standing, fiddling with a cast-iron gate that's getting between me and the beach.

'Here.' Jesse's hand is suddenly on mine, and a key is inserted into the lock, opening the gate and allowing me to pass through.

Ten wooden sleepers formed as steps and covered in sand and grass take me down to the beach. It's deserted, and as I look each way for any sign of life, I realise we're in a bay. There are no other properties in sight – no beach bars, no hotels, not anything. It really is just us, this beautiful villa, and the midnight blue warmth of the Mediterranean.

'Still on Central Jesse Cloud Nine?' he whispers in my ear, slipping his forearm around the tops of my shoulders and pulling me back to rest against his chest.

'I am. Where are you?'

'Me?' he asks, kissing my cheek softly and sliding his palm onto my tummy. 'Baby, I'm in paradise.'

I close my eyes on a contented smile and sink into his body, my hand finding his on my stomach, our fingers intertwining and feeling each other. Central Jesse Cloud Nine really is Paradise.

We spend the rest of the afternoon unpacking and taking delivery of groceries, and Jesse gives me a guided tour, showing me the six en-suite bedrooms, all with doors leading to a different part of the veranda. The kitchen, which is white and modern, has wooden stained worktops and little touches like the suspended wooden grid with cast-iron pans hanging over the cooking area to maintain the rustic feel of the villa. As an interior designer, I'm in awe. I couldn't have done a better job myself. The bedrooms are all plain-walled, but with sumptuous fabrics dressing the beds and billowing voile hanging at the windows. Sporadically placed canvases take the edge off the sparseness and all of the randomly scattered rugs break up the vastness of the flagstone flooring that runs through the entire villa.

Now we're sitting at the gigantic wooden table in the kitchen with a jug of iced water, and the questions are not prepared to stay in my brain for much longer. This place holds significance somewhere in Jesse's life and my curious mind is struggling to hold back.

He watches me with a small smile as I lift my glass to my lips before he proceeds to quench his own thirst, still keeping his eyes on mine. I'm desperate to ask, and he knows it, but he's making me suffer. 'Would you like something to eat?'

I can't prevent the surprised look from jumping onto my face. 'Are you going to cook for me?' There's no Cathy here, and he knows I hate cooking.

'I could've had staff, but I wanted you to myself.' He grins that roguish grin. 'I think you should look after your husband and fulfil your obligation as my wife.'

I cough a little at his arrogance. 'When you married me, you knew I hated cooking.'

'And when you married me, you knew I *couldn't* cook.'

'But you have Cathy.'

'In England I have Cathy to feed me, which is a good job as my wife doesn't.' He's serious now. 'In Spain I have my wife. And she's going to make me something to eat. You did a good job with the chicken.'

He's right, I did, but that doesn't mean I enjoyed it, although I'd be lying if I said that I didn't enjoy watching him eat it. I was looking after him for a change, and with that thought, I'm oddly keen to prepare him a meal. 'Okay.' I stand up. 'I'll fulfil my obligation.'

'Oh good. It's about time you did what you're told,' he says candidly, no smile, no humour. 'Get to it, then.'

'Don't push it, Ward,' I warn, leaving him at the table and making my way to the fridge. It doesn't take me long to decide what to cook. I grab some peppers, chorizo sausage, rice and mushrooms, along with some lamb cutlets, and transport them to the worktop before locating a chopping board and a knife.

I set to work, halving the peppers and deseeding them, and then chopping the mushrooms and sausage finely and frying it all off. I boil the rice, chop some fresh bread and pan fry the lamb. And the whole time he sits and watches me busy myself, with no offer of help and no attempt to make conversation. I'm halfway through stuffing the peppers when he appears in front of me, leaning across the counter from the other side. 'You're doing a great job, lady.'

I pick my knife up and wield it at him. 'Don't patronise me.'

I'm shocked when his relaxed face flashes black and the knife is snatched from my hand. 'Don't fucking wave knives around, Ava!'

'Sorry!' I blurt, glancing at it in his hand and quickly appreciating my stupidity. It's a nasty-looking blade, and I'm brandishing it about like it's a rhythmic gymnast's ribbon. 'I'm sorry,' I repeat.

He places it down carefully and seems to gather himself. 'It's okay. Forget about it.'

I gesture towards the table for anything to do other than apologise again. 'Do you want to lay the table?'

'Sure,' he says quietly, maybe thinking that he's gone a bit over the top; I don't know, but his withdrawn mood and my chastised state have formed a clear tension.

Jesse leaves me and quietly lays the table for two while I finish preparing dinner.

'Here.' I slide his plate in front of him, but before I can pull my hand away, he grabs it and looks up at me with sorry eyes.

'I overreacted.'

I feel better already. 'No, it's fine. I shouldn't be so careless.'

He smiles. 'Sit.' He pulls my chair out, but as soon as I've lowered myself, he stands. 'We're missing something,' he informs me, striding off and leaving me wondering where he's gone. It's not long before he's back, holding a candle in one hand and a remote control in the other. He finds some matches, lights the candle and places it in the centre of the table, then pushes a few buttons on the remote control, filling the villa with a distinct male voice. I recognise it immediately.

'Mick Hucknall?'

'Or God. Either will do.' He smiles as he takes his seat.

'You're willing to share your title?'

'He's worthy,' he replies casually. 'This looks good. Eat up.'

I acknowledge his nod at my plate with a small smile and carve my way through a piece of lamb, resisting the urge to brandish my knife again when Jesse leans over, looking at my meat. He's checking how well it's cooked. I help him out, turning my plate so he can see the centre of my lamb. I like my steak medium, but I love my lamb cooked thoroughly.

I stab a piece with my fork and bring it up to my lips. 'May I?' I ask, completely serious and with no hint of a smile on my face, which is good because I'm matching Jesse.

'You may,' he says, slicing through his own lamb and taking his first bite. He chews, nods and swallows. 'You can cook, wife.'

'I've never said I can't. I just don't like doing it.'

'Not even for me?'

'I don't mind,' I answer coolly.

'I like you cooking for me,' he muses. 'It's kind of normal.'

I pause and place my knife down. 'Normal?'

'Yes, normal. Like what normal married people do.'

'Normal, like the wife cooks and the husband eats? That's a bit chauvinistic.' I laugh, but he doesn't. He's still concentrating on his careful cutting and eating. He wants normality? Then he should try being a bit *normal* himself. But do I want him to be normal? He wouldn't be Jesse if he was normal. We wouldn't be *us* if he was normal. I take another bite of lamb to busy my mouth. We'll never be normal, not completely, and I hope we're not.

He shrugs, rests his cutlery on the side of his plate and sits back in his chair, slowly raising his eyes to mine as he chews purposely slow. What's going on in that head of his? The greenness of his gaze has me engrossed, making me slow my own chews down to mimic his. 'Isn't this normal?' he asks, his voice low and throaty.

'You mean having dinner together?'

'Yes.'

I shrug a little. 'Yes, this is normal.'

He nods mildly. 'What about if I spread you on this table during dinner and fuck you? Would that be normal?'

My eyes widen a little in surprise. I don't know why because that would be perfectly normal for us. 'Our normal is you taking what you want, when you want it. You can chuck in a meal cooked by your wife, if you like.'

'Good.' He collects his knife and fork. 'I like our normal.'

I frown at him. What was the point of all that? 'Is something worrying you?'

'No,' he answers far too quickly.

'Yes, there is,' I fire back, and I think I know what it is. 'Are you suddenly considering the possibility of no *wherever and whenever* with two babies around?'

'Not at all.'

'Look at me,' I demand, and he does, but he's looking at me in shock. I don't give him a chance to ask me who the hell I think I'm talking to. 'You are, aren't you?'

His shock turns to a glower. 'Wherever, whenever.'

'Not with two babies around.' I could laugh at him. He's suddenly well aware that his possession over my body is going to be curbed. I return to my dinner, delighting in this revelation. 'They'll need a lot of my attention.'

He points his fork at me. Not his knife, but his fork. 'Yes, your primary role will be the care of our children, but a close second, and I mean a very close second, will be for my indulgence.

Wherever, whenever, Ava. I might need to control my craving for you to a certain extent, but don't think I'm going to sacrifice devoting my life to consuming you. Constant contact. Wherever, whenever. That's not going to change, just because we have babies.' He stabs at a piece of lamb and yanks it off the fork with his mouth.

If wanting me to cook for him was chauvinistic, then I have no idea what that little speech would represent. 'Even if I'm knackered from night feeds?' I'm poking.

'Too tired for me to take you?' he asks, shocked.

'Yes.'

'We'll get a nanny.' His lamb takes another vicious stabbing, and I mentally laugh my socks off.

'But I've got you,' I remind him.

He sighs and drops his knife and fork to his plate. 'You do.' His fingertips go to his temples and start rubbing calming circles. 'You do have me, and you always will.' He reaches over and takes my hand. 'Promise me you'll never say "I'm too tired" or "I'm not in the mood".'

'You're the one who tells me I'm too tired!' I practically screech. 'It's okay for you to knock *me* back.'

'That's because I have the power,' he says frankly. 'Promise me.'

'You want me to promise you that I'm here for you to take as and when you please?'

He looks away, only very briefly, before returning thoughtful eyes to me. 'Yes,' he says simply.

'What if I don't?' I'm being insolent for the sake of it. I'll never be too tired for this man, but his sudden epiphany is really quite amusing. He should have thought about all of this before he nicked my pills.

He laughs, and then the arrogant swine only leans back and pulls his T-shirt over his head, revealing himself in all of his clean-cut perfection. He looks down at his chest, as if refreshing his own memory of just how incredibly flawless he is. My eyes are on that chest, too. I might even be salivating all over my lamb, but I'm defiantly resisting his tactics. I drink in his godliness, my eyes skipping over every hard piece of him, my mind making a mental note to refresh my mark. It's fading. 'You'll never resist this.' He gestures to his torso.

My eyes whip back up, seeing self-assured, bright greens. 'I'm used to it.' I rip my greedy stare away from the equal perfection of his face and back to my plate. My eyes are not happy and are pulling in my sockets to get another fill. 'It kind of gets the same old after a while,' I add as casually as I can.

He's on me in a second, pulling me from the table and taking me down to a rug. I don't get a moment to register what's happened until I'm barely breathing and he's coating me completely. 'You're a shit liar, baby.'

'I know,' I concede. I'm crap at it.

'Let's see how used to it you are, shall we?' He moves my arms to my sides and sits astride of me, pinning me in place. I'm immobile and suddenly very concerned by this situation. I've been here plenty of times before, and most of them I came out the other end a very unhappy girl.

'Jesse, please don't,' I beg, for very little purpose. He's in a trampling mood, his sudden realisation of how he might be sidelined sparking his animal instinct to stake his claim. He's like a lion.

'What?' he asks. 'You're used to it.'

He's fully aware that I'll never get used to it. I'll look at him this way, appreciate him this way and become consumed with desire this way for the rest of my days. And I can't wait. That desire is coursing through my veins right now. It's always lying dormant in the background, simmering gently, ready for a few right words or a touch. Then the simmering transforms into a fizzing, deep in my tummy, and then impatience, and then torturous pleasure until explosion, whether it's of the soft, rollover kind, or the mind-bending, screaming kind. I'm starting to fizz now. My tummy muscles are squeezing and he's probably aware because unlike previous encounters lately, he's resting on my stomach. Has he had enlightenment that he won't hurt his babies?

My current position and the relentless beat between my thighs isn't helped when he raises to his knees and starts unbuttoning the fly of his jeans. This is going to be painful. If he's going to go full force into dominant Jesse, then I want to make the most of it, and I have no hope of seizing the opportunity with my body and arms pinned down. I feel a yell of frustration brewing and as hard as I try to pull my insatiable eyes away from those abdominals as his hands work his jeans, I'm failing miserably. Used to it? Fucking ridiculous thing to claim.

'Jesse, let me up.' I don't bother wriggling because it will only tire me out, and I'm storing my energy for what I hope is to come.

'No, Ava.' He pushes the waist of his jeans down a little, revealing his tight, white Armani's. This is getting harder.

'Please,' I plead.

There's a glint of victory sparkling from his hooded eyes, even though we both know he's not done yet. 'No, Ava.' He slips his thumb into the waistband of his boxers.

I catch a glimpse of his dark-blond mass of hair and the unmistakable taut, smooth flesh of his cock. 'Oh God.' I close my eyes in hopelessness, hating him and loving him all at once. Keeping myself in darkness, I'm beyond mystified when I don't get the familiar bark to *open*. I'm not mystified for long, though. Not when I feel movement, and then the sensation of something solid and wet slipping across my lips. Natural instinct kicks in and my lips open, but I don't get mouth penetration, so I open my eyes to be met by his stomach from where he's dropped a hand by my head and is leaning over me. Glancing up to find his face, I know what look I'll see; I know it'll drive me insane with lust. And I know that I'll be able to do fuck all about it. But I still look anyway.

And there it is. My Lord, braced on one stupidly solid arm, his obscenely addictive eyes dropped low, his sickeningly long lashes fanning that stunning face and with a little flick of my eyes, I'm staring at that stomach and chest which should be deemed a hazard. With the added bonus of him holding himself, grazing my lips with the broad magnificence of his cock, I'm ruined. 'Mouth,' I demand calmly.

'What do I do to you, Ava?' he asks, clearly confident of the answer and teasing me with another dash of contact to my lips.

'You fucking cripple me!' I yell on a pointless writhe.

'Watch your fucking mouth,' he practically groans the words out, only heightening my simmering state *and* my aggravation.

'Please!'

'Are you used to me?'

'No!'

'And you never will be. This is our normal, baby. Get used to this.' He slides himself into my mouth on a moan, and I accept willingly, elatedly, eagerly. I moan around his invasion, I suck, lap and bite, but I don't have full control. He's retaining the power, but I don't care. It's contact.

'Keep it gentle, Ava.' He forces the words out, and I glance up to indulge in the strain on his face as he watches my mouth indulge on his arousal. 'I love your fucking mouth, woman.' His free hand creeps behind my neck and locks on my nape, holding me in place whilst he gently thrusts forward, slowly, evenly, deliciously. No hard necessary, but that's not to say he isn't fulfilling *his* obligation to be dominant Jesse. He's worked out the happy medium in our *normal* relationship, even if I haven't, but I'm beginning to get it, and he is doing a bloody fine job of showing me the way.

Biting down gently midway up his steel length, the telltale

signs of a regular throb, accompanied by the tensing of his legs, which are securing my arms, give me all the prompt I need. My licks and strokes become more forceful, ignoring his demand to keep it gentle. He's going to come. I moan around him, he bucks on a round of explicit language, but then he's not in my mouth any more. He pushes himself up to his knees, fists his swollen cock and watches me with parted lips as he finishes. I'm annoyed, but one of my favourite mental images of all time is being refreshed – the erotic, extraordinary vision of Jesse working himself to climax, but this time it's better because he has just reached up and swept his wet hair from his face, trailing his hand through his dirty-blond mass, ripping the muscles of his chest further. I nearly choke with satisfaction. Given a few more moments, I think I'd orgasm just watching this. Holy shit, he looks divine.

'Jesus!' he barks, resting back on his heels and yanking my top and bra down before positioning his erection between my breasts and spilling his seed all over my chest. He pants, sweating and wet, rolling himself around, spreading himself everywhere.

Marked.

'Wherever, whenever, baby,' he puffs, leaning down and hitting me with a forceful attack of his lips. I accept this willingly, too, letting him continue to take whatever he wants. 'Fucking perfect.'

'Hmmm,' I hum. It was perfect. *He* is perfect.

'Come here.' He sits up, rearranges my bra and top before standing and lifting me. He carries me to the table, puts me on my chair and points at my plate. 'Finish your dinner.'

'I didn't throw up,' I say, almost proudly.

'Well done.'

'Why didn't you come in my mouth?' I ask, as he buttons up his fly.

His serious face falters, but only a little. Taking his seat, he nods at my knife and fork in a silent instruction, and then takes his own. 'Might poison the babies.'

If I had a mouthful of lamb, I'd choke, but instead I splutter all over the place in a helpless fit of laughter. 'What?' I giggle.

He doesn't repeat himself, he just winks, and I fall in love that little bit more. 'Eat your dinner, lady.'

Grinning at my plate, I resume my meal, utterly satisfied, despite my lack of orgasm. I'm still bubbling slightly, but I'm not concerned. 'What are we doing tomorrow?'

'Well, I don't know about you, but I'm bingeing.'

'You're keeping me locked up in Paradise all weekend?' I don't mind, but it would be nice to go for a walk, perhaps, or maybe even dinner.

'I wasn't going to, but locks can be arranged.' He slips his fork into his mouth and pulls off a piece of stuffed pepper slowly as he looks at me with raised eyebrows. I'm putting ideas in his head.

There's no comeback from me. I just widen my grin, consumed with happiness as I continue my attempts to finish my meal.

'God, I love that fucking grin. Show me,' he demands.

I'm not grinning now. I'm smiling properly, and he blesses me with his one reserved only for me, twinkling eyes and all. 'Happy?' I ask.

'Fucking delirious.'

Chapter 24

I know I'm smiling in my sleep.

Opening my eyes, the first thing I see is a ginger biscuit, some folic acid and a glass of water. I smile, collecting the pill and swallowing before munching my way through the biscuit. I shuffle to the edge of the bed and don't bother with underwear or clothes. We're alone on a deserted beach, and I haven't forgotten his demand for me to come down to breakfast just like this every morning. I take my naked form out into the main part of the villa to find my Lord, but after a few moments of searching, no Lord. I notice the voile at the doors of the living area are flapping as the light wind gusts through, so I fight my way through the mass of moving material until I'm on the wooden veranda and taking a deep inhale of fresh air. Perfect. It's early because the sun is low, but the heat is intense, only slightly weakened by the breeze, which is whipping my hair all over my face. I fight to secure it in a loose, messy knot and once my vision is clear, I see him in the distance. He's running, and he's running in loose shorts, no T-shirt and no trainers. I lean on the wooden balustrade and happily watch him get closer and closer, his muscular frame shimmering under the morning sun. He could be a mirage.

'Morning,' I chirp when he's a few yards away, sweating and actually a little out of breath. This is unusual. He's a robot when running, never displaying any signs of fatigue or overexertion.

He grabs a towel that's draped over a railing and starts rubbing himself on a smile. 'Good morning, indeed.' His eyes travel down my nakedness, which is only slightly concealed by the posts that I'm standing behind. 'How do you feel?'

I have a quick think and do a bodily assessment, concluding that I feel perfect. I don't feel sick at all. 'Fine.'

'Good.' He approaches the pavilion and looks up at me. 'Give me a kiss.'

I lean over and peck his lips, his signature smell enhanced by the clean sweat riddling his body. 'You're soaked.'

'That's because it's fucking hot.' He pulls away. 'Breakfast?' He asks it as a question, but he doesn't mean it as a question. If I say no, then *without* question, I'd be growled at and possibly hauled in and force-fed.

'I'll make you breakfast.' I start walking across the veranda, towards our bedroom.

'Where are you going?' he calls after me.

'To put something on.'

'Hey!' he shouts, and I turn to see a face awash with disgust. 'Get your naked arse in that kitchen, lady.'

'Excuse me?' I laugh.

'You heard.' He's looking at me expectantly, daring me to defy him.

I look down at my bareness and sigh. He won't be making such demands when I'm fit to burst. I'll put him off his food, but for now, I'm comfortable in my skin and he's clearly comfortable looking at it, so I retrace my steps and enter the villa, receiving a swift slap on my backside as I pass Jesse.

If *our* normal is me preparing and eating breakfast with both of us butt naked, then I love our normal. If *our* normal is taking three hours to get ready because neither one of us can keep our hands off each other, then I *really* love our normal. If *our* normal is me putting on a summer dress and being looked at like I've totally lost my mind, then I'm not so keen on our normal.

'Think again, lady.' He rummages through my clothes,

cursing and scoffing to himself as he assesses and tosses each of my beach dresses aside. 'You've done this on purpose.'

'It's hot.' I laugh, standing in the centre of the room in my lace.

'But Christ, Ava!' He holds up a strapless playsuit with *very* short shorts.

'You said I have great legs,' I argue.

'Yes, you have great fucking *everything*, but that doesn't mean I want everyone to know it.' He chucks the playsuit aside and grabs a long, floaty black dress with spaghetti straps. 'My eyes,' he affirms. 'Just for my eyes.'

'What the hell is wrong with you?' I snatch the dress from his hands. 'You were fine with the gown at the anniversary party and my denim shorts.'

'I wasn't fine at all. I made an exception, but I saw the way men were looking at you.'

'I see how women look at you!'

'Yes, and could you imagine how they'd look at me if I was prancing around half naked?' He nods at the dress. 'You can wear that.'

'You're often shirtless,' I point out. 'You don't see *me* rugby tackling *you* to the floor to conceal your body. Lighten up!'

'No!'

Our scowls are in competition, but his has definitely got the edge. 'You're unreasonable,' I spit. 'I'm wearing what I like.' I chuck the black dress at him and retrieve my dusky-pink, halter-neck summer dress, stepping in and pulling it up my body.

'Why do you do this to me?' he asks impatiently.

'Because it's unreasonable for you to think that you can dictate my wardrobe, that's why.' I knot the dress behind my neck and smooth it down, ignoring the low, rumbling growl emanating from my unreasonable Lord. I'll never back down on this element of *our* normal relationship. 'It's not so bad.'

'You're too fucking beautiful.'

I smile and slip my feet into my flip-flops. 'But I'm *your* beautiful girl, Jesse.'

'You are,' he replies quietly. 'Mine.'

I take a calming breath and step into his chest. 'No one will ever take me away from you.'

He sighs. 'I know, but is it necessary to pick the tiniest dress on the fucking planet?'

I kiss his cheek. 'You're overexaggerating.'

'I don't think I am,' he grumbles, pushing his freshly shaved cheek into my lips. 'Can we compromise?' He squats and picks up a cardigan, and I start shaking my head.

'No way, Ward. I'll pass out.'

Making a ridiculously over-the-top point of demonstrating his exasperation, he drops it and rises from his squatting position. 'Fine, but I won't be held accountable if some prick looks at you funny.'

Paradise just gets better. Whilst letting Jesse have his way by keeping me locked up at the villa was really very tempting, I wanted to explore with him, walk along holding hands, have lunch and be together. I know he's taken pleasure from me in another way today. His arm around my shoulder has kept me snugly tucked into him and when we ate at a beach bar, he made me sit close to him so he could keep his contact.

It's dusk by the time we're bumping down the pot-holed road, back to the villa. The familiar fragrance hits my nose as we slip through the wooden gates and drive down the cobbled road beneath the canopy of green and white.

'Have you had a nice day?' he asks, shutting the engine off and looking at me almost hopefully.

'I have, thank you. Have you?'

'I've had the best day, baby. But now I get to pick what we do for the rest of the evening.' He unclips my belt and leans across to open the door for me. 'Out.'

I follow through on his order, ejecting myself from the soft leather. 'What are we doing?'

'We're going to play a game.' He's on my side of the car now, looking down at me with a crafty, raised brow.

'What sort of game?' I'm too curious, and it's obvious.

'You'll see.' My hand is grasped, and I'm led to the villa. 'Meet me on the rug in the lounge,' he instructs, dropping a kiss on my bewildered face and leaving me like a loose part by the front door.

My frowning face watches his back disappear out of the room, and with little else to do except follow through on his instruction, I drop my bag and make my way over to the designated rug, sitting myself down in the soft, thick pile. My curious mind is racing, but not for long. He reappears shuffling a pack of cards.

'We're playing cards?' I ask, trying not to sound disappointed.

'Yes.' His short, simple reply is an indication that we will, indeed, be playing cards, no matter how much I protest.

'Wouldn't you rather binge on me?' I try temptress tactics, with little confidence. I know when I'm going to win, and now isn't going to be one of those times.

He eyes me warily as he lowers his arse to the rug, leaning up against the back of the couch with his long legs spread at full length in front of him. 'We're playing strip poker.'

I'm promptly fidgeting in my seated position. 'I don't know how to play poker.' I'll lose, but is that such a bad thing? 'It won't be a fair game if I don't know how to play.' I decide that it will be a bad thing. He's smug, and I want to wipe that cocky look clean from his face. My competitive side races to the surface.

'Okay,' he says slowly, shuffling carefully to match his thoughtful word. 'How about pontoon?' He must catch my confused face because he smiles a little. 'Twenty-one? Stick, twist, burn?'

I look at him blankly. 'Nope, sorry. I have no idea what you're talking about.' I stretch my legs out and lean back on my hands. 'Snap?'

He laughs, that head thrown back, fanning temples laugh – the one I adore. 'Snap?'

'Yes, I'm really fast.'

'Ava, let's save Snap for when the babies arrive.' He chuckles to himself and deals us two cards each. 'Okay, I'm the banker and you need to take a look at your cards.'

I shrug and pick them up, noting a ten and a six. 'Okay.'

'What do you have?'

'I'm not telling you!'

He rolls his eyes. 'We'll call this a trial run. Tell me what you have.'

I hold my cards to my chest. 'A ten and a six,' I say suspiciously. 'Sixteen, then?'

'You add them together?'

He's going to regret this. He might be already. 'Yes, you add them together.'

'Right. In that case, I have sixteen.' I flash him my cards.

He nods his acknowledgment. 'So the winner's the one who is the closest to twenty-one when all players have made their move.'

'What moves?' I restrain my grin when he flops his head back, looking up at the ceiling in exasperation.

'The moves I'm about to explain, Ava.'

'Oh, okay. Explain away.'

His head comes back down and he blows out a tired breath. I bet he's wishing he had opted for bingeing. 'Right. You have sixteen and you need to get as close to twenty-one as possible, without going bust. Bust means over twenty-one. Got it?'

'Got it.'

'Good. With a total of sixteen, you should twist, which means I deal you another card. Got it?'

'Got it.'

He pushes another card toward me, and I pick it up stealthily, like he doesn't already know what I'm holding in my hand. 'What have you got?' he asks.

'A king.' I'm not a card genius, but I know that makes me bust. I throw my cards on the floor. 'I didn't want to twist.'

'You can't stick on sixteen, Ava.'

'But at least I wouldn't be bust!'

'No, but it's likely I'll beat sixteen, so you may as well risk it.' He turns his own cards over, revealing a jack and a queen.

'Twenty,' I confirm quickly.

'Correct. And I'll stick, so I win.' He gathers the cards back up and starts shuffling them again. 'Get it?'

'Oh, I'm gonna whoop your arse, Ward.' I rub my hands together and make myself comfortable.

He smiles at my competitiveness, probably thinking that I'm deluded. After all, Jesse Ward is amazing at everything. 'We need to talk about stakes, baby.'

'I'm not hungry, thank you. You've fed me enough today.'

His head falls back again as he laughs really hard. I'm trying to keep a serious face, but I so love him when he laughs. 'I mean what we're playing for.' His green eyes land on me. 'God, I fucking love you.'

'I know. What are we playing for?' I'm liking this game more and more.

'How many items of clothing do you have on?' His eyes run the full length of my body, as if he's mentally working it out.

Playing cards doesn't seem so bad now. 'Three. Dress, bra and knickers.'

'I have two.' He pulls at his t-shirt and his shorts.

'What about your boxers?'

'Obstruction,' he flips casually, dealing us two cards each. I absolutely know where this is going. No obstructions. 'The first one naked loses,' he grins at me. 'The winner takes the power. I'm being reasonable.'

I gasp and snatch my cards up carefully, holding them close to my face. He's as confident as ever, giving me an extra item of clothing. 'There is nothing reasonable about bargaining for the power in our relationship.' I glance down at my cards, seeing two sevens. 'I'll twist.'

He slides a card over to me, maintaining his grin. 'There you go.'

'Thank you,' I reply politely, pulling my card from the floor and placing it with my others. It's an eight. I dramatically huff and toss them between us. 'Bust,' I grumble.

He smiles and turns his own cards over, revealing a Jack and a nine. 'I think I'll stick,' he muses. 'You lose.'

I shake my head as I watch him put the cards down and slowly crawl over to me, his eyes burning into mine with rapt intention. My heartbeat is quickening at the sight of his prowling frame, and when he's up close, he slowly raises his hands to the back of my neck. 'Let's lose the dress,' he whispers, pulling the straps free of the knot. 'Up you get.'

I force myself to stand when all I want to do is collapse onto my back and let him take me right now. He can keep the power. I don't want it. Ever. I watch with lust-filled eyes as he grasps the hem of my dress and lifts it up over my head, standing as he rises and chucking it onto the couch when it's separated from my body.

Leaning into my ear, he bites my lobe. 'Lace,' he murmurs, blowing a soft stream of hot air onto my skin. I tense, despite my best efforts not to and, just like that, he leaves me standing like a built-up bag of desire and resumes position on his arse. 'Sit.'

I close my eyes and collect my senses. I need to be strong because this really is a game to him. I sit back down in my lace and, like the complete temptress I am, I spread my legs wide and lean back on my hands. 'Deal again, Lord.'

The knowing smile that creeps across his handsome face

indicates his awareness. His temptress is living up to her reputation. He deals the cards, I cautiously look, and then immediately declare my intention to stick. He nods thoughtfully and turns his own cards over. He has a nine and a queen. 'Stick.' He looks at me, and I grin, chucking my two kings down cockily before making my way over on my hands and knees.

I straddle his thighs and take the hem of his T-shirt. 'Lose the T-shirt,' I whisper, pulling it up. He lifts his arms willingly, and I throw it behind him, sighing and leaning in to kiss his chest. 'Hmmm, hard.' I grind myself into his lap wickedly, instigating a sharp intake of breath from him, but then I remove myself from his lap and resume my position across the rug. 'Deal.'

It's quite obvious he's fighting the urge to tackle me to the rug. He's really concentrating, and I'm really loving it. The view is improving with each hand I win, too. Just one more and he's mine, power and all.

He deals again, and I sweep my cards up, quickly calculating a total of fourteen. 'Twist, please.' I gesture for him to pass a card. A two. Total: sixteen. Crap, I really don't know what to do. 'Stick. No, twist!' He goes to pass me another card on a smile. 'No! No, I'll stick.' I wave away the card, and his smile turns into a grin.

'Indecisive?' he asks, taking his leaning body back upright, putting way too much emphasis on that chest.

I blink back my peeping eyes, determined not to lose my concentration. I'm not being distracted, but it's hellish resisting the urge to steal a look. Or even just gawp at it. 'No, I'm sticking,' I affirm snootily.

'Okay.' He's desperately fighting a smile as he turns his cards over. 'Hmmm, sixteen,' he muses. 'What to do?'

I shrug.

'I'll twist,' he says, turning a card over.

I don't know how, but I manage to keep a straight face when

he reveals a six. 'Oh dear,' I whisper, taking my eyes from his cards, up his torso, his neck, and then onto his lovely face. 'You risked it.' I chuck my cards at him – the ones that collectively total sixteen. 'I didn't. Lose the shorts.'

He examines my cards on a faint curve of his lips, shaking his head. 'You beat me, baby.'

'I have the power.' I start crawling my way over to him, not wanting to delay getting my hands on him. That was the longest card game ever. 'How do you feel about that?' I unzip the fly of his shorts.

He doesn't try to stop me. He pushes his back into the couch to raise his arse so I can negotiate them down his thighs, and with the revealing of his arousal, I struggle to contain myself.

'I'll ask you the same question,' he rumbles, low, throatily and with one hundred per cent sex in his tone.

'I feel powerful.' I throw his shorts over his head and take the pack of cards from his hand, placing them neatly to one side.

He reaches forward and rubs his thumb over my bottom lip, dragging it, his lips parting, his eyes flicking to mine. 'What has my little temptress got planned?'

I should push his hand away, but I don't. 'She's going to sur-render the power,' I whisper, placing my hands on his thighs and reaching up until we're touching noses. 'What does my god say to that?'

He smiles, that glorious smile. 'Your god says his temptress has learned well.' His big hands curl around my wrists and pull my hands up to rest on his shoulders. 'Your god says his tempt-ress won't regret surrendering to him.' His lips press to mine, and his tongue takes a slow sweep through my mouth. 'But this god and his temptress both know how our normal relationship works.' He cups me over my lace knickers and rests his forehead on mine. 'And it works perfectly.'

I bear down on his palm to get some friction. 'You're perfect.'

My lips find his and my hands automatically seek out his hair. I'm yanking at it again.

'I know,' he mumbles around my demanding lips, sliding his hands around my waist and onto my bum. 'I thought you surrendered the power.'

I couldn't stop if my life depended on it, and I'm mentally praying that he doesn't stamp his authority because I'm desperate, craving, needing. 'Please don't stop me.'

He groans, pulling me into him and showing no sign of halting this. He's letting me have my way with him. 'You know I can't say no to you.' He stands with me wrapped around him, and I don't even know it's happened. I'm too consumed, but when the cool night air attacks my bare back, I'm pulling myself into his body, holding tighter and kissing harder. My brain isn't given any space to think about where we're going. I don't care.

The light rushing sound of the night waves gently lapping at the shoreline is the first thing I hear. Then I smell the salty essence of the Mediterranean. There's a chill in the air, but the warmth of his body fitted snugly to mine eliminates any discomfort. I'm burning up. The wooden sleepers are taken with care as he carries me down to the sea's edge, but he doesn't take me into the water. He kneels and places me down on the soft, damp sand, ensuring our lips remain locked the entire time. My hands are wandering all over his muscular frame, my legs are writhing beneath him, and I'm fast losing my breath, my laboured breathing not helped when a gentle wave gushes up and breaks around my sprawled body, surrounding me in a shallow puddle of cool, salty sea water. My shocked, quiet yelp isn't containable. My fingernails dig into his biceps and my back arches to try and escape the freshness, my lace-covered breasts pushing into his bare chest.

'Shhhh,' he calms me, 'hush now.' His soft words relax me in an instant as he kisses his way into my neck, biting and sucking before he's kissing his way across my face again. 'I love you,' he whispers. 'I fucking love love, love, you.'

'I know.' My mouth skims his. 'I know you do. Make love to me.' It's what we need to do right now. No fucking. No hard. Just love.

'I never planned on doing anything else.' He's pulling at my lace and pushing my knickers down my legs. 'We'll call this one sleepy twilight sex.'

My hands are sliding up his arms until my palms are cupping his cheeks. His face is perfectly clear to me, despite the blackness surrounding us. Sleepy twilight sex may be a new favourite. 'Deal.'

His arm slips under the small of my back and lifts me a little so he can access the back of my bra. It's removed with one hand and slid down my arms where I leave it suspended between my two wrists that refuse to release his face. I want to keep my lips on his, the gentle caressing of his tongue on mine sending me right to the highest level of Central Jesse Cloud Nine. My nipples pucker further, tingling with coolness but mostly with desire. And then he's pulling his face from my hands on a moan and rearing back. He studies me for a few moments before sinking into me meticulously, perfectly, halting when he's only half submerged.

His face is unreadable, but those greens are telling a whole other story. They are seeping into the deepest part of me. 'All the way?' he asks, so quietly I almost don't hear him above the light rush of waves.

I nod, tipping my hips, and he inhales a shaky breath, quickly lifting me when another wave creeps up on us. I cry out at the coldness again, but his sudden full penetration is more of the cause. He's holding me against him as the water recedes, my cheek pressed to his throat, and then I'm on my way back down to the sand. My hands find their place on his shoulders and his forearms find their place on either side of my head. And we just look at each other. This in itself is beyond pleasurable. He's completely filling me, and I can feel him pulsating. I'm even contracting around him, but neither one of us has any urgent need to hurry this along. It's chilly, we're both wet, but we're perfectly happy. Nothing around us exists, just how we like it.

'Do you want me to move?' he drops his mouth to mine. 'Tell me what you want, baby.'

'Just you. However you come.'

'I come with uncontrollable love for you. Is that good enough?'

It's more than good enough. I kiss him instead of answering him, but he pulls away, his heavy, hooded eyes looking for a verbal reply. 'It's good enough.' I accept on a quiet sigh, feeling like I've probably just sanctioned his challenging ways. But it *is* good enough.

'I'm glad.' He rocks his hips, drawing a quiet intake of breath from me and strained neck muscles from him. 'You feel so fucking good. I don't know how I ever survived without this.' He gradually pulls out and pushes lazily back into me, pressing his lips to mine to capture my small cry of pleasure, mixed with shock as another wave surprises me. 'Now I live. And it's only for you.'

'I understand,' I say around his mouth, because I know that's his next question. 'I understand all of that.'

'Good. I need you to.' Out and in again, and there's a sigh and tensing from both of us. 'I love our normal.'

I smile, and squirm beneath him on another meticulous plunge. I love our normal, too. Our normal is Jesse loving me so violently, it drives him crazy. It's me returning that love. And it's me accepting him in all of his challenging ways. I'm so over it.

I'm not even feeling the coolness of the sea lapping around me now. Desire is coursing through my veins, heating my skin, and I'm grabbing on to every drive with every muscle I possess.

I equal his passion with my own, kissing him and feeling him, yanking at his hair and moaning. He's swaying those hips back and forth so precisely, so evenly, that each thrust is hitching me steadily closer to climax. The softness of his tongue exploring every part of my mouth and the hard velvet of his cock sliding in and out of me is utter ecstasy, as always.

I let my displeasure be known when he breaks our mouth contact, but he ignores me, pulling back to study me while he maintains his pace. 'I need to see you,' he breathes. 'I need to see those eyes smoulder when you come for me.'

'Jesse,' I'm panting. He won't have to wait very long at all. The switch is flicking, courtesy of my Lord and his expert ways. Knowing I'll get chastised if I close my eyes, I work hard to resist the temptation of throwing my head back and clenching them shut. It's hard when he's doing this to me.

He lifts his upper body and braces himself on his fists. 'Control it, Ava. Don't make me stop.' He increases his pace, never allowing his eyes to leave mine.

'Please, don't stop.' My hands find their way to his arse and grab on hard, pushing him into me.

'You know what to do, then.' He circles firm and deep, almost purposely making this more difficult for me. I bite back a cry, mustering up all of my strength to delay the inevitable until he's ready. This calls for deep, controlled breaths, so I swallow hard and begin a sequence of breath-regulating exercises. There is a faint shimmer of a knowing smile looking down at me, and he's quickening his strokes. His biceps are bulging, too, indicating a shifting of his fists in the sand where he's trying to gain more leverage to torment me with his punishing lovemaking. And God does he succeed. Every single time it just gets better and better.

I'm lying under him, soaking up his attentiveness, biting harshly on my lip, and I'm sizzling, bubbling, dying to let go. Through my wild sensuality, I'm searching for any sign that he may be close, and I begin to despair when I find nothing, but then his greens disappear behind his eyelids, only very briefly, and his hips jerk. He's struggling, and fearful that he might slow to gather himself, I quickly wrap my legs around his waist and use every leg muscle I own to push him into me. It's his downfall. He hisses, bucks again, and I shout my appreciation, moving my hands to his forearms and gripping hard.

'You little ... FUCK!' His head flies back and his smooth pace rapidly advances into faster strokes. I take the opportunity of his gaze away from mine to squeeze my eyes shut. I hold my breath, too. 'Eyes!' My darkness was brief. My lids are open again, and they are looking at a damp face of frustration. Frustration that he can't control it. 'Fucking hell, lady,' he pants. 'You want to come?'

'Yes!'

'I know.' He pistons into me, yells explicitly, time and time again, and then he barks, 'Come,' and I'm besieged, my whole body going into meltdown as it's attacked with violent shakes and is palpitating from the consistent bursts of release that just keep coming and coming and coming. I'm heated completely, his cum flooding me as he stills, moaning and grinding.

His breathing is sharp. My breathing is challenged. He's still braced on his arms and he's sweating profusely, while I'm rolling my head from side-to-side, almost disorientated from the intensity of my climax.

'You made me lose control, Ava,' he huffs down at me. 'Damn it, woman, you send me fucking crazy.'

My arms fall above my head into the wet sand, immediately noting another receding puddle of water, not that my body feels it. I'm scorching hot. 'You won't hurt them.'

He shakes his head, like he's also all disorientated, before he slides from within me and falls to his forearms, taking my nipple between his lips.

'That feels nice,' I sigh, finally closing my eyes for a reasonable length of time while he feasts on my breasts. 'Just keep doing that.'

'You taste so good,' he mumbles, latching onto the area where I know my mark to be and sucking deeply.

I happily leave him to his own devices while I concentrate on stabilising my breathing and racing heartbeat, but I'm still burning up. 'Take me into the water,' I pant. 'I need to cool off.'

He shakes his head and releases my breast to look up at me. 'No can do, lady.' He goes back to my chest with no more of an explanation.

'Why?' I press.

Each of my nipples are kissed before he brings his face up close to mine. His eyes are sparkling pools of mischievousness. 'It might freeze the babies.'

I don't laugh, but I do grin. 'It will not!'

My hair is pushed from my face and his hands creep up my arms until his fingers lace through mine above my head. 'How do you know for sure?'

I lift my head just to get my lips on him, the crazy, lovable arse. 'Even if that were true, which it isn't, right now my current body temperature is off the charts, so I'm probably roasting your babies as we speak.'

He gasps in an obviously dramatic display of horror and jumps up, pulling me to my feet. 'Fucking hell, lady. We need to cool you off.' He throws me up onto his shoulder and slaps my arse.

'Ouch!' I laugh, delighting in his playfulness. 'Go slow so I can get used to it.'

'Oh no.' He wades in quickly, leaving me fearing the worst. 'We don't have time to fuck about. We're at risk of having a pair of well-done babies.' He grabs my hips, instigating a yelp and a wriggle, but he has a firm grip of me. I'm held above him with my hips resting on his big palms, my hands on his shoulders, and I'm looking down at a crafty face that's trying to be serious.

I'm grinning so much, my cheeks are aching. 'Hello up there, beautiful girl.'

'Hi.' I'm bracing myself. I know what's coming, or I hope I know what's coming.

He loses his battle and blisters my skin with his smile, bending his arms and lowering me to plant a hard kiss on my lips. 'Goodbye, my beautiful girl.' His powerful arms straighten fast, and I'm launched into the black air on a squeal, my legs and arms flailing everywhere in deranged delight. I hit the water, still screaming, but quickly get stifled by the water as I go under. The dull muffle of frantic activity in the water surrounding me is definitely not just my doing, so I kick my legs urgently and work my way to the surface, emerging on a gasp and quickly doing a three-sixty turn to look for him. He's nowhere to be seen and apart from my fitful inhalations, it's deathly silent. I freeze as best I can, limiting my legs to a calm paddling beneath me. Damn it, where is he? Silent swells of water ripple away from me, and I can't work out if it's me causing the stir in the water, or something in the depths below – something tall, lean and beautiful, something that can hold its breath for a bloody long time. I don't know why, but I hold my breath, too, silently deliberating on my next move. Do I remain still and silent, or do I make a dash for the shore?

Dash, remain, dash, remain.

I release the stored air from my lungs. 'Shit, shit, shit.' I'm totally torn, my heart racing as I battle my indecisiveness, but then I hear a splash behind me and with no instruction at all, my legs kick into action. I swim like my life depends on it, like Jaws himself is in pursuit of me. I'm squealing like a girl, too. 'Oh fuck!' I yelp, piercing the night-time air with my filthy mouth, as my ankle is grasped and I'm pulled under. I'm a rolling mass of wild arms and legs, probably kicking and punching him, but I can't control it. It serves him right, anyway. My fright has turned into a little anger now, and I'm batting at the hands that are grasping at me. My eyes keep getting attacked with salt every time I attempt to open them, and my lungs are going to explode. And now his head is in between my thighs.

I break the surface and immediately release the air in my lungs on a furious shout. 'Jesse!' I'm on his shoulders being carted out of the sea, his arms locked over my shins on his chest.

'What's up, baby?' He's not even panting.

'You!' My hands smack his head a few times before I swoop down and grab his chin, yanking his head up. 'Let me see you,' I spit aggressively.

He laughs. 'Hello.'

'You're a menace.'

He seems to find his feet with no effort, rising from the water like some kind of otherworldly creature. 'You love me.'

I lean down, but I can't reach him. 'I want to kiss you,' I whine.

'I know you do.' In a stealthy set of coordinated moves, I'm whipped from his shoulders and lying across his arms in a nanosecond. 'And now you can.'

This grin feels like a permanent fixture on my face, and his sparkling eyes are deeply set and showing no sign of fading. We're so happy. Laid-back Jesse is full-on and drowning me in lust and roguishness. Central Jesse Cloud Nine doesn't get any better than this.

Chapter 25

I could get so very used to this. I could lie every morning and stretch happily, feel the breeze all over my nakedness and wander out onto the veranda to admire my god from a distance, running the curve of the bay. I could prepare him breakfast, despite the fact that I absolutely hate cooking, and I could sit naked at the table while he demolishes it with constant hums of approval around his fork before plunging his finger into a jar of peanut butter, which I'm sure he packed because it's Sun-Pat. I could open my mouth when instructed so he can feed me, and I could reach over and stroke his bare, sun-kissed chest, just because I feel like it. I could puddle on the chair when he winks and yanks me onto his lap to ravish me, and then continue with his breakfast with one hand while he holds me with the other, offering forkfuls of salmon to me. I could slip into my bikini within the privacy of Paradise, receiving no look of horror or demand to put something more substantial on, and go for a swim in the giant freshness of the villa's pool. I could be pulled out by my hand and dried off, then wrapped up and taken to the shower, where I'm soaped down and served in every shower-time way possible. *Every* shower-time way possible ... and a little more. I could get very, very used to this.

It's our last day in Paradise, and I'm feeling a little forlorn. It's our last day of indulging solely in each other, with none of the distractions or issues that are all currently awaiting us in London. I'm sitting on the bed with tissue wedged between my toes and a bottle of pink nail polish in my hand. It's gone noon. We've spent all morning doing all of *our* normal, and I'm now prepping and preening for an afternoon down at the port and a twilight dinner. I don't want to go home. I want to stay in Paradise for ever, just me and Jesse.

I look up, seeing Jesse rubbing his dirty-blond mass of wet hair with a towel. I lean back on my pillow and savour the delightful view. He's naked. I'm dribbling.

He saunters over and crawls up the bed until he's sitting on his knees by my feet. 'Let me.' The towel gets laid across his thighs and he takes my foot in his strong hands.

'You want to paint my toes?' I ask, a little amused at my manly husband taking on such a girly task. He flicks me an indifferent look, clearly not bothered by tending to his wife to this extent.

'I may as well get some practice in,' he informs me, straight-faced and all matter-of-fact. 'You won't be able to reach them soon.'

My foot lashes out on reflex, jabbing him straight in his stomach, not that it has the desired effect. He grins down at his lap and repositions my foot. 'I don't want to go home,' I say quietly.

'Me neither, baby.' He doesn't seem shocked to hear it, like he's read my mind, or clearly been thinking the exact same thing. He gives my big toenail a stroke down the centre with the brush, then one on each side.

'When can we come back?' I ask, watching as his concentration frown emerges. It makes me smile and momentarily forget my dispiriting thoughts.

'We can come back whenever you like. Just say the word, and I'll put you on that plane.' He wipes across the flesh at the base of my nail and sits back to observe his handiwork. It's not bad at all, considering his big hands and the tiny brush. He looks up at me. 'Have you had a nice time?'

'Paradise,' I muse, resting my head back. 'Continue.' I nod at my foot in his lap.

His eyes narrow playfully. 'Yes, my lady.'

'Good boy,' I sigh dreamily, relaxing into the pillow. 'What happens when we get home?'

He continues with the painting of my nails, not giving my question the acknowledgment it deserves. Something needs to be done, preferably by the police officially, not by Steve as a favour to a man he's pissed off.

'What happens is that you'll go to work and finally fulfil your promise to enlighten Patrick about Mikael.' He tosses me an expectant look, which I ignore.

'Do you think Mikael stole your car?'

'I have no fucking clue, Ava.' He places my foot down and picks up the other. 'I'm dealing with it, so don't worry your pretty little head.'

'How are you dealing with it?' I can't help the question. I really want to know because something tells me that, like most of Jesse's ways, it won't be conventional.

As I knew I would, I get landed with a warning look, and I'm mindful that by pushing this, I may very well get tossed off Central Jesse Cloud Nine before we arrive back in London.

'End of,' he says simply, and I know it really is.

So I relax and let him finish the intricate task of painting my toenails as I silently appreciate both his attentiveness and the fact that he's scrunched over, leaning down close to carry out his task, yet there is not a roll of fat on that stomach, whatsoever.

'You're done,' he declares, screwing the lid back on. 'I'm even amazing at this.'

I pull my feet up and lean over to take a look, half expecting to see a set of pink-coloured feet, but no. Jesse is, indeed, amazing at painting toenails. 'Not bad,' I flip casually, feigning the wiping of some stray polish that isn't even there.

'Not bad? I've done a better job than you'd ever do, lady.' He jumps up from the bed. 'You're so lucky to have me.'

'Aren't *you* lucky?' I ask incredulously.

'I'm luckier.' He winks, and I'm speedily dragged from my offended state on a sigh. 'Come on, lady. Let's go exploring.'

We pull off a roundabout and up to a security gate that leads down to a port. Jesse lowers his window and flashes a plastic card at a screen and the gate opens instantly, allowing him to drive through. 'Where are we?' I ask, edging forward in my seat to look down the road.

'This is the port, baby.' He proceeds at a crawl and turns onto a pedestrianised area, people mechanically moving to make way, not giving the DBS a second glance. I would've thought this strange, but I quickly register the dozens of prestigious cars, all parked in bays along the front. And not just the odd Merc or BMW. I'm looking at rows of Bentleys, Ferraris and even another Aston Martin, all screaming *billionaires*. My attention is speedily drawn from the row of expensive vehicles when I clock the rows and rows of boats. No, not boats. These are yachts.

'Fucking hell,' I whisper as Jesse slips into an empty bay.

'Ava! Please, watch your fucking mouth.' He heaves a tired breath and gets himself out of the car, making his way around to my side. I'm stuck in my seat, astounded by the bright whiteness of so many huge floating mountains on the marina. 'Out you get.'

I absent-mindedly eject myself with the assistance of Jesse's hand while keeping my eyes on the boats. 'Please don't tell me you own one of those.' I look at him with wide eyes. I don't know why I sound so shocked. This man is beyond wealthy, but a yacht?

He smiles and slips his shades on. 'No, I sold it many years ago.'

'So you did have one?'

'Yes, but I didn't have a fucking clue how to sail the stupid thing.' He takes my hand and leads me away from the car, to a pathway where we're safe from moving vehicles.

'Why did you buy it in the first place then?' I ask, looking up at him, but he just shrugs my question off and points out across the sea.

'Over there is Morocco.'

I follow the direction of his hand, but all I see is open water. He's trying to divert my enquiring mind. 'Lovely,' I say with lashings of sarcasm, just so he knows that I know his ploy.

'Sarcasm doesn't suit you, lady.' He pulls me under his arm and makes a meal of biting at my ear. 'What would you like to do?'

'Let's mooch about.'

'Mooch?'

'Yes, mooch,' I repeat, looking up at an amused expression. 'Like browse, peruse – mooch about.'

He smiles down at me, almost fascinated. 'Okay. I feel another Camden coming on.'

'Yes, exactly like Camden, but no funny sex shops,' I finish quietly.

Now he's laughing. 'Oh, there are plenty of funny sex shops on the back streets. Want to see?'

'No, I don't,' I grumble, reflecting back to our very own little pole-dancing treat by that leather-clad, dominatrix type. I inwardly gasp. A Sarah type. Holy shit, she looked just like Sarah, minus the whip, instead playing with a pole. Sarah may very well have a pole, who knows; but my sudden comprehension is overshadowing the similarities of the women. 'You didn't find that attractive, did you?'

My chin is grasped and pulled to face him. 'I've told you before. There's only one thing that turns me on, and I love her in lace.'

'Good.'

He kisses my forehead and takes a deep breath into my hair. 'Come on, Mrs Ward. Let's mooch.'

I'm thoroughly fed up with mooching by the time we're back on the marina front, and I know Jesse has humoured me to within an inch of his life, insisting on buying everything that I picked up or looked at in a bid to reduce my browsing time. This wouldn't have bothered me too much if it wasn't for the kind of stores in which we were mooching. This is no Camden. Yes, there were a few knick-knack stalls, but I was mainly directed into the abundance of designer stores, leaving me feeling a million times more conspicuous than I ever did in Harrods. The quiet, minimal spaces were dressed with just a few key pieces, not leaving much scope for mooching at all.

He's weighed down with bags now, and God bless him, he looks harassed. 'I'll put these in the car. Wait there.' He leaves me on the side of the pedestrianised area, coating my lips in Chapstick, while he goes over to the car to dump the bags. Then he makes his way quickly back over and grabs me. I stifle a yelp as I'm suspended in his arms and ravished. 'God, I've missed you.' His mouth slides over my freshly moisturised lips with ease as he takes me for all to see. As always, I'm oblivious to our location and company, letting him do as he pleases with me. 'Hmm, you taste good.' He pulls back and pouts, his own lips shimmering slightly from the transfer of my Chapstick.

'If you want to wear ladies' lipstick, then do it properly.' I reach up to apply, and he does nothing to stop me, even puckering to make the coating easier. 'Better,' I conclude on a smile. 'You're even more handsome with shimmery lips.'

'Probably,' he agrees, with complete ease, smacking his lips together. 'Come on, I need to feed my wife and peanuts.' He returns me to a vertical position and starts to reposition the slipping straps of my yellow sundress. 'These need tightening.'

Shrugging his fussing hands away, I lead on, pulling my own

straps into place and disregarding the grunts of protest coming from behind me. 'Where are you feeding me?' I ask over my shoulder, keeping up my stride. I'm not striding for long, though. My wrist is seized, and I'm suddenly pulling against a dead weight.

'Don't walk away from me,' he practically growls, spinning me around to face him. He's scowling while I'm grinning. 'And you can wipe that grin off your face.' He proceeds to tighten my straps, muttering some rubbish about an insufferable wife, who drives him fucking crazy. 'Better. Ridiculous dress.' He takes a deep breath of patience. 'Why do you insist on being so difficult?'

'Because I know it drives you crazy.'

'You just enjoy reducing me to a crazy madman.'

'You make yourself a crazy madman,' I laugh. 'You need no help in that department, Jesse. I've told you before; you do not dictate my wardrobe.'

His eyes burn with green displeasure, but I don't shy away from his hulking fierceness. I'm really rather brave. 'You drive me crazy,' he repeats, because he doesn't know what else to say.

'What are you going to do?' I ask smugly. 'Divorce me?'

'Watch your fucking mouth!'

'I didn't even swear!' I'm really laughing now.

'Yes you fucking did! The worse word, in fact. I forbid you to say it.'

Oh, now I've really got the chuckles. 'You forbid me?'

His arms fold over his chest in an act of authority, like I'm a bloody child. 'Yes, I forbid you.'

'Divorce,' I whisper.

'Now you're just being childish,' he huffs, just like a child.

'-ish.' I shrug. 'Feed me.'

He scoffs loudly and shakes his head. 'I should fucking starve you and reward you with food when you do what you're fucking told.' My shoulders are clasped, I'm turned around, and then guided to a seafront restaurant. 'I'll feed you here.'

We're shown to a table for two on the outside terrace and settled by a happy man with slicked black hair and a moustache to match. 'Drinks?' he asks in a thick Spanish accent.

'Water, thank you.' Jesse sits me down and tucks me under the table before taking a seat opposite and passing me a menu. 'The tapas are sublime.'

'You pick.' I hand the menu back. 'I'm sure you'll make a suitable choice.' My eyebrows are raised cheekily, and the menu is taken from my hand thoughtfully, but with no scorn or reproving look.

'Thank you,' he says slowly.

'You're welcome,' I counter, pouring us a glass of water each when the waiter places an ice-cold jug on the table. I down the whole glass in one fell swoop and immediately pour another.

'Thirsty?' He watches in astonishment as I make quick work of the second glass, nodding over the rim. 'Be careful,' he warns. I'm frowning over the rim, but unable to stop gulping the icy liquid. 'You might drown the babies.'

I cough a little on a laugh and place my water down to grab a napkin. 'Will you stop with that?'

'What? I'm just showing some fatherly concern.' He looks hurt, but I know better.

'You don't think I can look after our babies, do you?'

'Yes I do,' he retorts softly, with absolutely zero conviction. He really doesn't. I'm shocked, and my face probably shows it, even if he's refusing to meet my eyes so he can see for himself.

'What the hell do you think I'm going to do?' I regret the question the second it falls from my mouth, even more so when his head snaps up and I'm hit with a sceptical look. 'Don't,' I warn, my voice cracking and tears of regret immediately burning the back of my eyes. I work hard to blink them back, mentally beating myself up for my cold-hearted thoughts. I feel terrible enough all on my own, without Jesse enflaming the guilt.

He's sitting next to me in a heartbeat and pulling me into his side, stroking my back and burying his mouth into hair. 'I'm sorry. Don't get upset, please.'

'I'm okay.' I brush his concern away. It's plain to see that I'm not okay, but I can't lose control of my emotions in the middle of a restaurant for all to see. I'm already being stared at by a woman a few tables away. I'm in no mood for nosy parkers, so I flip her a look before pulling out of Jesse's chest. 'I said I'm fine,' I snap shortly, picking my glass up, just for something to do other than cry.

'Ava,' he says quietly, but I can't look at him. Will he ever let me forget this? 'Look at me.' He sounds harsher, firmer now, but I disobey, noticing that bloody woman still staring. I meet her eyes, enhancing my *fuck off* look, which quickly prompts her to return to her dinner. 'Three . . .'

I actually roll my eyes, but not because he's started the count-down. No, it's because I know I won't be getting any Jesse-style fuck or trample when he reaches zero.

'Two.'

It's like he's dangling a carrot that I'm never going to get a bite of. Stupid, I know, but the need for Jesse and all of his talent for fucking me into submission has become engrained in me, pregnancy only seeming to enhance my desire for it.

'One.'

I exhale tiredly and start fiddling with my fork, refusing to submit, probably only shortening his fuse.

'Zero, baby.' I'm snatched from my chair before my brain filters the final call of the countdown, and I'm on the floor, wrists pinned above my head and Jesse straddling my waist. My eyes are wide and the restaurant is silent. You could hear a pin drop. I'm staring up at Jesse, who is unashamed and most unconcerned by our surroundings. He's got me sprawled on the floor in a restaurant. What the fucking hell is he playing at? I dare not even look away from him. I can feel a million sets of shocked eyes drilling into the spectacle Jesse has created. I'm mortified.

'Jesse, let me up.' I wouldn't put much past him, but this? This is way past unashamed. Fucking hell, what if someone tries to pull him off me?

'I did warn you, baby.' His face is awash with amusement, while I'm simply horrified. 'Wherever, whenever.'

'Yes, okay.' I wriggle. 'You've made your point.'

'I don't think I have,' he says casually, making himself comfortable, suspending his face over mine. 'I love you.'

I want the ground to swallow me up whole. Ravishing me and kissing the living daylights out of me on a busy street is one thing. Pinning me to the floor in a busy restaurant is insane. 'I know. Let me up.'

'No.'

Oh God, I can't even hear the chinking of knives and forks, which tells me all eating has halted. 'Please,' I beg quietly.

'Tell me you love me.'

'I love you.' I grate the words through clenched teeth.

'Say it like you mean it, Ava.' He's not going to give up, not until I follow through on his stupid, unreasonable order to his satisfaction.

'I love you.' I sound softer, but still uneasy.

He eyes me suspiciously, and I'm beyond relieved when he shifts and pulls me to my feet, choosing to remain on his knees in front of me. I take my time straightening myself out, anything to avoid facing the masses of diners who are undoubtedly looking on in shock. After I've spent much more time than is really necessary brushing myself down, I chance a quick look around the restaurant, then proceed to die a thousand deaths on the spot. I'm tempted to run for it, but I notice Jesse still on his knees in front of me.

'Get up,' I say on a hushed whisper, despite the obviousness of being heard. It's still eerily silent.

He walks forward on his knees until he's flush with the front of my legs, and then slides his hands around to my arse, looking up at me with puppy dog eyes. 'Ava Ward, my beautiful, defiant girl.' My face is heating further by the second. 'You make me the happiest man on this fucking planet. You married me, and now you're blessing me with twin babies.' He slips a hand from my arse and onto my tummy, circling adoringly before dropping a kiss in the centre. There's definitely a few sighs from our spectators. 'I love you so fucking much. You're going to be an incredible mummy to my babies.' I can do nothing more than stare down at him as he makes his public declaration, the embarrassing fool. And there are more sighs. He kisses his way up my body until he's in my neck. 'Don't try to stop me from loving you. It makes me sad.'

'Sad or crazy?' I ask quietly.

He emerges from his hiding place in my neck and gathers my hair, draping it down my back before cupping both of my cheeks in his palms. 'Sad,' he affirms. 'Kiss me, wife.'

I'm not up for any further embarrassment, so I conform and give him exactly what he wants. This way I get to escape sooner. But then clapping starts, and I'm soon missing Jesse's lips on mine as he takes a bow and sits me back down. We're staying?

'I love her.' He shrugs, like that explains why he has just manhandled me to the floor and demanded a declaration of love, before announcing to a bunch of strangers that we're expecting twins.

'Twins!'

I jump at the excited, broken English of the waiter, who waves a bottle of champagne in front of us. 'You must celebrate.' He pops the cork and pours two glasses. I cringe. It's very thoughtful, but there's no way either of us are drinking it.

'Thank you,' I smile up at him, praying he doesn't hang around to watch us clink glasses and swig. 'That's very kind.' He backs away, leaving me assessing the surroundings. People have returned to their meals, some flicking fond looks every so often, but the interest seems to have died down. That woman is still staring, though. I frown at her, but I'm distracted when Jesse's hand lands on my knee. I turn and find a face full of mischievousness. 'I cannot *believe* you did that.'

'Why?' He pushes the champagne flutes away from us.

I'm about to argue my case, but I can feel eyes on me again, and I know who it is. I turn slowly, finding her staring again. She's quite a few tables away, and there are masses of people between us, but a small gap in the crowd is giving me a clear view, and it's obviously giving her one, too. 'Do you know that woman?' I ask, keeping my eyes on her, even though she's returned to her meal.

'What woman?' Jesse asks, leaning over me to see where my gaze is directed.

'There, the woman with the pale-blue cardigan.' I almost point across the restaurant, but quickly rein in my lifting hand. 'Can you see?'

After what seems like for ever has passed and he still hasn't answered me, I turn and watch as the colour drains from his face, leaving a pasty, shocked one in place of the tanned, content one.

'What's the matter?' I instinctively slap my hand on his forehead to gauge his temperature, noting with just a second's touch that he's stone cold. 'Jesse?' He's staring blankly past me in a complete trance. I'm worried. 'Jesse, what's wrong?'

He shakes his head, like he's shaking off concussion, and turns haunted eyes onto me. I can see that he's trying to look okay, but my husband is failing miserably. There's something seriously wrong. 'We're leaving.' He stands, knocking a glass over, attracting a little bit more attention. Throwing a pile of notes on the table, he wastes no time lifting my perplexed arse from the chair and leading me out of the restaurant.

He strides with complete purpose towards the car, virtually

pulling me along behind him. 'What is wrong with you?' I try again, but I know it's in vain. He has completely shut down.

The car door is opened, and I look up at him as he starts to guide me in, but I get nothing. No acknowledgment, no expression, no explanation. I do notice his shoulder tense and rise, though, and his chest is beginning to heave. He's looking past me, yet still trying to push me into the car.

'Jesse?' The unfamiliar female voice pulls my attention away from my spaced-out husband and to a woman behind me. *The* woman. I stare at her in confusion, feeling Jesse's hand grip me tighter. I can hear his breathing now, too. I'm completely bewildered, but I still manage to take her in, running my eyes up and down this stranger who has spent the best part of her time in the seafront eatery staring at me, or Jesse, or us. I'm not sure. But the longer I'm looking at her, the clearer it's all becoming.

Jesse tries to reposition me to get me in the car, but I shrug him off, too intrigued by who I'm looking at. 'Ava, baby, we're going.' He's not demanding or shouting at me impatiently, despite my defiance. It makes me want to cry.

'Jesse, son.' The woman steps forward and my fears are confirmed.

'You don't get to call me that,' Jesse says tightly. 'Ava, get in the car.'

I get in. That was all the confirmation I needed. I don't need to hear anything else, no shouting matches or explanations. That's Jesse's mum.

I shift my body in the seat and watch him make his way around the back of the car, feeling concerned when I see his mum hurry past the front to intercept him. I watch as she places a hand on his arm and he shrugs it off, I hear as she pleads for a chance to talk, and then I see as she presses her body up against the driver's door to prevent him from accessing the car. His hands fly to his hair and yank, the pain on his face breaking my heart. He won't physically remove his mother, which leaves him vulnerable out there. I can't just sit here and watch him struggle like this, so I get out and make my way around to Jesse and his mother, with nothing but determination coursing through me.

I stand in front of Jesse, like a protective shield, and look her square in the eye. 'Please, I'm asking you to move.'

He leans over me. 'You shouldn't be here. Why are you here?' Jesse's voice is broken and shaky, as is his body. I can feel the vibrations seeping into my back. 'It's Amalie's wedding weekend in Seville. Why are you here?'

Realisation dawns. I didn't read far enough into the invite to note a date or location, but Jesse obviously did. Why else would he bring me here, unless he knew his parents would be gone? But they *are* here. And it's sent Jesse spiralling into turmoil.

'It's your father,' she begins. 'The wedding, it got postponed because your father had a heart attack. Amalie tried to get in touch after you never replied to her wedding invite.'

Jesse's chest presses into my back. 'So tell me why Amalie tried to contact me? Why not you?'

'I thought you would answer your sister,' she replies quickly. 'I was hoping you would answer your sister's calls.'

'Well, you were wrong!' he roars over my shoulder, making me wince. 'You don't get to do this to me. No more, Mum. Your influence already fucked my life up, and now I'm making it right all on my own!'

She flinches, but she doesn't defend herself. Her green eyes – just like Jesse's – are all clouded and desperate. So many thoughts are racing through my brain, but my priority is Jesse and his obvious distress.

'Twins,' his mum whispers, reaching forward with her hand.

I freeze. I can't move. Her eyes are studying my stomach, and I see pain etched all over her wrinkled face. I'm pulled back, just avoiding a skimming of her hand on my tummy. It snaps me from my daze and makes me reassess the situation. It doesn't take long. I need to get Jesse away.

'Ava,' his voice has softened in my ear, 'please, get me out of here.'

My heart splits straight down the middle. 'I'm asking you nicely.' I look at his mother, whose eyes are still focused on my midriff. 'Please move.'

'It's another chance, Jesse.' She's sobbing now, but I don't feel any sympathy for her. Jesse doesn't speak. He remains still and quiet behind me. I think he might have fallen into a trance. Those few words have only heightened my determination and turned my building sadness into pure anger. I can't lash out at his mother, though.

I turn and slide my hand onto Jesse's arm. 'Come on,' I say softly, tugging at his arm. He lets me take him. I'm guiding him for once, and I make fast work of it. I'm determined to remove my husband from this situation which is causing him anguish. I've only ever seen him like this a handful of times and every one of those times has ended in heartache. I'm not prepared to set him or myself up for any further difficulties in our relationship.

I open the passenger door and gently guide him in, while he stares blankly at the thin air in front of him. I'm more than re-lieved when I see Jesse's mum come around the front of the car because it means I can hurry around the back and jump in the driver's seat. The first thing I do is locate the door locks and flick the switch before I search Jesse for the keys. I've never driven on the wrong side of the road before, or on the wrong side of the car, but now is not the time to get myself in a panic over something so trivial. I start the DBS up and barely look behind me as I reverse carelessly out of the space before whacking it into first and pulling away a little more cautiously. I chance a look in the rear-view mirror and see a man taking Jesse's mum in his arms. His dad.

My eyes do a quick check of the road ahead, noting the exit gates, but I don't have chance to panic about finding the card that will open them. They shift automatically and I'm getting further away from Jesse's parents by the second. I glance at him, and I don't like what I see – a troubled man, staring blankly out of the window, showing no emotion. If he was angry I would feel better, but he's not. The only familiarity is the deep crevice across his brow and the cogs of his complex mind spinning out of control. Strangely, these little traits offer me some comfort. What he could be thinking about, however, does not.

Another chance? That's what she said. I can't blame Jesse for his meltdown, not when his mother has just suggested that everything can be righted by the birth of his own twins. That's cruel and selfish, and it will never make up for the years of sorrow and betrayal that have come before.

These babies and I are Jesse's chance of happiness, not his parents' opportunity to right all of their wrongs. If she intends to use my babies as some sort of family therapy, then she can think again.

The familiar fragrance of Paradise finally has me relaxing completely as I make my way up the cobbled driveway to the villa. He gets out of the car and strides towards the veranda, leaving me to follow tentatively behind. I don't know what to do. I know we won't be talking, so I need to do what instinct is telling me and that's to just be there for him. Not fish for information to ease my own inquisitive mind.

Following him into the villa, I find him standing in the middle of the room. I'm quiet as I approach behind him, but he doesn't flinch when I slide my hand into his. He knew I was close, as he always does. I lead him into the bedroom and start to unbutton his shirt. There is no sexual tension ricocheting between us, or heavy, desperate breaths. I'm just looking after him.

His head is dropped, he's completely despondent, but he lets me undress him until he's standing before me naked and quiet. I go to direct him to the bed, but he stands firm and turns me back to face him, then sets about unzipping my dress and pulling it over my head, encouraging me to lift my arms. I let him do his thing, anything to drag him from his melancholy state. I stand quietly while he sees through his task, unhooking my bra before kneeling and taking my knickers down my legs. I'm lifted to his body, my legs finding their place around his hips, and he positions himself on the bed, back against the headboard so I'm sitting on his lap, pressed against his chest. He's not prepared to have any space between us, which is fine by me. His arms are completely encasing me, his nose is in my hair and his heartbeat is slow and steady under my ear. This is all I can do, and if need be, I'll do it until the day I die.

Chapter 26

I feel different this morning. I'm on my back, but I'm not sprawled across the bed with a light breeze tickling my naked skin, and I'm unable to stretch. It takes a few seconds to register why. I'm cocooned beneath Jesse, who is half lying on me, half off, so he isn't putting pressure on my tummy. His face is nuzzled in the space between my jaw and my shoulder, his palm is flat on my abdomen and his hot, minty breath is heating my neck. My rousing brain speedily kicks into gear, reminding me of the events of last night, the pain, the anguish and the shock. Paradise was turned upside down.

My fingers slip into his hair as I gaze up at the ceiling and massage gently. This man has a troubled history, but I'm fixing all of that hurt and suffering. I'm his little piece of heaven, and I'll never allow him to fall back into his hellish, hollow past.

As I lie there giving myself a little mental pep talk, I feel the slight flicker of his long lashes against my neck, but I remain quiet, allowing him to have his thinking space, my fingers keeping up the gentle twisting of his hair.

'I would never have brought you here if I had known.' His raspy voice breaks the silence. 'I never wanted my life with you to be stained by my past.'

'It hasn't affected us,' I assure him. 'So please don't let it.'

'They have no place in my life, Ava. Not before, and even less now.' His hand starts a slow movement across my stomach.

His babies will not replace Jake. They will not ease Jesse's parents' guilt. And I know for sure they'll never be reason for reconciliation. Some things are unforgivable, and your parents doing anything other than loving and supporting you are just a few of them. My dad has always said that he could never tell me what to do, only advise me. He has said he would never force my hand in anything, knowing it would make me unhappy. He said he would always be there, despite my choices, and he would make things better if it was the wrong choice. And he did. Many times. That's what parents do.

'You don't need to explain anything to me. You and me.' I repeat his words to enforce my own.

He rolls onto his back and pulls at me, encouraging me to crawl onto his chest. I find my way and start my slow, light trailing of his scar. 'This place was Carmichael's,' he says quietly. 'It was part of his estate, as was the boat.'

'I know.' I smile to myself.

'How did you know?'

'Why else would you have a villa so close to where your parents live?'

I can't see him, but I know he's smiling. 'My beautiful girl is frightening me.'

'Why?' I ask, frowning into his chest.

'Because she's usually so demanding for information.'

I have to agree, but I've found out more since I convinced myself to keep my trap shut than I ever did when I was stamping and screaming. 'There can't be anything else you could tell me that would convince me to run away from you again.'

'I'm glad you've said that.'

If there was anything he could say that would make me stiffen and wish I could retract my words, then that would be it. I know I'm not going to like what I'm about hear. It's like I'm unintentionally pulling confessions from this man.

'Ava?' he says quietly.

'What?'

'I need to tell you something.' He goes to move, but I make

myself a dead weight, ensuring optimum difficulty for him, not that it makes a blind bit of difference. I'm removed from his chest with minimal effort and turned onto my back. He straddles my waist, but doesn't rest himself fully on me, and chews his lip for a few moments while I look up at him, a sceptical expression plastered all over my face. I know knowledge is power is the sensible option, but given what Jesse has presented me with in the knowledge department, it scares the fucking life out of me.

He takes my hands and holds them tightly. 'I've had Sarah at The Manor while we've been gone.'

'*What*?' My head lifts and my throat is instantly hoarse.

'She's dealing with things while I'm gone. John can't do it on his own, Ava.'

'But Sarah? You said she was gone, end of!' I'm livid. My blood is instantly boiling and it's heating my face, all thoughts of absconded parents and painful histories eradicated at the mention of *her* name. 'Why, after everything she's done, would you allow that?' I snatch my hands from his and try to push him away. 'Get off!'

'Ava, will you calm down!'

'Why? Worried I might injure your babies?' I spit at him.

Those words just changed his concerned look to one of displeasure. He's scowling at me, but I couldn't give a toss. 'Don't talk fucking shit.' He manages to seize my flailing hands and secure them above my head.

'You think it!' I yell in his face. 'Your constant monitoring and overprotectiveness tells me all I need to know.'

'I've always been overprotective, so don't brandish that card, lady!'

He's right, he has, but I'm pissed off and I'll use anything against him, which reminds me that we've steered off course a bit. 'She goes, or I do!'

He actually rolls his eyes. I don't appreciate it. I buck myself, and he releases me, but it's because he doesn't want me to hurt his babies. It makes me madder. 'Ava, I was in a mess, you refuse to work for me, and I need someone who knows what they're doing.'

I stop and swing round. 'So she's working for you again?' I don't believe this. Her compassionate little speech at the coffee house stood for shit. She's probably delighting in this.

He gets up and walks towards me.

'Stop where you are, Ward!' I point my finger in his face. 'Don't try to placate me or convince me that this is all fine because it fucking isn't!'

'Watch your fucking mouth!'

'No! She's in love with you. Do you know that? Everything she has done really is because she wants to take you away from me, so don't even *think* about trying to convince me that this is a good idea.'

'I know.'

I snap my mouth shut and retreat a little. 'What do you mean, you know?'

'I know she's in love with me.'

'You do?'

'Of course I do, Ava. I'm not fucking stupid.'

I scoff. 'You obviously are! You'll trample anyone who tries to take me away from you, yet right under your nose, she's doing the best job and you're choosing to ignore it!' I swing around and stamp my way into the kitchen. I need some water to soothe my scratchy throat.

'I didn't just let it go unsaid, Ava. I had it out with her and she admitted and regretted it all.'

'Of course she regrets it. She failed! She's probably regretting not doing a better job!' I slam my glass down on the worktop. 'And you may as well have let it go unsaid. Did you offer burial or cremation?'

His face screws up. 'What?'

'The usual option you give people who hurt me. Did you offer it to Sarah?'

'No, I offered her a job in return for her word that she'll never interfere again. I told her that if you say so, she's out.'

'I say so!' I shout. 'I say she's out!'

'But she hasn't done anything.'

I look at the thick-skinned idiot across the worktop in disbelief. 'She's not done anything?'

His eyes close and he exhales long and wearily. 'I mean she's not done anything since I reinstated her. And you rewarded her with a tidy crack to the jaw for the stuff that came before.'

'Why are you doing this? You know how I feel, Jesse.'

'Because she's desperate, Ava. She has no life past The Manor.'

'You feel sorry for her?' I ask more calmly. I love everything about this man, except his sudden empathy for all of these women who are trying to sabotage our relationship.

'Ava, first of all, I want you to calm down because it's not good for you or the babies.'

'I am calm!' I screech, lifting my glass with wobbly hands.

He sighs and cocks his head to crack his neck, almost like he's alleviating some stress. I have no idea what he's so stressed about. Let me tell him that I'll continue to work for Mikael and see what reaction that sparks. It's the same principle, kind of.

He walks over to me, takes the glass from my hand and picks me up, placing me on the worktop. My jaw is seized and pulled up to meet his face. I maintain my scowl, looking at him through pissed-off eyes.

'Sarah has nothing. I kicked her out when she came clean and thought no more of it.' He takes a deep breath. 'Until John spoke with her and she was saying all kinds of fucked-up shit, the most worrying part mentioning death being better than living her life without me.'

My suspicious mind instantly makes me think that it's

another ploy to nab him. I can't help it. 'Attention-seeker,' I snipe, still scowling. Her past actions are a clear indication to what lengths she'll go to.

'I thought so, too, but John wasn't so sure. He found her. She'd slashed her wrists and taken a pile of painkillers.' He raises his eyebrows as I recoil. 'It was no cry for help, Ava. There was no attention-seeking about it. John only just got her to the hospital in time. She wanted to die.'

My brain is failing me on all counts. There are plenty of sensible questions that I should be asking, but nothing is coming to me. I'm blank.

'I don't want another death on my conscience, baby. I live with Jake's every single day. I can't do it.'

I choke on sympathy. 'She came to see me,' I say. I don't know where it comes from.

'She told me.' He reaches up and cups my cheek. 'But I'm surprised you never mentioned this before.'

What can I say? That Sarah's words were, in fact, the reason for my clarity? That she was the reason I turned up at The Manor in such a state and confessed my pregnancy? 'I didn't think it was important,' I answer feebly.

'It was Sarah who told Matt about my drinking.' He starts biting his lip.

I recoil further, and his hand drops from my face. That's how Matt found out? 'Is that how you knew I was collecting my clothes from Matt's, too?'

He nods. 'She said she'd overheard you on the phone, telling someone you were intending to pick your stuff up. I was too mad to piece it together. I saw red, acted on impulse and asked questions later.'

So her list of misdemeanours goes further. I desperately do not want to feel sorry for her. 'She said she couldn't work for you any more,' I tell him. 'So how come she is?'

'I asked her. I'll never find someone else to do the job, which means I'll have to do it, and I'm not prepared to give up my time with you. And you should know, she only accepted on the condition that you were okay with it.'

So the future of Sarah has been placed in my hands? If I say no, will she try to top herself again? And if I agree, will I be facing another round of Sarah trying to split us up? 'You're not giving me much of a choice,' I mutter. I'm trying and failing to be logical here. I don't want to lose Jesse to The Manor's demands at the best of times, not least to piles of paperwork that will stress him out. I'll never see him, but if I accept this, then I'm accepting what she has done to us, and I don't think I can do that, not even when she's tried to kill herself. But Jesse's words keep running on repeat in my head.

I live with Jake's every single day. I can't do it.

And I can't do it to him. My anxieties are justified, but Jesse's guilt isn't, and I can't put him through any more than he's already dealt with. It would be cruel and selfish. I love him too much.

He cups my cheeks again and pierces me with green eyes full of sincerity. 'I'll tell her it's a no-go. I'm not prepared to see you so unhappy.'

I crumble on the inside. He's prepared to live with the potential of further blood on his hands, even though none of this is his fault, just to keep me happy? I shake my head in his grasp. 'No, I want you with me more than I want her gone.'

'You do?' He sounds surprised.

'Of course I do, but you have to promise me something.'

'Anything. You know that.' He kisses my forehead.

This is not strictly true because he wouldn't ask this of me. I'm trying to disregard the mitigating circumstances, but it's hard to ignore a woman who has attempted suicide because my husband doesn't want her. 'When the babies arrive, you won't be at The Manor day and night. You'll be with me as often as you can. I don't know if I can do this.' The fear of being alone with twins is scaring me. One baby was frightening enough. Two babies? I'm terrified, and he needs to know.

His lips curve at the edges. He finds my panic funny? 'Ava, you'll have to bury me six feet under before I have it any other way. You can do it because you have me.' He wraps me in his arms and pulls me off the counter so I'm left little choice but to cling onto him with my legs around his naked hips and my arms around his naked shoulders. 'We're going to be okay.'

'I know,' I admit. I'm feeling needy, like I'm seeking constant reassurance. He'll always give it to me, but he must be slightly concerned by my anxiousness. I'm hardly showing any motherly tendencies. Shouldn't it be the woman reading the books and buying folic acid?

'Let's not fight. It makes my heart split in pain, and I don't want you stressing out. We have to watch your blood pressure.' He paces back to the bedroom.

I link my fingers at the nape of his neck and lean back so I can see him. 'I'm confiscating that book.'

He grins at me. 'That's *my* book, and I'm keeping it.'

'We need to make friends.' I straighten my back, pulling my body into his so my nipple is at his mouth. 'Did you read the part of the book that says a husband should service his wife as she demands?'

He bites down gently and swirls his tongue in a deliciously slow rotation, spiking a moan from me and a chuckle from him. 'I did, but our plane is scheduled for take-off in two hours. I need more time, so I'll service you when we get home. Deal?'

'No deal,' I retort, thrusting my chest to his mouth again. 'I want to stay in Paradise.'

'You're incorrigible, and I love it.' I'm lowered to the bed on a disgusted snort. 'But we need to catch that flight.'

'I need you.' I grasp his cock loosely, teasingly, and he jumps away.

'Ava, when I have you, I like to take my time.' He plants a chaste kiss on my lips. 'Pack.'

I flop back on the bed in complete pregnancy-fuelled exasperation. My time in Paradise is up.

Chapter 27

It's the morning after we arrived home and I'm not a happy bunny. He's woken, gone for a run, showered and dressed, all without me, but he left my ginger biscuit and folic acid by the bed with some water. I'm standing in front of the floor-length mirror in my lace, drying my hair, when I see him in the reflection, strolling into the bedroom. He's not shaved and he has on my favourite grey suit, black shirt and tie, but it doesn't improve my mood, even if he does look edible.

'Morning,' he chirps, all happy and awake.

I flip him a scowl and chuck my hairdryer on the floor before stalking into the wardrobe to find something to wear – something I know he won't approve of. I exit the wardrobe and slip my feet into my black suede heels, and then head straight for the bathroom. I'm aware of his large frame to the side of me, following my every move, and I snatch a quick look as I pass, seeing his hands resting lightly in his trouser pockets and an amused expression on his face. I don't humour him with my time or silver tongue, instead finding my way to the bathroom mirror and making fast work of my make-up.

He walks in and comes to stand behind me, his fresh-water loveliness smacking me right in the nose. 'What do you think you're doing?' he asks, still displaying amusement on his face.

I pause, mid-mascara application, and pull back from the mirror. 'I'm putting my make-up on,' I answer, knowing this is not what he means.

'Let me rephrase that. What do you think you're wearing?'

'A dress.'

His eyebrows hit his hairline. 'Let's not start the day on a bad note, lady.' He holds my black pencil dress up. 'Put the dress on.'

I take a deep breath of calm and turn to take the dress before exiting the bathroom without a word. I'll put the dress on, but only because I'm worked up enough. Not only have I been snatched from Paradise, but, as predicted, I've also been tossed off Central Jesse Cloud Nine. London does our relationship absolutely no favours. No, let me rephrase that. Jesse in London does our relationship no favours.

I go out of my way to make the biggest deal of demonstrating the inconvenience he's causing, not that he's bothered. He stands patiently and observes as I remove my unauthorised dress and replace it with the one he's sanctioned. Reaching behind my back, I grasp the zipper and pull it up my back, but I only get halfway before I lose my grip of the little piece of metal. I quickly locate it again, but the same thing happens.

I close my eyes, hating having to ask the smug arse for assistance. 'Will you zip me up, please?'

'Of course,' he chirps, and the next second he's pressed against my back, his mouth at my ear, instigating a ferocious wave of treacherous tingles to ride through me. My hair is grasped and draped down my front before he takes the zip and tugs. 'Oh dear.'

'What? Is it broken?'

'Urm ...' he tries again. 'No, baby. I think you may have grown out of it.'

I gasp, completely horrified, and turn to see my back in the mirror. There's a good inch of bare flesh revealed and the material is *not* stretchy. I sag on the inside and out. And so it begins. All of the pregnancy side effects will be accelerated because I have two peanuts, not one. I refuse to cry, although I could, quite easily. I need to embrace this. I need to match Jesse in the enthusiasm stakes. It's all right for him; he's still going to be a god at the end of all this, whereas my body will probably be ravaged. I turn to face him, finding an apprehensive face around a chewed lip. He thinks I'm going to disintegrate. 'Can I put my other dress on now?' I ask quietly.

He visibly relaxes and even fetches my other dress for me, helping me out of the now too small one and into the newly authorised one. 'Beautiful,' he says, 'I need to scram. Cathy's downstairs and she's made you breakfast. Please eat it.'

'I will.'

He can't hide his surprise at my easy submission. 'Thank you.'

'You don't have to thank me for eating,' I mutter, grabbing my bag and making my way out of the bedroom.

'I feel like I should thank you for everything you do without arguing with me about it.' He follows me down the stairs.

'If you were still fucking sense into me, then I would argue.'

'Are you pissed off because I didn't service you this morning?' he asks, amusement rife in his tone.

'Yes.'

'Thought so.' He grabs my hand and swings me around so my body crashes against his hard chest. Then he eats me alive. I'm taken with purpose and conviction, and I don't stop him. It'll never make up for the sex we didn't have this morning, but it might quench my thirst until later. 'Have a nice day, baby.' I'm spun back around and my arse is slapped before I'm guided to the kitchen archway. 'Make sure my wife eats her breakfast, Cathy.'

'I will, boy.' She waves a whisk over her head, but doesn't turn around.

'I'll see you later. And don't forget to speak with Patrick.' He strides out without waiting for confirmation that I will, indeed, talk to Patrick. I know my time is up on that matter.

'Ava, you look so well!' Cathy sings at me from across the kitchen. 'All glowing and fresh!'

'Thanks, Cathy.' I smile at her kindness. 'Can I take my bagel with me? I'm running a little late.'

'Of course.' She starts wrapping it in cling film. 'Did you have a nice time?'

My smile broadens as I approach her to collect my breakfast. 'We had a lovely time,' I say, because we did, despite the last, horrific evening.

'I'm so glad. You both needed a break. Tell me, are the biscuits working?'

'Yes.'

'I knew they would. And twins!' She shoves my bagel in my bag and clasps my cheeks. 'Do you realise how lucky you are?'

'I do,' I answer, actually meaning it. 'I should get going.'

'Yes, yes, you go, dear. I'll get started on the washing.'

I leave Cathy sorting whites and darks, and board the lift after punching in the new code. I'm quickly delivered into the foyer of Lusso, where I find Casey sorting out the post. 'Morning, Casey,' I greet as I bounce past.

'Mrs Ward! You're back.' He joins me as I head for the brightness of outside. 'Did you have a nice time?'

'Casey, you don't need to call me Mrs Ward. We had a great time, thank you.' I slip my shades on and retrieve my keys from my bag. 'How are you enjoying the new job?'

'More now you're back.'

I skid to a halt. 'Pardon?'

He blushes terribly and starts fiddling with the envelopes in his grasp. 'That came out wrong. Sorry. It's just, well, did you know that you're the only woman in the whole building?'

'Am I?'

'Yes. All these rich businessmen don't say a word. They just grunt at me or make demands down the phone. You're the only one who takes the time to speak. I appreciate it, that's all.'

'Oh, okay.' I smile at his awkwardness. 'You mean rich businessmen like my husband?'

He blushes further. 'Okay, now I'm just digging myself a hole.' He laughs uncomfortably. 'It's just nice to see a cheerful face around here again.'

'Thank you.' I smile, and he returns it, his steel-blue eyes twinkling. 'I'd better be going.'

'Sure. I'll catch you later.' He backs away before turning and strolling off casually, back to his desk. I need to get my backside in gear. It's my first day back, and I'm going to be late. I need to be in Patrick's good books today.

I don't even falter in my steps when I emerge from Lusso and see John waiting for me. He doesn't shrug apologetically like he usually would, either. I had fully expected this. 'How are you, John?' It's good to see him again. I've missed the big, friendly guy.

"S'all good, girl.'

I jump in and secure myself with the seatbelt, watching as John takes his seat beside me on a frown.

'You're not going to kick up a stink today?' he asks, his voice plagued with laughter.

'I think I'd be signing my own death warrant if I did,' I answer drily.

John laughs, shifting his big body in the seat before starting his Ranger Rover up. 'I'm glad. I was under strict instructions to manhandle you with optimum care if you resisted.' He looks across at me through his black wraparounds. 'I didn't want to resort to that, girl.'

I grin at him. 'So are you my assigned bodyguard now, then?' I know if there was anyone else Jesse would trust me to, it would be John.

'If it keeps that motherfucker happy, I'll do whatever he wants.' John swings out of the car park. 'Are you and the babies okay?' He keeps his eyes on the road.

'Yes, but now there are three of us for Jesse to get his knickers in a twist over.'

'Crazy motherfucker.' He laughs, revealing his gold tooth. 'How are you feeling?'

'Do you mean being pregnant, or after the accident?' I keep my eyes on him, gauging his reaction. I want to know if there have been any developments since we've been away.

'Both, girl.'

'Fine on both counts, thank you. Any news on Jesse's car?' I sweep straight in. I'm comfortable enough with John to ask what I want.

'Nothing for you to worry about, girl,' he answers coolly. I might be comfortable enough to ask, but I need to remember that John is also comfortable enough to brush me off. 'How was Paradise?' he asks in a blatant change of subject tactic.

'It was paradise,' I muse. 'Until we bumped into Jesse's parents.' I'm not sure if I should be divulging this, but I've said it now and judging by the look that's just flashed across the ever cool giant's face, I've shocked him. I nod my head, confirming that he heard me right, and his shiny forehead wrinkles above his shades. 'Amalie's wedding got postponed because Jesse's dad had a heart attack,' I continue. John must be aware of the wedding, the invite, and Jesse's parents living near to Paradise. He's been around for ever, according to Jesse.

'Henry had a heart attack?' he asks, surprised. 'And what went down?'

'What went down?'

'Yes, did they speak? How was Jesse?' John sounds really curious, which is pricking at my own curiosity.

I spill it all while he drives me to work and when I'm done, he nods his head thoughtfully.

'Was that it?' he asks.

'Yes, I got him away from her. He was so upset.'

'And afterwards, he didn't drink?'

'No,' I sigh. 'But I have a feeling he would have, had I not been there.' I keep seeing his face, the face that resulted in binge drinking and whippings. 'Did you know them?'

'Not really. I don't ask questions.'

I'm nodding to myself. As well as being around for ever, John was Carmichael's best friend, so he must know more than he's letting on. 'How's Sarah?'

He shifts and turns that menacing face to mine. 'Better than she was.'

I wilt in my seat. I have nothing to say to that, so I shut up, unwrap my bagel and let John drive me the rest of the way in silence.

I audibly sigh when John pulls up at the kerb.

'What's up, girl?'

I gather my bag and exit the car before I can convince John to drive me to The Manor. 'It's time to advise my boss of a certain Danish client.'

'Oh,' he says slowly. 'Good luck.'

I think I actually blow the sarcastic sod a raspberry. 'Yeah, thanks, John,' I quip, slamming the door and hearing that deep baritone laugh getting quieter as the car door comes between us. I take a deep breath of confidence and stride into my office. Tom's screech is the first thing I hear. 'Oh my God! Ava!'

Then I hear Victoria. 'Oh wow, you have a real tan!'

Then I see sparkling Sal, sparkling again. 'Ava, you look so well.'

Then I clock my desk and stop dead in my tracks. Balloons . . . everywhere. With babies on them. There's a pack of nappies on my desk, too, and a *How To* guide on becoming a mother. But the worse thing of all, and I pick them up to check I'm seeing right, are the gigantic maternity jeans lying across the back of my chair, or covering my chair completely, more to the point. As if my morning wasn't depressing enough, with my dress not fitting and the lack of a Jesse wake-up call, I've now been reminded that I'm going to look like a whale. He really has told everyone. I'm going to kill him.

'I knew it!' Tom scurries over to my desk. 'I knew you were pregnant. But twins! Oh wow, this is so exciting! Will you name one after me?'

I discard the maternity wear and flop into my chair. I've been here two minutes and I've already had enough. Double babies means double excitement, as well as double weight gain and double anxiety. 'No, Tom.'

He gasps dramatically. 'What's wrong with Tom?'

'Nothing,' I shrug. 'I just won't be naming any of my babies it.' He snorts his disgust and stomps off, without even wishing me congratulations.

'Congratulations, Ava.' Sally bends down and hugs me. I knew I could rely on Sal. 'Coffee?'

'Please. Three sugars.' I return her hug, getting Sal's great tits thrust in my face from my seated position. 'How are you, Sal?'

'Amazing!' she gushes, dancing off to the kitchen. I quickly conclude that Sal's love life must be back on track.

'Where's Patrick?' I ask no one in particular because there's no one standing at my baby-infested desk any more. Tom is sulking across the office, obviously ignoring me, and Victoria is daydreaming, staring at me. 'Hello.' I wave my hand at her.

'Oh, sorry! I was just wondering what shade you would call that.'

'What?'

'Your tan. I'd say deep bronze.' She scribbles something down, and I know it says *deep bronze*. 'So, babies now?'

I take instant defence to her tone. 'Yes.' My short, snappy answer pulls her head quickly from her writing pad and the long blond locks get flicked over her shoulder as she smiles. If it's fake, then she's doing a great job. 'Congratulations, Ava.'

'Thank you.' I smile, doing a terrible job. 'And thanks for all this.' I gesture to the balloons wafting around my head.

'Oh, that was Tom.' She returns to her computer.

'Thanks, Tom!' I throw a pencil across the office, catching him a treat on the side of his head, knocking his glasses off kilter. He gasps in shock. 'Sorry!' I press my lips together to suppress my laugh.

'Workplace bullying!' he squawks, and I lose the battle to keep quiet. I start jerking in my chair as Sally places my coffee in front of me on a frown, and then turns to see what I'm laughing at. She starts chuckling, too.

'Where's Patrick, Sal?' I ask, having not got any answer from Victoria.

'He'll be in at noon,' she answers. 'He's not been around much.'

'No?'

She shakes her head, but says no more and returns to the pile of invoices at the filing cabinet.

'Ava,' Tom begins, straightening out his fashion specs. 'You need to call that Ruth. She hounded the office phone yesterday.'

My laughing abates fast. 'What did she say?' I ask casually, riffling through my bag for my phone when it occurs to me that I've still not turned it on. It's been off since Thursday morning when Jesse impounded it.

'Not much.' He straightens his aqua tie. 'Everything's fine with the works. I kept your appointment with her on Thursday, but she wasn't impressed to see me.'

I shrink into my chair on a wince as my phone comes to life in my hand and immediately starts alerting me of dozens of missed calls, texts and e-mails. I filter through, responding to Kate's *Welcome home!* text, and my mum's *Call me when you're settled* text, before counting the missed calls from Ruth. There are eleven, but despite the bombardment of calls from her, it's the two missed calls from Mikael that start my heart pumping fast. I can't avoid this any longer and for the first time, I sit and think hard about who could be responsible for drugging me and trying to run me off the road. And then there are the dead flowers. They were from a woman, I don't doubt it for a moment, which leads me to the same conclusion: Mikael couldn't possibly be responsible. He's a businessman, and a respected one at that. But what about the CCTV footage from the awful night when my drink was spiked? It was Mikael, I'm certain. Maybe the incidents aren't connected at all. My money is on Coral, the ex-lover, or perhaps Sarah. The flowers came after Sarah's apology, though. So did the car chase. Is she playing games still? I drop my phone to the desk. My brain aches.

I twiddle my pencil, scanning my mind for my next move. It doesn't take long. I swipe my phone up and dial Mikael. I don't even register it ringing before his smooth, mildly accented voice comes down the line. 'Ava, how very good to hear from you.'

'I'm sure,' I reply drily. 'Did you manage to sort your divorce out?' I go straight for the jugular and judging by the silent span of time that follows my question, I've succeeded in my strategy.

'I did,' he says cautiously.

'Oh good. What can I do for you, Mikael?' I'm stunned by my own confidence. I could be dealing with a lunatic here, and I'm talking to him with absolutely no respect, as a client *or* as a potential lunatic.

He laughs lightly. 'It's time we met, don't you think?'

'No, I don't,' I retort briskly. 'I think we both know that our business relationship is over, Mr Van Der Haus.'

'Why ever would that be?'

His question stops me in my tracks, but I soon gather myself. 'You said it was very interesting that I'd been seeing Jesse for about a month-ish.' I'm not shying away from this.

'Yes, except now you're married to him and expecting his twins. I'm broken-hearted, Ava.'

I don't gather myself so quickly this time. How the hell does he know? 'Mr Van Der Haus ...' I'm sure to keep my voice down, scanning the office constantly. This isn't the time or the place, but I've started now. I'm not finishing this conversation until I've said what needs to be said. I get up, beating away balloons, and pace into the conference room, shutting the door behind me. 'Is this about Jesse and your wife?' I know I hear a falter in his breathing, and it boosts my confidence. 'Because I already know, so you're wasting your time.'

'Oh, Mr Ward's been confessing?'

'Your ex-wife turned up at Jesse's home, Mikael. I'm sorry for what has happened, but I don't see what this is going to achieve.' I'm not sorry at all, but maybe, just maybe, I can make him see sense.

He laughs, and it prickles at my deeply bronzed skin. 'Ava, I couldn't care less about my ex-wife. She's a money-grabbing whore. I care only for your well-being. Jesse Ward is not the right man for you.'

I flinch at his harsh referral to his wife and rest my backside on the edge of the conference table. 'And you are?' I stammer over the words, mentally scolding myself for showing any hesitance. He cares for my well-being?

'Yes, I am,' he says candidly. 'I won't entertain other women behind your back, Ava.'

I nearly drop my phone. He knows that, too?

'Nevertheless,' I'm desperately trying to find my stride again, 'I think too much has happened for us to continue working together.'

'Too much has happened?' he asks. 'And you know what he got up to when he left you?'

'Yes,' I grate, wondering how the hell he knows. I've managed to keep that issue quiet. 'My relationship with Jesse has nothing to do with you, Mikael. I know what he did.' It kills me to say it. 'I'll be speaking to Patrick and withdrawing from the Life Building project. You're welcome to take my designs and have someone else see the contract through.' I hang up and exhale a relieved breath. I don't know why I feel like a weight has been lifted when I've still got to tell Patrick, and listening to Mikael for the last few minutes has stirred more questions. I'm not sure whether I would put my life on it, but I don't think he would go to the extremes of drugging me and trying to ram me from the road, not if he wants to take me away from Jesse so I can be with him. What use am I dead? I laugh out loud in my own little private moment of comprehension. Someone tried to kill me. This is insane.

My phone dances in my hand and a quick glimpse at my screen tells me my day has only just begun. Dealing with Ruth Quinn at the moment, though, doesn't seem like such a chore. 'Hi, Ruth.'

'Ava!' She sounds surprised. 'You never said that you were going away.'

'Last minute, Ruth. Is everything okay?'

'Yes, fine, but I've changed my mind on the cabinets for the kitchen. Can we meet to discuss?'

'Of course.' I only just suppress my sigh. 'I've got piles of paperwork to get through, so can we say tomorrow?'

'Twelve?' she counters, not demanding today, which is a pleasant surprise.

'I'll see you then, Ruth.' I hang up feeling empowered, like I'm taking charge of things rather than letting them take charge of me.

I land at my desk and spend the rest of my Tuesday clearing the build up of paperwork.

Six o'clock comes around fast, and I'm the last to leave the office. Patrick didn't return to work as planned, but called to assure me that he'd be in tomorrow. I'll talk to him then, but I'm disappointed. I feel the compulsion to rid myself of this burden without delay.

I get straight into the big black Range Rover without a sigh, falter, or complaint. 'Hi, John.'

'Girl.' He pulls off into the traffic. 'How was your day?'

'Constructive. Yours?'

'Magnificent.'

I get the feeling he's being cynical. 'Where are we going?' I slouch back in my chair, hoping he says Lusso, but I won't hold my breath. Jesse would've collected me himself if we were going home.

'The Manor, girl. How did it go with your boss?' He turns his covered eyes to me, a curious look flickering across his face.

'It didn't. He wasn't in today.'

'That'll please the crazy motherfucker.' He laughs.

I smile my agreement. I know it will.

I jump out the second John pulls to a stop and take the steps fast, pushing my way through the doors. 'He said to wait in the bar for him, girl,' John calls to my back, but I pretend not to hear him. I'm not waiting in the bar. After having him to myself for three whole days, my first day back at work has been the longest ever. I hotfoot it past the stairs and through the summer room before John can catch me. The usual gatherings of members are here, but I don't hang around to gauge the reaction to my presence.

I steam straight into Jesse's office, without knocking and without stopping to think that I could be barging in on a business meeting. I've had some shocks when doing this before.

And I'm shocked now.

Chapter 28

'Dan?' I say warily, staring at my brother's back. He's sitting opposite Jesse at his desk, and he turns at the sound of his name. 'What are you doing here?' The sudden astronomical consequences of his visit hit me hard.

'Hey, kiddo.' He stands, smiling, and makes his way over to me, stooping to hug me. 'Congratulations.'

'I might get to tell someone myself soon,' I grumble, landing Jesse with a reproachful look over my brother's shoulder. He shrugs sheepishly and pouts before mouthing *I love you.*

'So what are you doing here?' I repeat, cocking my head at Jesse, but he just shrugs again and remains quiet. It's a novelty.

'Making amends.' Dan releases me and runs his hand through his dark mop. 'I didn't want to go home without sorting this out.'

'Oh?' I look at Jesse again, who just shrugs ... again. 'So you're friends?'

'Something like that. Anyway, I need to shoot. I'm meeting Harvey up west.' He turns to Jesse. 'Thanks.'

'No problem.' Jesse nods, not bothering to be civil and stand to see Dan out. That and all of the nonchalant shrugs are increasing my suspicion.

'When are you heading back?' I ask when he's facing me again.

'I'm not sure. Depends on flights. I'll call you, okay?' He kisses my cheek and heads past me, meeting the big guy at the door. John shakes his menacing head at me before escorting my brother from Jesse's office.

I point my suspiciousness at Jesse. 'What was all that about?'

'What?'

I walk over to the sofa and drop my bag down before taking the seat my brother has just vacated. 'Look at me.' Those three words always do the trick, but not because he's obeying me. It's because he's always shocked to hear them. I don't care. He can look at me stunned all he likes. 'Why was Dan here?'

He stands and picks his phone up from the desk. 'He apologised.'

I laugh in his face. Dan would never apologise, not to Jesse. I've known him my whole life, and I know he's far too proud to back down. 'I don't believe you.'

'That makes me sad, baby.' He pulls a solemn face, which raises my suspicions further. 'Now, tell me. What did Patrick say?'

I know my suspicious glower has just transformed into guilt, and it's me evading *his* eyes now.

'You've not told him, have you?' he asks with an edge of anger in his tone. 'Ava?'

'He wasn't in the office,' I blurt quickly. 'But he will be to-morrow, so I'll speak to him then.'

'Too late, lady. You've had your chance. Again and again and again.'

'That's not fair,' I argue. 'I told Mikael I won't be working with him any more, so you can't say I'm not trying to resolve this.' I know immediately that I've made a grave mistake when his shoulders stiffen and his greens widen.

'You did what?'

'I don't think he drugged me, Jesse. He said he wanted me, so why would he hurt me?' I need to shut the hell up. Those words have just made his mouth drop open.

'What the fucking hell are you doing talking to him?' He

rests his fist on the desk, like a silverback gorilla getting ready to charge. It makes me sit back in my chair.

'He knows that you've . . .' I start a frantic tap on my front tooth with my nail, 'entertained other women while we've been together.' I hold my breath, knowing that I'm increasing the building fury.

'We agreed never to speak of that again.' He virtually grinds the words out, his jaw tense to snapping point.

'It's hard when people keep reminding me of it.' I'm leaning forward now, finding a momentary spurt of bravery. 'How does he know?' I figure the answer out before he can deny even knowing it. The chewed lip and quite a few other things, mental comprehension, mainly, bring me to a fast conclusion. Mikael's ex-wife. 'She was one of them, wasn't she?' I ask. His eyes close, and I stand up and lean across the desk, mirroring his threatening stance. He doesn't need to reply. 'You said *months*. You said you hadn't been with her for months, that you didn't understand why she was suddenly sniffing around. You've slept with her more than once, too!'

'I didn't want to upset you.' He's still hostile. It's a blatant defence mechanism.

'Tell me. Did you call them up and have them make a queue outside your door?'

'No, they hear that I'm on the drink and they're like flies around shit.'

'I hate you.'

'No you don't.'

'Yes, I do.'

'Don't make my heart crack, Ava. Does it matter who it was?'

'No, what matters is that you lied to me.'

'I was protecting you.'

'And it's hilarious that every single time you do that, you end up hurting me.'

'I know.'

'So, have you learned?'

'Every fucking day.' He grabs my jaw aggressively, but says softly, 'I'm sorry.'

'Good.' I nod decisively in his hold, suddenly registering that our faces are now touching as we both lean in over his desk. We're burning each other with angry gazes, mixed with a ton of lust. 'How did this happen?' I ask the question out loud when I was only intending on thinking it.

'Because, my beautiful girl, we're meant to be stuck together. Constant contact. Kiss me.'

'I've accepted that you're an arsehole, so there's no need to try and get me submitting to your touch now.' I will, though.

'I missed you, baby.'

I climb up onto his desk and inch my way closer on my knees until I'm wrapped around him and my lips are all over his. Stupidly, I've missed him, too. One working day after Paradise and I'm feeling hard done by – short changed. I've been suffering Jesse withdrawal and now I've finally got my next hit. 'I wish you were pure and untouched,' I mumble, trailing my lips over every inch of his face. Of everything, this I wish the most – that no one came before me, or even during me. I've forgiven him, I truly have, but I'm struggling to forget.

'I am.' He sits down in his leather chair and jostles with me until I give in and let him sit me on his lap. 'The most important part of me is untouched.' He takes my hand and twirls my rings for a few thoughtful moments before flattening my palm and placing it on his chest. 'Or it was until you stepped into my office. Now it's being stamped all over and is exploding with pure love for *you*.'

I smile. 'I like feeling it beating.' I move in, opening his jacket up and lowering my ear to his shirt. 'I like hearing it, too.' It's one of the most comforting things in the world.

His arms wrap around me and pull me in closer. 'How was your day?'

'Crap. I want Paradise.'

He laughs and kisses the top of my head. 'I'm in Paradise whenever I'm with you. I don't need a villa.'

'You were more relaxed in Paradise.' I say it how it is. I know being back in London will slowly draw my neurotic control freak back to the surface.

'I'm relaxed now.'

'Yes; that is because I'm sitting on your lap, coated in you,' I reply sardonically, earning myself a little dig in the hollow space above my hips. I laugh and turn myself around on his lap so I'm facing his desk. 'How was *your* day?'

His hands slide around onto my tummy and his chin rests on my shoulder. 'Long. How are my peanuts?'

'Fine.' His notepad catches my eye. 'Why's my brother's name written down there?' I reach forward to pull it closer, but too slowly because it's soon whipped from under my nose and shoved in the top drawer of Jesse's desk. I pull my hand back on a shocked jump at his fast movement. 'Daniel Joseph O'Shea?' I frown to myself, thinking I definitely saw numbers on that paper, and it wasn't a telephone number. 'Why have you got Dan's bank account number written down?'

'I haven't.' He quickly dismisses my question, and he's tense. Damn him, he hasn't learned at all.

I remove myself from his lap and place myself to the side of him, punishing him with a stare equal to his *don't push it* glare. 'I'm giving you three seconds, Ward.'

His lips press into a straight, aggravated line. 'The countdown is mine,' he claims, childishly.

'Three.' I even hold three fingers up, in the most provoking fashion possible. I'm just as bad as he is. 'Two.' I lose a finger, but I don't get to one or zero because I have an obvious moment of lucidity. 'You're giving him money!'

'No.' He shakes his head in the most unconvincing way

possible, shifting his feet in his seated position. He's becoming as bad at lying as I am.

'You're a shit liar, too, Ward.' I swivel on my heels and make a run for it, mainly to catch my brother before he leaves, but also to escape Jesse before he catches *me*.

'Ava!'

I take no notice of the threatening shout of my name, and break into a full-on run when I reach the summer room. I pass the kitchens, the bar and the restaurant and skid on my heels when I find Dan standing by the huge round table in the entrance hall. He's not doing anything or talking to anyone, he's just standing there looking confused. John is here, too, and I know why that is. It's the same reason why John accompanied *me* everywhere in the early days. I watch in apprehension as Dan looks around and John tries to usher him on, but he's not shifting, not even for the big guy.

Jesse's chest hits my back, and I'm picked up and turned in his arms. He's not happy. 'For fuck's sake, woman! You'll give the babies brain damage! No running!'

If I wasn't so concerned by my brother's location and behaviour, I would laugh at the crazy idiot holding me firmly in his arms. 'Get a grip!' I wriggle free and swing around, finding Dan watching us. His brow is completely furrowed, and John looks on edge.

Dan takes a leisurely gaze around the entrance hall again, then his inquisitive eyes land on Jesse. 'If this is a hotel, then where's the reception area?'

'What?' Jesse's tone is impatient, almost defensive, and I wish it wasn't. It's a dead giveaway and I'm praying for him to think up something quickly.

'Where do your guests pick up the keys to their room?' He looks up at John. 'And why the need to have a gorilla escorting me everywhere?'

I cringe, Jesse tenses, and John growls. My brother is a bit quicker on the uptake than me. I'm wracking my blank mind for something, anything, but it just isn't happening. I, or we, have been caught completely off guard. And then I hear a voice and it's the only voice in the world that I would wish *not* to hear right now.

Kate.

I visibly sag on the spot, and I feel Jesse's hand on the small of my back. Why isn't he saying anything? I watch and listen in horror as Kate and Sam dance down the stairs, giggling, feeling each other up and generally looking all sexed up. This is a disaster. I can't help elbowing Jesse in the ribs, a silent demand to say something. Oh God, please say something!

Kate and Sam are completely oblivious to the silent audience awaiting them at the bottom of the stairs, as they fondle and pet each other, saying inappropriate things, of which one sentence definitely included the word *dildo*. I'm in hell, and no one has even said anything, except my delinquent best friend and her cheeky chap of a boyfriend, not that they are aware . . . yet. I'm stuck in limbo. It's the closest I've come to watching a train crash, all very slowly. Dan and The Manor; Dan and Kate; Dan and Sam; Dan and Jesse. The shit is going to hit the fan in a big way.

'Oh!' Kate's delighted shriek echoes around the entrance hall, followed by Sam's sexed-up growl. Then they land at the bottom of the stairs in a messy bundle of entwined arms and frantic lips, eating each other alive. They should have stayed in the suite because they are nowhere near done. 'Sam!' She laughs and falls back over his arm, catching my eye, her happy face beaming further, until she clocks my brother. She's not laughing now. In fact, she looks close to seizure. She scrambles up and slaps a disgruntled Sam away before smoothing down her wild red hair and pulling at her dishevelled clothes. But she doesn't say anything and neither does Sam as he looks to and fro between the quiet observers.

Dan breaks the screaming silence. 'Hotel?' He's drilling holes into Kate and Sam at regular intervals, back and forth, before turning his questioning eyes to Jesse. 'Do you often let your friends carry on like this in your establishment?'

'Dan.' I step forward, but I don't get very far. Jesse places himself in front of me.

'I think you should come back to my office.' Jesse's voice is intimidating, as is his body language.

'No thanks.' Dan almost laughs, keeping his eyes on Kate. I've never seen her looking so uncomfortable, and Sam must be wondering what's going on. 'You're whoring it up at a brothel?'

'What the fuck?' Sam shouts. 'Who the fuck do you think you're talking to?' Sam's moving forward, but Kate catches his arm, pulling him back.

'This is no brothel, and I'm no whore.' Her voice is shaky and unsure as she holds onto Sam. I want to jump to her defence, but no words are forming and Jesse saves me the trouble, anyway.

He approaches Dan, wraps his palm around the nape of my brother's neck and leans in, whispering something in his ear. It's the most threatening act possible. I don't even want to consider what he has said, especially when Dan shows his willingness to follow Jesse's lead, with no further persuasion. I go to follow, too; I want to hear this, but I'm halted.

'Wait for me in the bar, baby.' He tries to turn me, but I'm feeling a little defiant. I'm not happy with Jesse taking Dan to his office alone.

'I'd like to come.' I have no faith in my feigned confidence.

I'm picked up and taken to my stool. 'You'll stay put.' He kisses my cheek like it will appease me. It won't. My eyes are throwing daggers right at his back as he stalks out of the bar in long, even strides.

'Ah!' Mario's happy voice draws my attention away from my husband's disappearing back. 'Look at you, all ... how you say?

Like a flower. Blooming!' He clucks my cheek across the bar and passes me a bottle of water. 'No more Mario's Most Marvellous for you!'

I grunt but smile, taking a long swig of the icy water, leaving Mario to go and tend to other members. Sam wanders in, looking all chirpy and with his dimple in its usual spot. I'm confused. 'Hey, Mama!' He has a cheeky rub of my stomach. 'How are you feeling?'

'Fine . . .' The word trails from my mouth slowly. 'Where's Kate?'

'Ladies',' he replies quickly, waving Mario for a beer.

I look past him, wondering if I should go and see her. 'Is she okay?'

'Yeah, she's fine.' He doesn't look at me, but I have a feeling he knows there's a face full of confusion focused on him. He looks out of the corner of his eye to me, and then sits on a sigh. 'I know you all think it, but I'm not stupid.'

My back straightens. 'I don't think you're stupid.' I defend myself. He's a little oblivious, maybe, but not stupid.

He smiles. 'I've worked out Kate and Dan. I know why she called it off with me, and I know that something went down at your wedding.'

I know I look as guilty as sin, and I'm wondering if Kate is aware of this. 'Why have you kept quiet?'

'I don't know.' He tips his bottle to his lips, clearly pondering that, too. 'She's a great girl.' He shrugs.

I nod thoughtfully, smiling on the inside. I could happily bang their heads together. I could also cry for Sam. Something tells me he's never shared his orphan history with many women, if any, but Kate knows and whilst they both act so casual and carefree, I know there are a whole lot of feelings here that both seem to be playing down. 'I think I'll go and find her.' I stand and give Sam a shoulder rub – a silent gesture of understanding, to which he responds with a cheeky grin, leaning down and whispering some mushy rubbish to my navel before he lets me leave.

I push the door of the Ladies' open and find Kate braced over the sink, her red hair completely concealing her face as she looks into the bowl. 'Hey.' I tread carefully, not wanting her to go on the defensive.

She pulls her head up with some effort and shows me glass blue eyes full of despair. 'Do you think I'm a whore?'

'No!' I'm shocked that she would even ask. A little reckless perhaps, but never a whore. I'm very suddenly seeing the ladies of The Manor in a different light. I know for sure that many of them are only here for one purpose and that purpose is a tall, lean god who is no longer available. Memberships are being cancelled to prove it, as well as some of the relentless ones taking things further. Like drugging me, or trying to run me off the road, or sending me a threatening note. Suddenly, it becomes a very frightening thought that any one of these women could be behind this. Has Jesse got any inkling?

'What the hell have I got myself into, Ava?' Kate's question snaps me from my disturbing thoughts.

'Love?' I blurt before I can think of whether or not it's a good thing to say. Her wide blues tell me it's not. 'You're going to deny it again, aren't you?'

'No,' she whispers. 'I think we're past all that bullshit.'

'We're past it?' I laugh. 'Kate, we were past it weeks ago.' I'm completely exasperated, but so relieved. My blind friend has finally seen the light. 'He's at the bar, and he . . .' I pause, quickly reining in what I was about to say. I'm not forewarning her that Sam knows about Dan. That's for them to sort out.

'He what?' She looks all panicky, which just reaffirms my decision to hold back.

'He's waiting for you.'

Her whole body relaxes and an air of contentment seems to form a haze around her. 'So I should go?' she asks, looking for reassurance. It's rare to see her doubt herself or ask for encouragement or guidance.

'You should go,' I confirm on a grin. 'You have to take a chance, Kate. I think you'll be surprised where Sam leads you.'

'Do you?'

'I really do.' I smile and take my unsure friend in my arms and squeeze all of the uncertainties out of her. 'Please go and talk to him. And let him talk, too.'

'Okay,' she agrees. 'I will.' She pushes me off her, pulling a disgusted face. 'Quit with the slushy shit.'

'Of course, it's all me.' I turn to the mirror, along with Kate, and we both start rubbing under our eyes.

'What do you think Jesse is saying to Dan?' Kate's question reminds me quickly that they're alone.

'I don't know,' I say on a frown, 'but I'm going to find out. You good?'

'Fan-fucking-tastic.' She drops a quick peck on my cheek and leads the way from the Ladies', she going right towards the bar, me heading left to Jesse's office.

I burst in, my eyes almost closed, like I'm protecting them from the certainty of seeing my brother held against the wall by his throat. He's not, though. They're in the same seated positions as the last time I walked in on them.

'Why are you taking money from Jesse?' I ask assertively in an attempt to make both of them see that I mean business. I definitely don't mistake the rise and tense of Dan's shoulders. He might have rumbled Jesse's establishment, but I've rumbled this little agreement. 'Are you going to answer me?'

Dan doesn't, but Jesse does. 'Ava, I told you to stay put.'

'I'm not talking to you,' I counter fearlessly, spiking an incredible scoff of disbelief.

'Well, I'm talking to you.'

'Shut up.' I approach the desk and poke Dan in the back. '*You're* keeping quiet. Have you nothing to say?'

'See what I have to deal with?' Jesse's palms face the heavens in hopelessness.

I flip Jesse a scowl and smack my brother on the shoulder. 'Speak. What's going on?'

'I'm broke,' Dan says quietly. 'Jesse's agreed to help me out.'

'You asked?' I blurt in disbelief. That's brash, given the history of my husband and brother's relationship.

'No, he offered, and there were no strings attached . . . until ten minutes ago.'

'You're bribing my brother?' I swing my gaze to Jesse, whose hands are now forming a thoughtful steeple in front of his mouth. 'You've paid him to keep quiet?'

'No, I've lent him some money and added a little clause to the contract at a later date.'

I'm appalled, but stupidly relieved. Jesse said my parents would never know, and he's ensuring that he keeps his promise. 'What about the surf school? And why haven't you asked Mum and Dad? They would've lent you some money.'

'We're not talking a few quid, Ava. I'm up to my eyeballs. I got myself a massive loan to fund my share of the business and my partner did a runner with it. I'm fucked.'

I crumble. 'Why didn't you say anything?'

'Why do you think?' He looks truly humiliated. 'I was turned over, Ava. I have nothing left.'

My sorry eyes fall back on Jesse, who's remaining extremely quiet, but studying me closely. 'How much?' My question makes my husband look all uncomfortable, and Dan is shifting in his chair next to me, which can only mean one thing. 'Five thousand? Ten thousand? Tell me.'

'Just a few,' Dan interjects before Jesse can tell me himself. I don't believe him for a moment.

'Jesse?' I push, holding him in place with a determined glare. I need to know how much trouble my brother's in.

His eyes break from mine for a few moments and aim for

Dan before he takes a deep breath and starts rubbing his temples. 'I'm sorry, Dan. I'm not lying to her. Two hundred, baby,' he says on a long exhale. I might need some temple rubs myself. I'm hoping by two hundred he means pounds, but I know I'm hoping in vain. I stagger back in shock and Jesse is out of his chair in the blink of an eye. He looks mad.

'Damn it, Ava.' He holds me in place by my shoulders. 'Are you okay? Are you dizzy? Do you want to sit down?'

'Two hundred thousand!' I yell. 'What sort of bank lends two hundred thousand?' I shrug a faffing Jesse away as my shock allows for the information to sink in, turning my disbelief into anger. 'I'm fine!'

'Don't push me away, Ava!' he yells back at me, taking my elbow and leading me around his desk. I'm pushed gently onto his massive office chair. 'Don't be getting your knickers in a twist, lady. It's not healthy.'

'My blood pressure is fine!' I snap petulantly, but I suspect it's probably just gone through the roof. 'Two hundred thousand? No bank in their right mind would lend that sort of money for a surf school!' They would laugh in anyone's face if they rocked up with a request on that scale. How much can a few surfboards cost?

'No, you're right.' Dan's shrinking further into his chair, making himself smaller and smaller. It's an indication of how he feels – small and stupid. 'A loan shark would, though.'

'Oh God!' My head falls into my palms. I know how they work. 'What were you thinking?' I can feel Jesse's palm rubbing soothing circles into my back, but it doesn't soothe me at all.

'I wasn't thinking, Ava,' he sighs.

I uncover my face, just so Dan can see the disappointment on it. I thought he was smart. 'Is that the only reason you came home?'

'They're looking for me.' Dan's defeated face yanks at my

heart strings. 'You don't get away with non-payment with these types.'

'You said you were doing well,' I remind him, but I get no explanation, just a shrug. 'Just stay here.' I sit forward in my chair. 'Don't go back.' I hear Jesse's quiet laugh and see Dan's soft smile. Both reactions to my remedy are not being taken seriously. They are also a clue that both men find my naivety endearing. I don't see a problem, though. Australia is on the other side of the planet.

'Ava,' Dan sits forward, too, 'if I don't go back, then they will come here. I've already been warned, and I believe it. I'm not putting Mum, Dad or you at risk and ...' Dan's interrupted mid-sentence by a cough from over my shoulder, pulling his stare from me to Jesse. I don't need to turn around to know what expression will be on my husband's face. Dan continues. 'These people are dangerous, Ava.'

My head hurts, and Jesse's hand rubs are becoming firmer. I rest my head back on the chair and look up at Jesse. 'You can't just deposit that kind of money into a bank account. Isn't it laundering? I don't want you involved, Jesse.' I feel terrible saying that, given my brother's sorry situation and knowing Jesse is his only hope, but we have enough of our own issues without Dan adding to them.

He smiles down at me. 'Do you honestly think I'd do any-thing to put you and my babies at risk?' He nods at my stomach. 'I'm transferring enough money into Dan's account to get him back to Australia. I have the details of an offshore account where I'll transfer the two hundred. They won't know where the money has come from, baby. I wouldn't do it otherwise.'

'Really?' I'm looking for reassurance.

'Really.' His eyebrows rise and he lowers to kiss my cheek. 'There are ways. Trust me.' His confidence makes me wonder if this is something he's handled before. I wouldn't be at all surprised.

'Okay,' I concede, accepting his kiss before feeling his face. 'Thank you.'

'Don't thank me.'

I look across the desk to my brother, who has noticeably eased up. 'Have *you* thanked my husband?' I ask, suddenly feeling a little resentful.

'Of course,' Dan retorts, offended. 'I never asked, Ava. Your husband's been doing some digging.' Dan's tone shouldn't be, but it's accusing.

'Has he?' I swing my eyes upward. 'Have you?'

He almost rolls his eyes, like he thinks I'm stupid for not seeing something was amiss myself. 'I know a man in the shit, Ava.'

'Oh,' I whisper. This is too much. I feel exhausted. 'Can we go home?' I ask.

'I'm sorry.' Jesse pulls me up from his chair and does a quick scan of my body and face. 'I've neglected you.'

'I'm fine, just tired.' I sigh and pull my depleted form over to Dan. 'When are you leaving?' I sound short and stroppy, but I can't help it. I know exactly why Jesse is doing this, and it's not just to keep Dan quiet. That was an essential add-on when needed. He's doing it firstly because he won't risk the Australian mafia turning up in London, and secondly because he knows I'll be a wreck if anything happens to Dan, which is highly likely if Jesse doesn't get him out of the diabolical situation that the idiot has got himself into.

'Tonight.' Dan stands. 'They'll be on their way over if I'm not back by Thursday, so I guess this is goodbye for a while.'

'You weren't going to tell me you were leaving?' I ask.

'I would have called you, kiddo.' I can sense his shame, but it doesn't ease the hurt. 'I'm not your favourite man any more,' he adds on a smile. I'm not going to disagree. He's not. He always was, even during my relationships with Matt and Adam, but not now. My favourite man is currently holding my tired body up and massaging my tummy with his comforting touch.

'Take care.' I force a smile.

'Can I?' he asks for Jesse's permission with his arms open, stepping forward.

'Sure.' Jesse's hand reluctantly leaves my stomach, but he still holds me until Dan has me in his embrace.

I don't want to, but I do. I let a few tears escape and soak into Dan's jacket as I return his tight clinch. 'Please be careful,' I beg.

'Hey, I'll be fine.' He holds me at arm's length. 'I can't believe your husband owns a sex club.'

I smile as he rids my cheeks of tears with his thumb and kisses my forehead. 'Look after her.' Dan puts his hand out to Jesse, who takes it without even a snort of disgust at my brother's insulting demand. He just nods and reclaims me before Dan has fully released me.

'You can tell them the money will land in their account before the week is out. You have the proof.' Jesse's fingers work through my hair softly as he speaks. 'And no trouble when you leave.'

I know what that means, but I don't know what the proof is. My washed-out mind is too exhausted to even ask. I watch as Dan nods his acceptance and then strides out of Jesse's office, not looking back.

Chapter 29

'I want to show you something,' Jesse says as he collects me from the car outside Lusso. 'Do you want me to carry you?' I don't know why he's asked me because I'm draped across his arms before the question registers in my useless brain.

'What do you want to show me?' I ask, resting my head on his suit-covered shoulder. These are the first words I have spoken since watching Dan leave Jesse's office, and not because I haven't been spoken to. I couldn't even muster up the strength to growl a warning at Sarah as we passed her in the entrance hall of The Manor. She smiled awkwardly, refrained from laying her wandering hands all over Jesse and stepped back, almost warily, like she was fully expecting a backlash from me. The surprise was clear when I ignored her presence, choosing to walk on and leave Jesse to talk business with her. And I know that's all it was and all it ever will be. Business.

'You'll see.' He strides into the foyer of Lusso, and I smile when I hear Clive's cheerful voice. He's not as easy on the eye as our new concierge, but I'll always favour Clive's age-worn and jolly face, rather than Casey's fresh, pretty one.

'Congratulations!' he chants. I'm not surprised. Either Jesse really has broadcasted it, or Cathy's been getting excited. 'Wonderful news!' His voice is getting closer as I'm carted across the marble towards the elevator. 'Let me get that for you, Mr Ward.' He jumps in front of Jesse and pushes in the code for the penthouse lift.

'Thanks, Clive.' Jesse sounds just as cheerful.

'Very good, Mr Ward, very good. You look after yourself, Ava.' His instruction is stern, and I smile fondly as his crabby face disappears when the doors meet in the middle.

'You let Clive call me Ava,' I point out casually.

He looks down at me with raised, cautionary eyebrows. 'Your point being?'

'Just saying.' I find the muscle power to curve my lips into a grin, my husband's possessiveness providing the amused strength necessary.

'I'm ignoring you.' He's fighting his own grin as we exit the lift and he lets us into the penthouse, kicking the door shut behind me.

'You won't be able to carry me soon,' I grumble, holding on extra tight. I'll miss it so much, but when I'm bursting at the seams and double the size, I can't envision being carried with such ease, like I'm just an extension of his own body.

'Don't worry, lady.' He kisses my forehead and turns to push his back into his office door. 'I've already increased the weights I'm lifting in preparation.'

I gasp and reach up to pull his hair. 'Hey!' I'm placed on my feet, but I still have hold of his hair.

'You're a savage, lady.' He laughs, his head lowered to prevent the pull. 'Are you going to let go?'

'Say sorry.'

'Sorry.' He's still laughing. 'I'm sorry. Let go.'

I release him and kick my shoes off. 'Why are we in your office?'

'I wanted to show you something.'

'What?' I ask. He looks shifty all of a sudden, uncomfortable and all boyish. 'What's up with you?'

'Turn around,' he commands softly, resting his hands in his pockets.

I look at him questioningly, but he remains silent and his frown line remains fixed in place. He's concerned, which makes me concerned, and very, very curious. I slowly pivot, wanting to close my eyes, but far too inquisitive to do it. And then the wall slowly comes into view, and I stop breathing. A choked gasp flies from my gaping mouth, and I know I've taken a step back because Jesse's chest is pressed up against me. I can't even take it all in. My eyes run from one side of the large wall, the length of his office, to the other end.

It's completely coated in . . . me.

Every square inch is me. Not framed pictures or canvases or photographs. It's wallpaper, although you would never know it. Each seam is so incredibly perfect, it looks like one giant piece of art – an homage to me, and the biggest piece, the centrepiece, is me spread on the cross in our room at The Manor. I'm naked, my eyes are dropped low and my lips are parted. My hair is a mass of glossy waves, framing my lust-filled face, and the sensual vibes pumping from my body in the still shot is tangible. I can feel it as I'm standing here.

My gaze starts to drift, absorbing it all. There's too much, and I'm gasping again as I spot a motion shot of my back as I rush down the steps of The Manor. It wouldn't be particularly strange, but I can clearly see the head of a calla lily extending from the side of my fleeing body. And I register my dress. It's my navy pencil dress. It's the dress I wore to my very first consultation with Mr Jesse Ward.

'That was the first one I took,' he murmurs. 'It became a bit of an obsession after that.' His voice is quiet and unsure. I swing around, my mouth still gaping. I can't possibly speak. He's biting his lip, watching me closely. I swallow and turn back to the wall.

The Ava Wall.

I'm everywhere. I'm at the launch night of Lusso; I'm sitting on the bench at the dockside after our encounter; I'm in the shower, the kitchen, on the terrace. I'm in Harrods' changing rooms, and I'm sitting on my stool in the bar at The Manor. I'm kitted out in my biker leathers, and I'm storming away from him in an oversized, cream knitted jumper. I smile, noting so many shots of my back from where I'm running away from him, probably after I've received the countdown or I'm having a strop. I'm naked in countless, or just in lace. And then there's me in handcuffs on the bed, and another of me swimming in the pool at The Manor. I'm laughing with Kate; I'm brushing my hair from my face; I'm eating lunch in Baroque; I'm dancing with my friends, and I'm tapping my front tooth with my fingernail. I also see myself slouched in the passenger seat of the DBS, clearly drunk. I'm running towards the Thames and I'm collapsed on the grass in Green Park. I'm pushing a trolley around the supermarket, I'm getting changed into my baggy shit, and I'm brushing my teeth. I'm asleep on the jet and standing on the veranda in Paradise. I'm poking about on the market stalls, kicking the sand on the beach and cooking breakfast in the villa. We only returned from Spain yesterday. How did he do this? I'm asleep in his bed and asleep in his arms – there are so many of me asleep in his arms. Every facial expression imaginable and every habit I have is displayed in one of these pictures. It's like my life in images since I met this man. And I wasn't aware of any of it. He really is obsessed with me, and if I had known about this in the early days, like when he persistently pursued me, I think I would have run faster and farther. Not now, though. Now I'm just reminded after a tiring day of this man's love for me.

I'm unaware that my feet have taken me to the foot of the wall. I'm slowly walking the length of it, absorbing it all, each flick of my eyes finding another picture that I didn't see before.

'Here.' Jesse's quiet husk pulls my bewildered eyes from the Ava Wall, and to a black permanent marker pen. That alone makes me smile. 'I want you to sign it.'

I take the pen and look up at him, unsure if he's playing or not. 'Sign it with my name?' I ask, a little confused.

'Yes, wherever.' He waves at the images.

I glance back at the wall and laugh lightly, still dazed by what I'm confronted with. I step forward and pop the lid from the pen, looking for a spare space to scribble my name, but then I spot the first shot that he ever took of me and I approach it, armed with my pen. Smiling to myself, I write beneath the shot of me fleeing The Manor.

Today I met you.
This day was the beginning of the rest of my life.
From this moment, I was your Ava x

Then I make my way over to the image of me sitting by the docks on the launch night of Lusso.

Today I realised how deep I was.
And I wanted to be so much deeper with you.

I move along the wall to the picture of me drunk in Jesse's car and smile as I write;

Today I learned that you can dance. I also admitted to myself that I was in love with you, and I think I might have told you too.

I'm in my stride now. I quickly locate the picture of me in the chunky jumper, after he manhandled me into the damn thing.

Today I found out that I'm just for your eyes.

Then I'm writing underneath the picture of me walking naked from the bedroom after I found him collapsed at Lusso, and after he showed me how he does his talking.

Today I learned that I'm for your touch and for your pleasure only. But my favourite part of today was when you told me that you love me.

My pen drifts over to the shot of me handcuffed.

Today you introduced me to the retribution fuck.

I quickly scan the wall and find a picture of me walking in front of him through the foyer of The Ritz.

Today I found out how old you are . . . and that you don't like being handcuffed.

I can't stop. Each and every image brings a thought, and I

find myself marking picture after picture with my memories in words. He doesn't stop me. I just keep going, like I'm writing a diary of the last few months of my life. I don't need to record it, each and every moment is etched on my brain, good and bad, but these are all good. And there are so, so many of them.

My hand is aching by the time I reach my final picture – my final picture for now, anyway. I'm sure I'll be thinking of more captions to add. It's the one of me standing on the veranda in Paradise. I push my pen to the wall.

Today I decided that you're right. We will be okay.
And yes, I do have a bump . . . ish,
and I love you for giving it to me.
I'll always love you.
End of.

Replacing the lid on the pen, I take a deep breath and finally face my Lord, bumping into his chest and getting a waft of his fresh, minty scent. I look up at him, finding a straight face and clouded green eyes. 'I'm done,' I whisper quietly, but he's not looking at me. He's studying all of my captions, his eyes travelling across the wall and pausing every now and then to read what I have written.

He takes the pen and moves towards the picture of me fleeing The Manor, and then gets up close and personal with the wall. I can't see what he's writing, and I shift to try and look around his body, but he's too close. He finally moves away, and I see it, scrolled across the top of the image.

Today my heart started beating again.
Today you became mine.

I press my lips together and watch as he moves across to an image of me seated in the long grass of The Manor's grounds in my wedding dress, top to toe in ivory lace and with the sun shooting bullets of light through the trees behind me. I'm looking away, probably at the photographer. Again, Jesse gets up close to the wall, and then moves away, chewing the end of the pen. He's drawn a perfect halo above my head and written:

My beautiful girl.

My defiant temptress.

My lady.

My angel.

My Ava.

I smile and step forward, taking the pen from his mouth and dragging him from his daydream. I replace the lid and drop it to the floor, then gracefully climb up him until I'm wrapped around his big body.

His palms are cupping my bum and his eyes are burning into mine. 'Ava, today has been the longest fucking day of my life.'

Those words have me pushing his suit jacket from his arms and my lips crashing to his, ravenously.

'Easy,' he warns gently, moving each arm in turn so I can rid him of his jacket. 'What's the rush?'

I force my lips to slow their devouring of him – easier said than done when I haven't had him for two full days. 'It's been too long,' I mumble, pulling at his tie, probably strangling him in the process, but I'm not releasing his lips to confirm it.

He places me on my feet, breaking our kiss, and pulls his tie over his head before kicking off his Grensons and socks. His eyes are ablaze and virtually burning my dress from my body. 'Take your dress off.'

It takes me three seconds flat to unzip my dress and pull it up over my head, leaving me standing in my lace. My hand slides onto my navel, my rings sparkling as I rub slow circles around my belly button. A piece of me and a piece of Jesse, two pieces, in fact, are growing inside me, and the very thought has me overcome with a sudden sense of warmth that I've never felt before – a warmth that deepens when Jesse's hand lies over mine and he stoops down, nuzzling my face so he can access my mouth.

'Incredible, isn't it?' he asks, reattaching me to his body with an effortless pull of my upper thighs.

'Just like you.'

'And you.'

'Show me how incredible you are. I've forgotten.' I provoke his arrogance with those words and bow my back, lifting myself higher to him so he has to drop his head back to maintain our kiss. The low rumbling growl emanating from deep inside him travels through our joined mouths and warms me further.

He starts walking from his office through the vast openness of the penthouse, where I'm laid on the huge corner couch and my backside is pulled to the end so my lower body is propped up on the arm. He removes his trousers and boxers, revealing the beauty of his cock, hard, ready, and within touching distance, but he kneels down at the end of the couch, taking it clean from my view. I don't have time to complain. My knickers are removed, my legs are pulled apart and his mouth is on the inside of my thigh fast, kissing gently, shifting to the other thigh and teasing softly. Forward and back he goes, moving from one side to the other, getting higher with each set, his hands spreading me further as he makes his way to my pulsing centre.

'Jesse.' I take in air, my legs needing to move. My hand flies up to grasp the leather on the backrest of the couch, my other cupping the back of his head.

'Have you remembered how incredible I am?' he asks seriously, pulling back and blowing over my raw flesh.

'Yes!' My hands are twitching as his cool breath spreads over me and travels down my thighs. 'Shit!' I try to close my legs when I feel the first dash of contact from his tongue on my clitoris, but he's just teasing me, giving me a taste of what's to come, and my legs are going nowhere, except where he decides, which is wider, making me sensitive, more open and more frenzied.

'Mouth, Ava.' His tongue enters me and then licks an unspeakably delicious stroke up my middle. I cry out, my head thrashing from side-to-side. 'Incredible?' He's cocky and sure, and has earned that privilege. 'Tell me how it feels, baby.'

My fisted hand that is now clenching at his hair should tell him all he needs to know – that and my inaudible mumbling. I'm seeing stars, my belly is aching and my poor legs are unable to move. And then his fingers are inside me and my hands leave the sofa and his hair in favour of my own head. My stomach muscles are rigid as I lift my upper body up to try and quench the charging surge of pressure that's descending from my tummy to my core. I decide in my fevered bliss that I want to see him, so I prop myself up on my elbows and gaze down the length of my body, seeing his palm resting on my stomach, while his fingers fuck me slowly.

'Tell me,' he pushes, sweeping through me with agonising precision.

'It feels like you were made to fit me.' My words are even and as sure as the expression on his face. He thinks that, too.

He smiles and leans in, tenderly kissing my sensitive skin before rising to his feet and grasping me under my thighs, lifting my lower body to position himself. I find my upper body lifting, too, my hands palm down behind me so I have the best view of him entering me. And it really is the best view. We both focus on his rigid cock as he brings it to me, meeting my entrance and hovering for a while, just skimming my damp void, teasingly. I'm ever impatient, my lower legs curling around his lower back and pulling him to me, but he's going nowhere. Not until he says so. And he doesn't say so. He just smirks that almost undetectable smirk while he keeps his eyes down, still teasing me with irregular and torturous skims of his slippery head across the very tip of my oversensitive small nub of nerves. He's killing me, and I'm dying to lie back down, but I'm too engrossed by his cruel pleasure.

'Shall we try penetration?' he asks, but he still won't look at me. I'm going out of my mind, but that defiance in me, coupled with his self-assured attitude, has me determined to match his poise.

'If you like.' My calm, aloof words have his greens leaving their rapt focus point on a surprised twinkle.

'If I like?' He pushes into me, only very slightly, but enough to force me to repress a moan. 'What about if *you* like?' In a little further he goes. I know my lips have just parted, and I know my chest is expanding fast. I'm held in place with one arm while his other hand reaches forward and yanks the cups of my bra down. Each nipple is given a sharp pinch, and I bite back a scream of pleasure mixed with intense pain. 'My beautiful girl is trying to play it cool,' he muses, adjusting his grip of me, ready to pound forward. 'It's a shame she's shit at feigning casualness.' He doesn't pound forward, though. He eases in lazily, and my head rolls back on a groan. 'That's more like it.' He's completely submerged within me now, the tip of his impressive cock brushing my womb. 'Show a bit of appreciation, Ava.' He extracts himself, and this time he really does pound forward, surprisingly hard. My arms begin to shake, followed by my head in despair.

'Again,' I demand. He's teased me too far this time. 'Again!'

'That depends.'

'On what? You said it doesn't always need to be hard.' I'm battling to catch my breath, swallowing repeatedly. 'Then you do this to me. Have you finally read the part of the book that confirms you won't hurt the babies?'

'Yes.' He strikes with utter accuracy, buckling my arms, but then holds still again. 'It's a good book.'

'It's a good book now.'

'It was always a good book, but it did say you must listen to your body.' He slides out again and pushes forward on a moan.

'I'm listening, and it's saying harder.'

'The babies are protected. I read that.' He hisses and blows out a controlled breath. 'And I can spank you, apparently.' His palm collides with my arse on a loud smack, and I yelp.

'You've already slapped me!' I remind him on a shout as he re-enters me.

'But I didn't think you were pregnant then.' *He* reminds *me* on another sharp assault of his palm across my bum. 'Good?'

'Yes!' I persuade my head to lift and when it does, I go dizzy with gratefulness. My tongue leaves my mouth of its own accord and journeys across my bottom lip slowly, enticingly. 'You look amazing,' I breathe, watching each finely tuned muscle on his abdomen bunch and his biceps bulge from holding my lower body to him.

'I know.' He grinds smooth and slow.

'Oh God!' My arms finally give in, collapsing and leaving me flat on my back.

'I know,' he agrees. 'I fucking know.'

'Jesse, I'm going to come.'

'I'm not!' Out and in he slides all over again. 'Are you listening to your body, Ava?'

'Yes! And it's telling me I need to come!'

Slap! 'Don't be fucking smart!' He swivels, pulls free completely and slips his cock straight up my centre, instigating a stupidly satisfying friction of his flesh against mine. He's shaking. I can feel it travelling through his arms and into my legs, but he maintains his silky smooth thrusts. 'Fuck, I need to be all over you.' My lower body is dropped and my hands grasped, pulling me up to his standing body with an easy tug. I'm on the rug, beneath him in no time at all, my nipples being teased by his tongue and his hand between my thighs, guiding himself back to me.

Now that I can feel his skin, I notice just how sweaty he is. My hands are feeling out every inch of him. 'Kiss me,' I plead, and he doesn't mess about. Our mouths are together, he's sliding back inside me, and our bodies are touching in every place possible. His momentum is perfect, and I'm rocking my hips up to meet him on every drive, capturing the spikes of pleasure that each one of his plunges is instigating. My hands land on his arse and my nails dig into his solid cheeks as he ravishes me with his mouth, our tongues dancing wildly and hungrily.

'I think . . .' he's on my cheek, pushing on, 'you should . . .' now he's at my neck, then he's biting at the lobe of my ear, 'quit your job.'

I shake my head, tipping my hips up on a long, happy moan. 'No.'

'But I want to spend every day doing this. Give me back your mouth.'

I turn my head into to him. 'You'll have to wait until I get home.' I'm biting his lip now and pushing my hands into his arse to gain some friction.

He bites me back. 'Wherever, whenever.'

'Except when I'm at work. Deeper.'

'Oh, so she can make the demands, then?' He doesn't go deeper, the bastard.

'I'm not quitting my job.'

'And how do you expect to look after my babies if you're working?' He asks the arrogant question around my mouth on a painfully perfect rotation of his hips.

'But you want me at home to do this, not to look after your babies.'

'Now you're just being awkward.' He abandons my mouth and leans down to bite my nipple before kissing his way back up my body. 'Deeper?'

'Please.'

'Okay.' He goes deep. Very deep. So lusciously, amazingly deep.

'Hmmmmm.'

He stills and concentrates on kissing the life out of me. 'Do you see? I'm giving you what you want.'

He most definitely is, but I know where this is going, and it's called a sense fuck without the brute force. I need to be careful here. 'Ohhhhh!' I'm tinkering on the edge of orgasm obliteration, but this is so nice – just steady lovemaking, feeling each other and taking our blissful time.

He swallows my sated moan, continuing to explore my mouth, like he's never had it before. Our sex sessions, whether steamy or romantic, hard or soft, are always like the first time all over again. 'You should show your gratitude.' He leaves my mouth and braces his upper body on his arms. 'Don't you think?' He looks down between our bodies as he rears back, and I look down, too, seeing the full length of him emerging from my passage. 'Look at that,' he sighs and holds himself, just breaching my opening, then he looks up at me. 'Just fucking perfect.' He sinks in, smooth and slow on a long rush of hot breath that warms my face, even from his raised position. I'm starting to tremble and my useless arms fall back over my head. 'She's beginning to pant,' he states, dropping to his forearms. 'She's trembling all over.' His hips falter in their meticulous assault and judder forward.

I'm holding my breath now, tensing everywhere ready to ride out my climax.

'I think she wants to come.'

I start shaking my head, even though I mean to nod and scream *yes*. I'm squirming under the hard, cut beauty of his body, our sweaty skins blending and sliding. My redundant arms and hands are rapidly rising, deciding all on their own that there is something they'd like to do. My fingers thread through that dirty-blond mass and grip hard.

'She definitely wants to come.' He sounds self-assured and cool, but his own body is having a fit of spasms as he tries to maintain his stable tempo. He's failing on every level. His hip movements have become unpredictable, indicating his pending orgasm and his fast loss of control. 'Fuck!'

And that word seals the deal. He's way past the point of return, so I seize my opportunity, pulling harder on his hair and reaching up to sink my teeth into his sweat-glistened shoulder in an attempt to suppress my scream of release and encourage his. It works, as I knew it would.

'Fuck, fuck, fuck!' He's working harder and faster into me, burying his face into my hair. 'Now, Ava!'

I'm done for. I unclamp my teeth from his flesh and join him in his frantic oblivion of raw, carnal pleasure, throwing my arms around his neck and rolling my hips up to meet the last thorough thrash of his body into mine.

He collapses onto me carefully, but grinds slowly as he nibbles on my neck through his laboured breathing. 'Please quit,' he begs. 'Then we really can stay like this for ever.'

I can't find my vocal cords, except to mumble some objection, which I do with an increase of pressure of my arms around his neck.

'Was that a yes?' He licks up the salty skin of my cheek and across my lips. 'Say yes.'

'No.'

'Stubborn woman.' He pecks my lips and rolls onto his back, ensuring he remains snugly inside me and I'm comfortable on his lap. 'We need to renew our vows.'

I frown and take a few moments to gather enough air in my lungs to form a sentence. 'We've not even been married a month.'

My hips are seized and I tense, but then I watch as his eyes drift onto my stomach and his warning look transforms into a smile as he shifts his threatening hands to my small-ish bump and starts caressing it. 'Yes, only a month and you've already forgotten a significant part of your promise.'

'You can take your *obey* and swivel on it.' I manage to get those words out just fine. I also manage to lift my heavy arms and wrap my palms around his neck.

He feigns a choke on a grin and pulls me down by the tops of my arms, curling his big palms around *my* neck. We're both ready to strangle each other. 'Who'd win?' he asks, getting nose to nose with me.

'You.'

'Correct,' he agrees. 'I'm thirsty.'

I give a little shake of his neck, making him laugh. 'I'll get some water.'

'You can't pick and choose when you fulfil your wifely duties.' He pushes me from his strewn body and lifts slightly to catch a slap of my arse as I walk away. 'Water, wench!'

'Don't push it, Ward,' I caution, snapping the cups of my bra back over my breasts and taking my mostly naked form into the kitchen.

'Don't even think about coming back in here until I can see your breasts again, lady!' he shouts after me.

I have the biggest grin on my face as I open the fridge and collect two bottles of water. I also snatch another item that's sitting all on its lonesome on the bottom shelf. I'm grinning again.

'Didn't you hear me?' Jesse's affronted tone is the first thing to hit my ears when I reappear. He's staring at my bra-covered chest.

'I heard you.' I drop the bottles on the couch and keep my Jesse surprise behind my back.

He's still flat on his back and he's looking up at me with suspicious green eyes. 'My wife has a crafty look on her beautiful face.' He slowly sits up and positions his back against the couch, then pats his lap. 'And she's hiding something from me.' He reaches behind him and grabs a bottle of water, having a long swig before screwing the lid on slowly.

'Crafty-ish.' Taking his cue, I lower onto him and shift

forward when he drops the bottle and cups my arse with both big palms.

'There's no "–ish" about it.' One of his hands leaves my bum, but only for long enough to yank the cups of my bra down again. Then it's firmly replaced. 'What are you hiding?'

'Something,' I tease, moving to the side when he tries to crane his neck to get a peek. 'No,' I warn, and he huffs a little before resting back against the couch. I unscrew the lid behind my back and drop it before presenting the jar to my god, whose curious eyes have just sprung wide open in delight at the sight before him.

'I'm in control.' I grin.

His eyes widen further but this time in outrage. 'Oh no. Not where that's concerned. Forget it, no way, never.' His hand makes a grab for it, but my stealthy move whips it from under his nose.

'Relax,' I laugh, pushing him back against the couch. The urge to cuddle him overwhelms my teasing streak when I see his concerned frown wriggle its way onto his brow, and that bottom lip is being nibbled away as he watches my hand move slowly to the jar and my finger disappear within the depths of creamy goo. I actually grimace as my finger squelches back out, and I know my nose has just wrinkled in disgust at the sight of a huge dollop all over my index finger.

'Don't tease me with it, baby.' His eyes are fixated on my coated finger, and they follow my trail as I bring the gloop down and wipe it all over my nipple. It's freezing cold and disgusting, but the look of thorough exhilaration that has just landed on my rogue's face is enough of an incentive to battle forward.

His eyes flick to mine. 'Oops.' I grin as his head leisurely creeps forward, all slow and casual, which is absurd because I know he's dying to clean it all off, and not just because he wants my breast in his mouth.

The hum of happiness has me giggling and writhing under

his hot tongue. 'Holy fucking shit.' He laps away, making a completely over-the-top spectacle of demolishing my breast with his tongue before flopping back and licking his lips. 'I didn't think it could taste any better. More.'

I'm grinning like an idiot as I delve back into the peanut butter. I hold my finger up. 'Would sir like the right breast or the left breast?'

His face is truly torn as he swings his eyes from one breast to the other. 'I don't have time to waste. Slap it on both.'

I laugh, but follow through on his urgent order, and he's on me again before I've barely removed my finger from the smothering of the first breast. 'Unravel your boxers, God.' My nose falls into his hair as he ravishes me and bites my nipple for my cheek. 'Ouch!'

'Sarcasm, lady.'

'Tasty?'

'I'm never eating it any other way again, so now you do have to quit work because I need you to be available to lick when I please.' He surfaces with a smear on his nose, and I home right in to suck it off. 'I thought you hated peanut butter?'

'I do, but I love your nose.' I kiss the end and resume my position. 'Will you do something for me?'

His facial expression changes considerably. He's all wary again, but I'm not hiding anything this time, only a plea, which he'll soon hear. He relaxes a little and strokes up the sides of my body. 'What do you want, baby?'

'I want you to say yes before I ask,' I demand quietly and very unreasonably, but we've broached this before, and I got nowhere.

'You've been trying to butter me up.' His lips tip at the edge, and I screw my face up in irritation, placing the jar beside us.

'That's a crap joke.'

'Pick the jar back up, lady.' He's not grinning any more. 'We're not done yet.'

I roll my eyes and re-dunk and re-smear. 'Happy?'

'Ecstatic.' My nipple is clean in no time at all. 'Now, tell me what you want.'

'You have to say yes,' I press, with absolutely no faith in my strategy. Even if he does say yes, he'll soon retract it if he wants to.

'Ava,' he sighs. 'I'm not agreeing to anything without knowing what I'm agreeing to. End of.'

I pout. 'Please.' I drag the word out and slide my freshly coated finger into his mouth.

'You're adorable when you sulk,' he mumbles. 'Just tell me.'

'I want you to revoke Sam and Kate's memberships to The Manor.' I blurt it all out quickly and hold my breath. I'm desperate for Jesse to help me out here. I know Sam and Kate seem to have hit a significant point in their relationship, and I hope they talk, but without the temptation of The Manor, they stand a far better chance. I brace myself for his *none of our business* speech, but it doesn't come. Nothing comes, actually. He doesn't scoff, and he doesn't refuse. He's just looking at me on a small smile.

'Okay,' he shrugs and dives into the jar with his own finger, spreading it on my breast.

'What?' I know I'm displaying a look of complete confusion, which is absolutely fine because I'm really confused. I didn't even need to morph into temptress.

'I said okay.' He's on my breast again, while my eyes are looking down at the back of his head.

'It is?' I should be showing my appreciation, not questioning him on his reasonableness.

His perfect smiling face appears in my line of sight, and his palms surround my cheeks. 'Sam already cancelled.'

I gasp. 'I thought you were finally doing as you're told.' I should've known, but my disgruntled state doesn't detract from the happy knowledge that they will be pursuing a conventional relationship. I'm delighted.

Jesse is standing and laying us back down on the sofa in an instant. 'I always do as I'm told. Come here.' The jar is taken from my hand and placed on the floor beside the couch, and then I'm pulled down to his chest. 'Snuggle,' he exhales contentedly.

I snort in disbelief at his ridiculous claim before nuzzling myself right up into his neck and resuming my usual skimming of his scar with my fingertip.

'Are you warm enough?' he asks, snaking his legs with mine and completely engulfing me with his strong arms.

'Hmmm.' I sigh and close my eyes, relishing in every element of his loveliness – his scent, his touch and his heart beating against mine.

Chapter 30

My sweet dreams are interrupted by coughing. I think it's coughing. It sounds like coughing, but neither my brain nor my body are ready to greet the day yet, so I dismiss the raspy choke and push myself further into the hardness beneath me.

There it is again, and it's becoming hard to ignore. In fact, it's irritating the hell out of me. Peeling one eye open, the first thing I see is Jesse's serene beauty. My irritation subsides, and I reach up to catch a feel of day number three stubble.

There's that cough again. I think nothing of turning to locate the source of the noise, exposing a full-on frontal of nakedness to . . . Cathy.

'Oh shit!' I splatter myself back on my front against Jesse's chest, the abrupt movement stirring him. 'Jesse!' I whisper, like she won't hear me. 'Jesse, wake up!'

He's smiling before his eyes open and his wandering hands cup both my bum cheeks and squeeze in acknowledgment to my voice. 'If I open my eyes, I'm going to see big chocolate fuck-me ones, aren't I?' His voice is all deep and husky, and coupled with those words would usually have my stomach clenching with sexual anticipation. But not this morning.

'No, you're going to see big, wide, disturbed ones,' I whisper. 'Open your eyes.'

He does. He reveals his greens on a furrowed brow and looks over my shoulder when I cock my head. 'Oh. Morning, Cathy.'

'You two love birds need to buy some pyjamas.' Cathy's amused tone makes me cringe further. 'Or at least keep your underwear on. I'll be in the kitchen preparing breakfast.'

I hear her scurrying footsteps leaving our naked display, and I exhale in despair, dropping my head back onto his chest. He's chuckling. 'Morning, baby.' He shifts his legs so they spread and my body falls between them. 'Let me see your face.'

'No.' I push it further into his neck, like my embarrassment might disappear if I hide for long enough.

'She's all bashful.' He's grinning. 'Shall we get you upstairs?'

'Yes,' I grumble, knowing full well that time must be knocking on with Cathy's presence, not that I care. It's like I'm trying to get myself sacked so I don't have to give Jesse the satisfaction of quitting because he demanded it.

I sit up cautiously and check for Cathy's whereabouts, then laugh loudly when Jesse sits up, too, popping his head over the back of the couch to check. He looks at me, eyebrows raised, slightly bemused by my little outburst. 'What's tickled you?'

'You look like a meerkat!' I giggle, falling back and completely exposing myself. Through my uncontrollable fit of chuckles, I reach up to arrange my bra over my chest, because that's really going to save my modesty when I'm knickerless. 'Wind your neck in!' I laugh.

He snorts a mixture of amusement and umbrage at his hysterical wife and gently pushes my body away to free his legs before standing and taking hold of my shaking body. I'm tossed up onto his shoulder, still laughing and now with the glorious view of his solid arse as he strides toward the stairs. 'Where I'm from, that means something entirely different.' He slaps my arse. 'It is you who needs to be doing the winding.'

'I know what it means. I was being ironic.' I run my palms over his back. 'And there will be no winding of necks here.'

'A man can live in hope.' He takes the stairs two at a time, but I don't jump and jolt all over his shoulder and he doesn't puff or pant. No, he flies up the backlit onyx staircase like some sort of freakishly fit paratrooper. 'There.' He places me on my feet and turns the shower on. 'In you get.'

'I hope you're going to lock your office door now,' I say, as a mental image of Cathy's sweet, innocent face turning to horror pops into my mind's eye.

He laughs. 'Only for our eyes, baby. I have a key and I've hidden one among the piles of lace in your underwear drawer. Okay?'

'Okay,' I agree. I'm really late already, but that doesn't stop me from stepping forward and grasping his morning erection. He flinches, and I smirk as I circle my thumb slowly over the broad head, keeping my eyes on the throbbing rod of flesh.

'Ava,' he warns weakly, stepping back, but that just means he gets a full-on stroke of my hand down the length. He hisses and his palms lift to cover his face. I've got him. He rubs his cheeks in a gesture that suggests it might restore some control. 'If I don't take you now, my cock is going to be aching all day long.'

'Take me,' I say quietly, remembering the words so well. I step forward to close the gap he's made, and his palms come down, his face full of recognition.

'Oh, I will,' he replies, picking me up and placing me on the vanity unit. 'You can't escape now.'

'I don't want to.'

'Good.' He leans in and kisses me sweetly. 'I like your dress.'

'I'm not wearing one, so we can't lose it.'

He smiles around my lips, and I open my eyes, finding bright-green pools of sincere happiness. 'Fond memories?'

'Very. Can you pin me against the wall now?' I've always found him irresistible, but this incessant need to constantly have him is taking my life over. I'm late for work, I couldn't give a shit, and I know he won't either. His smile broadens and his face slowly starts drifting toward mine again, his eyes holding mine. His lips part. My lips part. He's making me be patient. I'm struggling.

On the launch night of Lusso, it was a jangling of the door handle that whipped our heads to the side in shock. This time it's Cathy's distressed shouting. My back straightens, and I'm snapped right out of my wanton condition.

Jesse has disappeared before my eyes and I'm sitting in the bathroom, still on the unit, wondering what on earth is going on. I quickly jump down and run into the walk-in-wardrobe, grabbing the first shirt that I can find, before sprinting over to the chest to retrieve some knickers, while shoving my arms in the sleeves of Jesse's shirt and buttoning it on my way. I'm halfway down the stairs when the front door comes into view, and I see Jesse in just his white boxers removing Cathy from the doorway, where she's doing a good job of keeping whoever is on the other side out.

'I thought it was Clive,' she wheezes, clearly exhausted from her battle.

'Cathy, I'll deal with it.' He places her to the side and gives her arm a reassuring rub as she straightens her apron and hair.

'Who the hell does she think she is?' she spits nastily. I've never seen Cathy cross before.

'Cathy,' Jesse placates her gently. 'Please, go and sort out some breakfast for Ava.' He's whispering as he effortlessly holds the door shut, like he doesn't want me to hear him, but the persistent banging from the other side is letting him down.

I look on as Cathy marches off, hissing and spitting to herself, and then my eyes fall on Jesse as I reach the bottom of the stairs. He's spotted me, and the wary look all over his face instantly has me on edge. 'What's going on?' I ask.

'Nothing, baby.' He tries to smile but fails miserably. He's all jittery. It doesn't sit well. 'Cathy's making your breakfast. Go.'

'I'm not hungry,' I reply flatly, staring him down.

'Ava, you didn't eat last night. Go and have some breakfast.' His tone is altering to impatient by the second and all the while, the banging continues.

I can't believe he honestly thinks that his demand for me to eat is going to pull me away from the mystery behind the door. 'I said I'm not hungry.' I stand firm, my eyes burning red rings of furious fire into his greens.

The door jolts, and Jesse lets out a frustrated growl, his jaw ticking wildly as he looks up to the heavens for strength. I would like to think that it's the tenacious idiot hammering on the penthouse door who's causing his mounting anger, but I know it's me. 'Ava, why the fuck can't you do what you're told?' His head drops, and I know instantly he means business. 'Go. And. Get. Your. Breakfast.' He speaks each word slowly and concisely, but I mean business, too.

'No.' I steam forward, not in the least bit bothered by my half-naked body, and grasp the door handle. I pull, for what use it is, which is none at all. 'Jesse, let go of the fucking door!'

'Watch your—'

'Fuck off!' I snap, yanking at the door like a deranged, hormone-pumped pregnant woman.

'Ava!' He holds it in place as I fight pointlessly to pull it open. I'll never win, but I'm not backing down. No way.

But then we both freeze in place when a voice interrupts our spitting match, and it's neither of ours. If I was a little cranky before, I've just been catapulted into the realms of psychotic. There will be no need for him to open this door because at any moment I'm going to be flying around this apartment like the Tasmanian Devil himself, and I'll smash it down.

I look up at him with clenched teeth. He visibly sags. 'What the hell is she doing here?' I use his lapse in concentration and his defeated hold to my advantage and pull the door open, coming face to face with Coral. 'What the hell are you doing here?' I hiss, looking her up and down in utter contempt. Her hair is tied up today, her short black bob giving her a pathetic excuse for a ponytail – such a bitchy thought, but it's going to be the first of many, I can feel it. And they might not *just* be thoughts.

She blanks me completely and looks straight at my bare-chested god. Why the hell didn't he put some jeans and a T-shirt on? 'I need to speak to you.' She sounds determined. 'Alone,' she adds, flicking an impertinent look at me. Her fortitude will be of zero help. She'll have to rip him from my dying hands before I leave them alone.

'You've got more chance of having tea with the queen,' I snarl. My fury is building by the second, and I absolutely cannot control it. 'What do you want?' I feel Jesse's hand rest lightly on the small of my shirt-covered back. It's a silent demand to calm myself down. It'll never work. The more I look at this impudent hussy, the angrier I'm getting, if that's possible. I feel like a pressure cooker set to explode. 'I asked you a question.'

'Ava.' Jesse's calming voice just infuriates me further. 'Calm yourself down, baby.' His palm slides around to my front to hold my tummy. He's worried about my blood pressure, the anxious fool. My blood pressure should be the least of his worries. Blood spilt, that's what he should be concerned about.

'I'm calm.' I'm clearly not. 'I won't ask you again.' I push Jesse's hand away from my stomach, but he doesn't let me get away with it. He pulls me back so I'm slightly behind him, and then holds his arm out to the side in silent warning. It won't work, but he starts speaking before I can wrestle his arm out of my way.

'Coral, I've told you before. It's never going to happen.' His tone is tinged with anger, but after my little performance, I can't be sure if his fury is for my benefit or Coral's. 'You need to fuck off and find someone else to stalk.'

I'm mentally cheering him on, even though I'm sure that I'm in for it when she concedes and clears off. I must look ridiculous in Jesse's shirt, my hair a wild mass, yesterday's make-up on, and restrained by my virtually naked husband.

Coral's eyes cross from Jesse's to mine a few times before she settles her smug stare on my god again. I don't like that look. It's bold, and I'm sure her next words will be, too. She's going nowhere until she's said what she came to say, and I'm annoyingly curious of what that is exactly.

'Have it your way.' She shrugs nonchalantly and holds a piece of paper out to Jesse.

'What the fuck is that?' he barks.

'Take a look for yourself.' She flaps the paper, encouraging Jesse to take it. I can't help it; my neck is craning to try and see for myself, but his arm pushes me back again.

He snatches it, and I watch as his head drops to look, then I look at Coral, who is performing the best sly smirk I have ever had the pleasure of witnessing. My eyes are on Jesse's back, which is stiff as a board, his muscles protruding, indicating his tension.

'What is it?' The question I don't want to ask just slips right out. But he doesn't answer.

Coral does, though. 'That is a scan picture of his baby.'

I know I stagger back, and I know he has turned to steady me, but everything is a blur. 'Fucking hell.' His worried voice is nothing but a drowned out rush of noise, and I know it's because all of the blood is draining from my head. I feel dizzy. 'Shit, Ava.' My feet disappear from under me, but I don't hit the floor. I've not passed out. I've been scooped up, and in a split second, I'm sitting on the couch with my head being pushed between my legs. 'Breathe, baby. Just breathe.' His palm is on my head, rubbing soothing, fast, anxious circles. 'What the fuck are you playing at?' he yells away from me. 'You stupid fucking woman! I've not slept with you for months!'

'Four months, and I'm four months gone.' She answers quickly and proudly. 'Do the maths.'

I need to get my breathing under control because the rush is still whirring and the black is starting to set in. I'll fall flat on my face if I stand.

'You can't be,' Jesse snaps anxiously, sounding far too unsure. 'Fuck!'

This is it. That baby will be born before either of mine and knowing Jesse's desperation for a child, he'll take the first one he can lay his hands on. He'll leave me. I'll be alone with two screaming babies and no help. My babies will be fatherless. Who's going to rub my feet when they're swollen? Who's going to love me in lace when I'm covered in stretch marks? Who's going to make me eat when I'm not hungry and feed me folic acid and lick peanut butter from my breasts and paint my toe-nails when I can't reach them? I start to choke on panic, but then my eyes fall onto the little piece of paper that Jesse has dropped to the floor in favour of tending to me. He didn't look at that picture like he did of our babies' picture. He didn't drop to his knees or grab Coral to hug her. What is wrong with me? I feel like a mixed bag of overexaggerated emotions. I stoop and pick up the black-and-white scan picture. I'm being watched, by both of them, but I take my time, firstly noting Coral's name. This is definitely hers. But what isn't on this scan picture is a date. Neither is there an estimated gestation. I study the picture more closely.

'Ava, what are you doing?' Jesse asks, trying to get me in his field of vision, but I ignore him.

'Yes, what are you doing?' Coral hisses.

I point at the picture. 'I'm just trying to figure out whether you're four or five weeks' pregnant,' I muse, keeping my eyes on the picture. 'I'm guessing just four.'

'I'm four *months*. Not weeks.'

'No you're not.' I look up at Jesse. He's holding his breath. 'When was the last time you slept with her?'

'Four, five months.' He shakes his head, his frown line doing a worried dance across his forehead. 'Ava, I can't think that far back. I didn't exist before you.' His hands rest on the tops of my thighs and squeeze. 'I always used a condom; you know that.'

'I know,' I agree, but there is one other possibility and it kills me to ask, especially in front of this interloper. I clench my eyes shut. 'Was she one of the . . .' I swallow around my words. 'Did you . . .'

He stops me from my struggling. 'No.' He says the word softly and secures the nape of my neck in his palm. 'Look at me,' he demands, just as softly, and I do. I lock eyes with him and he shakes his head, only very faintly. 'No,' he repeats.

I nod on a quiet exhale and offer a small smile of trust. There is no need for a confession because he has nothing to confess. Our quiet exchange of understanding almost makes me forget that Coral is standing nearby.

'You're going to stay with him when he's having a baby with another woman?' she asks on a laugh. 'Where's your self-respect?'

'I'm going to trample now,' I tell him quietly, looking for his permission this time.

He smiles and drops an accepting kiss on my cheek. 'Knock yourself out, baby. But please, let's just make this one a verbal trample.' He nods at my tummy, and then stands and turns a contemptuous look onto the brazen slut, but he doesn't say anything. He's leaving this one to me.

'What are you two talking about?' Her smugness is disintegrating by the second. She has no idea what to make of this.

I join Jesse in his standing position and look up to him. 'Get me your picture.'

My question pulls his condemning eyes from Coral down to me. He's looks at me all gone out. 'What picture?'

I roll my eyes. 'The one that you carry everywhere. I'm not stupid. Where is it?'

'In my suit jacket,' he admits sheepishly.

'Go and get it.'

'No. I'm not leaving you with her.' He doesn't even grace *her* with a look this time.

'"Her"?' Coral blurts incredulously. 'Is that the way you're going to speak to the mother of your child?'

He swings around violently. 'You are not the fucking mother of my child, you deluded freak!' His anger is building again. I need to remedy this once and for all.

I leave them and head straight to Jesse's office, finding his suit jacket where he discarded it last night, and rummage quickly through his pockets, finding a neatly folded wedge of notes and his phone before locating the picture from his inside pocket. It's a little worn; no doubt from being transferred from pocket to pocket. I exit hastily armed with exhibit B and find the distance between Jesse and Coral has closed. Jesse is still in the same location, but Coral is moving forward.

'We had something special, Jesse.' She goes to touch him, but he yanks his arms away.

'Special?' he laughs. 'I screwed you for a while. I fucked you and then kicked you out. How the fuck is that special?'

'You came back for more. That has to mean something.' Her tone is hopeful. She really is deluded. 'You made me need you.'

Those words prickle at my skin. I want to interrupt, but I want to hear how he responds to that.

'No, you made yourself need me. I barely even spoke to you when I was screwing you. You were a piece of meat that was handy to have on call.' He moves in and leans down, making her pull back slightly. Jesse's tone is full of venom, and intended to be. He's doing a damn good job at trampling all over her himself. 'You're just like the rest of them, but even more desperate. Get a good seeing-to and you think your life depends on it.'

I almost laugh. My life really does depend on it, even more now I'm a raging bag of pregnant hormones.

Jesse looks her up and down, and I get a glimpse of the conceited man who treated women like objects for so long – the man who drank, fucked and threw them out.

'What the hell makes you think that I'd leave my wife for you?'

'Because I'm having your baby.' The smugness has fallen away completely now. She knows she's losing the battle.

'You're lying,' he retorts, but there is definitely an element of uncertainty in his tone.

'She *is* lying,' I interject, uncomfortable with seeing Jesse so close to her, even if he is snarling in her face.

'I'm not. You have the proof there.' She points at the picture in my hand.

'Yes, I do.' I turn it around and push it in her face. 'This is a six-week scan picture.'

She frowns 'No, it's a four-*month* scan picture.'

'This isn't your baby, Coral.'

'Whose is it then?' she asks slowly. She's beginning to catch my drift.

'This is my baby.' I look at the tatty piece of paper fondly. 'And Jesse's.'

'What?'

'Well, I say baby. What I actually meant was *babies*. You see, we're having twins, and I know you're trying to pull a fast one because this really is a six-week scan picture. And there are two peanuts here, smaller than your one blob, I know, but I can get a feel for it. I don't know. Maybe it's motherly instinct.' I shrug. 'Is that all?'

Her mouth is slightly agape and whilst I'm still reeling on the inside, I'm beyond proud of myself for maintaining my composure. Jesse is right. I can't go rolling around on the floor, as much as I'd love to rip her hair out.

'Unless you can miraculously produce the missing strip that'll confirm your dates, I think we're done?' I give her an expectant look, but she's saying nothing. I throw her picture into the space between us. 'Now fuck off and go find the real father of your spawn.' I don't remove my eyes from her and I won't until that door is shut and she's firmly behind it. 'Are you leaving, or do I have to drag you out?' I ask, stepping forward.

She bends and picks her picture up before backing out of the door, her eyes flicking nervously from Jesse to his deranged, pregnant wife, and as soon as her body is over the threshold of the penthouse door, I slam it in her face, then turn to look at my ex-whore of a husband. He's chomping nervously on that bottom lip and maybe I shouldn't be, but I'm mad with him, too. I steam past him and up the stairs, finding the shower still flowing when I arrive back in the en suite. Stripping down, I scrub my teeth, then step in and make no rush to get done quickly. I've been up for less than half an hour and I already feel like it should be the end of my day.

My eyes are closed as I rinse my hair, but I can feel him behind me. He's not touching me, but I know he's there. And he's all worried. I can sense the anxious vibes shooting into my wet back. The evidence of his uncertainty at Coral's claim just reinforces my concern. Have I now got to add *potential baby mommas* to my list of things that could cause us issues? We've been back from Paradise for just two days, and I'm mentally exhausted already. A life of peace and comfort, that's what I want and need, and every time I think we're close to exactly that, something jumps up and obliterates it.

The familiar feel of the natural sponge connects with my back, as does his palm with my tummy. He's cautious, and he should be. 'Jesse, I'm not in the mood.' I step away from him and finish rinsing my hair. He doesn't know what to do, so as usual when he finds himself in this situation, he tries to win me back over with his touch. I expect to hear a snort of disbelief or even a scorn for denying him, but I don't. I do, however, feel his hand slide back around my stomach. 'I said I'm not in the mood,' I snap harshly, shrugging him off and grabbing a towel to dry myself.

'You promised you'd never say that,' he murmurs sullenly.

Securing myself in the towel, I glance up and see him standing under the pounding water with his hands hanging limply by his sides. 'I'm late.' I leave him, with trepidation written all over his face, to get myself ready for work.

For the whole twenty minutes it takes me to get ready, Jesse sits on the bed, cautiously watching me, cogs spinning, teeth nibbling. I'm just about to exit the bedroom when he blocks the door, all dopey-eyed and sad. 'Baby, my heart's splitting. I hate fighting with you.' He makes no attempt to close the distance between us.

'We're not fighting.' I brush off his solemnity. 'You need to get the code on the lift changed. And find out how she got up here, too.' I walk out, but barely make it to the top of the stairs before the warmth of his palm is around my wrist, stopping me from going anywhere.

'I will, but we need to make friends.'

'I'm dressed. We are not making friends now.'

'Not properly, no. But don't make me spend all day knowing that you're not talking to me.' He drops to his knees in front of me and looks up. 'The days are long enough already.'

'I'm talking to you,' I mutter.

'Then why are you sulking?'

I sigh. 'Because a woman has just invaded our home and tried to stake a claim on you, Jesse. That is why I'm sulking.'

'Come here.' He pulls me down and wraps me in his arms. 'I love it when you trample.'

'It's tiring,' I mumble into his chest. 'I really need to go.'

'Okay.' He kisses my hair and pulls back, securing my cheeks in his hold. 'Tell me we're friends.'

'We're friends.'

He blasts my moodiness with his smile – my smile. 'Good girl. We'll make friends properly later. Go get your breakfast. I'll be two minutes.'

'I need to go,' I remind him, glancing down at my Rolex. 'It's eight-thirty already.'

'Two minutes,' he repeats, returning me to standing. 'You'll wait for me.'

'Hurry up then!' I push him away and go to find Cathy in the kitchen. She's wrapping a bagel and still muttering under her breath. She soon stops when my presence is noted.

'Ava.' She scurries over, wiping her hands down her apron. 'I tried to stop the vindictive little minx!'

Something tells me Cathy has had an encounter with Coral before. 'Don't worry, Cathy.' I smile and give her a rub of her arm. 'You know her, then?' I press lightly.

'Oh, I know her, and I don't like her.' She starts muttering again as she returns to the island to finish wrapping my breakfast. 'She's been turning up for months, pestering my boy and claiming poverty. I told her! I said, look here, you conniving little tramp! Leave my boy alone and try fixing your marriage.' I smile as I watch her aggressive hand movements, virtually bashing away at my bagel. 'I don't know how many times my boy has sent her packing. Hell hath no fury like a woman scorned.' She looks up at me. 'Have you taken your folic acid?'

'No.' I walk to the fridge and collect a bottle of water before taking the pills that Cathy hands me, followed by a ginger biscuit. 'Thank you.'

'You're welcome, dear.' Her wrinkled face grins. 'You certainly put her in her place.' She laughs and retrieves my bagel, and then stuffs it in my bag. 'You eat that, I mean it.'

'You sound like Jesse.' I down my pill.

'He cares, Ava. Don't condemn him for that,' she scolds me lightly, looking over my shoulder. 'Here he is, and he's dressed!'

'I'm dressed,' he laughs, straightening his tie. 'As is my beautiful wife.'

I roll my eyes, but I don't feel embarrassed at all. She's seen it all before, and Coral's visit has taken the edge off any mortification. 'Can I go to work now?'

He pulls his collar down and rubs his three days' worth of stubble. Two minutes didn't give him time to shave. 'Have you taken your folic acid?'

'Yes.'

'Have you had your breakfast?'

I tap the side of my bag.

'You better eat that,' he warns, taking my hand. 'Say goodbye to Cathy.'

'Bye, Cathy!'

'Bye, dear. Bye, my boy!'

I'm a little wary when we leave the penthouse, and even more wary when we step out of the elevator into the foyer of Lusso, but she's nowhere to be seen. Clive is, though, and I wince as we pass, knowing he's about to cop it in a big way.

'Morning, Ava. Mr Ward.' The old boy's cheerfulness is going to be short-lived once Jesse lets loose.

'Clive,' Jesse begins, 'how the hell did a woman make it past you and up to the penthouse?'

The confusion on Clive's face is clear. 'Mr Ward, I've just come on shift.'

'Just?'

'Yes, I relieved the new boy . . .' he glances down at his watch, 'only ten minutes ago.'

I cringe further. It's Casey who'll be copping it. Chancing a peek at my man, I note a look of pure irritation. Casey might do well never to return. 'When's he back on shift?' Jesse asks shortly.

'I finish at four,' Clive confirms. 'Did he do something wrong, Mr Ward? I have advised him of protocol.'

I'm pulled towards the sunlight outside. 'For what fucking use it's done,' Jesse mutters. 'John's taking you to work,' he tells me as we emerge.

'When do I get my Mini back?' I ask, spotting the big guy across the car park, leaning up against the driver's door.

'You're not. It's a write-off.'

'Oh,' I say quietly. I love my Mini. 'Well, when do I get to drive myself to work, then?'

Jesse opens the passenger door of John's Range Rover and lifts me in. 'When I find out who stole my car.'

'Why aren't *you* taking me to work?'

He pulls my seatbelt across and secures me before dropping a kiss on my forehead. 'I have a few meetings at The Manor.'

'Then why did you make me wait for you?' I ask on a scowl.

'So I could put you in John's car and remind you to speak with Patrick.'

I know I audibly groan. 'You're impossible.'

'You're beautiful. Have a good day.' He kisses me once more and shuts me in, giving John a brief nod before making his way to the DBS. I'm suspicious of that nod and when John climbs in next to me, I make sure I direct my suspiciousness at him.

'What's up, girl?'

'Him.'

'Nothing's changed, then.' He laughs that deep, rumbling laugh.

'No, nothing has changed.'

Chapter 31

I'm a whole hour late for work, but I'm not going to get away with it today. Patrick is here, and he's standing over my desk when I finally burst through the door.

'Flower?' His round face is questioning. 'What time do you call this?'

It's one of the only times I've seen a displeased look on my boss's face. 'I'm sorry, Patrick.' I can't lie and feed him any rubbish about a client appointment, so I leave it at just an apology.

'Ava, I know your life has been moving pretty quickly lately – congratulations, by the way – but I need dedication.' He takes his comb from his inside pocket and sweeps it through his silver mop.

I'm a little shocked. *Congratulations, by the way*? That was hardly sincere. 'I'm sorry,' I repeat, because I'm stumped for anything else to say. He goes back to his office, shutting the door behind him.

I collapse in my chair and decide, wisely or not, given my boss's annoyance, to call Kate. A friendly voice. That's what I need to hear right now.

She grunts down the phone in greeting.

'Are you still in bed?' I ask, firing up my computer.

'Yep,' is the one-word, swift reply that shoots down the phone.

I smile. 'Is a certain cute, messy-haired, dimpled-faced man with you?' I pray for a yes, then hear shuffles and definitely a giggle, making my smile widen. I might have wanted to hear a friendly voice, but this will do the trick, too.

'He is.'

'Okay, I'll go.' I have things to share, but I'm more than happy to hold off.

'No, Ava!'

'What?'

'Wait!' she demands. I hear more shuffling, definitely a few slaps and then a door close. 'I just wanted to know how you got on with Dan.' She's whispering, for obvious reasons.

That wipes the smile clean from my face. Kate doesn't need to know the gory details. I'm just as ashamed of my brother as he is of himself. 'Fine. It's fine. He's gone back to Australia, and Jesse convinced him to keep quiet.'

'I feel responsible.'

'Kate, he'd already worked it out before you made the entrance of the year.' I can joke about it now. 'Did you and Sam talk?' I ask tentatively, tapping my pen furiously on the table and wondering if there's still scope for a bit of head bashing.

'Yes, we talked. He knew about Dan.' She pauses, and I know she's waiting for a shocked gasp from me, but too much time has passed for me to fake one now.

I try, anyway. 'Really?' I practically shriek, receiving three sets of wide, startled eyes shot straight to me from every corner of the office.

'Whatever, Ava,' she mumbles. 'I felt like such an idiot. He's not as daft as I thought.'

'I know,' I agree. 'So, everything is okay?'

'Yes, everything is fine. Perfect, in fact.'

I'm smiling again. 'No more Manor?'

'No more Manor,' she confirms. 'How are you? Throwing up? Achy legs? Any stretch marks?'

'Not yet.' I look down and notice my hand resting on my stomach. 'I might not be the only one getting all of those things, though.' I prick her curiosity. There's no way in hell I'll ever keep this one to myself.

'Ooohhhh, who's preggers?' she asks, obviously intrigued. 'Not boring Sal?'

'No!' I look over at boring Sal and instantly register that she is, in fact, boring Sal again. I cave on the inside for her.

'Who then?' Kate's impatient voice pulls me back to her pressing need for answers.

'Coral.'

'Fuck off!'

'No, Coral is pregnant and she claims it's Jesse's.'

'*What?*'

I pull my phone away from my ear, certain that the whole office, perhaps even the whole of London, heard her. 'It's not, though.'

'Wait, wait, wait.' I hear the unmistakable scraping of a chair across her kitchen floor. She's sitting herself down. 'How do you know?'

'Because she tried to pass off a peanut as a walnut.'

'What the fucking hell are you on about?'

I sigh and continue filling Kate in while absent-mindedly scrolling my e-mail account. 'She has a scan picture. She's claiming it's a four-month scan, but it's clearly not and she's cut all of the evidence away – the date, everything.'

'The crafty fucking bitch! Is she that desperate?'

'Very. She's four-ish weeks, maximum. I swear to god, Kate, I was this—'

'Hold up!'

'What?'

'Fucking hell! *Sam!*' she shrieks, and I jump in my chair.

'Will you stop yelling in my ear?' I hear thundering foot-steps, then the sound of a door crashing open. 'Kate?'

'Ava, fucking hell! Drew slept with Coral.'

I sit up in my chair. 'When?'

'Oh, about four or five weeks ago.'

'How do you know?'

'Sam told me. Drew was rat-arsed; Coral nabbed him. The poor bloke knew nothing about it and probably wouldn't if Sam hadn't turned up at his place. He caught her sneaking out.'

'Oh shit.' I'm not scrolling my e-mail casually any more. I'm tapping my pen wildly on the side of my desk. 'How did she think she'd get away with it? I mean, the baby would be three months overdue!'

'Desperate people do desperate things, my friend. Sam's on the phone to him now. Are you okay? That must have been a shock, even if she was lying.'

'Yeah, I'm used to shock with Jesse.' I brush it off with the apathy the whole episode deserves. Drew won't be able to, though.

'Good. You need to be careful now, don't you?' She asks it sweetly as a question, but there is a tinge of menace in there, too.

'I do, I am, and I will. Listen, I'd better go. Lunch tomorrow?'

'Perfect. Call me.' She hangs up, and I cast a sceptical gaze around my office. It's only ever this quiet when I'm here on my own. I glance over my shoulder to Patrick's office and see his door shut. I'm dying to call Jesse and offload my new knowledge, but I would be pushing my luck further and I know Sam will be calling him, anyway. I should prep for my meeting with Ruth Quinn.

At eleven-thirty, Patrick still hasn't come out of his office and I'm feeling nervous when I knock on his door. I wait for his okay and when it comes, I poke my head around and smile sweetly. 'I have an appointment with Miss Quinn.'

'Fine. You need to be back by two. We're having a meeting.' His tone is clipped, and he doesn't look at me, choosing to keep his attention on his computer screen.

'Okay.' I shut the door with care and leave the office bewildered and concerned, being greeted by a moped courier at the door. 'Delivery for Ava O'Shea.' His voice is muffled through his helmet.

'That's me,' I murmur apprehensively, the sound of my maiden name sending a chill down my spine.

'Sign here, please.' He thrusts a clipboard under my nose and I sign away, taking an envelope from him when I'm done. I don't want to accept this delivery, but when John pulls up, the courier jumps on his bike and zooms off down the road without another muffled word. It's not until John leans over and pushes the passenger door open that I realise I'm frozen in place, still with the envelope in my hand.

'What you got there, girl?' he asks, his smooth, shiny forehead creasing above his wraparounds.

'Nothing.' I stuff it in my bag and jump in, pulling my seatbelt on. 'What are you doing here?'

He pulls straight into the traffic and starts the therapeutic tapping of his palm on the steering wheel. 'You have an appointment, girl.'

My inquisitive eyes bore into the side of his head. He can't possibly know that because I've ensured my work diary remains under lock and key, just like my mouth. 'How do you know?' For the first time since I've known this big, menacing, black man, he looks awkward, and he's refusing to look at me. 'He's making you follow me, isn't he?' His tapping increases momentum, and I give him time to think about his answer, but I can tell by the look on his face that he knows I've got him.

'Girl, someone tried to ram you off the road. You cannot blame him for being a little jittery. Where am I heading?'

'Lansdowne Crescent,' I reply. 'So what's your excuse for all of the other times he's stalked me?'

'I don't have one. Those times he was just a crazy motherfucker.'

I laugh and John joins me, his neck retracting just how I

like it. 'Don't you get bored?' I ask, thinking that he must see me as a royal pain in the arse. This definitely can't be in his job description.

'No.' He quits with the laughing and turns to me, smiling fondly. 'That crazy motherfucker isn't the only one who cares about you, girl.'

I have to press my lips together before my stupid pregnant emotions get the better of me and I let out an embarrassing sob. 'I don't mind you, either.' I shrug his affection off because I know he'll appreciate that, and his quiet laugh confirms it.

'I've been reading,' he informs me, leaning over and opening the glove compartment. He takes a book out and hands it to me before resuming tapping the wheel.

I read the title, and then again to make sure I have it right. 'Bonsai trees?'

'That's right.'

I start flicking through the pages, admiring the pretty little trees and imagining John bent over one, delicately clipping at the fragile branches. 'It's a hobby?'

'Yes, very relaxing.'

'Where do you live, John?' I don't know where the question comes from. John and Bonsai trees would never be two things that I would naturally put together, but with this strange, new knowledge, I'm compelled to know.

'Chelsea, girl.'

'Alone?'

'All alone.' He laughs. 'Me and my trees.'

I'm astonished. I would never have thought it. This is a man who on first sight I thought was a member of the mafia – this huge, black, mean-looking geezer, who patrols The Manor, keeps overexcited men, and perhaps women, too, in their place, and now I find out that he lives with trees? Fascinating.

'Are you going to wait outside for me?' I ask him playfully when he pulls up outside Ruth Quinn's house.

His gold tooth flashes, and he reaches over to take the book. 'I might read a few pages, girl.'

'I'll be as quick as I can.' I jump out and dash up the path to Ruth's home.

The front door is open before I even knock. 'Ava!' She sounds far too happy to see me.

'Hi, Ruth. How are you?'

'Fabulous! Come in.' She looks over my shoulder on a slight frown and ushers me in quickly.

I let her be curious because explaining John will take too long, and I don't want to stay any longer than is necessary. I need to keep this as professional as possible.

She leads me down the corridor, into the kitchen. 'Did you have a good weekend?' she asks.

Brilliant and awful. It seems like light-years ago. 'Yes, thank you, and you?' I settle myself at the huge oak table and get my files out.

'Wonderful,' she sings, taking a seat next to me.

I smile politely and open her file. 'So, what did you want to discuss? Cupboards?'

'No, don't worry about the cupboards. We'll stick with the original. Now, the wine fridge, remind me: did we opt for the single or double width?'

If that is what she's dragged me here for, I will be most upset. 'Double,' I say slowly. I'm not at all comfortable. She could have called for both of those points. My phone starts ringing from my bag, but I ignore it, even though it's 'Angel'. I don't plan on being here for much longer, and there is absolutely no need for me to be, so I can call him back as soon as I escape. 'Was that all?' I ask dubiously. My phone rings off, then starts again immediately.

'Do you want to get that?' she asks, looking at my bag.

'It's fine.' I shake my head mildly. She doesn't know it, but it's in disbelief. 'Was there anything else, Ruth?'

'Urm ...' She looks frantically around the kitchen. 'Yes, I've changed my mind about the walnut floor,' she says, dragging a magazine over from the other side of the table. 'I quite like this.' She points to an oak alternative on the cover of the magazine.

I start to voice my reasons for sticking to walnut when my phone cuts me off. My shoulders sag.

Ruth pushes my bag towards me. 'Ava, perhaps you should answer. Whoever it is obviously wants to talk to you.'

I close my eyes in a give-me-strength gesture and reach into my bag to retrieve my phone before getting up from the table and making my way into the hall. 'Jesse, I'm in a meeting. Can I call you back?'

'I'm having Ava withdrawal,' he murmurs. 'Are you having Jesse withdrawal?'

'Is there a cure?' I ask on a grin, knowing damn well what the cure is.

'Yes, it's called constant contact. What time are you finishing work?'

'I'm not sure. I have a meeting at two with Patrick.' I glance over my shoulder and see Ruth flicking through the design magazine. She may not be paying any attention, but she must be able to hear me. Maybe that's a good thing. I'm happily married, most of the time. And I'm pregnant, too. Should I slip that into the conversation?

'Oh good. You're finally going to see through on your promise to talk with Patrick,' Jesse says.

'Yes.'

'Well, it won't take that long, will it?'

'No, probably not, but it doesn't matter because John will be waiting for me, won't he?' I answer his question with my own.

'He will.' I can hear his grin in his tone. 'How are my babies, lady?'

'*Our* babies are fine,' I realise immediately what I've just said, and I also notice my hand caressing my belly. 'Jesse, I need to get back. I'll see you later.'

'What am I supposed to do until later?'

'Go for a run.'

'I already did that,' he counters proudly. 'Maybe I'll go shopping.'

'Yes, go shopping,' I encourage him, hoping he lands in *Babies R Us* and doesn't emerge until gone six. 'I love you.' I end the conversation on something that'll placate him for a little longer.

'I know,' he sighs.

'Bye.' I smile and hang up, making my way back to the kitchen. 'Sorry about that.' I wave my phone as I sit back down. 'So, oak then?'

She looks lost in thought as she studies me for a while, and then her stare drops to my tummy, which is tucked neatly under the table. I know she must have heard.

I start scribbling down a load of complete nonsense. 'I'll get a price on the oak. The fitting and labour will be the same, but I'll check it out, anyway. Are you sure we're ditching the walnut?' I wait for her confirmation, but when I've run out of things to write and she still hasn't answered, I look up and find her still daydreaming. 'Ruth?'

'Oh, sorry! I was miles away. Yes, please do.' She jumps up. 'Ava, I'm so sorry. I've not even offered you a cup of tea. Or maybe wine. We could have a cheeky lunchtime wine.'

'No, honestly. I don't drink.'

'Why?'

Her abrupt question increases my unease. 'Not in the week. I don't drink in the week.'

'I see. Yes, we can all get a bit carried away.' She smiles, but it goes nowhere near her blue eyes. 'How's your husband?'

I can't help the sharp inhale of breath. Not when she's linked alcohol, getting carried away, and my husband all in two close sentences. 'He's good.' I start to pack my things away, keen to leave. She may have innocently touched a nerve, but she's still gazing longingly at me, and it's becoming unbearable. 'I'll get those quotes and call you.'

I make to stand a bit too hastily and catch my heel on the leg of the chair, causing me to stumble slightly. She's on me in a second, holding my arm to steady me. 'Ava, are you okay?'

'Yes, fine.' I collect myself, trying my hardest not to appear uneasy, but now she has hold of me and she's not letting go. In fact, she's trailing her hand up my arm. I tense from top to toe as it makes it to my cheek and strokes me gently.

'So beautiful,' she whispers.

I should move back, but I'm too shocked and my lack of recoil is allowing her to caress my cheek to her heart's content. 'I should go,' I say quietly, finally letting some sensibility filter into my brain. I step back and her hand falls away, a shimmer of embarrassment washing over her face.

She laughs and looks away. 'Yes, perhaps you should.'

I hurry down the hall to the front door and swing it open. John spots me rushing down the path and jumps out of his Range Rover. 'Ava, girl?' he questions as he runs a quick all-over scan of me, checking I'm physically okay. Once he's satisfied himself that I am, he looks past me and slowly reaches up to remove his sunglasses. I slow my escape and turn to see what's caught his interest, seeing the front door to Ruth's home close as I do.

'What's up, John?' I ask, feeling better now that I'm away from my friendly client, who now just seems creepy.

'Nothing, girl. Get in the car.' His glasses are replaced and he nods at me, so I climb in and wait for him to join me. He slides in and turns to face me. 'What's got you in a state?'

I sag and pull my seatbelt on, feeling a little stupid. 'I think I have a female admirer.'

I expect a laugh or at least a shocked gasp, but I get nothing, just a nod of acknowledgment and a face that turns away from me. 'Something else to send the motherfucker crazy,' John rumbles drily. 'What's her name?'

'Ruth Quinn. She's strange.'

He nods thoughtfully. 'Back to the office?'

'Please, John.' I throw my bag between my feet, dislodging the envelope that I tucked neatly in there earlier. It pokes out, reminding me of its presence, and I reach down, curiosity getting the better of me.

'What's that?' John asks, nodding at the brown A4 envelope that I'm holding.

'I'm not sure.' I sound as apprehensive as I feel. 'A courier delivered it.' I'm being totally honest because if this turns out to be another warning, then I'll be telling Jesse anyway, so it's of no consequence if John knows, too. I peel the seal and pull out a piece of card and as soon as I clock the cut-out letters, I lose my breath.

'What is it?' John asks, his voice laced with concern.

I can't speak. As I stare down at the message, assembled with various newspaper and magazine cuttings, my casual disregard of my previous warning seems quite reckless.

'It's another warning,' I manage to splutter through my racing breath. I feel sick.

'Another?'

'Yes, I had one with some half-dead flowers. I just chucked it in the bin and put it down to a jilted ex-sexual conquest.' I open the window to get some needed fresh air.

'What does it say?' John keeps flicking his sunglass-covered eyes over to the piece of card that I've dropped in my lap. I read the message to him.

I told you to leave him.

A frustrated curse shoots into the air. 'What did the other one say? Was it like that one?'

I try and collect my scattered thoughts and attempt to

recall the exact wording of the other message. 'Something along the lines of me not knowing him. They said they did.' I shake my head in frustration. 'I can't remember. The other was handwritten.' I'm furious with myself for getting rid of it when I should have been sensible and told Jesse. He's got Steve investigating the car incident and my drugging and, stupidly, I kept something from him that could've assisted in dealing with this. It may have sent him off the deep end initially, but the long-term benefits to him knowing far out-weigh the meltdown that would be guaranteed – the meltdown he's going to have very soon because now he *will* know, and I'm going to be facing a seriously pissed off male. I've been so stupid.

'Okay, girl.' He doesn't say I've been foolish, but I know he's thinking it.

'I thought it was Coral,' I say quietly.

'Even after the dressing down that you gave her this morn-ing?' He's restraining a small smile, I can tell.

'No, I thought it was Coral before. Not now.'

'Do you want to tell him, or should I?' John asks seriously. I know what he means. No further elaboration is required and when he looks at me and nods at my pleading face, I know he understands. 'I'll tell him, girl.'

'Can you try to calm him down, too?'

'If we were talking about anything else, I'd say yes. But this is you. I'm not promising anything.'

I sigh, but I appreciate his frankness. 'Thank you. Are you going back to The Manor?'

'No, girl. I'll call him. You just get done at work, and I'll be waiting for you.'

'Okay,' I agree, feeling anxious, stupid and way too vulnerable.

The office is still uncomfortably silent when John drops me off. No one acknowledges me when I pass through and Sally doesn't offer me a coffee, so I dump my bag and head through to the kitchen to make one myself.

I'm just tipping my third sugar into the mug when my shoulders rise and tense at the sound of my beloved husband's ringtone. If I could get away with it, I'd ignore him, but he'll be calling the landline and failing that, charging into the office. Abandoning my coffee, I take deep breaths of courage as I go in search of my phone. This isn't going to be a call that I can take in the openness of my office, so I hurry to the conference room and close the door behind me before connecting myself to what will be a raging mass of angry male.

'Please don't shout at me!' I blurt down the line, immediately holding the phone away from my ear once I've made my plea.

I was right. 'What the fucking hell were you thinking?' he yells. 'You stupid, stupid woman!'

My eyes close, and I quietly accept his rant, keeping my phone at a safe distance.

He's breathing erratically between scorns. 'I've been pulling my fucking hair out, trying to work with Steve and figure this shit out, and all along you had a handwritten threat?' I hear a door slam. 'And you tore it up? Evidence, Ava. Fucking evidence!'

'I'm sorry!' I'm close to tears.

'Fuck!' Silence falls after his curse, and I can see a clear mental image of him slumped in his office chair, rubbing a furious circle on his temple with his fingertips. 'Tell me you're not leaving that office this afternoon.'

'I have a meeting with Patrick. I'll speak to him about Mikael.' I'm trying to tell him what I know he wants to hear.

'This isn't the work of Mikael, Ava,' he says more calmly than I know he's feeling. 'Steve confirmed that Mikael has been back and forth to London over the last few weeks, but completely legit. He couldn't have drugged you and he couldn't have been driving my car because both of those times he was in Denmark.'

'What about the man in the CCTV footage?' I ask tentatively.

'I don't know, Ava,' he sighs. 'My car was found yesterday. Steve's looking into it. The tracker's been deactivated.'

I rest my tired arse down on one of the plush chairs surrounding the conference table. 'Should I come to The Manor after work?' I ask.

'No, John will take you home as soon as you've spoken to Patrick. I'll meet you there. Given this new information I've *just* found out, I've got Steve swinging by.' His sarcasm doesn't go unnoticed and neither does the edge of anger. I don't point out that my working day may not be over after I've spoken to Patrick because it will serve no purpose other than instigating further growling down the phone. I really do need to play by his rules this time. 'Don't leave that office, and once John's taken you home, you stay put. Do you understand me?'

'I understand,' I whisper.

'Good girl. I'll speak with Steve, but I'm out of here the second I'm done.'

'I love you,' I blurt urgently, like I won't ever get to tell him again.

He sighs. 'I know you do, baby. We'll have a bath when I'm home. Deal?'

'Deal,' I agree, his soft words and promise of tub-time making me feel a little better.

He hangs up, but I don't take my phone from my ear. I know he's gone, but I hold it there for a few moments anyway, maybe hoping that I'm mistaken and his deep husk will instil some further reassurance.

It's only when the door to the conference room swings open and Patrick appears that I finally pull my mobile away and accept he's gone.

'There you are.' He doesn't look impressed as he stands holding the door open. 'Are you ready?'

'Yes.' I go to rise, but he waves me back down.

'No, stay there. We're having the meeting in here.' He shouts through to the others and one by one, they filter in, all puzzled and all deadly quiet. Something is going down; everyone can obviously sense it.

There are no trays of tea brought in by Sal and there are no fresh cream cakes to dive into. Patrick looks tired and harassed, whereas we all look majorly confused by this sudden change in meeting etiquette. What happened to the usual relaxed affair, where we all huddle around our boss's desk and stuff our faces with cake while Patrick brings himself up-to-date on client progress?

'Right.' He sits his big body down in a chair at the head of the table and undoes his suit jacket to prevent the pull over his rounded stomach. 'I've not been here much lately, and I'm sure you're all wondering why.'

We all murmur our acknowledgment.

'Well, there is a perfectly good reason,' he continues. 'And I'm now in a position to disclose it. It has been tough keeping you all in the dark. You all know I value each and every one of you, but things needed to be ironed out and finalised.' His hands rest on his stomach and he relaxes back in his chair. My eyes travel from Tom to Victoria to Sal, and back again a few times, trying to gauge their reaction to the news of news, but they are all just staring blankly at Patrick. 'I'm retiring,' he sighs. 'I've had it.'

There is a collective hum of relieved breaths coming from everyone, except me. If he's retiring, then what happens to Rococo Union? Have none of them thought of that yet?

'You've all still got your jobs. I've made sure of that.' More collective sighs. 'But I can't do it any more. The rat race is wearing me out, so Irene and I are moving up to the Lake District.'

My first thought is . . . Patrick full time with Irene? What is he thinking? And my second thought is . . . who am I going to be working for? I don't have to wait long to find out. The door opens and Mikael walks in.

Chapter 32

'Meet the new owner of Rococo Union!' Patrick sings.

Tom and Victoria swoon a little, but Sally is definitely with me in the shock department. We're both visibly choking on thin air, but while I know damn well why I am, I have no clue what's gotten into Sal.

'Of course, you already know him in some capacity,' Patrick continues. 'Mr Van Der Haus and I have been thrashing out a deal over the last few weeks, and we've finally settled on mutually agreeable terms.'

'And I can't wait to get stuck in,' Mikael smiles, ignoring the other members of staff and keeping his blues right on me.

I predict that the hum of agreement comes from only three people in this room. I don't agree and it doesn't look like Sal does, either. There will be nothing coming from my mouth because my throat has closed up. I watch him round the table and shake hands with Patrick before formally introducing himself to my colleagues. When he makes it to Sal, he barely looks at her and she burns bright red and looks down to the floor.

She's been seeing Mikael!

My mouth gapes as I watch her fidget. That is how he knows I'm married. That is how he knows I'm pregnant and that I'm pregnant with twins. That is how he knows everything!

The room is suddenly filled with Massive Attack's 'Angel' and everyone looks at me, sitting in the chair like a statue, holding my phone limply in my hand.

'Would you like to take that?' Mikael asks on a smile, which

I don't reciprocate. Then the office door bursts open and John steams in, panting and doing a quick assessment of the scene that he's just barged in on. Now I can safely say that my career at Rococo Union is over.

John steps forward, with no regard for the people all looking wide-eyed at him, and grabs my phone from my lifeless hand, answering it quickly. 'She's fine.'

My stunned brain gets up to speed with what's happening as I watch John pace the conference room. Everyone is watching him, but no one is questioning him. He must have seen Mikael enter the office and called Jesse. I almost want to yell at the big guy, but the latest stroke Mikael has pulled is the nail in the coffin for me and my employment at Rococo Union – that and the huge, mean mafia-type stomping around the conference room.

Mikael doesn't need an interior design company. This is ridiculous, and crossing the line of obsessive … a bit like my husband did.

John looks at me and nods, me nodding back because speech still hasn't found me. Then he hands me the phone, and I look at him in horror. I can't have what I know will be a heated conversation with Jesse here and now. I push myself back further into the chair, but John gives me a look to suggest that I'm not going to get away with it. Jesse wants to talk to me, and I know I'm going to get nowhere refusing.

Nervously taking the phone, I stand up and leave the room. 'Jesse?'

'What the *fuck* is he doing there?' He's rampant, probably yanking chunks of hair from his head.

'He's bought the company.' I say the words quietly and calmly.

He's hyperventilating down the phone. 'Get your bag, get John, and leave. Do you hear me?'

'Yes,' I confirm quickly, knowing I have no other option.

'Do it now while I'm on the phone.'

'Okay.' I let my phone leave my ear and re-enter the office, getting six sets of eyes pointed straight at me. The tension in the air is heavy as I pick my bag up and look at John, who nods again.

'Ava?' Patrick's familiar, concerned voice pulls my eyes to my boss, or ex-boss.

'I'm sorry, Patrick. I can't work for Rococo Union any more.'

'Why ever not? Exciting things will be happening. Mikael has assured me that you'll be made a profit-sharing director. I made it part of the deal, flower.' He's standing now and approaching me with a wrinkled brow. 'It's an amazing opportunity for you.'

I smile and glance at Mikael. He seems to be speechless himself now. 'I'm sorry, I should've said that I can't work for Mikael.' Now all eyes are on the Dane. 'Mikael has been actively pursuing me for some time. He won't take no for an answer.' I swing my bag onto my shoulder. 'Sal, he's been using you to keep tabs on me. I'm sorry.'

She's hiding her face, but I can see that she's crying. I feel terrible for her.

'Are you so desperate that you'd destroy someone as sweet as Sally?' I ask Mikael. 'Are you so desperate to get revenge on a man that you'll buy the company his wife works for?'

'Revenge on that womaniser is just an advantage. I've wanted you from day one.' He confirms Jesse's suspicions in that one sentence. 'He doesn't deserve you.'

'He does deserve me, and he has me. He'll always have me. We've fought off bigger issues than you, Mikael. Nothing you can tell me will ever sway me from my decision to be with him.' My body might be shaking, but my voice is steady and firm. 'I have nothing more to say to you.' I turn to leave, but stop briefly at the door. 'I'm sorry, Patrick,' I say, but my boss is too stunned to speak.

John follows me, his giant hand set firmly on my back. I feel sad, but strangely resolute.

'Ava.'

The light Danish accent that I used to find quite sexy now just makes my skin crawl. John tries to push me on, but a stupid sense of curiosity has me fighting against the big guy's strength and turning towards Mikael.

'He fucked other women when he was with you, Ava. He doesn't deserve you.'

'He does deserve me!' I scream the words in his face, and he steps back, shocked.

John's hand moves to my arm, but I shrug him off. 'Ava, girl?'

'No! No one gets to pass judgment on him, except me! He's mine!' I scream. I've forgiven him, and given the chance, I could probably forget. 'You're blinded by resentment.'

'It's more about you.' The Dane flicks a cautious glance at my bodyguard.

I laugh and shake my head. 'No, it's not. I'm married and preg—'

'And I still want you.'

My mouth snaps shut, and John lets out a warning growl. 'The girl is taken.' He tries to manoeuvre me onward, but I'm fixed in place.

'Did you drug me?' I ask, but the horrified look that instantly invades his pale face tells me what I need to know.

'Ava, I would never hurt you. I've bought this company for you.'

I shake my head on a disbelieving laugh. 'You're consumed with the need for vengeance. You don't even know me. We've shared no intimacy, connection, or special moments. What's wrong with you?'

'I know a good thing when I see it, and I'm prepared to fight for it.'

'You'll be fighting in vain,' I say calmly. 'And even if you succeed in your attempts to break us – which you never will – you
couldn't have me afterward.'

His skin gathers on his forehead when he frowns. 'Why?'

'Because without him, I'm dead.' I turn and leave my workplace, knowing I'll never return. I'm a little sad, but knowing
what's waiting for me past this point in my life puts the biggest
smile on my face.

When I'm settled safely in John's Range Rover and we've
pulled away from the kerb, I register my phone in my hand and
remember that he's on the other end of the line. I don't want to
hear him, I want to see him. 'Jesse?'

It's silent for a while, but I know he's there. His presence
travels through the line and kisses my skin. 'I don't deserve you,'
he says quietly. 'He's right, but I'm too selfish to give you up to
someone who does. We'll never be broken and you'll never be
without me, so you'll be living forever, baby.'

Tears stab at my eyes and I think of how grateful I am that
he is such a selfish man. 'Deal,' I whisper.

'I'll see you in the bath.'

'Deal,' I repeat, because I know I'll never manage more than
one word without coughing all over them. He hangs up and I
lose myself in thought as I watch London fly by the window.

'Let's get you in, girl.' John parks and jumps out, leaving me to
unbuckle and join him at the front of his car.

'You don't have to escort me in,' I say, but he pulls a face that
suggests he does. 'Jesse's told you to sweep the penthouse, hasn't
he?'

'Just a little check, that's all, girl.' He takes my elbow and
leads me into the foyer of Lusso.

I'm surprised to see Casey here, but he's not in uniform.
'Hi, Casey,' I call as I'm led past, not being given a moment to

converse, or maybe warn him that he's going to be facing the wrath of Jesse very soon. I do notice how smart he looks in his suit, though, and I definitely spot the look of alarm on his face at the sight of the big guy escorting me. John punches the code in and stands back to let me enter the elevator before he joins me. He taps the code in again.

'You know the code?' I ask, hoping to God he doesn't know the significance of the code.

He smiles down at me, and I can't work out if it's a knowing look or not. 'The motherfucker was sensible this time, but you'd think he would be a little bit more creative.'

I cough a little, thinking just how creative Jesse can be when he reaches that zero. Wonderfully creative, in fact. Mind-blowingly creative. I need to run that bath, but as the doors of the elevator open, I uncharitably remember that it's early and Cathy is more than likely still faffing around the penthouse.

Letting us in, I immediately head to the kitchen and dump my bag on the island, but I find no Cathy, so I set off upstairs in search of her, set on relieving her for the rest of the day.

'Ava, girl.' John's thundering footsteps come after me. 'Let me check.'

'John, really?' I stop and let him pass.

'Peace of mind,' he rumbles. 'Quit with the complaining.'

I let him open and close doors while I prop myself up against the glass banister, arms folded across my chest, patiently waiting. There is no way I should be whining about this, given our surprise visitor this morning.

'All clear,' he grunts once he's done.

I watch him stomp off downstairs. 'No Cathy?' I ask his back.

'No Cathy,' he confirms, heading for the penthouse phone system, but his mobile starts ringing before he makes it to the landline. 'Yes?' he grunts, detouring into the kitchen. 'We're here now. Cathy's already left, but I'll stay until you arrive.' His voice is getting quieter as the distance between us grows, but I know he's talking to Jesse. 'Blue door, needs painting,' John says on a purposed hush. I can still hear perfectly, though. That's the disadvantage to having such a low, rumbling voice. He may sound menacing, but he can't whisper for shit. 'Lansdowne Crescent. I can't be sure. I only got a glimpse, but if it's not her, then she has a doppelgänger.'

I'm walking towards John's voice. His attempt to keep this from my earshot, coupled with the mention of Ruth Quinn's address and the fact that John obviously recognises her, makes me need to see his face to gauge his expression. I know it's not going to be good, not when he's talking to Jesse, which means Jesse knows Ruth Quinn. My blood is running colder the nearer I get to John's low, hushed tone.

'There's no one there?' John's pacing the kitchen at the far end. 'Ruth Quinn. I already told you. I know my eyesight isn't as good as it used to be, but I'd put my life on it. You need to call the police, not go looking for her, you crazy motherfucker.'

My blood is ice and my body frozen in place as I watch John turn slowly and register my presence. He might be black, but he has definitely just paled. 'Who is she?' I ask him.

His huge chest expands and he reaches up to take his glasses off. I wish he had left them on because the rare sight of his eyes has just confirmed my fears. They are worried, and the big guy doesn't do worried. 'Jesse, you need to get your arse back here. Leave it for the police to deal with,' he says, and I hear Jesse's angry yell down the phone.

'Who is she?' I grate, my breathing starting to accelerate. I'm anxious and panicking, but I don't know what about.

John sighs, defeated, yet he still doesn't answer, instead turning his back on me. 'It's too late. She's standing right here. You'd better come home.'

I hear an angry yell, and I think I catch the sound of something hitting something, like a fist on a front door – a worn, blue front door. I can feel my patience fraying. My lack of knowledge of something I should know about is reheating my frozen veins fast.

John hands me the phone, and I don't delay swiping it from his hand. 'Who is she?' I remain calm and clear, but if I don't get an answer, then I'll be raging very quickly. And it'll be the blood pressure-raising kind of furious.

He's heaving down the phone, his purposeful, thumping footsteps evident in the background. 'I'm not sure.'

'What do you mean?' I'm shouting. He didn't answer, not satisfactorily. He knows who Ruth Quinn is.

'I'm on my way home. We'll talk.'

'No, tell me!'

'Ava, I didn't want to say anything until I was sure it's her.' The screeching of tyres makes me wince. 'I'll explain when I can sit you down.'

'I'm not going to like this, am I?' I don't know why I'm asking. Even the big guy looks all concerned by what's transpiring.

'Baby, please, I need to see you.'

'You didn't answer my question,' I remind him quietly, resting myself on a barstool. 'What else could you possibly have to tell me, Jesse?'

'I'll be home soon.'

'Will it make me run?'

'I'll be home soon,' he repeats and hangs up, leaving me with John's phone suspended limply by my cheek and a stomach churning with trepidation. The penthouse phone screeches, making me jump, and John thumps his heavy feet across the kitchen, now with his glasses back in place. I won't waste my breath trying to extract any information from him.

He returns to the kitchen, looking too fraught for such a menacing man. Now I'm *really* worried. 'I'm needed downstairs. You'll lock the door behind me and you won't answer it unless I call you to say it's me. Where's your phone?'

'What's happening?' I stand, starting to shake.

'Where's your phone?' he presses, taking his own from my trembling hand.

'In my bag. John, tell me.'

He tips the contents of my bag out and quickly locates my mobile. He sits it neatly on the island and picks me up, placing me gently on the stool. 'Ava, now isn't the time to argue with me. There's someone the concierge is suspicious of and I'm just going to check it out. It's probably nothing.'

I don't believe him. Nothing suggests I should; not the tone of his voice or his body language. Everything is suggesting that I should be terrified, and I'm beginning to feel it. 'Okay,' I agree reluctantly.

After nodding and squeezing my shoulder affectionately, he carries his big body from the kitchen, and I soon hear the front door close, leaving me still shaking and with a racing mind. I just want Jesse. I don't care what he's got to tell me. I clench my phone and run up the stairs to the bedroom, quickly locating the key to Jesse's office from my underwear drawer before rushing back down and making quick work of unlocking the door. I know I'll feel better when I'm sitting in his big office chair, like he's wrapped around me in a sense.

I burst through the door, frenzied and out of breath.

And the first thing I see is a woman.

She's standing in the middle of the room, staring at my wall.

Ruth Quinn.

My legs buckle, making me stagger forward and my heart stop in my chest. But my dramatic entrance and gasp of shock doesn't seem to faze her. She maintains her rapt stare, not giving me a second glance. She's spellbound and if it wasn't for Jesse and John's recent words and reactions to this woman, then I would be thinking that she not only has a crush on me, but she is insanely obsessed.

Too much time has passed before my brain registers that I should be running, but when I slowly start stepping back, she looks at me. She looks hollow, not the usual bright-eyed, fresh-skinned woman whom I've become used to. It has only been a few hours since I've seen her, but you would think it was years.

'Don't bother.' Her voice is cold and carrying an air of loathing, and it immediately eliminates any thoughts I had that this woman is crushing on me. Now I know, with absolute certainty, that she hates me. 'The lift will be out of action and Casey will stop you on the stairs.'

I might be in shock, but those words register loud and clear. So does the mental flashback of Casey in his suit . . . and in the CCTV footage from the night I was drugged. I even manage to ask myself the sensible question of how the hell she got in the penthouse, let alone Jesse's office.

Then she's dangling a bunch of keys in front of her. 'He made it too easy.' She throws them on Jesse's desk, and my eyes follow their path until they clatter and eventually still. I don't recognise the set, but I'm not stupid enough to wonder what they're for. 'Your husband's stupidity and my lover's desperate need to make me happy has almost made this boring.' She looks back to the wall. The Ava Wall. 'I think he's a little obsessed with you.'

I remain exactly where I am, racing through my options. I have none. No escape, no chance of anyone getting to me and with the new concierge keeping guard, I'm helpless.

The tip of her finger meets the wall where Jesse has written something. 'My heart started beating again?' She laughs, a cold, sinister laugh, increasing my already potent unease. 'Jesse Ward, the obnoxious, woman-using arsehole is in love, married and now expecting twins? How perfect.'

I'm facing another scorned ex-lover, but this one is on a whole new level. She hates him, and in turn, hates me. Frightening clarity, plus the way she has now turned and is staring at my stomach, informs me that she also hates our growing babies. My fear has just catapulted to the highest level, and I know for certain that my babies and I are in grave danger.

I acknowledge her getting closer, but I don't acknowledge that I'm moving, too. Not fast enough, though, because she's in front of me in seconds and now stroking my stomach thoughtfully.

Then she draws her hand back and punches me. I scream, my body folding over protectively, my arms wrapping around my tummy, instinctively trying to protect my babies.

She's screaming, too, grabbing at my hair and yanking me from Jesse's office into the openness of the penthouse. 'You should have left him!' she shouts, pushing me to the floor and kicking me accurately.

Pain slices through me and my eyes tear up, flowing freely. If I could get my mind past the incredible pain and shock, then I think I could find the strength to find my anger. She's trying to kill our children.

'What is it about the immoral bastard that has you hanging around, you pathetic bitch!' She pulls me to my feet and slaps me around the face, but the raging sting and flaming skin won't pull my arms from my stomach. Nothing will, not even the need to fly back at her. I even have my phone in my hand still, but I can't risk giving her clear access to my stomach.

My overloaded brain is urgently trying to guide me, give me instruction, but all I can think to do is accept her derangement and pray that all three of us come safely out the other end. If I've ever thought that I might have been in hell, then this moment is proving me wrong. This is below the lowest level of the underworld.

Her fist connects with my forearm on an angered, frenzied scream and my body concaves on a frightened, painful one. I'm not going to get through this. I'm nowhere near dead, but the look in her eyes through my hazy vision tells me she won't stop until I am. She's demented. Completely unhinged. What the hell did he do to this woman?

The front door crashes open and she's suddenly gone from in front of me. I struggle to turn, still clutching at my stomach, still crying in agony. I see her back disappear into the kitchen, and then my welling eyes land on Jesse. His whole body is heaving. He's run up the stairs, and his fist is visibly swollen. His frantic eyes are running all over my body, his forehead is pouring with sweat and his face is a mixture of pure, raw terror and incensed, body-shaking anger. It takes him a few moments to gather himself, and I can see he's torn between tending to me or dealing with the crazy woman who's broken into our home. I can't talk, but I'm mentally screaming at him to do the latter. A choked sob escapes my mouth, prompting him to shake further then break into a full-on sprint into the kitchen. My feet instinctively fly into action, and wisely or not, I follow him. Now every modicum of fear is for him.

I skid to a halt, seeing Jesse standing across the room, then I quickly locate Ruth across the breakfast bar from him. We're standing in a perfect triangle, all breathing heavily, all flicking eyes to each other, but Ruth is the only one brandishing a knife. My phone drops from my hand, clattering loudly, but it doesn't draw her attention. The huge blade glimmers as she turns it casually in her hand. It's pointed in my direction, but the sight of the evil, razor-sharp metal doesn't just make my fear rocket. It also makes my eyes fall onto Jesse's abdomen in horror.

'Oh my God,' I whisper, so quietly I know that I've not been heard over the distressed rush of breaths coming from all three bodies in the room. He said that it happened in the car accident. That's what he said. I search my brain, trying to locate the exact words, but I don't find them because they're not there. What's there, though, is the silent conclusion that I drew myself. I'm horribly mistaken in my assumption and the real reason is standing here now, playing threateningly with a knife – a knife I know that she's prepared to use. I don't think anything else I could face will terrify me more. Now all four of us are in danger.

'Nice to see you, Jesse,' she spits, steadying her stance by shifting her feet further apart. She's getting ready to pounce.

'No, it's not,' Jesse replies calmly through his laboured breathing. 'Why are you here?'

She smiles coldly. 'I was happy to let you wallow in misery, drink your life away, and try to fill the void that *you* created by mindlessly fucking about, but then you went and fell in love. I can't let you have happiness when you've destroyed mine.'

'I've paid tenfold for my mistakes, Lauren.' His referral to Ruth has my head snapping from the shiny blade to Jesse's sweaty face. Lauren? 'I deserve this.' It's almost a plea, and it slices straight through my heart. He's trying to convince himself that he deserves me and the thought of him seeking approval from this deranged woman momentarily makes me forget about the dull ache in my stomach and the heated sting of my face. I feel anger simmering.

'No you don't. You took my happiness, so I'll take yours.' She waves the knife at me and Jesse shifts nervously, his haunted greens flicking over to me briefly before settling back on Ruth – or Lauren. I don't even know.

'I didn't take your happiness.'

'Yes!' She screams. 'You married me, and then left me!'

I gasp and swing my eyes to Jesse. He's chewing his lip, his eyes darting constantly between me and ... his ex-wife? He was married? I'm choking on nothing, my mind racing in circles and failing to comprehend what I've just heard.

Ruth looks at me, snapping instantly from her angry outburst and smiling. 'You didn't know? Well, there's a surprise. It might also explain why you've stuck around.'

Her smugness teamed with Jesse's despair cripples me completely. 'Nothing can break us.' My words travel through the air and wipe the smile from her face, but they also make Jesse noticeably tense. I hold his wary gaze and determine from the emptiness in it that he disagrees. My head starts shaking mildly, my bottom lip trembling. The feeling of my palm sliding across my stomach is comforting, but the look on his face isn't. His eyes fall from mine to my navel and a wave of desperation travels slowly across his face.

'I'm so sorry,' he murmurs. 'I should have told you.'

He really has saved the best shocker till last, but I don't care. I mean it. Nothing can break us. 'It doesn't matter,' I try to reassure him, but I can see defeatism swallowing him up.

'It does matter,' Ruth spits, pulling our attention away from each other and back to the knife-wielding, psychotic bitch who has invaded our lives. 'She knows nothing, does she?'

I hope she's mistaken. I hope Jesse nods and explains that I know everything. The Manor, the drinking, now her ... everything. But his head starts to shake, quadrupling my uncertainties.

'She doesn't know about our daughter?' The room starts to spin, and Jesse goes to move. 'Stay where you are!' Ruth shouts, flicking the knife to him.

'Ava ...' He desperately needs to get to me. I know I'm swaying on the spot as I try to let that information sink in. He has a daughter? My life is ending here and now. That tips the iceberg of shocks from this man. He's trying to compensate for his lack of involvement in her life.

'Yes, we were married and he left me when I was pregnant,' she spits.

'I was forced to marry you *because* you were pregnant. I didn't want to and you knew it. We were seventeen years old, Lauren. We fooled around *once*.' His voice is broken and unsure, like he's trying to reassure himself that he did the right thing.

'Don't blame your decision on your parents!' She's burning with fury again, her hand shaking uncontrollably.

'I was trying to right my wrongs. I was trying to make them happy.'

The room is still spinning wildly while I try to piece together what I'm hearing. I can't make any sense of it, especially now when I'm in such a hazardous situation. Through my confusion and alarm, I do, however, realise the importance of keeping myself safe. I need to get out of here. I start to back away, hoping her attention and anger will remain on Jesse as I quietly attempt my escape. I know this is going to end with her gunning for me, not Jesse. She wants to punish him, and she's going to do that by making him live without me. She's got it all worked out and so have I.

'Don't move!' she screams, halting me dead in my tracks. 'Don't even *think* about trying to leave because this knife will be in him before you make it out the door.' That threat foils my plan completely. 'You've not even heard the best part, so it would be nice if you stick around to hear me out.'

'Lauren,' he grates in warning.

She laughs – a sly, delighted laugh. 'What? You don't want me to tell your young, pregnant wife that you killed our daughter?'

He's moving fast now, nothing will stop him, and I know it's because I'm swaying, set on free-falling to the ground. My world has just exploded, splintering into a million pieces along with my overloaded mind. But I register her moving, too. I register the knife coursing towards me fast, and with absolute intent. And I also register Jesse coming between me and the blade. He manages to break my fall before tackling Ruth to the floor and punching her straight in the face on an infuriated roar. She laughs. The psychotic bitch just laughs, goading him, pushing him on with her hysterical fit of amusement.

'I didn't kill my daughter!' he punches her again, the sound of his fist colliding with her joyful face sending shockwaves through me.

'You did. The moment she got in that car you sent her to her death.'

'It wasn't my fault!' He's straddling her, trying to control her flailing hands.

'Carmichael should never have taken our daughter. You should've been watching her! I spent five years in a padded cell. I've spent twenty years wishing I'd never let you see her. You left me without you, then you killed the only piece of you I had left! I'll never let you replace her! No one else gets a piece of you!'

Jesse roars and with a last reinforced swing of his fist, he knocks her out cold. I'm scrambling into a sitting position, watching his whole body convulsing with exhaustion and anger. I heard and fully comprehended every single word that they just shouted at each other, and I'm shocked, but I'm saddened more than anything else. Every tiny little piece of pure craziness I have endured since meeting this man has just been justified. All of his overprotectiveness, unreasonable worry and neurotic behaviour have just been explained. He doesn't think he de- serves happiness, and he *has* been protecting me. But he's been protecting me from himself and the darkness of his history. It wasn't him in that car with Carmichael. It was his daughter. All of the people he has truly loved throughout his life have died tragically, and he thinks he is responsible for each and every one of them. My heart bleeds for this man.

'Nothing will break us,' I sob, trying to stand, but not making it past my knees. He thought this would but it won't. I'm re- lieved. Every little thing is making perfect sense to me now.

He heaves his tall body up from the floor and turns foggy- green, tormented eyes on me. 'I'm so so sorry.' His chin is trem- bling as he starts to walk to me.

'It doesn't matter,' I assure him. 'Nothing matters.' I hold my arms out to him, desperate for him to know that I accept him and his history, no matter how shocking and dark it might be. A sense of serenity travels between our bodies, like a silent, mutual understanding as I wait for him to get to me.

My impatience is growing. He's taking too long, seeming to get slower and slower with each step he takes until he collapses to his knee on a strangled gasp and clenches his stomach on a hiss. My confused eyes search his face for some clue of what's wrong, but then he pulls his jacket back, revealing a blood-soaked shirt and the knife submerged in his side.

'NO!' I scream, finding my feet and rushing to his side. My hand hovers over the handle of the knife, not knowing what to do. 'Oh God! Jesse!' He falls back, choking, his palm patting at his wound around the blade. 'Oh God, no no no no no. Please no!'

I collapse to my knees, all searing pain in my stomach and across my face being shifted straight to my chest. I'm struggling to breathe. I pull his head up onto my lap and madly stroke his face. His greens are getting heavy. 'Don't close your eyes, Jesse,' I shout, frenzied. 'Baby, keep your eyes open. Look at me.'

He drags them open, the effort clear. He's panting, trying to get words out, but I shush him, resting my lips on his forehead, crying hysterically. 'Ava . . .'

'Shhh.' I gain a second of rationality and start riffling through the inside pocket of his jacket, quickly locating his phone. It takes three scrambled attempts to key in the same digit three times, and then I'm screaming down the phone, shouting instructions and begging the woman on the other end to hurry. She tries to calm me down, she tries to give me instructions, but I can't hear her. I hang up, too distracted by Jesse's paling face. He looks grey, his body is completely limp and his dry lips are parted, wheezing in shallow breaths. His laboured breathing doesn't blank out the eerie silence surrounding us, though.

'Jesse, open your eyes!' I yell. 'Don't you dare leave me! I'll be crazy mad if you leave me!'

'I can't . . .' His body jerks as his eyes close.

'Jesse!'

He opens them again and his arm tries in vain to lift, but he gives up, letting it flop back down to the floor. I can't stand the sound of him struggling to breathe, so I grab his phone and dial my mobile, hearing 'Angel' start from a few feet away. I rock him, unable to control my sobbing. Every time my phone stops, I dial again, repeating over and over and over, the sound of his track dulling down the sound of his raspy wheezes. He's staring blankly up at me. There's nothing in his eyes. I search for anything, but there's nothing.

'Unbreakable,' he murmurs, his eyes getting heavy until he loses the battle to keep them open.

'Jesse, please. Open your eyes.' I desperately try to part them. '*Open!*' I scream the word at him, but I'm pleading to nothing.

I'm losing him.

And I know this because my own heart is slowing, too.

Chapter 33

I haven't looked into those eyes for two weeks. It's been the longest two weeks of my life. Any notions of desolation or misery that have come before this point in my life have been trampled all over by the feelings crippling me right now. I'm lost. I'm helpless. I'm missing the most important part of me. My only comfort has come from seeing his peaceful face and feeling his warm skin.

Four days ago the doctor removed his breathing apparatus. I can see him better now, all bearded and pasty, but he refuses to wake up, even though he surprised them by breathing on his own, albeit shallow and strained. The blade sliced clean through his side, puncturing his stomach, and his lung collapsed during surgery, complicating matters. He has two perfect mars on his perfect torso now; the new one a neat slice rather than the jagged mess that she made of him the last time. I've watched it be re-dressed daily and watched them drain the build-up of blood and nastiness from behind the wound. I'm used to it already, the imperfection a horrid reminder of the worst day of my life, but now another part of him to love.

I've not once left his bedside. I've showered in seconds when my mum physically put me in there, but each time I've made her swear to scream if he stirs. He hasn't. I've been told each day by the same doctor and surgeon that it's a waiting game. He's strong and he's healthy, so he has the best chance, but I can't see an improvement since they left him to breathe on his own.

Not one hour passes without me begging him to wake

up. Not a minute passes without me kissing him somewhere, hoping the feel of my lips on his skin will spark something. It hasn't. Each day my heart slows more, my eyes become sorer and my tummy is growing larger. Each time I take a split second to look down at myself, I'm reminded that my babies may never meet their father, and that is an injustice far too cruel to accept.

'Wake up,' I demand quietly, my tears beginning to roll again. 'You stubborn man!' I hear the door open and turn to see my mum through my hazy vision. 'Why won't he wake up, Mum?'

She's at my side in a second, working around my refusal to move so she can hug me. 'He's healing, darling. He needs to heal.'

'It's been too long. I need him to wake up. I miss him.' My shoulders start to shake and my head collapses onto the bed in hopelessness.

'Oh, Ava.' My mum is despairing, feeling helpless and useless, but I can't make anyone else feel better when I'm in desolation myself. 'Ava, darling, you need to eat,' she says softly, encouraging me to lift from the bed. 'Come on now.'

'I'm not hungry.'

'I'm making a list of your disobediences, and I'll be telling Jesse about each and every one of them when he comes round,' she threatens, her own voice quivering as she presents me with a light boxed salad.

The silly notion that eating will please him is the only reason I open the box with one hand and start picking at the cherry tomatoes.

'Beatrice and Henry have just arrived, darling.' Mum's voice is wary, but I'm past the contempt I feel for Jesse's parents. I have no room for any feelings, except grief. 'Can they come in?'

I selfishly want to refuse. I want him all to myself, but I couldn't prevent the papers from splashing the news of a stabbing all over London. News travels fast, even across Europe. They arrived two days after Jesse was admitted, his mum and sister emotional wrecks and his dad just silently looking on. I could detect the regret in his blank face, which is scarily similar to Jesse's. I heard all of the explanations, but they didn't really sink in. In the endless, quiet time I've had, just sitting here with nothing to do but cry and think, I've drawn my own conclusion. My conclusion is simple: Jesse's own guilt for many tragic things that have happened in his life has pushed his parents away. They may have been a contributing factor, with their pushy ways and demands for his cooperation, but with common sense and knowing my challenging man and now everything else, too, I know his own stubbornness was what essentially caused this rift. By distancing himself from everyone who reminded him of his losses, he thought it would ease the guilt – the guilt he should never have felt in the first place. He didn't give himself the chance to be surrounded by the people who love him and who could have helped him. He waited for me to do that.

'Ava?' My mum's voice and shoulder rub drags me back into the room which is too familiar to me.

'Just for a few minutes,' I agree, giving up on my salad and pushing it away. Mum doesn't argue with me, nor does she try to negotiate more time for them. I've allowed them five minutes here and there, but I've not allowed it privately.

'Okay, darling.' She disappears from the room and a few moments later, Jesse's mum, dad and sister quietly enter. I don't acknowledge them. I keep my eyes on Jesse and my mouth firmly shut as they crowd the bed. His mum starts to weep, and I see Amalie in my peripheral vision comforting her. His dad definitely brushes at his face. Three sets of eyes, all green, all glazed, and all grief stricken, are staring at my lifeless husband.

'How has he been?' Henry asks, moving around the bed.

'The same,' I answer, reaching up to brush a stray blond hair from his forehead, just in case it's tickling him in his sleep.

'And what about you, Ava? You need to take care of yourself.' He's speaking softly, but sternly.

'I'm fine.'

'Will you let us take you for something eat?' he asks. 'Not far, just down to the hospital restaurant.'

'I'm not leaving him,' I affirm for the millionth time. Everyone has attempted and everyone has failed. 'He might wake up, and I won't be here.'

'I understand,' he soothes me. 'Perhaps we can bring you something, then?'

His concern is genuine, but not wanted. 'No, thank you.'

'Ava, please,' Amalie presses, but I ignore her plea and shake my head, digging my stubborn heels in. Jesse would force-feed me, and I wish he could.

I hear a collective sigh, then the door opens and the night-nurse enters, pulling the familiar trolley, loaded with a blood pressure machine, thermometer and endless other equipment to check his stats. 'Good evening,' she smiles warmly. 'How is this fine specimen of a man today?' She says the exact same thing every time she starts her shift.

'He's still asleep,' I tell her, shifting only to give her access to Jesse's arm.

'Let's see what's going on.' She takes his arm and loads his bicep with the material band before pressing a few buttons and triggering the automatic inflation of the device. Leaving it to do its job, she takes his temperature then checks the printout from his heart monitor and notes down all of her findings. 'Just the same. You have a strong, determined man, sweetheart.'

'I know,' I agree, praying for his continued endurance. He's no better, but he's no worse either, and I have to hang on to that. It's all I have. The nurse injects some medication into the driver on his arm before changing his catheter bag and drip, then collecting her things and leaving the room quietly.

'We'll leave you in peace,' Henry pipes up. 'You have my number.'

I nod my acknowledgment and let them all attempt to rub

some comfort into me, then watch as they take turns kissing Jesse, his mum going last and spilling tears on his face. 'I love you, son,' she murmurs, almost like she doesn't want me to hear, like she thinks I'll condemn her for having the cheek. I would never. Their anguish is enough of a reason to accept them. My mission is to restore Jesse's life to what it should be. I'll do anything, but I don't know if he'll be around to accept it and appreciate it.

More tears fall.

I look up and watch them filter out, passing Kate, Sam, Drew and John at the door. Civil hellos and goodbyes are exchanged, and I can't help the tired sigh that slips from my mouth at the arrival of more people. I know they are all just worried about Jesse and me, but the effort to answer questions when I'm asked requires energy I just don't have.

'You good, girl?' John rumbles, and I nod, even though I'm clearly not, but it's easier to let my head fall up and down rather than from side-to-side.

I look up and offer a small smile, noticing the bandage from his head has been removed. He beat himself up for days, but what could he do when Casey called him down under false pretences and caught him off guard, clouting him around the head with an iron bar as he left the lift?

'I'm not staying,' John continues. 'I just wanted you to know that they both appeared in court today and both have been remanded.'

I should be pleased, but I can't even find the strength for that, either. I've answered endless questions that have been thrown at me by the police, and Steve has been a regular, keeping me up-to-date on their findings. It's quite simple. Ruth, or Lauren, is the psychotic, ex-wife of Jesse, and Casey is her pussy-whipped lover, who did exactly what she asked in an attempt to please her. 'Okay.' I look up, registering four more sets of eyes, all sympathetic. I'm sick of seeing it. 'I don't mean to be rude, but I don't have the ener . . .' My voice trails off, my spare hand reaching up to dab at my sore eyes again.

'Ava, go home, have a shower and get some sleep.' Kate pulls a chair up next to mine and drapes her arm around my shaking shoulders. 'We'll stay. If he wakes, then I'll call you immediately. I promise.'

I shake my head. I wish they would all give up. I'm going nowhere unless Jesse is with me.

'Come on, Ava. I'll take you,' Drew volunteers, stepping forward.

'There, see?' Sam joins the persuasion party. 'We'll stay and Drew can take you home for a while.'

'No!' I shrug Kate off. 'I'm not fucking leaving, so just stop it!' I look straight to Jesse, waiting for my scorn, but nothing. 'Wake up!'

'Okay.' Kate treads gently. 'We'll stop, but please eat, Ava.'

'Kate,' I sigh tiredly, trying my hardest not to lose my temper. 'I've eaten some salad.'

'I don't know what else to do.' She stands and steps into Sam's arms when he opens them. Drew looks at me sorrowfully, and I'm reminded that he must be having a tough time himself at the moment, dealing with a woman who used him to try and trap my husband. I've heard the odd word from Kate when she's tried to distract me with conversation, but I don't know the full story. I do know that Drew has committed himself to the situation, though. Not to Coral, just the baby, a commendable thing to do, given how she's deceived him.

'We'll go,' John prompts, turning to the others and virtually pushing them from the room. I'm grateful, just managing to be courteous enough to croak a goodbye before returning all of my attention to Jesse.

My head rests back down on the bed and I fight the heaviness of my eyes for the longest time until my defiance fails me. They slowly close, sending me to a land where I'm refusing to do anything he asks me, just so he resorts to his touching tactics. I'm in a happy place, reliving every moment with this man, all of the laughter, passion and frustrations. Every word exchanged and every touch between us is on replay through my mind. Each second, each step we've taken together and each time our lips have met. I don't miss a moment. His tall, lean body rising from his desk the first time I met him, his beauty growing with every pace he took towards me until his scent saturated me when he leaned in to kiss me. And his potent touch which sparked the most incredible feelings within me. It's vivid, it's clear, and it's blissful. From the moment I stepped into that office, I was destined to be with this man.

'My beautiful girl is dreaming.'

I don't recognise the voice, but I know it's him. I want to answer him, take my opportunity to tell him so many things, yet my desperation still doesn't help me find my voice. So I settle for the lingering echo of his words and his continued touch, gently caressing my cheek.

A loud bleeping sound stuns me from my happy slumber and my head flies up hopefully, but I find his eyes are still closed and his hands are where I've held them – one in mine and the other draped lifelessly by his side. I'm disorientated and wincing at the screaming noise, which I soon realise is his drip, shouting that he's out of fluids. Pulling myself up, I reach up to call the nurse, but jump when I hear a muffled moan. I don't know why I jump; it's low and quiet, not at all frightworthy, but my heart is racing anyway. I watch his face closely, thinking that perhaps I've imagined it.

But then his eyes move under his lids and my heart rate increases. 'Jesse?' I whisper, dropping his hand in favour of his shoulder so I can shake him a little, which I know I shouldn't be doing. He moans again and his legs shift under the thin cotton sheet. He's waking up. 'Jesse?' I should be calling the nurse, but I don't. I should be shutting that machine up, but I don't. I should be talking quietly, but I'm not. 'Jesse!' I shake a little more.

'Too loud,' he complains, his voice broken and dry, his eyes going from relaxed closed to clenched closed.

I reach over him and punch the button on the machine to shut it up. 'Jesse?'

'What?' he grumbles irritably, lifting his hand to clutch his head. Every fear and grief-stricken emotion flows freely from my body and light engulfs me. Bright light. Hopeful light.

'Open your eyes,' I demand.

'No. It fucking hurts.'

'Oh God.' My relief is incredible, almost painful, as it courses like lightning through my depleted body, bringing me back to life. 'Try,' I beg. I need to see his eyes.

He groans some more, and I can see him struggling to follow through on my unreasonable order, but I don't relent. I need to see his eyes.

And there they are.

Not as green or addictive, but they have life in them and they are squinting, adjusting to the subtle glow of light in the room. 'Fucking hell.'

I've never been so pleased to hear two words. It's Jesse and it's familiar. I stupidly dive on him, kissing his bearded face, only stopping when he hisses in pain. 'Sorry!' I blurt, pushing myself away and causing him more discomfort.

'Fucking hell, Ava.' His face screws up, his eyes closing again.

'Open your eyes!'

He does, and I'm beyond thrilled to see him scowling at me. 'Then stop inflicting fucking pain on me, woman!'

I don't think I've ever felt so happy. He looks terrible, but I don't care. He can keep the overgrown facial hair. He can swear at me every second of every day.

'I thought I'd lost you.' I'm sobbing again as overpowering

relief takes hold and my cheeks fall into my palms to conceal my wrecked face.

'Baby, please don't cry when there's fuck all I can do about it.' I hear his shifting body, followed by a string of bad language. 'Fuck!'

'Stop moving!' I scold him, wiping my sniffling face before pushing lightly on his shoulders.

He doesn't argue with me. He relaxes back into his pillow on an exhausted sigh, then lifts his arm and focuses on the needle hanging out, before taking a confused glance around at all of the machinery surrounding him. I see understanding settle across his face and his head whips up, his eyes wide and frightened. 'She hurt you.' He struggles to sit up, hissing and wincing as he does. 'The babies!'

'We're okay,' I assure him, forcing him back down to the bed. It's hard. His sudden realisation has injected some strength into him. 'Jesse, we're all okay. Lie down.'

'You're okay?' His hand lifts and feels its way through thin air until he finds my face. 'Please tell me you're okay.'

'I'm fine.'

'And the babies?'

'I've had two scans.' I rest my hand over his and help him feel me. It relaxes him completely, my words assisting, too. His eyes close, making me want to prod him to open, but I let him rest them. 'I should call the nurse.'

'No, please. Let me wake up before they start poking me about.' His hand slides from my cheek to the nape of my neck and he applies a light pressure, silently telling me to come closer.

'I don't want to hurt you,' I protest, pulling against him, but his face strains and his strength increases. 'Jesse.'

'Contact! Do what you're told,' he snaps drowsily. Even now, when he's clearly in tremendous pain, he's impossible.

'Are you in much pain?' I ask, lowering myself gently to his side.

'Agony.'

'I need to get the nurse.'

'Soon. I'm comfy.'

'No you're not,' I almost laugh, working around his wound to gently rest against him. I'll give him five minutes, then I'm getting the nurse, and there is nothing he can do to stop me – literally, for once.

'I'm glad you're still here,' he murmurs, using more valuable energy to turn his face into mine and kiss me. 'I'd have given up if I didn't constantly hear your defiant voice.'

'You could hear me?'

'Yes, it was strange and fucking annoying when I couldn't tell you off. Will you ever do what you're told?' There is no humour in his tone. It makes me smile.

'No.'

'Thought not,' he sighs. 'I have some explaining to do.'

Those few words make me tense. 'No you don't,' I blurt, trying to pull away from him so I can get the nurse, but I'm going nowhere.

'Fuck!' he spits. 'Fucking, fuck, fuck, fuck!' He's still fighting against me, the stupid man, but I'm the one who relents, more concerned for him than he is for himself. 'Just stay put and listen,' he demands harshly. 'You're not going anywhere until I've told you about Rosie.'

Rosie. The name signifies unbearable heartache and years of self-torture. He should have confessed this long ago. It would have explained so many of his neurotic ways.

'Lauren was the daughter of my mum and dad's good friends,' he begins, and I brace myself, realising that I'm about to get the whole story. Not just the bits that I'd like to hear about his daughter, but the parts about the psychotic woman who nearly robbed him from me. 'I'm sure you can imagine the type – well-bred, rich, and highly respected in the snotty community that we were forced to tolerate. We fooled around once and she ended up pregnant. We were seventeen, young and stupid. Can you imagine the scandal? I'd really done it this time.' He shifts, flinching and cursing some more. 'Emergency meetings were called between Lauren's family and my own, and her father demanded I marry her before word got out and ruined both of our families. Jake had not long died and I went along with it, hoping my compliance might build some bridges with my parents.'

I clench my eyes shut and hold on to him a little tighter, remembering our visit to my parents and his reaction to my mother implying that he'd married me because I was pregnant.

'The joint effort of both families did an amazing job of convincing the community that we were hopelessly in love.'

'She was,' I whisper, knowing the direction in which this story is heading.

'And I wasn't,' he confirms quietly. 'I was married off and moved into her parents' country estate within a month. Everyone was happy, except me.' His fingers play idly with my hair, and he draws a painful breath before continuing. 'Carmichael gave me an escape, and I finally plucked up the courage to call a halt on the whole diabolical farce, but when Rosie arrived, I was determined to be a dad. That little girl was the only person on the planet who loved me for me, no expectations or pressure; she just accepted me in her innocence. It didn't matter that she was a baby.'

All of this is filling me with immense pride, but this story doesn't have a happy ever after. And it crushes me.

'She was a real daddy's girl,' he says fondly. 'I could do no wrong, and I knew I never would in her eyes. That was enough to make me evaluate the lifestyle I'd slipped into while Lauren was pregnant. Carmichael got the best solicitor involved to try and gain me full custody because he knew that she was my redeemer, but Lauren's family dug up every dirty little secret, from Jake, to The Manor, to my brief lifestyle from when I'd left Lauren until Rosie was born. I didn't have a hope.'

'And your parents had moved to Spain by then?' I ask.

He jerks on a hiss as he laughs quietly. 'Yes, they escaped the shame I'd brought on the family.'

'They abandoned you,' I whisper.

'They wanted me to go with them. Mum begged, but I couldn't leave Rosie full time with that family. She'd be frowned upon as an illegitimate child, even though she had me. Not an option.'

'So then what?'

'Rosie was three and I made the worst mistake of my life.' He pauses, and I know he's munching on that bottom lip. 'I slept with Sarah.'

'Sarah?' I'm frowning heavily into his neck. How does Sarah play any part in this?

'Carmichael and Sarah were together.'

'They were?' I'm scrambling with care from his hold now, but this time he lets me. He *is* chewing that lip and he's holding his breath, too. 'Sarah and Carmichael? But I thought he was a playboy.'

'He was. With a girlfriend . . .' he flinches as he inhales, 'and a child.'

'What?' I'm sitting up fully now. 'Go on,' I push. This story isn't taking the direction that I thought it would at all.

He takes another long, painful breath. I should tell him to stop and rest, but I don't. 'Carmichael walked in on me and Sarah. He hit the roof, got the girls, and left.'

Oh good Lord. 'The girls?' I ask. I don't know why. I know who the girls are.

'Rosie and Rebecca.'

'Your Rosie and their Rebecca,' I whisper. 'The car accident?'

He nods mildly and screws his eyes shut. 'I didn't just kill my uncle and my daughter. I killed Sarah's girl, too.'

'No,' I shake my head. 'That can't be your fault.'

'I think you'll find that my poor decisions have been the cause of everything, Ava. I've fucked up on so many levels so many times, and I've paid for it, but I can't pay for it now, not now that I have you. What if I make a bad decision again? What if I screw up again? What if I'm not done paying?'

His demand for compliance on everything is crystal clear. Too clear. He really does live in terror, but it's far worse than I ever imagined. He blames himself for everything, and maybe his carelessness played a small part, but ultimately he's not responsible. He wasn't driving the car that hit Jake. He wasn't driving the car with the girls. He didn't want to get married and he definitely wanted to be a proper father. And Sarah? That has totally floored me. She had a child with Carmichael, but was in love with her boyfriend's nephew? Fucking hell, this is complicated stuff. Sarah really does have nothing, and after losing both her daughter and her lover, she sought solace in The Manor, a little bit like Jesse did. Two tortured souls drowning themselves in whips, sex and drink, but never in each other. That was Jesse's choice, though. Not Sarah's.

'You are more than done paying.' My eyes land on his stomach. He's paid physically and mentally, and it's made my husband a neurotic control freak now that he has something he cares about again.

Me.

'When did she hurt you before?' I ask, needing that final piece to secure this colossal puzzle and lay it all to bed.

'After Rosie died she tried so hard to make me see that we needed each other. She had always been a little unpredictable, but when I continually rebuffed her advances, she really started behaving erratically. We're talking full-on bunny-boiler style.' He smiles at me, but I can't smile back. She's tried to kill him twice. This is no laughing matter.

'Did she get pregnant on purpose?'

'Probably.'

'And she stabbed you?'

'Yes.'

'Did she go to prison?'

'No.'

'Why not?'

He's sighing again. 'Her family got her help and kept her away from me in exchange for my silence.'

'But look at the mess she made of you.' I point to his old scar. 'How did you pass that off?'

'It's pretty superficial.' He looks down at his stomach. 'She did a better job this time.'

'You didn't even go to hospital, did you?' I'm horrified. That is one nasty scar and far from superficial. 'Who stitched you up?'

'Her dad. He was a doctor.'

'Oh my God!' I move and collapse onto the chair. 'And where were your parents whilst all of this was going on?' I sound like a lecturing fishwife, but holy shit, where did it end?

'They'd already returned to Spain.'

'Jesse . . .' I snap my mouth shut, trying hard to think of what I can possibly say, before I blurt out just anything. As always, I'm blank. This man renders me speechless on every level. 'Your mum in Spain.' I think hard. 'Second chance?' She hadn't been referring to Jake at all. She'd been referring to Jesse's lost daughter – a chance for him to be a good father again.

'You really do know everything now.' His dry voice is still disjointed and his searching eyes are looking for mine. But he won't let our gazes connect. 'Are you leaving me?'

If my heart was breaking for him before, then now it's just shattered. That simple, perfectly reasonable question and the unsure tone in which he's asked it has tears stabbing painfully at the backs of my eyes. 'Look at me,' I demand sharply. He does, showing me unthinkable hurt. It cuts so deep and the tears roll freely. So do his. I know I'm his saviour now. I'm the key to redemption for him. I'm his angel. 'Unbreakable,'

I weep, crushed by sadness for this man. Two weeks of emptiness has been flooded by happiness, but soon replaced with sorrow.

He gasps, but I'm not sure whether it's in pain or relief. 'Hold me,' he begs, weakly lifting a heavy arm out to me. The no-contact will be killing him, especially when he has to depend on me to feed his need.

Gingerly crawling onto the bed again, I settle carefully around tubes and dressings. I'm pulled in closer. 'Jesse, be careful.'

'It hurts more if I'm not touching you.'

His fingertip connects with my chin and pulls my face up to his, and I reach up to catch a stray tear before running my palm all over his overgrown face. 'I love you,' I say quietly, pushing my lips gently to his.

'I'm glad.'

'Don't say that.' I pull back and hit him with a disappointed glare. 'I don't want you to say that.'

His confusion is clear. 'But I am.'

'That's not what you usually say,' I whisper, giving his too long hair a warning yank.

My savageness tips the corner of his lips. 'Tell me you love me,' he demands, probably using far too much of his energy to sound stern.

'I love you.' I comply immediately, and he breaks into his full-on, glorious smile, reserved only for me. It's the most incredible sight, even if there are tears accompanying it and he's a little too washed out.

'I know.' He kisses me sweetly, then hisses, losing his momentum, then rides out the pain to kiss me again.

'I'm getting the nurse now,' I tell him determinedly. 'You need some painkillers.'

'I need you,' he grumbles. 'You're my cure.'

Reluctantly releasing his lips, I prop myself up and clasp his face in both hands. 'Then why are you still tensing and hissing in discomfort?'

'Because it fucking hurts.'

I give him one last peck and peel my body away from him before rearranging the sheets over his waist. Whilst it's horrible seeing him so weak and helpless, the thought of looking after him and nursing him back to health is something I'll cherish.

'What are you smiling about?' he asks, lifting his arms to let me tuck the sheets in.

'Nothing,' I reach over and finally press the call button for the nurse.

'You're going to love this, aren't you?'

I pause mid-plump of his pillow and break out into a smile when I catch his disgruntled face. He's a big, powerful man, who has been reduced to a weak, injured soul. This will be hard for him. 'I have the power.'

'Don't get used to it,' he grunts, just as the door swings open and the nurse hurries in.

'Oh! Oh my!' She's by his bed and checking the machinery in a second, faffing around and feeling for his pulse. 'Welcome back, Jesse,' she says, but he just grunts some more and looks up to the ceiling. 'Feeling groggy?'

'Shit,' he confirms. 'When can I go home?'

My eyes roll, and the nurse laughs. 'Let's not get ahead of ourselves. Eyes, please.' She gets the pen light from her pocket and waits for my grouchy Lord to drop his greens for her, and when he does, she falters slightly before resuming medical duties. 'Your wife has told me all about these eyes,' she muses, flicking the pen from one to the other. 'They really are quite something.'

I smile proudly and raise on my tiptoes to look over her bending body, finding him grinning from ear to ear. 'Is that all she told you about, nurse?' he asks cheekily.

The jolly woman cocks a warning eyebrow. 'No, she's told me about that roguish grin, too. Bed bath?'

He recoils on a grimace, and I laugh. 'No, I'll shower.'

'No can do, young man. Not until the doctor checks you over and we remove your catheter.' She is putting him firmly in his place.

His horror increases, and the nurse lifts his catheter frame to demonstrate the obstacle. The mortification all over his handsome, hairy face is really quite a picture. 'For fuck's sake,' he mutters, dropping his head back to the pillow and closing his eyes to hide from his embarrassment.

'I'll call the doctor.' She chuckles as she leaves the room and I'm once again alone with my poor, dependant husband.

'Get me out of here, baby,' he begs.

'No way, Ward.' I pour him some water and stick a straw in the plastic cup, then put it to his dry lips. 'Drink.'

'Is it bottled?' he asks, eyeing up the jug on the side.

'I doubt it. Stop being a water snob and drink.'

He takes a few sips. 'Don't let that nurse give me a bed bath.'

'Why not?' I ask, placing the cup on the unit next to the bed. 'It's her job, Jesse, and she's been doing it very well for the past two weeks.'

'Two weeks?' he blurts. 'I've been out for two weeks?'

'Yes, but it felt more like two hundred years.' I rest my backside on the edge of the bed and take his hand, twirling his wedding band thoughtfully. 'Don't ever complain to me about having a long day again.'

'Okay,' he agrees. 'She hasn't really been sponging me down, has she?'

I smile. 'No, I have.'

I'm stunned when his eyes sparkle and he pouts playfully. How can he even think about that? 'So while I was naked and unconscious, you were . . . fondling me?'

'No, I was washing you.'

'And you didn't have a sneaky touch?'

'Of course.' I brace my hands on either side of his head and float my face over his smug one. 'I needed to lift your limp dick to get to your saggy balls.' I'm not able to prevent my grin, especially when his eyes widen before narrowing fiercely. This is a man who prides himself on his body and sexual capabilities. I shouldn't tease him like this.

'I'm in hell,' he mutters. 'Fucking hell on earth. Get me a doctor. I'm going home.'

'You're going nowhere.' I kiss him chastely and leave him brooding and muttering on the bed while I nip to the loo. It's the first time in weeks, probably my whole life, that I've carried out the mundane chore with a huge smile on my face. My heart is beating strongly in my chest. I might even be giving our babies a headache.

When I re-enter his room, the doctor is examining Jesse. I stand quietly to the side while listening to the questions and one-word answers that are exchanged between the two men. I make mental notes and watch carefully as the doctor redresses the wound and removes the drains. He seems happy with the healing and delighted with Jesse's alertness. The doctor isn't so keen to remove Jesse's catheter, though, and not even a five-minute heated exchange of words between them convinces him.

'Maybe tomorrow,' he tries to appease Jesse. 'We'll see if you're up for a little walk about tomorrow. You've just come round, Jesse.'

'What about this, then?' Jesse indicates the needle in his arm, but the doctor shakes his head and Jesse snorts his disgust.

After seeing through his observations, the doctor leaves and I settle back in the chair. 'The more you cooperate, the sooner you'll be released.'

'You look tired,' he says, changing the subject and directing the concern onto me. 'Are you eating?'

'Yes.' My traitor fingers dive into my messy hair, totally giving me away.

'Ava,' he moans. 'Go now and get something to eat.'

'My mum fed me a salad. I'm not hungry now.'

His eyes widen at the mention of my mum. I know what's coming. 'What have you told them?'

'Everything,' I admit. I blubbered my way through it all while my mum soothed and hushed me. She was quietly tolerant. It was bizarre. 'Except your four-day absence.'

He nods thoughtfully, almost acceptingly. He must know I could never have avoided it. 'Okay,' he says quietly. 'Go and get something to eat.'

'I'm not hun—'

'Don't make me tell you again, lady,' he snaps. 'Piss bag or not, I'll march you down to that fucking restaurant myself and shove some food down your throat!'

I wisely halt all further arguments. I'm really not hungry, but I know he absolutely would, so I drag my tired body from the chair and retrieve the twenty that my dad left for me in Jesse's bedside cabinet. 'I'll get you something, too.'

'I'm not hungry.' He doesn't even look at me. He's lost in thought. He's ashamed, but he shouldn't be. I'm not, so neither should he be.

His mood and my affronted state goes nowhere near to dampening down the elation dancing through me. The presence of his arrogance and challenging ways really is a sign that I have my Jesse back. I wouldn't have him any other way.

Chapter 34

I'm munching my way through a Dairy Milk as I round the corner that leads back to Jesse's room, and I halt as soon as I see Sarah hovering outside Jesse's door. She goes to take the handle, but pulls back again, then turns, deciding to leave, but spots me and freezes, looking out of place and awkward. I haven't seen her here since Jesse was admitted, and I thought she had stayed away, but seeing her now, hanging around the corridor, I realise that she's probably been here most days. I know if I had seen her before, I might have lashed out in grief, but not now. I'll never forgive her for what she's done, but having learned of her history, I'd be inhuman if I didn't feel some compassion for the woman. She lost a child. It's tragic and she's put up a hard-faced front to protect herself. She wanted Jesse. She saw a reason to unite and soothe each other's grief, whereas he saw her as a reminder of what he lost because of a poor decision. Two suffering souls who used each other in different ways, except Jesse found his salvation elsewhere. And Sarah still wants him to be hers.

'Are you okay?' I ask, not knowing what else to say to her. I've shocked her with my question. She looks tearful, but she's trying to keep up a hard persona. I quickly realise that she doesn't know he's awake. I'm sure John has been keeping her informed, but he doesn't know either. 'He's come round.'

Her eyes snap to mine. 'He's okay?'

'He will be, if the stubborn idiot listens to the doctor.' I hold up a miniature jar of peanut butter that I found in the restaurant. 'And eats.'

She smiles. It's a nervous smile. 'I hope you've got more than one of those.'

'Ten.' I lift my arm where a paper bag is dangling. 'But it's not Sun-Pat, so he'll probably reject it.'

She actually laughs, but stops quickly, and I know it's because she thinks it's inappropriate. It probably is, not because the situation isn't funny, but because she's laughing *with* me.

'I know everything, Sarah.' I need her to appreciate that my empathy is only because of my new knowledge. 'I'll never forget what you tried to do to us, but I think I understand why you did it.'

Her red lips part, her mouth falling open in shock. 'He told you?'

'About your little girl. About Rosie. About Carmichael, the car accident and why the girls were with Carmichael in the first place.'

'Oh.' Her eyes fall to the floor. 'It's always been ours.'

She means their story and connection. And I've severed it. I *do* feel sorry for her, but nothing will ever make me stand down. Not scorned ex-lovers, high-class sex clubs, drink problems, psychotic ex-wives, the shock of a lost daughter, or the desolation of Sarah. Neither will the madness that surrounds all of those reasons. This man has thrown everything at me, and I still don't plan on going anywhere. Unbreakable.

'Can I see him?' she asks quietly. 'I'll understand if you refuse.'

I should refuse, but compassion prevents me. I need closure on this, and she does, too. 'Sure. I'll wait here.' I sit myself down on a hard plastic chair and watch her disappear into his room.

I don't need to hear what will be said. I have a good idea, anyway, so instead I finish my chocolate bar, my body thanking me for the instant sugar hit.

'Ava?'

I look up and see Jesse's mum and sister hurrying down the corridor. 'Hi.' I speak around a mouthful of chocolate.

'The nurse said he's awake. Jesse's awake.' Beatrice looks over at the door, then back to me.

I nod and chew fast, swallowing so I can give her the information she needs. 'He's fine. Grumpy but fine.'

'Oh, thank you, Jesus!' She turns and throws her arms around Amalie. 'He's going to be okay.'

I watch as Amalie smiles over her mum's shoulder at me. 'Grumpy?'

'Or stubborn – whichever.' I shrug on a smile, and her green eyes glimmer in understanding.

'The latter, for sure,' she confirms, holding her sobbing mother in her arms. 'It's good to see you eating.'

'Where's Henry?' I ask.

'Just parking the car. Would you mind if we see him?' Amalie asks.

I'm very abruptly hit with the hard realisation that Jesse doesn't know they're here. And I have no idea how to handle it. After our last encounter with his parents, I should avoid subjecting him to the potentially stressful situation, but my conniving mind is jumping all over the fact that he can't escape. And whilst I might be taking a huge risk, I know it will be my only opportunity to get them in the same room together. He will *have* to listen. If he doesn't like what he hears, then so be it, but I've watched his family grieving. I saw it clearly, even through my own grief. Now is the time to put all wrongs right, no matter who is to blame.

This is what I hope, but it's his choice, and I'll stick by whatever he decides.

'I haven't had the chance to tell him you're here yet,' I explain, almost apologetically. 'As soon as he woke, the doctors were on him and now a friend's in there.'

'Can you do that?' Beatrice breaks away from Amalie and

retrieves a tissue from under the cuff of her cardigan. 'Can you tell him we're here?'

'Of course, but—'

Amalie cuts me off. 'We don't want him upset, so don't push it.'

'You'll try, though.' Beatrice clasps my hands pleadingly. 'Please, try hard for me, Ava.'

'I will.' I feel the pressure, but I also feel the desperation that's seeping from every pore of this lady. I'm the key to her reconnecting with her son. She knows it, Amalie knows it, and I know it.

We all turn when the door to Jesse's room opens and Sarah steps out. She's been crying, and as she lifts her hand to wipe her eyes, the sleeve of her jacket rides up and I see a bandage around her wrist. But I'm distracted from this when I feel the hackles on Jesse's mother rise.

Sarah's tear-drenched eyes widen in shock. 'Beatrice?' she splutters, shutting the door.

'What the hell are you doing here, you vindictive bitch!'

'Mother!' Amalie yells, shocked.

I'm shocked. Sarah is definitely shocked, and then the door to Jesse's room swings open and he's standing there, shocked. I gasp and rush over to him, noting he's wrapped in a thin sheet at the waist and has dragged his drip and catheter frame with him. 'Jesse, for God's sake!'

'Mum?' He looks so confused and a little unsteady.

Jesse's mother's screwed-up face of hatred softens immediately at the sight of her son looking so pale and weak. 'Oh, Jesse, you stupid man. Get back in bed now!'

I look up and find nothing but puzzlement on his bearded, dazed face, and then I turn, seeing Beatrice clearly fighting her motherly instinct to put him back in bed herself. This is an incredibly bizarre situation, but as I watch Sarah skulk off quietly and see Amalie and Beatrice scanning Jesse's tall frame worriedly, I quickly snap back into action. 'Give me five minutes, Beatrice,' I say, pushing Jesse back into the room and shutting the door behind me. 'What do you think you're playing at? Get in bed!'

His mouth falls open to yell at me, but soon snaps shut again when he starts to sway.

'Oh shit!' I'll never catch him. 'Shit, shit, shit!' I drop my bag and frantically guide him back to the bed, but I can do nothing more than let him collapse in a heap of hard muscle. 'You're an idiot, Ward.' I'm so mad with him. 'Why can't you do what you're bloody told?' I sort his drip and catheter out before heaving his heavy legs into place and re-covering him with the sheet.

'I feel pissed,' he slurs, lifting his arm and draping it across his head.

'You got up too quickly.'

'What are they doing here, Ava?' he asks quietly. 'I don't want to see them.'

I quickly check his dressing before sitting on his bed and pulling his arm away from his hiding face. He looks at me with beseeching eyes. It kills me, but I'm going to try anyway.

'You have me, and I'm all you need, I know that, but this is a chance to put everything in your life right. Just give them a few minutes. I'm here for ever, no matter what, but I can't let you pass up an opportunity to find peace in this part of your life, Jesse.'

'I don't want anything to ruin what I have.' He grates the words through his clenched teeth, squeezing his eyes shut.

'Listen to me.' I grab his cheek and wiggle it, prompting him to open his eyes. 'After everything we have been through, do you really think there is anything else that could possibly fracture what we have?' If *that* is his only concern, then I'm even more determined to repair this. 'It'll be done on your terms. We'll take it slow, and they will accept it.'

'I only need you.' He slips his hand under my T-shirt and finds my tummy. 'Just you and our babies.'

I sigh, placing my hand over his. 'You don't have to want something to need it, Jesse. We're having twins. I know we have each other, but we'll need our families, too. And I'd like our children to have two sets of grandparents. We're not normal, but we should make our children's lives as normal as possible. It won't change us or what we have together.'

I can see him grasping my logic. His pale face mulls over my statement until he nods lightly and gingerly pulls me down, engulfing me with his arms. I relax into him, thankful that he will at least attempt to do this. I won't hold my breath for an instant remedy or reunion, but it's a start.

'Tell me you love me,' he says into my hair.

'I love you.'

'Tell me you need me.'

'I need you.'

'Okay.' He releases me. 'Plump my pillow, wife. I need to be comfy for this.'

I ignore his insolence and make him comfy. 'I'm going to give you some privacy.' I tell him, standing and making my way to the door.

'You're not staying?' he blurts, his green eyes bulging in panic.

'No. I don't need to. You'll be fine.' It takes every effort not to sit and hold his hand through this, but he needs to do it for himself. I might have played the babies card, but my reasons are far deeper than the need to have more family around us. Jesse needs to heal physically *and* mentally. Forgiving his parents will play a massive role in that.

I open the door and smile at Beatrice and Amalie, who have since been joined by Henry. I say nothing. I leave the door open for them and lose myself for a time while I let a lost family find themselves again.

Chapter 35

I'm in Paradise.

After Jesse got the all-clear from the doctors a full week after he awoke, we left the hospital, me leading him. He refused the wheelchair that was delivered to his room, which I wasn't surprised about at all. My big, strapping man had been laid up for three weeks, dependant on others to care for him, so I couldn't deny him the dignity of walking out of the hospital, even if it took us an hour. We returned to Lusso, where Cathy fussed and flapped around like a mother hen, ensuring cupboards were full, washing was done, and the whole place looked like it did on the launch night before it had been lived in. Then I gave her a few weeks off. We needed privacy in our home. I needed to look after Jesse. I needed to nurse him back to the man I know and love.

The first week was a washout. Streams of constant visitors plagued the penthouse, including Jesse's parents. It's still odd and a little strained, but I can see a light in my husband's eyes that I never have before. It's different to the sparkle of lust or the deepening in anger. This is peace.

The police paid numerous visits during that first week. It was probably too soon, but Jesse insisted on getting the chore out of the way so we could resume *our* normal. Patrick stopped by with my work colleagues, expressing his sincere apologies for putting me in such an awful situation, but he wasn't to know, and neither was poor Sal. She's well and truly back to dreary, plaid-skirt-wearing Sal, but she seemed happy enough. Mikael

withdrew from the deal to buy Rococo Union and Patrick offered me my job back, but I politely declined and Jesse didn't
try to convince me otherwise. I can't return to work, and I really
don't want to.

For the following three weeks after that first hectic one, there
was constant contact, just how he likes it. We bathed every
morning and indulged in hours of tub-talk. I re-dressed his
wound, he rubbed Bio Oil into my tummy. I cooked breakfast,
he fed it to us – both naked. He read his pregnancy manual out
loud, I listened intently. He chose to skim past the parts that
would put his ridiculous worries to rest, and I chose to snatch
the book from his hand and read those parts aloud to *him*. He
would scowl, I would grin. He wanted lots of sex, but I didn't
want to hurt him, which is ironic after the constant battle we've
had in this aspect of our relationship since I've been pregnant.
It's been hard. My raging hormones are not improving.

Now, four weeks later, I'm spreadeagled on the bed in the
main bedroom of Paradise. I'm naked and I'm basking at the
highest level of Central Jesse Cloud Nine.

'Comfy?'

My head lifts so my eyes can locate the whereabouts of my
Lord, finding him standing in the doorway of the bathroom,
naked, just how I like him.

'No, because you're not in here with me.' I pat the mattress,
and he blasts me with his smile, reserved only for me. He doesn't
lie next to me, though. He spreads my legs and crawls up between my thighs, resting his freshly shaved chin on my growing
tummy and looking up at me with those glorious greens.

'Good morning, my beautiful girl.'

'Good morning.' My fingers seek out his wet hair, and I sink
further into the bed on a contented sigh. 'What are we doing
today?'

'I have it all planned out,' he declares, nibbling on my midriff. 'You will do what you're told.'

'Does it involve cards?' I enquire casually, but far too hopefully. I'll ensure that I lose this time, so there will be no need for the transfer of power.

'No.'

I'm disappointed. 'Does it involve sleepy twilight sex?'

I feel him grin around the flesh that he's nibbling on. 'Maybe later.'

'Then I'll do whatever you want,' I advise him, my thighs clenching at the thought of sleepy twilight sex, and my mind wishing the day away so later gets here faster.

'Your day starts right now, Mrs Ward.' He plants a set of loud kisses around my belly button before sitting up and straddling me. He reaches over to the bedside cabinet and retrieves an envelope. 'Here.'

'What's this?' I ask on a frown, gingerly taking it from him. I don't like surprises from this man.

'Just open it.' My nerves increase when he commences nibbling that lip and I see cogs starting to fly.

I'm not sure that I want to open it, but curiosity is drowning my apprehension, so I slowly pull it open, flicking eyes back and forth between Jesse and the envelope. Slowly pulling out the piece of paper, I unfold and read the first line.

Haskett and Sandler Property Management

That means nothing to me. I read on, but I can't make head or tail of the legal lingo. I can make sense of the obscene amount of numbers that follow the pound sign halfway down the page, though.

'You've bought another house?' I blurt, looking over the paper at him. I say house but judging by the figure, which I now notice has the words 'For the sum of' written next to it, it could be a castle . . . or maybe even a palace.

'No, I've sold The Manor.' The lip biting has just sprung into the realms of cannibalism. He's chomping furiously as he gauges my reaction to that statement.

'You've what?' I'm trying to sit up, thinking maybe being upright might lessen the shock, but I won't find out because I'm being pushed back down to the bed.

'I've sold The Manor.' He lies down over me and clasps the sides of my face in his big palms.

'I heard you. Why?' I don't understand. I planted the seed, I know, but I never expected him to take a bit of notice.

He smiles down at me and lowers his lips to mine, teasingly. I'm desperate to know what has instigated this, but I'm also desperate, as always, for his magic mouth. I drop the document and fall straight into the rhythm he's set, finding his big shoulders and feeling my way up to his jaw. I'm distracted for now, but he won't get away without an explanation on this. The Manor is all he knows, even if he's not utilising the facilities any more.

'Hmmm, you taste heavenly, lady.' He bites my bottom lip, pulling back so it drags through his teeth lightly.

'Why?' I press, keeping him close to me and wrapping my thighs around his narrow hips. I'm not letting go until he spills.

He gazes at me thoughtfully for a few moments before drawing breath. 'You know when you're a kid? At primary school, I mean.'

'Yeah,' I say slowly, my brow scrunched up, my eyes undoubtedly inquisitive.

'Well . . .' he sighs. 'What the hell would I do if the babies asked me to go in for one of those open days these schools have?'

'Open day?'

'You know, when daddies stand up and tell their kids' classmates that they're a fireman or a copper.'

I squeeze my lips together, desperate not to laugh at him when it's clearly a worry.

'What would I say?' he asks seriously.

'You'd tell them you're The Lord of The Sex Manor.' It's no

good. I'm laughing. God love this man. My fast-disappearing hipbone is grasped and my laughter increases. 'Stop!'

'Sarcasm doesn't suit you, lady.'

'Please stop!'

I'm released and recovering from my bout of hysteria when I catch his concerned expression. He really is worried. 'You would tell them that you own a hotel, just like we'd tell the babies.' I can't believe I'm trying to give him an out.

He rolls onto his back, and I quickly resume position and sit myself on him. He grasps the tops of my thighs and looks up at me. 'I don't want it any more.'

'But it was Carmichael's baby. You wouldn't sell it when your mum and dad demanded it, so why now?'

'Because I have you three.'

'You'll always have us three, anyway.'

'I want you three and nothing to complicate that. I don't want to lie to our babies about my job. I would never allow them to spend any time there, which means my time with you and the babies would be limited. The Manor is an obstruction. I don't want any obstructions. I have a history, and The Manor should be part of it.'

I feel untold relief and the smile invading my face is proof of that. 'So I get you all day every day?'

He shrugs sheepishly. 'If you'll have me.'

I dive on him, smothering him all over his wonderfully handsome face. But I'm quickly sitting up again when I think of something. 'What about John and Mario? And Sarah? What about Sarah?' I have no loyalty to the woman, despite my compassion, but I don't want her attempting suicide again. However, John and Mario I love.

'I've spoken to them. Sarah's taking up an opportunity in the US and John and Mario are more than ready for retirement.'

'Oh,' I say in acceptance, but I suspect they've all picked up a tidy little sum for their services to The Manor, no matter in what capacity they served. 'And will the members renew under the new owners?'

He laughs. 'Yes, if they like playing golf.'

'Golf?'

He smiles. 'The grounds are being converted into an eighteen-hole golf course.'

'Wow. What about the sports facilities?' I ask.

'They're all staying. It'll be pretty impressive. Not much different to my set-up, except the private suites really will be hotel rooms and the communal room will serve as a conference room for businesses.'

'So that's it, then?'

'That's it. Now, I need to get you ready for the rest of your day.' He goes to sit up, but I pin him back down.

'I need to freshen up my mark.' I point to his pec, where my perfect circle has nearly disappeared. Then I look down at my own barely visible bruise. 'And you need to work on mine, too.'

'We'll do it later, baby.' I'm lifted and placed on my feet. 'Go take a shower.' He slaps my bum, sending me on my way, and I wander off without complaint and with a stupid smile on my face. No Manor, no Sarah and Jesse all to myself . . . and the babies.

After soaking myself under the lovely hot water and shaving everywhere, I dry my hair roughly and start rummaging through the wardrobe for something to wear.

'I've picked something,' he says from behind me, and I turn to see him wearing a pair of loose swimming shorts, holding up a short lace sundress.

'It's a bit short, isn't it?' I run my eyes up and down the delicate piece of clothing, with tiny straps and a floaty skirt.

'I'll make an exception.' He shrugs and unzips it before holding it at my feet. By that little statement, I assume we're not going anywhere public. I watch him kneel before me so I can step into the dress, and he secures me before standing back and clasping his chin in his hand thoughtfully. 'Cute.' He nods in approval and takes my hand, pulling me to the double doors that lead to the veranda.

'I need shoes.'

'We're paddling.' He dismisses my concern and leads on, walking around the veranda and over the grass until we're at the gate that leads down to the beach. 'Can we paddle on our backs?' I ask cheekily, and he stops, looking down at me with amused eyes.

'Pregnancy does wonderful things to you, Mrs Ward.'

I know my forehead has just wrinkled. 'I always want you this much.'

'I know you do. You're missing something.' He produces a small calla lily from behind his back and tucks it behind my ear. 'Much better.'

I reach up and feel the fresh flower, smiling up at him a little bemused, but far too content to enquire further. He winks, kisses my cheek and leads on, turning when we get to the sleepers to ensure I take them carefully. 'Watch that piece of splintered wood,' he says, pointing to a jagged edge on one of the sleepers. 'Careful.'

'You should have let me put some shoes on, then,' I say, skipping that step and leaping down to the next.

'Ava, no jumping. You'll shake the babies up.'

'Oh, shut up!' I laugh, jumping my way down the rest of the steps until my feet are warm and sinking into the golden sand. 'Come on!' I start to run down to the shore, but as soon as my head lifts from my feet to look where I'm going, I stop dead in my tracks.

They are all looking at me. Every single one of them. My eyes run down the line of people, noting everyone I know, including Jesse's family. I gasp, a little delayed, and swing round, finding Jesse towering over me, looking down at me on a smile.

'What are they doing here?' I ask.

'They're here to witness me marrying you.'

'But we're already married,' I remind him. 'We are, aren't we?' I'm suddenly considering the possibility of him announcing that we're not married at all, that The Manor, in fact, had no licence.

'Yes, we are. But my mum and dad missed our day, and we should have done it this way before.' He takes my hand and tugs my reluctant body gently, until I follow his lead down to the shoreline, where both of our families and all our friends are waiting, all smiling, all relaxed. They part, letting Jesse pull me through, and I look at each of them in turn, but all I get are happy faces. I can do no more than shrug a little, demonstrating my surprise. It's only now that I register Jesse's shorts are white and so is my sundress. We're getting married again?

I'm positioned in the wet sand with the gentle waves lapping at my feet, and then we're greeted by a man who looks as relaxed in his attire as Jesse, me and all of our guests. I'm quiet and accepting as he welcomes us and joins our hands in the space between our close bodies. I repeat the words being asked of me as I look up into Jesse's addictive eyes and smile around each and every word I say to him. I reaffirm everything. I renew my promise to love, honour and obey him and I reach up to kiss him gently on his luscious lips when I'm done. I'm on autopilot, just doing what is asked of me, but not because I don't know what else to do, but simply because it's what I'm supposed to do. Despite everything, I entrust myself to this man. He leads the way and I follow. Because I know it's where I belong.

When it's his turn to speak, the registrar steps away and Jesse moves in closer, lifting both of my hands with his and resting his lips on them, leaving them lingering for the longest time. 'I love you,' he whispers, stroking his thumbs where his lips have just left. 'An eternity with you wouldn't be enough, Ava. From the moment my eyes fell on you, I knew things would change for me. I plan on devoting every second of my life to worshipping you, adoring you and indulging in you, and I plan on making up for empty years without you. I'm taking you to Paradise, baby.' He stoops and clasps me under my bum, lifting me high so it's now him looking up at me. 'Are you ready?'

'Yes. Take me,' I demand, running my hands into his hair and giving it a yank.

'Oh, I took you long ago, Mrs Ward. But right now is where it really begins.' He kisses me hard. 'No more digging to get beneath me. You know everything there is to know. And no more confessions because I have nothing left to tell.'

'I think you have,' I whisper, nuzzling into his neck and taking a hit of him in all of his fresh-water, minty loveliness.

'I do?' he asks, carrying me into the glimmering coolness of the Med.

'You do. Tell me you love me.'

He pulls back, green eyes sparkling, my smile gracing his perfect mouth and his dirty-blond hair a glorious, dishevelled mess with my hands tugging demandingly at it. 'I love you so fucking much, baby.'

I smile, dropping my head back and closing my eyes as he starts spinning us in circles, the sun warming my face and his body close to mine warming everywhere else.

'*I know!*' I scream, laughing before we're under the water and homing straight in on each other's lips. I cling onto him like my life depends on it because it absolutely does.

This is it. This is us. This will be our normal for ever and ever, no more shocking discoveries and no more confessions. His two perfect mars on his insanely perfect stomach are a constant reminder of our journey together, but the relentless gleam of happiness in his shockingly green eyes is a continuous reminder that I still have this man.

And I always will.

Bonus Scene from Jesse's perspective

Life is good. Actually, it's fucking amazing. Constant contact. And I've had it for six straight months. If this is my Angel's idea of Central Jesse Cloud Nine, then it's my most favourite place in the world, too.

Her pregnant belly is perfectly round, and I've definitely noticed it drop over the past few weeks. I've also noticed an air of tranquillity floating around her in recent days. It's the most beautiful sight. Nothing will ever beat the vision of her glowing face as she potters around the penthouse with my babies growing inside her. I think she might be at that nesting stage. I've read about it. Everything is spotless, but she keeps going over the same routine, even after Cathy's seen to it all. She seems to have developed a bit of a growl, too, so I've stopped trying to intervene with her pregnancy habits – the best habit of all being me. I'm close to fucking exhaustion, not that I would dream of telling her so, or dream of denying her. If she wasn't so irresistible herself, I might feel used and abused.

Kicking my feet up onto my desk, I rest my head back and stare at my wall, smiling when I hear the Hoover kick in upstairs. Works are still under way on the new house, our little manor, but I'm keeping the penthouse. Everywhere I look, Ava is there, whether it be one of those irritating scatter cushions, a huge lump of furniture ... or her face splashed all over my office wall. My eyes only. That'll never change.

A smile of utter contentment spreads across my face but soon drops away when I jump at the sound of an almighty crash above my head. What the fuck was that? I fly up from my chair, my heart pounding instantly. 'Ava!'

I sprint from my office and take the stairs four at a time, crashing into our bedroom, my eyes darting all over the place until they land on my girl. She's clutching her tummy.

'Ava, fucking hell!' I'm by her side in a second, my hands running all over her face. She turns those deep-chocolate eyes onto me. They're full of fear. I'm starting to shake, despite my best effort to remain calm and collected. 'Fucking hell! Is it time?' I barely get the words out. Fuck me, I've been preparing for this, training myself to be all calm, but I can't stop my damn heart from clattering in my chest. 'Shit, Ava, tell me! Is it time? Are the babies coming?'

She straightens, releases her tummy and grins that little fucking grin. 'No.' She takes my hand and kisses my wedding ring. 'But it'll never get old.'

I practically crumble to the floor in relief. 'Damn it, Ava, you'll fucking kill me off!'

She gasps again, her hands resuming position on her bump.

'Oh no!' I laugh. 'You have to leave at least ten minutes between pranks.' She's taking this too far now. But then I hear an audible pop followed by a gushing sound. 'What the fuck was that?' I look down, seeing liquid running down her bare legs. My heart beats up to my throat and chokes me. I can't breathe.

'My waters.' She exhales, then doubles over on a shriek that nearly bursts my eardrums. 'Fucking hell, Jesse!'

I don't know what to do. She's not playing now, I'm certain, and rather than gathering her hospital bag and calmly walking her to the door, I scold her instead. 'Ava, watch your fucking mouth!'

'Oooooohhhhh, shit!' She starts panting, short, sharp breaths, just how we practised. 'Fucking hell! Ward, you'd better get some fucking earplugs. *Fuck!*'

'Ava!' I'm useless, just standing here doing nothing except registering her string of foul language.

'Jesse.' She's still panting. 'Remember how we practised this a million fucking times?'

Yes, we did, but I can't remember a fucking thing. Phone! I scoop her up and go in search of my mobile, taking the stairs fast down to my office.

'Jesse, leave me on the bed!'

'I'm not leaving you alone, lady.' I burst into my office and place her in my chair, immediately swiping up my phone and calling the big guy. 'John! It's time, it's time!' I start pacing up and down, my eyes darting to Ava every few seconds and noting a pained, sweaty face. 'They're too early! Fuck, they said four weeks early, not six!'

'I'm on my way. Do you remember the drill?' John asks me calmly.

'No! I can't remember fuck all!'

'Is she okay?'

'I don't know!' I yell, just as Ava lets out a strangled gasp.

'You?' he asks. I can hear humour in his tone. He's laughed his way through this pregnancy.

'Shit, John, I'm fucking useless,' I admit, making it to Ava and stroking her sweaty brow as she draws long breaths.

'You need to time the contractions, you stupid motherfucker.'

'Right!' I immediately glance down at my watch. 'Hurry up.' I hang up and swivel my office chair so she's facing me. 'Tell me when the next one comes, baby.' I crouch between her thighs.

'Now!' she screams in my face, nearly knocking me on my arse. 'Fuck fuck fuck!'

I hold back on my scorn for fear of being punched in the face and stand her up like we practised, placing her hands on my shoulders and watching my Rolex over her head. Her short nails sink into my flesh through my T-shirt as she braces herself on me and wails and moans. She even sinks her teeth into me, and it's the only time in the history of our relationship that the action hasn't made my cock immediately hard.

I can do no more than whisper encouraging words in her ear, accept her vicious scratching and biting, and hold her up. And the whole time, my heart pounds with fear and excitement. It's time to meet my babies.

'Twenty-four fucking hours!' I yell, doing an aboutturn and marching back down the corridor. 'This can't be fucking normal!' I'm scowled at by a passing couple, but I couldn't give a fuck. 'What the hell are you looking at?' I yell, making them walk faster to escape the loon prowling the hospital corridor.

John shakes his head and strides over, grabbing my shoulders with his big palms and holding me in place. 'Calm the fuck down, you stupid motherfucker.'

'I am!' My hands find my hair and yank. 'It's too fucking long. She's exhausted, John. Fucking hell, when is enough enough?'

'You heard the midwife. It's all perfectly normal and she's doing great.' He knocks my jaw with his big fist on a laugh. I don't know what he finds so fucking funny. 'You need to calm the fuck down and get back to your girl.'

'Oh Jesus, John, I don't know if I can take any more. It's killing me.' I feel like a complete wanker for saying such a thing, given the pain my angel is going through, but fuck me, I've never felt anything like it. I'm powerless.

He shakes me and lands me with a furious glare. 'Pull your shit together, Jesse. She needs you.'

Those words snap me straight out of my meltdown. She needs me. I barge back into the room, just as the midwife shouts, 'Push, darling!'

'Jesse!' she screams, her head flying forward, her face bright red. 'Where the *fuck* have you been?'

The midwife doesn't bat an eyelid at Ava's foul mouth, instead cocking her head at me to shift my arse. 'Mr Ward, you're of no use in the corridor.'

My eyes are wide, my body frozen on the spot until the midwife shakes her head in exasperation and comes to retrieve my static body from the doorway, guiding me over to the bed and placing me next to Ava.

'Pull yourself together, for goodness' sake,' the midwife says calmly, like my wife isn't in fucking agony. 'Okay, Ava,' she places a reassuring hand on Ava's bent knee, 'we'll have a few more goes, and then we might need to think about other options, darling.'

'No!' Ava snaps, then commences panting again. 'I'm having these babies naturally!' I don't have the mental power to tell my eyes to roll. She's insisted on no drugs and no scars, my stubborn, beautiful girl.

The midwife starts laughing. 'Things don't always go to plan during labour, Ava. Especially when twins are involved.'

'There's another coming!' she puffs out fast spurts of air and holds her hand out to me. 'Jesse!'

My hand flies out and clasps hers and I move right in, doing what feels right. I put my face straight into her wet neck, crowding her completely. 'I love you,' I whisper, like an idiot, not knowing what else to say. 'What the fucking hell did I do to deserve you?'

She moans into my neck, rolling her head from side-to-side. 'Make it stop. I can't take any more.' Her lips push into my flesh, her fists clamping in my hair.

'One last try, baby.' I turn my face into her to find her lips, kissing her softly. There are no sparks of desire, just pure, raw love. 'Together, okay?'

She nods against me and resumes her nuzzle in my neck. Then I feel her whole body tense; her mouth opens against my throat and her grip of my hair crosses the line into violence. She screams, her teeth sinking into my flesh, one hand pulling my hair, the other digging into my bicep. I blank it out, all of the pain she's inflicting on me, even though I'm certain it's nothing compared to what she's experiencing right now ... which means she must feel like she's being fucking tortured. I clench my teeth. Fucking hell! I'm yanked about, released from her punishing bite so she can scream some more before her teeth go straight back in and her nails scratch at me, my hair probably coming out in fistfuls.

'That's it, Ava!' the midwife shouts before calling for her colleague's assistance. 'Oh my, we have a girl!'

Those words hit me like a sledgehammer. I can't feel anything now, not a thing, but I can hear. A rush of activity is happening behind me, Ava is still intermittently screaming, my heart is pounding in my ears ... and there's something else – something that has just injected further life into me. A baby crying. I have a little girl. I'm a daddy again.

'Another push, Ava. Come on, girl!' The midwife sounds excited.

'No more,' Ava cries in my ear. 'Please.'

Through my numb state, I inject some strength into my muscles and use everything I have to squeeze some comfort into her, nestling into her hair and latching onto her neck with my teeth. I lightly bite her before kissing her, lightly biting and kissing, again and again and again. I can't talk – can't speak any words of encouragement, so I focus all of my attention on touching her, feeling her, speaking to her through our contact. It's our silent language, in which we are both fluent. She returns my squeeze, acknowledging me, and then lets out an ear-piercing yell. It's an angry yell. And it goes on and on until she eventually sags beneath me, every harsh grip she has of me loosening to allow me to relax into her.

There's another cry.

'A boy!'

My heart has just burst, an incredible sense of peace and serenity engulfing me.

We both remain huddled on the bed, Ava heaving, me unable to hold my tears any longer. I sob relentlessly into her neck. My exhausted heart is showing no sign of letting up and I know it probably won't for the rest of my life. I haven't even set eyes on them yet. I haven't smelled them, felt them or told them how much I love them. But my heart is beating faster than ever before, and I never would have thought that possible. Now I have three angels.

'Mr Ward?'

I hear the distant voice, and I know I should be jumping up, but I can't move and when a few moments pass and I'm still frozen in place, I feel Ava shift under me. 'Can we have a few moments?' she asks.

'Of course,' the midwife says softly.

'Are they okay?'

'They're perfect, Ava. Have your moment, but don't be too long. You're a mummy now.'

'Thank you.' Ava's voice is soft and calm as she resumes her hold of me and sighs into my neck, softly stroking my hair and dropping small kisses on my skin every now and then. No words need to be spoken – not for a very long while. It's her comforting me now. And I need it. I need to keep hold of her. It's one of the only ways I can be sure that all of this is real. She eventually pulls back, searching out my clouded eyes, and as soon as hers land on mine, reality is confirmed. My reality. I'm not dreaming. 'Go and meet your babies,' she says, smoothing her small palm down my rough cheek. 'It was twenty-six years before I found you. Don't make them wait for you a moment longer than they have to.' She pecks my lips and then looks over my shoulder and I muster up the courage to slowly turn and finally introduce myself to my babies.

*

'Let Daddy tell you a story,' I whisper. 'A story about a defiant little temptress and a godlike creature. That's me, by the way. The god. The temptress is your beautiful mother.' I look down at my babies lying on my bare chest, one curled on each pec, both sleeping peacefully. I push my lips to the tops of their heads in turn, closing my eyes and inhaling them into me, like it might make me physically closer. Maddie stirs, and I still as she nuzzles her face into me, her eyes shut tight, her little fists balled by her tiny mouth. And then Jacob whimpers in response, performing the same little string of movements before they both settle together. Damn it, I'm going to fucking cry again.

'You okay?'

I look up and find Ava standing in the doorway of the nursery, only one of my shirts covering her petite frame. 'Shhhh.' I cock my head gently, urging her to come and join me. She pads softly across the carpet and eases down next to me, working around the babies to push her lips into my cheek. 'I'm telling them a bedtime story.'

Her head rests on my bicep, her palm spread across both of our babies' little rumps. 'Does it have a happy ever after?' she asks quietly.

'It does,' I sigh.

'Can I listen too?'

I smile and nestle my face between the babies' heads again, taking another hit of that incredible baby scent. 'There was this man,' I begin quietly. 'Good-looking fucker, fit, toned, confident, strong . . . pretty much amazing at everything—'

'Except cooking,' she interrupts, turning her mouth onto my bicep and gently sinking her teeth in.

'Except cooking,' I agree, my smile widening. 'He was a little lost when she found him. She was his angel.' Her face turns up to me and our eyes lock as she reaches up to kiss me. 'This man was quite taken by the angel,' I say against her lips, feeling her smile. She cuddles back into my side on a sigh and I resume my own nuzzle between my babies' heads. 'Every time she was near, this funny feeling came over him and he had no idea what to make of it. It kind of sent him a little crazy.'

She hums quietly and begins stroking my forearm.

'She was too beautiful for words,' I whisper. 'And this man had seen some beautiful women in his time.' I smile when she nudges me, but she doesn't say anything. 'But this woman was something else. He didn't think she could be real, but when he looked into her eyes, something happened.'

'What happened?' she asks quietly, snuggling closer, warming me further.

'His heart started beating again.' I know she knows this, but her tender kiss on my arm confirms she likes hearing the words. 'For the first time in for ever, he felt alive.' Jacob stirs, rubbing his nose into my bare chest on a tiny whimper.

Ava's palm shifts to his back and starts circling softly. It settles him immediately. 'Shhhh,' she breathes. The sight of her natural way with them only enhances my constant sense of bliss.

I watch my three angels settle again and take a long pull of breath. 'He knew she wanted him,' I say on a steady exhale.

'How?'

'Because those eyes told him so. Every time he looked into them, he saw salvation for him and addiction for her.'

'She's still addicted to him,' she proclaims, making me smile.

'I know. She couldn't resist him, and that was the only hope he had. He made it his mission objective to turn that addiction into need and if he could do that, then he hoped that need would turn into . . . love. He wanted to look after her for ever. Nothing and no one existed any more – just her and the incredible feelings they shared. She smiled and set his heart alight. She spoke and made his ears ring with pleasure. She touched him and he would stop breathing for a few moments before his heart speeded up some more. She became his everything.'

'Those feelings are still incredible,' Ava murmurs, sounding sleepy.

'It's still bliss, baby. Total gratification. Absolute, complete, earth-shifting, universe-shaking love.' I drop my gaze down to my perfect babies and sigh, my eyes brimming with tears of pure, powerful love. 'And now we get to share that love with these two little people and live happily ever after.'

Epilogue

Five Years Later

Fuck me, how long have I got to endure my home being bombarded and my wife and babies being hogged? Too fucking long, that's how long. I should snatch their gifts and throw them a piece of cake before shutting the door in their face. I smile on the inside, picturing Elizabeth's face if I did exactly that. This is going to be painful, and to rub salt into my moody wounds, we have school friends this year, too. And their mothers – lots of women, who have taken Ava up on her offer to stay, if they would like to. And, of course, they would like to.

My stroppy feet are pounding down the staircase of our lovely little manor, as I button up my shirt and chew my lip, thinking of any excuse to avoid this. I come up with nothing. My babies are five years old today, and not even Daddy's amazing negotiation tactics will convince them that a party is a bad idea – not now that they have their own minds. I've tried for the last four years and fallen flat on my face, but only because my beautiful wife always intervened on their behalf. I know this year, though, if I got them alone, I could break them down with something. Skiing again, perhaps?

Hitting the bottom of the stairs, I take a quick glimpse in the mirror and smile. I get better-looking every day. I've still got it, and she still can't resist me. Life is fucking good.

'Daddy!'

I spin around, and my hard muscles liquefy as I watch my baby boy running down the stairs, his dark-blond hair a tousled mess around his handsome little face. 'Hey, birthday boy.' His greens sparkle as he launches himself at me, the good-looking little fucker. 'Whoa!' I laugh as he slams into me, crawling up my body.

'Guess what?' he asks me, eyes wide with excitement.

'What?' I'm not feigning interest. I really am curious.

'Nana 'Lizabeth said we can sleep at her house tonight. She's taking us to the zoo tomorrow!'

I try to conceal my scowl and match his excitement. 'Nana 'Lizabeth lives too far away, and Daddy likes taking you to the zoo,' I say, throwing him up onto my shoulders and turning back towards the mirror. 'See how handsome we are?'

'I know,' he replies flippantly, making me smile. 'Nana and Pappy live ten minutes away. I timed it on Mummy's phone.'

I'm swiftly reminded that my dear mother-in-law does, in fact, live ten minutes away. The beauty of Newquay couldn't keep Elizabeth and Joseph away from their grandchildren – or *my* babies, more to the point. 'Hey, I was thinking . . .' I go for subject change, or distraction tactics – whichever. 'We should go skiing again.' I'm speaking in a stupidly over-enthusiastic voice, hoping to snare him.

'We already are.' His little hands rest on my forehead, covering the frown that's just jumped into place.

'We are?'

'Yes, Mummy said so, and she said not to listen to you if you try to put us off our party.'

My shoulders sag, and I make a mental note to deliver on one retribution fuck, the conniving little temptress. 'Mummy needs Daddy's money to do that.' I'm shameless.

'Why don't you want us to have a party, Daddy?' His little forehead matches mine in the frown department, and I instantly feel like a bag of shit.

'I do, mate. I just don't like sharing you,' I admit.

'You can play, too.' He reaches down and kisses my rough cheek. 'Mummy will be pleased.'

'Why will she?' I know why she'll be pleased. She's intercepted me. Make that two retribution fucks – one for her interception and one for her smugness.

'Because you've not shaved.' He rubs his palm up and down a few times, and I smile at my handsome little man before striding towards the kitchen.

I halt at the doorway and spend a few moments drinking in the sight of my angel frantically stirring a big mixing bowl of some brown shit, the curve of her perfect arse holding me rapt. Fucking perfect. My little man doesn't pester me to push onward. He just sits happily on my shoulders, waiting for his spellbound father to snap back into action. He's used to me daydreaming, especially when his mother's around. I have no fucking clue what I've done to deserve this woman and these beautiful kids, but I won't be arguing with the destiny gods.

'Shit!' She curses as a blob of chocolate flies up and lands on her olive cheek.

'Mummy! Watch your mouth!'

She swings around, armed with a wooden spoon lathered in chocolate, and scowls at my grinning face before turning her big brown orbs onto our son. 'I'm sorry, Jacob.'

My grin widens and her scowl deepens. I'm so smug, and I'll pay for it later. She can't play the defiant little temptress with our babies around, and I love it. 'What you making, baby?' I ask, lifting Jacob from my shoulders and placing him on a stool. I hand him my phone to play with before heading to the fridge and collecting a jar of Sun-Pat.

'Peanut butter cups.' She's all flustered, but I'm not offering my help. She knows I'm shit at cooking, and I'm not making this easier. Next year, I'm predicting skiing.

I'm behind her, looking down into the bowl, and I'm thinking that I might stick to jars. God bless her, she's tried a million times, but she'll never match my mum's famous peanut butter cups. 'How many jars of my peanut butter have you wasted on that?' I ask, pushing myself into her back and not missing the opportunity to feel her neck out with my lips. She smells too good.

'Two.' She pushes the bowl away. 'I want Cathy back.'

I laugh and spin her around, pushing her into the worktop, the wooden spoon waving in my face. I'm firming up, damn it. I can't help it. I lean in, as I watch her watching me, and lick her cheek clean.

'Don't start something you can't finish, Ward,' she whispers on a husky, alluring voice. I'm solid now.

Fucking hell!

She pushes me away on a knowing grin. 'I need to finish. Guests will be arriving.' She's smug again, earning herself a third retribution fuck. She knows what she's doing – she knows there will be no countdowns or trampling with the babies around.

Or baby.

'Where's Maddie?' I discreetly adjust my groin area before facing my baby boy, who's oblivious to the goings on around him. It's not unusual to see Daddy loving Mummy. I've had to seriously work on my control, though.

He doesn't look up from my phone, but I can see his little face screw up in disgust. 'She's putting on her party dress. It's all frilly. Nana bought it.'

My eyes roll, knowing that I'm going to find my baby girl looking like candyfloss has exploded all over her. 'Why does your mother think *my* daughter needs to look like she's been attacked with the pink stick?' I sit myself next to Jacob and put the jar between us so he can help himself. And he does. His chubby little finger dives right in and scoops out the biggest dollop. My chest swells with pride, and I exhale around my own finger, looking back up to Ava for an answer.

Her eyebrows are high as she shakes her head at Jacob on a

fond smile, but then her eyes are on me and she's not smiling any more. What did I do? 'Don't wind her up, Jesse.'

'I won't!' I laugh. I bloody will, and I'll enjoy every moment of it.

'Nana calls you a menace.' Jacob looks up at me, his finger still hanging from his mouth. 'She said you always have been and always will be. She accepts it now.' His little shoulders shrug.

A burst of laughter escapes and now Ava is laughing with me, her dreamy chocolate eyes sparkling, her succulent lips begging me to take them. Then she ditches the apron, revealing her tight, tidy little figure. I'm not laughing now. I'm panting and reaching under the table to try and bash myself down. It's a constant fucking battle. 'I like your dress.' My eyes take a lazy jaunt down the length of her black fitted dress as I plan on how I'll remove it later. I might be kind and let her wear it again, she really does look amazing in it, but by later, I know I won't be in any fit state to take my time.

'You like all of Mummy's dresses,' Jacob pipes up tiredly, snapping my eyes from that body – the one that sends me insane with want.

'I do,' I agree, giving his messy mop of blond a ruffle. 'Speaking of dresses, I'm going to find your sister.'

'Okay,' he agrees, turning his attention back to my phone and dipping his finger again.

I jump up and go in search of Maddie, taking the stairs two at a time and bursting into her pink-infested room. 'Where's my birthday girl?'

'Here!' she squeals, appearing from her Wendy house.

I nearly choke on thin air. 'You are *not* wearing that, little lady!'

'Yes, I am!' She runs across the room when I start marching towards her.

'Maddie!' What the fucking hell? She's five! Five fucking

years old, and I'm already ripping hot pants and cropped T-shirts from her tiny body. Where the fuck is that frilly pink thing?

'Mummy!' she screams, as I catch her ankle on the bed. She can scream the fucking house down. She is *not* wearing that. 'Mummy!'

'Maddie, come here!'

'No!' She kicks me – the little sod kicks me and dashes out of the room, leaving me a pathetic heap of stressed-out daddy on her pink, fluffy bed. I've been outdone by a five-year-old little girl. But that little girl is the daughter of my beautiful wife. I'm fucked.

I stand and straighten myself out before going in pursuit. 'Don't run down the stairs, Maddie!' I yell, practically throwing myself down them after her. I watch her tiny little hot-panted arse disappear into the kitchen as she searches for the back-up of her mother.

I skid to a halt and watch her scrambling up Ava's body. 'What's going on?' Ava asks, looking at me like I've lost my mind. I might have.

'Look at her!' I wave my hands at my baby girl like a deranged screwball. 'Look!'

Ava places her on the floor and crouches down, pushing my baby's chocolate waves over her little shoulders and pulling the hem of that ridiculous T-shirt down. She can pull it down all she fucking likes. It's not staying on my baby's body. 'Maddie,' Ava's gone into pacifying mode, something, perhaps, I should have thought about before blurting the death words. I should have learned by now: don't tell Maddie no. It's rule number fucking one. 'Daddy thinks your T-shirt is a little small.'

'I do,' I cut in, just for clarification. 'Way too small.'

My little lady flips me a scowl. 'He's being unreasonable.'

I gasp and point an accusing glare at Ava. She has the decency to look apologetic. 'See what you've done?'

'Daddy has the power!' Jacob sings, halting any chance I had of scoring a win.

It's Ava who's gasping now. 'You need to remember, Ward. These little ears hear everything.'

I do the sensible thing and shut the fuck up. My wife can't hide her exasperation, and I don't expect her to. I expect her to remove that pathetic excuse of a T-shirt from my baby girl's tiny body.

'He can't dictate my wardrobe!' Maddie fires across the kitchen, her chubby arms folding across her little chest. I look at my defiant temptress, noting she's failing to hide that fucking beautiful grin.

Fucking hell! My hands fly to my hair and yank. I'll have none of the fucking stuff left soon, especially when Ava gets her hands on it. I momentarily forget my turmoil and smile, mentally feeling her tugging at it while I slam into that beautiful body. But I'm soon back to reality with my little lady drilling displeased brown eyes into me.

I watch as Ava reasons with her before grasping her little shoulders and turning her toward me. 'Maddie is ready to compromise.' Ava tilts her head with a *humour her* look.

It doesn't make me feel any better. I've humoured Maddie before, and it resulted in me carting her out of Waitrose over my shoulder while she screamed the place down and kicked me to death. I look back to Ava with pleading eyes, pouting like an idiot, but she just shakes her head and gently urges my wilful little lady towards me.

She's smiling at me now, her arms reaching up for me to take her. She melts my fucking heart but Jesus Christ, what the hell am I facing in the years to come? I'll be bald or maybe even dead. Or I could be in prison because if any little fucker lays his hands on her, I'll rip their fucking heart out. I scoop her up and leave Ava to help my easy-going boy put his Converses on.

'Dad, you need to calm down. You'll give yourself a heart

attack.' She snuggles into my neck and my raging, crazy love for my defiant little lady is fully restored. But my wife gets her fourth retribution fuck of the day.

'It's Daddy. And you need to stop listening to your mother.' I take the stairs fast and burst into her room, throwing her on the bed. My heart bursts, listening to her squeal in delight before she jumps straight up and starts bouncing up and down, her long, chocolate locks flying all over the place. 'Right.' I rub my hands together in an attempt to make what I'm about to suggest exciting. Where will I find her jeans and jumpers? I pull her pink wardrobe doors open and start skimming through the rails, immediately laying my hands on something full and frilly. I pull it out and hold the hideous thing up. She mirrors my look of disgust. 'Your nana needs to stop buying you dresses.'

'I know.' She sits down and crosses her legs. 'Will you trample her today, Dad?'

'Daddy,' I retort, shoving the dress on the top shelf, out of sight. 'I might do.'

'It's funny,' she giggles.

'I know.' I pull out a cute little sailor dress. There are no sleeves, but I'll find a cardigan. 'How about this?'

'No, Dad.'

'Daddy. What about this?' I present her with a lemon, shin-length brocade thing, but she shakes her defiant little head. 'Maddie,' I sigh. 'You are not wearing that.' God give me fucking strength quick before I wring her stubborn little neck.

'I'll wear tights.' She jumps up and pulls the drawer of her pink chest open. 'These ones,' she says, holding up some candy-striped things.

I tilt my head on an agreeable nod. I can work with that. 'What about the T-shirt?'

She looks down and strokes her little belly. 'I like this one.'

'Then how about we buy it in a bigger size?' I'm compromising. I pull down a long-sleeved, mint-green T-shirt covered in love hearts and hold it up, all keen and smiley. 'I love this one. Make Daddy happy.' I'm fucking pouting like a sad, desperate twat, and I can tell her five-year-old mind thinks I'm a twat, too.

'Okay,' she sighs heavily. This is stupid. She's the one humouring *me*.

'Good girl.' I pick her up and stand her on the bed. 'Lift.' She throws her arms in the air and lets me rid her torso of the half T-shirt before replacing it with the green one that I love so much. Then I get her out of the shorts and cover her little legs with the delightful candy-striped tights before replacing the little denim things. 'Perfect.' I stand back and nod my approval, then collect her silver Converse hi-tops from the wardrobe. 'These?' I don't know why I'm asking; she refuses to wear anything else.

'Yep.' She falls to her cute little butt and holds her foot up for me to slip them on. 'Daddy?'

I tense from head to toe at the sound of the name I'm constantly demanding she call me. She wants something. 'Maddie,' I reply slowly, cautiously.

'I'd like a little sister.'

I nearly fall on my arse with laughter. Another girl? Fuck me, you'd have to drug me and string me up to extract my seed. Not a fucking chance, no way in hell, never, no way.

'What's so funny?' She looks at my laughing face, all puzzled.

'Me and Mummy are happy with just you two,' I pacify her, quickly getting the other shoe on, eager to escape this room *and* the conversation.

'Mummy wants another baby,' she informs me, and my shocked eyes fly up to serious chocolate ones. Ava wants another baby? But she hated pregnancy. I loved it. She hated it. I loved everything about it, except the birth. She really got her revenge during that hellish twenty-four hours. I was stabbed with nails, yelled at constantly and threatened with divorce on numerous occasions. And her mouth was like a fucking sewer. But what killed me the most was seeing her in so much pain and being unable to stop it. I could do fuck all about it, and I *never* plan on putting her through that again.

'We just need you two,' I affirm, lifting her from the bed and placing her on her tiny, silver-coated feet.

'I know.' She runs off laughing. 'Mum said your eyes would bug and they did!'

I actually laugh, but not because it's funny. It's not. It's because I'm so fucking relieved. I could never refuse Ava if she did want another baby, not after my fucked-up, creative way of getting us our adorable carbon copies of each other. I smile, a full-on smile, the one I save only for my babies. I'm so glad I hid those pills.

It really is the longest afternoon of my fucking life. Dozens of kids run around screaming, and their mothers pretend to be watching their offspring, but I'm under constant surveillance by the desperate bunch of bored housewives. Maybe I should ditch the personal training and invest some time in advising the husbands of these women how to please them – lessons in various degrees of fucking, perhaps. I'm nodding thoughtfully to myself when my mum appears in my line of sight. She's got that look, and I know I'm about to be lectured.

'Son, take it easy.' She eyes up the bottle of Bud in my hand, prompting me to take a swig.

I walk over to her and tuck her anxious body into my side. 'Mother, stop your fussing.' I start leading her over to the decking, where my father, Amalie and Doctor David are all sitting, chatting happily. My babies couldn't keep my parents away, either.

'I just . . .' She stammers over her words, placing her wrinkled palm on my stomach and rubbing lightly. 'I just worry, that's all.'

I know she does, but she has no need to. I can enjoy a few beers, just like the rest of them, and I can do it in a relaxed atmosphere with my family. I still don't touch the vodka, though. 'Well, I said you shouldn't, so you won't. End of.' I encourage her to take a seat next to my father. 'Do you want a beer, Dad?'

He looks up at me on a smile. 'No, son. I promised Jacob a few bounces on that inflatable thing.' He points across the lawns and I turn, seeing dozens of kids, pumped up on E-numbers, jumping and screaming on the bouncy castle.

'Good luck!' David laughs, resting his hand on his pregnant wife's bulging belly. I smile fondly and watch my dad slowly make his way over to Jacob, who's frantically waving for his granddad. And then I spot Elizabeth kneeling in front of Maddie, tying her locks in fucking bunches.

'Leave her alone, Mum!' I shout across the garden, earning myself a filthy look from Elizabeth and a giggle from my little lady.

'Trample, Daddy!' Maddie shrieks, batting her nana's hand away from her hair and running off to reclaim her tree house.

I'm grinning as I watch Ava's long-suffering mother pull herself to her feet. I can't help it. She turns a frighteningly dirty look on me, making me grin further. Nothing gives me greater pleasure than rubbing her up the wrong way, but she doesn't do a bad job of returning the favour, so I'm not going to beat myself up about it. I'll just keep enjoying it.

'Why did your daughter have to be like you?' she yells across to me.

I nearly spit my beer out. 'Me?'

'Yes, you! Challenging!'

I scoff. She has to be joking. 'I think you'll find that my little lady is the prodigy of *your* daughter. Defiant!'

She huffs and puffs, straightening out her blouse before heading to the kitchen to help Ava. Challenging? The stupid woman doesn't know what she's fucking talking about.

Leaving my mum with Amalie and David, I stroll over to our friends, who have all, unsurprisingly, taken up residence by the bar.

'My man!' Sam slaps my back and John nods as I dip so Kate can kiss my cheek.

'Everyone good?' I ask, collapsing into one of the chairs. 'Where's Drew?'

Kate laughs, pointing to the bouncy castle where Drew is scrambling through the masses of kids to find his daughter. 'He's making sure that Georgia returns to her mother with no cuts or bruises.'

'Talking of kids,' I point my bottle between Kate and Sam, and fail to maintain my seriousness when John's body starts shaking, making the whole fucking house vibrate behind me with that deep, rolling laugh.

'Jesse,' she breathes, exhausted by the constant question. 'I've told you. There is not a maternal bone in this body.'

'You manage my babies all right,' I point out. She's great with them.

'Yes; that is because I get to hand the adorable creatures back to you when I'm fed up with them.' She grins, and I match it, raising my bottle for her to chink.

'I'm going to find my wife.' I stand back up, keen to locate her and advise her on what exactly I plan on doing to her later.

Where is she?

I find her in the kitchen with Cathy, who has taken over food preparations. 'There's my boy!' my old housekeeper sings, reaching up to kiss my cheek before exiting the kitchen with a tray full of tiny sandwiches, crusts cut off. 'I'll tell Clive to gather the children. Wonderful day!'

Watching her leave, I turn slowly until my eyes find what they're looking for. She's watching me closely, and those eyes are smoking out. She'll never get enough of me.

'I've missed you.' I stalk forward, placing my bottle on the worktop as I pass. The tea towel is dropped from her hands, and she's leaning back on the counter, willing me on, the little temptress.

I'm not gentle. I grab her and pin her to the wall, my mouth falling to the sweet flesh of her neck. 'Jesse, don't,' she exhales, arching herself into my chest.

'Later, I'm ripping this dress off and I'm going to fuck you into next year.'

She moans, raising her bare knee and rubbing it lightly over my solid cock.

Control, control, control. Fucking control!

'Deal,' she wisely agrees, not that she has a choice. Wherever, whenever, she knows that. But not fucking now.

I growl my frustration and rip my body from hers. 'I fucking love you.'

'I know.' She smiles, but it doesn't make her eyes sparkle like usual.

'What's up, baby?' I hunker down to get my face level with hers. 'Tell me.'

She sighs and flicks me almost nervous eyes. 'I wish Dan was here.'

It takes every ounce of my love for this woman not to roll my eyes or growl in frustration. The bloke rubs me up the wrong way, I can't help it. 'Hey, you know he's fine,' I remind her. Fuck me, the prick's cost me near on half a fucking million since I've known him, not that I will ever share that with Ava. She knows about the first bailout, but not the subsequent two. She'll only get her knickers in a twist. He just can't keep himself out of trouble. 'It's too hard for him.' I say what I know will ease her. 'With Kate and Sam, you know.'

'I know,' she agrees. 'I'm being stupid.'

'No, you're not. Kiss me, wife.' I need to distract her. She doesn't waste any time. She's on me immediately, moaning into my mouth and yanking at my hair. It always works. 'You taste delicious.' I'm growling. Fucking hell, I'm going to lose my fucking mind. I bite her lip and push my hips into the curves of her perfect body. 'I'm getting rid of them,' I declare. 'Fucking imposters.'

She grins that fucking grin, hardening me further. 'Stop being unreasonable.' She laughs. 'It's your babies' day.'

'There is nothing unreasonable about me wanting you and my babies all to myself.' I try to focus on cooling down my raging hard-on, but with my body pushed up to hers, those eyes begging for me to claim her, it's fucking impossible. 'I can't look at you,' I mutter, stepping away and exiting the kitchen sharply before I bend her over the countertop.

I'm about to trample the party.

I virtually kick the last people out, who happen to be Ava's parents and they're taking my babies for the night, so I'm delicate-ish. I lean into the back of Joseph's car, my heart pounding happily at the sound of my babies giggling when I take turns to smother them. 'Be bad for Nana.' I wink, get another collective giggle, and then a scold from Elizabeth before shutting the door and sprinting back into the house on the prowl.

'Ava?' I shout, poking my head around the kitchen door. 'Ava?'

'You have to find me!' She laughs, but I can't figure out from which direction that silky voice came.

Damn it, she's playing fucking games. 'Ava, don't make me crazy mad,' I warn. Where the fuck is she? 'Ava?' She's silent now, and so copping it when I get my hands on that body. 'For fuck's sake!' I yell, taking the stairs four at a time and crashing into our bedroom. 'Ava?'

Nothing.

I stand in the middle of the room contemplating my next move. It doesn't take me long. 'Three.' I say it evenly and with optimum confidence. I am confident. She can't resist me. 'Two.' I keep still, listening for any sign of movement. Nothing. 'One,' I say quietly, my cock twitching wildly. I know she's near.

'Zero, baby,' she whispers from behind me, her seductive voice pulling the corners of my lips up. I turn and nearly stagger back at the sight of her standing before me, in just a small pair of lace knickers. Fuck me, she gets more beautiful every day. Despite my urgency, I take my time absorbing her in all of her flawlessness, my eyes dragging over her firm, perfectly formed breasts, over her ridiculously flat stomach and down those fabulous legs. I'm throbbing as I watch her slide her lace down her thighs, and I take my time unbuttoning my shirt and removing my jeans. She doesn't seem to mind. Her big brown eyes are enthralled by my leanness. Nothing changes.

'Do you like what you see?' My voice is low and tempting, although this woman needs no tempting when it comes to me.

Her lips part and her tongue creeps along her full bottom lip. I'm rigid. Everywhere. 'I'm used to it,' she whispers, her eyes flicking across my chest.

I'm on her in a flash, my mouth attacking hers with brute force, and she doesn't stop me. She never will. Her legs wrap around my hips, her arms around my neck and she's all mine again.

'How loud do you think you'll scream when I fuck you?' I ask, ramming her up against the wall, breathing in her face.

'I'd say quite loud,' she pants, grappling at my hard back before shifting her hands into my hair and yanking, hard.

I smile, rear back and slam into her, my head falling back on a yell, my hearing saturated by the sound of her screaming. My heart beats wildly in my chest.

I don't demand to see her eyes any more. I don't need to check she's real.

As long as my heart keeps beating, I'll know that she is.

End of.